# The Twelfth of April

# The Twelfth of April

## Roy Doliner

CROWN PUBLISHERS, INC.
NEW YORK

Copyright © 1985 by Roy Doliner
All rights reserved. No part of this book may be reproduced or transmitted in any form or by any means, electronic or mechanical, including photocopying, recording, or by any information storage and retrieval system, without permission in writing from the publisher.
Published by Crown Publishers, Inc., One Park Avenue, New York, New York 10016 and simultaneously in Canada by General Publishing Company Limited
Crown is a trademark of Crown Publishers, Inc.
Manufactured in the United States of America
Library of Congress Cataloging in Publication Data
Doliner, Roy.
The twelfth of April.
I. Title.
PS3554.045T8   1985      813'.54      84-28500
ISBN 0-517-55735-5
10 9 8 7 6 5 4 3 2 1
First Edition

*To the Memory of Ruben Reyes-Vallis*

# A NOTE FROM THE AUTHOR

Was Franklin Delano Roosevelt's death natural or was something more sinister involved?

Some years ago—it was while I was still in school and first learning of the hectic activity of Soviet agents in Washington before, during, and immediately after the Second World War—I realized how precisely Roosevelt's death fitted into Stalin's postwar plans. What a neat thing it was, and how Uncle Joe must have smiled, how his fish eye must have gleamed, when the news was brought to him.

Because the immense gain to the Soviets was so obvious, I wondered why Soviet complicity had not occurred to anyone else. Did Roosevelt die of cerebral hemorrhage or was he killed? Had there been a cover-up? Certainly conspiracy was in the air at the time. And certainly a lot was covered up.

The decisive evidence is forty years old and long turned to dust. But old files are being opened all the time, and in them are revelations and tantalizing clues, and it is remarkable how unwaiveringly the finger points to Uncle Joe.

# The Twelfth of April

# Prologue

I still have the *New York Times* dated April 13, 1945. It's on my desk, yellow after all these years. Let me begin by telling you what it says:

The *New York Times*
Warm Springs, Ga., April 12, 1945
END COMES SUDDENLY AT WARM SPRINGS
Even His Family Unaware of Condition as
Cerebral Stroke Brings Death to Nation's Leader

PRESIDENT FRANKLIN D. ROOSEVELT'S LAST WORDS WERE, "I HAVE A TERRIFIC HEADACHE."

HE SPOKE THEM TO COMDR. HOWARD G. BRUENN, NAVAL PHYSICIAN.

MR. ROOSEVELT WAS SITTING IN FRONT OF A FIREPLACE IN THE LITTLE WHITE HOUSE HERE ATOP PINE MOUNTAIN WHEN WHAT WAS DESCRIBED AS A MASSIVE CEREBRAL HEMORRHAGE STRUCK HIM.

DR. BRUENN SAID THAT HE SAW THE PRESIDENT THIS MORNING AND HE WAS IN EXCELLENT SPIRITS AT 9:30 A.M.

"AT ONE O'CLOCK," DR. BRUENN ADDED, "HE WAS SITTING IN A CHAIR WHILE SKETCHES WERE BEING MADE OF HIM BY AN ARTIST. HE SUDDENLY COMPLAINED OF A VERY SEVERE OCCIPITAL HEADACHE (BACK OF THE HEAD).

"WITHIN A VERY FEW MINUTES HE LOST CONSCIOUSNESS. HE WAS SEEN BY ME AT 1:30 P.M., FIFTEEN MINUTES AFTER THE EPISODE HAD STARTED.

"HE DID NOT REGAIN CONSCIOUSNESS, AND HE DIED AT 3:30 P.M. (GEORGIA TIME)."

THE ARTIST SKETCHING MR. ROOSEVELT WAS N. ROBBINS OF 520 WEST 139TH STREET, NEW YORK.

ONLY OTHERS PRESENT IN THE COTTAGE WERE COMDR. GEORGE FOX, WHITE HOUSE PHARMACIST AND LONG AN ATTENDANT ON THE PRESIDENT; WILLIAM D. HAMMETT, PRESIDENTIAL SECRETARY; MISS GRACE TULLY, CONFIDENTIAL SECRETARY; AND TWO COUSINS, MISS LAURA DELANO AND MISS MARGARET BUCKLEY.

While that's what was written, the truth is different. The portraitist was a Russian woman and nowhere is that mentioned. There is no person named N. Robbins who lived at 520 West 139th Street. The real portraitist was introduced to Franklin Roosevelt by his intimate friend, a woman he loved for many years and who was with him in the cottage in Warm Springs on April 12, 1945. I call her Julia Winters. Roosevelt was to have lunch with Julia that day. Her face was perhaps the last thing he saw before he died. But nowhere does her name appear in the official story.

It's all very strange. The President of the United States died suddenly and quite conveniently for his enemies. His personal physician said that his health was fine, but no autopsy was ever done.

Perhaps all of the truth will never be known. By the time I arrived in Warm Springs that afternoon, Julia Winters had been whisked away and the official story was already in place. I know of certain crimes, but also of love and loyalty. I'm old, and time is short. I better get to it. What follows is my truth, a human truth, my testimony.

Irina Markova<br>May 7, 1970

# one

MOST OF MY FATHER'S PROPERTY WAS SEIZED IN THE REVO-
lution, and bit by bit he sold what was left to keep us alive. By the fall
of 1921, only one thing of value remained, a diamond, which he took
out of hiding and gave to me.

"Take it," he said. "Take it and leave Russia. Your life is ahead of
you."

It was a square-cut stone, yellowish in color, and heavy in the palm
of my hand. I cared little for gemstones and knew nothing about them,
so it seemed to me a dull and useless thing to be of such value as to
actually provide the chance for a new life.

When I asked my father how much it was worth, he didn't answer
directly or look me in the eye. "It's an excellent stone," he said, finally. "Of the first quality."

My father knew about such things, and I had always relied on him,
but I've not forgotten that he didn't look me in the eye, and I wonder
about it even now. "You merely have to take it to Zurich," he said.
"I'll give you the name of a man who'll buy it, no questions asked."

Even though it was still possible to get an exit visa, and a ticket on
the train to Zurich, there was a lot of red tape, and the time dragged
by. I went through many changes of heart. I was twenty-one, but had
already finished medical college and was eager to intern abroad; in
Russia, even after the Revolution, it was hard for a woman to get a post
in a hospital. But most of all, I was eager to be on my own, and to
begin the adventure of life. On the other hand, I was the only daughter, and I loved my mother and father and was often happy and contented with them. I suffered because I was abandoning them, and
feared that if I left it would be for good and I would never see them
again.

We were still together at Christmas, although there were no pres-
ents, not much to eat, and little wood for the stove we used to heat our
apartment. But we tried to be gay and look back on happier times. We
still had our piano, I suppose because there was nobody to buy it, and
my mother played and I danced with my father. The piano was out of
tune and had a tinny sound, but that only added to the fun. My father

1

managed to get half a bottle of vodka and even persuaded my mother to have a glass, and we all got tipsy. We put aside the thought that I'd be leaving soon.

My birthday was just after the new year—my father always said I'd been expected just at the end of the nineteenth century, but stubbornly refused to arrive until the twentieth—and it was on my birthday that I got my exit visa, and after that a ticket on the Zurich train. My mother sewed the diamond into the lining of my coat, I had my papers, and finally the day came that I was to leave.

I woke up early, before light, but my father was already awake. I doubt if he had slept at all. It was bitter cold—all the wood had run out—and he sat huddled in his coat, scarf, and hat in a chair by the window, staring absently at the shuttered houses along the street, the snow falling heavily, the flakes turning silver and dark, swirling outside the window.

He didn't hear me come in, but was far away in his own thoughts. He seemed old and worn out, his face deeply lined and a weary and tragic look in his eyes. It broke my heart to see him then, and it breaks my heart now, a lifetime away, just to remember it.

I kneeled beside his chair and took his hand. He guessed what I was thinking and put his fingers to my lips, so that I couldn't say it.

"You've got to go," he said, and repeated what he had said when he gave me the diamond. "Your life is ahead of you."

I knew that he was determined that I go, but even so I wonder how I found the resolve to leave. I certainly did love him, and my mother, and I knew how they loved and relied on me and how difficult life in Petrograd had become for them. But in truth I wanted to go; I was young, and life called.

As there was no cab to take us to the station, we walked, bundled up against the cold, my father and I taking turns with my suitcase. My mother was frail, and my father looked after her, and as we trudged along with our heads lowered into the blowing snow, he had to keep a tight grip on her arm. We had to stop at every corner for her to catch her breath. I became impatient, afraid that I'd miss my train. My father was also anxious that I not miss the train, but he never hurried my mother or lost patience with her. He kept hold of her and looked after her, and when we came to the bridge over the Neva, the freezing wind nearly knocking us off our feet, we put my mother between us, and together my father and I held her up, managing somehow to drag my suitcase as we made it across the bridge and finally arrived at the Finland Station.

2

The platform was crowded with people, some there only to get out of the storm. There was hardly any room to move, and no place to sit. I saw loved ones come to say good-by, perhaps forever, clinging to each other, and in every face the same pinched expression of cold, hunger, and misery. It was the same when I looked into the faces of my mother and father, who had also come to say good-by.

I said something about selling the diamond and sending them tickets to Zurich. I promised we'd be together again. I even spoke of happier times ahead. But when I looked into my father's eyes, I saw he was without hope.

A train whistle sounded in the distance, and some in the crowd began to shout that the train was coming; everyone began to push toward the edge of the platform. There were more blasts from the whistle, and as the crowd came closer, I saw the smoke from the locomotive against the sky. In the surging mob, my father kept a tight grip on my mother. Soon I heard the clack of wheels on the old track and the rattling of the old carriages. I lifted my suitcase and started for the end of the platform, but my mother clutched my hand, as if to hold me back. The train pulled into the station and stopped with a loud hissing and·a jet of steam from its brakes. I pulled free of my mother and plunged into the crowd, fighting my way to the edge of the platform. There were shouts and people shoving. The crowd closed in on me, trapped me, and I had to push and shove back with all my strength. There was an ear-splitting whistle, and more steam, and, in a panic, I fought my way through the mob to the train.

Just then, I caught sight of a Red Guard with a rifle slung on his shoulder, standing on the top step of the car just ahead of me. I handed up my suitcase to him, took hold of the rail, and pulled myself on board. There was another blast of the whistle, more steam rose from the locomotive, and the brake was released. I was on the train, which had begun to move.

Below me on the platform, I saw hundreds of strange faces, all of them staring up at the train, all of them shouting, waving, or crying. And in those hundreds of strange faces, I saw my mother—she was calling my name—and my father, my beloved father, and I shouted his name. I shouted, "Father! Father!" But the train whistle blasted again, and my voice was lost in the shouts of everyone else.

The train picked up speed and the faces became a blur. I clung to the rail with one hand and to my suitcase with the other. The train sped under a bridge and came out alongside a frozen lake. The faces on the platform were gone. My mother and father were gone. I never saw them again.

# two

I ARRIVED IN ZURICH WITH SEVEN FRANCS, AND THE DIA-
mond, which I had carefully removed from the lining of my coat.

My father had given me the address of a shop owned by a man he
knew, a man he said could be trusted, and my first problem was to find
it. At the time I knew only a few words of German, but luckily there
was a city map on the wall of the Haupt Bahnhof. The shop turned out
to be a distance away, across the Meinster Bruck, and by now my
suitcase felt as if it were filled with bricks. I was tired and hungry, and
it had begun to snow. When I look back on the difficult times of my
life, it seems always to be raining or snowing, and I seem always to be
worn out and looking for a place to get warm and dry. Remember that
I'm an old woman now, although my mind is as sharp and clear as it
ever was. But I'm writing about things that happened over sixty years
ago. Perhaps, if some smart-alec dug up the *Zurcher Zeitung* for February 3, 1922, he'd be able to show that the sky was clear, and that the
sun was shining. But what of it? Look anywhere you want for such
truth; it'll be found only in memory. So let it be snowing the day I
arrived in Zurich and let it be cold, mercilessly cold.

Finally, I found the shop and went in, dripping wet and still carrying the suitcase. The first thing I noticed were the number of clocks, a
dozen or so, ticking away on shelves along one wall, and a glass case
filled with pocket watches. Two men were there, facing each other
across a wooden table. The smaller of the two, the proprietor of the
shop, wore a pair of glasses with a jeweler's lens attached by a wire to
the frame; and through it he was examining the case of a pocket watch.
The other man was seated with his long legs crossed, smoking a Russian cigarette. The proprietor had just said something in German; I
caught the word *gold*, and the name of the man with the cigarette:
Bogdonov.

Just then he noticed me, and stood up, sweeping off his hat and
making a formal bow. He was a gentleman, a Russian to be sure.
Vladimir Bogdonov, a huge man, well over six feet, but bony, with a
long face like a horse, and with a great bent nose. I fleetingly thought

4

there was something of the artist about him, something theatrical, and I imagined even something of the charlatan.

He gave me a keen look and with a smile said in Russian, "Emil, please see to the young lady."

He was far from being handsome, certainly not in any conventional way, but he had a face that stood out. There was humor in it and one noticed it, and wondered about it, and from that first moment I was attracted to him.

But I was careful not to smile or glance at him, or offer him any encouragement at all. Because he had taken my measure and spoken in Russian, I used my German, my awful German. "If you are Herr Lowenstein," I said to the shopkeeper, "I have a matter of business." I tried to explain why I had come, and about my father and the diamond, but I couldn't find the right words in German and got lost in the grammar.

I stammered and stood like a fool, bedraggled from the days of sitting up on the train, and from the long walk in the rain, and I sneezed twice and dripped rain on Herr Lowenstein's carpet. I'd overheard my mother say of me, "Well, she's no beauty," and I thought of the sad truth of my mother's words while I dug in my pocket for a handkerchief to blow my nose.

From behind me, Vladimir came to my rescue. It was his first rescue, it came just at the right moment, and I think I knew even then it wasn't to be the last time he'd pull my ashes out of the fire.

"Please be at ease," he said. "We're émigrés too, and we often speak Russian." He pulled up a chair for me. "Emil, perhaps the young lady would like a cup of tea."

I was longing for a cup, but refused. Vladimir ignored my refusal, and with a nod sent Lowenstein off for the tea.

"Have you just come from Russia?" Vladimir said. "From Petrograd? How is it?"

I spoke and Vladimir listened. I was shy and thought myself awkward, and had a difficult time with strangers, even with people I'd known for years. But I was able to speak easily to Vladimir. He pulled his chair near mine, leaned forward, fixed his gray eyes directly on me, and all of my awkwardness left me. I never worried that he had noticed my nose, and thought it too short, or that the tip of it was red. My ears weren't too big and my hair not a mousy color, and I was woman enough to see something stir in Vladimir's gray eyes, and woman

5

enough to return his gaze, and impudently respond with a suggestive flicker of my own.

Herr Lowenstein returned with sweetened tea, which I drank, and felt much better. I took the diamond from my purse and gave it to him. He put it under a strong light and studied it through the lens at the end of the wire attached to his glasses. I felt no apprehension. "An excellent stone," my father had said. "Of the highest quality." I expected shortly to be told that I was rich.

But I kept my eyes fixed on Lowenstein's face; Vladimir kept his eyes fixed on Lowenstein's face. Not a breath was drawn, not a sound in the shop, not a clue from Lowenstein, who impassively turned the diamond under the light.

At last Lowenstein put down the diamond, coughed and cleared his throat, raised his eyes to the ceiling and lowered them to the floor, and even clasped his hands before rendering his decision. "A poor stone, very poor," he said. "Worth almost nothing."

I was certain there'd been a mistake. He'd spoken in German, and I glanced quickly at Vladimir, but Lowenstein repeated the decision in Russian. "In today's market, I couldn't give it away," he said.

"But my father knows stones," I said. "He's an expert."

"Then he surely knew this one was no good."

"My father . . ." I was shocked and bewildered. "How can it be?" I said.

I don't remember what was said after that, or what Lowenstein did, or Vladimir. I don't remember taking back the diamond, or grabbing hold of my suitcase. I remember only running out of the shop, my face burning with shame. I had been betrayed; my father had betrayed me, and I was humiliated. I ran across the street and kept running until I found myself on a bridge looking down at the canal.

I had no money, no job or prospect of one, no friends to call on, or relatives outside of Russia. There was no chance of going back to Petrograd—I had neither visa nor ticket—and I wouldn't have gone if I had had one. My father had betrayed me. He had lied to me, his "excellent stone of the first quality" had turned out to be worthless. I looked down at the freezing water and thought of jumping in.

But could I actually have jumped in? Could my life have ended there and then? I was scared, soaked to the skin, hungry, flat broke, and bewildered at what I thought was my father's betrayal. I could have jumped. I gripped the wall above the river and looked down. I was on the edge, another minute and I might have done it.

But I heard steps on the bridge and looked up from the river, peering through the mist and rain, and there was Vladimir. He had arrived just in the nick of time, with his broad magician's hat and soaring nose, holding out his hand to me.

"You ran out of the shop so suddenly and didn't tell me how to get hold of you," he said. "And the diamond, you left it behind."

"It's not worth a single franc," I said.

I took it from Vladimir, and if he hadn't stopped me I'd have thrown it into the river. "How could my father have lied to me?" I said. "How could he have sent me off with a worthless stone?"

"If you'd known it was worthless, would you have gone? Would you have had the courage?"

"I don't know. I certainly wanted to get away, to be out of Russia and on my own."

"But it was a hard decision. Were you afraid?"

I hesitated: It was unlike me to speak openly, even to intimates, and I had just met Vladimir. But I was drawn to him and felt I could trust him. "I was afraid to leave," I said. "I told myself I stayed out of love for my parents. But it wasn't true. It was fear that kept me—fear of going out on my own."

"Then the diamond gave you courage," Vladimir said. "It was the push you needed, and your father knew that. He knew what you were thinking, because he loved you." He was again looking deeply into me with those gray eyes, which were darker with the light reflected from the river. "And now that you're here, and on your own without money, now that the worst has happened, you have nothing more to fear."

"Nothing?"

"Of course not."

He had hold of my suitcase. "All you are is hungry." With his free hand, he gripped my arm, and with my suitcase dangling at the end of his great fist, and me running to keep up with him, we went to a restaurant run by a Russian, who claimed to be a count.

I wanted to know if he really was a count. "Who knows?" Vladimir said. "His cabbage soup is good, and his pancakes delicious."

"So we'll make him a count," I said.

With a full stomach, things always look better, and it was easy to talk to Vladimir, although I learned little about him. His answers to my questions were evasive. Yet I didn't think he was a crook, although he certainly kept a lot to himself. Right from that first night, eating the count's pancakes, I knew he was one of those men with a secret life. I'd never get to the bottom of Vladimir, and so never be sure of him, but that only made him more attractive to me.

He asked about my family, my background. "I am Irina Natalina Markov. My father is a lawyer," I said. "But he's forbidden to practice."

"Why is that?"

"Before the Revolution, he owned land," I said. "A farm near Kolpino."

"South of Petrograd, on the Neva?"

"Do you know it?"

"It's lovely."

"Well, it's gone. The Bolsheviks seized it. They said it was to be given to the peasants. But when I saw it last, the house was empty, the windows smashed, and the furniture taken away. In the fields nothing had been planted." I shook my head, trying to rid myself of the memory of the untended fields and the ruined house. "The Revolution started out grandly," I said. "But so little has come of it, and so much has been destroyed."

"Then you're opposed to them?"

"The Bolsheviks?" It was a test; Vladimir's glance was friendly, even affectionate, but still I was being examined, judged. "Opposed to the Bolsheviks?" I said. "Yes, of course."

"And the Czars?"

"We'll never go back to that."

"A republic then?" he said. "A progressive Russia?"

"Is it possible?"

He shrugged and said, "Do you believe in miracles?"

"It's a miracle that I'm here."

"Why have you come?"

"To get on with my life," I said. "I graduated from the medical college in Petrograd, and want experience here in a hospital as an intern."

"It's not so easy here for a woman," he said.

"It wasn't easy in Russia," I said. "All I want here is a foot in the door, to get a job as an intern."

"An intern here will take some doing," he said. "You'll need a work permit. There are things you can do in the meantime. Do you know any languages?"

"You've heard my German," I said. "And my French is only a little better, but I know English."

He looked up at that. "How good is your English?"

8

"I tutored at the university."

"That's a start," he said. "I may have someone, an American, who from time to time needs translations from the Russian. But you would have to be discreet."

"I can keep my mouth shut."

"A rare talent, particularly among émigrés."

That night Vladimir found me a room, and loaned me money to pay for it. I promised to pay him back. "With the first money I earn," I said. "The very first."

"Not the very first," he said. "You have to hold on to it awhile." He made a joke of it, but I could see he was serious. "One day I may need help, and then I'll come to you. Will you remember to help me?"

"Yes."

"Do you promise?"

"Of course."

"Then I better get you a job right away, one you can do without papers. And a place to live."

My room that first night was just below the roof, an attic with a sloping ceiling and a single window looking out on the roofs of other houses. I had a writing table and a chair, a basin to wash in, a chest for my clothes, and even a little mirror. I slept on a narrow bed opposite the window, which was tall and arched, like those in the tower of a castle, and through it, lying on my side, I saw the chimneys on the roofs and a church steeple against the sky. This was the first place I'd had of my own. It was complete and perfect, and in it I was able to imagine a complete and perfect life; it was exactly the room I'd always wanted.

Before going off to sleep, I thought of my mother and father and saw their faces as they were at the train station. I was to relive that moment often. I see the station still, and their far-off beloved faces. But that first night in Zurich, looking out at the rooftops, the church steeple, and the sky, I put aside my past and thought only how wonderful to be free and on my own finally. It didn't matter that the diamond was worthless and I had no job and no money. I was confident. Life had begun at last.

Vladimir came for me in the morning. He'd found me a job with a wealthy St. Petersburg family named Roykov. The name was familiar to me. Before the Revolution they had lived in a great house on Krasnaya, which I'd often passed with my father. Now they lived in Weinberg Strasse, at the end of the tram line. Vladimir had persuaded them to hire me to look after the two young Roykov girls and teach them English. I was to be given room and board and twenty francs a month.

I never found out how Vladimir had arranged things so quickly, although I soon learned that he was in touch with all the Russian émigrés and made it his business to know what was going on. I thought only of how reluctant I was to leave the attic room; but of course I needed a job, and was grateful to Vladimir, as the arrangements with the Roykov family were ideal. They were good-natured, generous people, liberals of the old school, but clever enough to have sent most of their money out before the Revolution. Their house on Weinberg Strasse was always full of people—relatives and impoverished émigrés—most of whom did little but gossip, play cards, eat, and drink at the Roykovs' table, and create secret societies designed to overthrow the Bolsheviks. The old imperial general, Belensky, a permanent guest of the house, went so far as to set up a Russian government in exile, with himself as its head, and received emissaries and petitioners in his bedroom on the third floor.

But not all the Roykovs' guests were vain and self-deluding, like the general; there were even some who had fought against the old regime. By this time the first of the disillusioned Bolsheviks had arrived in Zurich, and some came to the Roykovs' to be fed and given a warm bed. These had served the Revolution, and fought for it, and lived to see it betrayed by Lenin. They had escaped prison, but were hunted by Lenin's secret police, the Cheka. They looked around with disbelief, trying to grasp the simple fact that they had survived, that they were alive. It was in their eyes when they tasted food, or listened to our conversation, that miracle of normal life. I tried to imagine what they had endured. When they spoke—and most were reticent, but when they did speak—it was to describe the hunger and suffering of the people, the betrayal of the ideals of the Revolution, and the ruthlessness of Lenin.

All faced the need to begin another life. Vladimir was trusted by them, and through him I was trusted by them to carry messages and write letters in English for those who knew only Russian. They needed new passports, and money from the Roykovs, with which they slipped away to France, England, and America. In time they created an informal network, which came to be called Living Memory.

It was a circle that I soon felt at home in. As a girl I had been bookish, shy, and unpopular at school. I discouraged young men because I felt none could be attracted to me. But I liked the attention I got at the Roykovs', and even began to flirt a little. Alone in my room, I examined myself in a mirror. My eyes were large and dark, my hair was nearly black, and my skin had a fine healthy glow. I have always had good teeth, and a firm jaw with a distinctive cleft in the center of my chin. My figure in those days was slim, but full, as a woman's ought to be.

"Do you believe in miracles?" Vladimir had said.

I said I did, and it was true; I had changed from an ugly duckling into an attractive woman.

Vladimir was responsible. I had changed because of him, and for him. Every Sunday, my day off, I'd take the tram to the station opposite the Haupt Bahnhof, where I'd meet him and go around with him.

It began to bother me that I knew so little about him, and that when I asked him questions, he answered with tall tales about himself. One day he was born in Baku on the Caspian Sea, and another time in the Caucasus, in Tibilisi. He was a nobleman, and the son of a peasant. He had fought in the 1914 war, and then been an officer in the White Guards. One time he told me, with a straight face, that he had been a priest. Well, he was some priest, my Vladimir. That was one I didn't believe, although I believed most of what he told me. I was quite swept away by him, and in that first stage of love, I was ready to believe whatever he told me, and ready to do whatever he told me and to learn whatever it was he had to teach me.

When I went around with him on Sunday, I saw that he was well known, and it pleased me to see that he was respected. He showed me articles he'd written for the Russian-language papers in Zurich and Geneva, and even for one in Paris. I knew that he sometimes acted as a broker for the Roykovs or other rich émigrés, and he often acted as go-between when they bought or sold jewelry, real estate, or works of art.

One Sunday in the Café Odeon, he introduced me to the painter Claire Balaban. I had heard of her, and seen portraits she'd done of Madame Roykov and the children. She was small and thin, with hair cut short like a boy's and a white, anxious face. She smoked one cigarette after another and drank Pernod. Her hands were large and very strong, less an artist's hands than a workman's. I'd heard that in her youth she'd been a revolutionary, that she'd known Lenin in Zurich. As we talked I learned that she had been born in Moscow, but that her mother was French and she had lived much of her life in Switzerland and France, and studied in Paris.

"And now you live here," Vladimir said, "in Zurich, and paint portraits."

"Yes, and also have a job."

"Then you must have a Swiss work permit." Vladimir's manner was friendly, as it had been when he'd questioned me. But there was a difference. I was getting to know Vladimir. Behind that friendliness was suspicion. He distrusted Balaban.

"I'm an artist, don't forget," she said. "And I've got a job teaching painting. For that a permit is easier to come by."

"Why is that?"

"I teach art as a technique of psychological therapy," she said, "a method of self-healing for the mentally distressed. I've been specially trained, and the need at the sanatoriums here is considerable."

"So you were given a work permit."

"Yes. I suppose being a French citizen also helped."

"Is that what you are—a French citizen?"

"Because of my mother. Under French law . . ."

"Of course, your mother. That would make all the difference," Vladimir said smoothly.

After that I didn't see Claire Balaban for a while. She seemed to have disappeared. My days were taken up by the Roykov children. I'd borrowed medical books from the library and every night I studied them. The licensing exam was known to be a stiff one, so every spare minute I spent with my medical books. But Sunday afternoons, I still found time to be with Vladimir.

One Sunday as I was leaving, a guest at the Roykovs' gave me a letter to pass on to Vladimir. It was sealed and addressed to a relative of his in Moscow.

When I asked Vladimir about it, he said, "It's possible to get messages in without going through the regular mails. And to get them out as well."

I knew that all the mail in and out of Russia was examined, and in many cases was not delivered at all. Letters to my mother and father were unanswered, and I suspected they never got them.

"If your parents are at their old address, I'll see your letters are delivered," Vladimir said. "We still have friends in Russia." Then he gave me one of his inscrutable smiles and said, "These are secret friends. That is the way with us, with Russians. There are the police, and the spies for the police, and the rest of us who have our secret friends."

"And which are you?" I said. "Not the police?"

"No."

"Or a police spy?"

"Well, one doesn't know. One can never be sure." He had begun to tease me, which made me furious. It was patronizing; I was a woman, and not always to be taken seriously. "I'm not a police spy," he said. "I don't work for Little Lenin." And again he teased me. "But what about you? Are you a spy for the Cheka?"

"You can be sure of one thing," I said. "If I were a Chekist, you'd never know it. I could easily fool you, and outsmart you, because you're a big, conceited ass."

He saw that I was genuinely angry and tried to make it up to me, and stopped teasing me. I'd served notice on him that I wasn't to be patronized by him or any other man; from then on he treated me with respect, and my love for him deepened and became permanent.

But I still knew little about him, and the more I saw of him the less I knew, and the more mysterious his life seemed.

One day in the middle of the week, I was given a holiday with the children and tickets to a visiting circus. The tent had been pitched in the park next to the Mythen Quai. It was the first circus I'd seen in years, and I enjoyed it as much as the children. The menagerie was fascinating—lions, tigers, and even an elephant, which I had seen before only in a picture book. Because we were on a holiday, the children, who'd been raised in Zurich, insisted I speak German with them. All week I taught them English, and now they took over, and were having a wonderful time listening to me trying to explain about the animals in German, with my Russian accent, making all sorts of comical mistakes.

And while all of that was going on, I glanced across the park, and there was Vladimir. He didn't see me, and I didn't call to him. I don't know why exactly—curiosity, I suppose, suspicion, even jealousy, the need to know what he was up to when we were apart.

He was with another man, a stranger to me, a foreigner. I was too far away to hear what they were saying, or even the language they spoke. But there was something in the way the stranger stood, with his chin thrust out and his hands jammed into his trouser pockets, and something about his clothes that made me think he was English or American. He looked small beside Vladimir, but he must have been average size, or even a little better, a stocky man with light reddish hair.

The children were distracted by one of the clowns from the circus, who mingled with the crowd and led the children off playing a penny whistle. I was alone. I could have called out to Vladimir, or gone over to him. I nearly did; but something held me back; it was the way the

13

two men were talking, or rather the way the stranger was talking and Vladimir was listening, and listening intently. He was being given an explanation; he was being given instructions. The stocky red-haired man was laying things out for Vladimir, giving him orders; then I saw him take Vladimir's arm—it was done in a friendly way, but he did firmly take hold of Vladimir's arm—and they walked off without noticing me, still deep in conversation.

Shortly after that Vladimir gave me the first of the translations to do. These were speeches by Lenin delivered to the Central Council of the Committee of Commissars, and printed in *Pravda*. I thought them boring, wordy in the later style of Vladimir Ilich, and repetitious, but innocuous enough, part of the public record. They were dated and took place over a period of years. I couldn't imagine who'd be interested, some scholar or student? And then I noticed that with the pages of Lenin's rhetoric, tacked on without comment, were the minutes of meetings that were designated secret, pages of figures for steel and cement production, bushels of wheat and corn. Mixed with all of this were confidential memos signed by Lenin himself, giving detailed instructions to his ministers, ambassadors, and even secret agents of the Comintern in Europe and Asia.

I translated these as I did the others, and passed them to Vladimir without comment. I was curious, more than curious; I burned to know how they had been acquired, and what Vladimir's game was. But I said nothing. If it was a spy's game, the first rule was secrecy.

Eventually, Vladimir brought up the confidential memos and asked me what I thought of them. "There are rumors that Lenin is sick," I said. "I think it may be true—at least he's begun to think about who will succeed him."

"Who is it to be? What do you think?"

"Not one person," I said. "Not even Trotsky. He wants a committee."

"Not Stalin?"

"Stalin last of all," I said. "Lenin fears Stalin, and despises him. The language of the memos is formal and restrained, but his hatred of Stalin comes through."

"He doesn't say he hates him," Vladimir said.

"Not in so many words, but it comes through. Stalin is crude, a person without culture. That's Lenin's opinion, and it's there in the Russian."

"And in your English version?"

"I was careful to get it in."

"You're doing an excellent job," Vladimir said. "I was told to commend you."

"By whom?" I said. "The man you meet in the park, the red-haired Englishman?"

"He's American."

"I saw you with him the day of the circus."

"Were you spying on us?" Vladimir shook his finger at me and smiled, a mischievous smile. "You should have come over and been introduced. Winters would have been charmed by you. His name is Winters. Andrew Winters."

After that I was given more translations to do, but not boring speeches printed in *Pravda,* no more tables of statistics dealing with the grain harvest or cement production. There was a secret memo from Lenin to Stalin, reprimanding the *crude* Georgian for a rudeness to Lenin's wife, the beloved Krupskaya.

The final memo was from one of the physicians attending Lenin, Mikhail Auerbach, writing to the Central Committee on the condition of Lenin's health. Lenin had suffered a series of strokes; although his mind remained clear, his speech was slurred and his right side practically paralyzed.

I knew Auerbach—I had studied neurology under him at the medical college. He was cautious and skilled, a scientist without politics. From the medical facts in his memo, it was certain that Lenin was dying.

Yet I couldn't believe it. Outside of the Kremlin nothing was known of Lenin's illness. He was already immortal, a man made of iron. I wondered if the memo were genuine. And then the news swept Zurich. Lenin was dead.

For the émigrés, everything stopped; Lenin was dead. At the Roykovs', the talk was of a second civil war, of the collapse of the Bolshevik government, of returning to St. Petersburg; some people even began to pack their bags. General Belensky met with his emissaries and sent off cables. Only Living Memory wasn't fooled. They knew Stalin, and knew a worse terror was about to begin.

The first chance I had to slip away, I took the tram to Zurich, and went directly to Vladimir's rooms; they were empty. He had packed up in the middle of the night without a word to his landlady, to me, to anyone. Among the Russian émigrés, no one knew or would say where he had gone. I was angry at him for not letting me know he was leaving, for not trusting me. I thought of asking someone in Living Memory, but decided it was best to say nothing. I simply went on with my work, tutoring the children and studying whenever I could.

Lenin had died in late January, and at the end of March I took my licensing exam. I came away thinking I had done poorly, remembering only those questions I hadn't known. I was certain I had failed, certain I'd never be able to practice medicine in Switzerland. It was a dark time. My father had raised me with a certain idealism, and I had left Russia with the hope of doing well. But I had failed. I lost all of my new-found self-confidence. And how I missed Vladimir, the only person I could confide in.

Two months passed. The licensing committee was known to be slow, but it was said that the longer it took, the more likely one had failed. My spirits sank even lower.

Then on June 4, 1924—a date that I'll never forget—a letter arrived for me from the Board of Medical Regents. Madame Roykov brought it to me. She knew all it meant to me, and her eyes were filled with anxious sympathy. I took the letter and ran to my room. I needed to be alone. But my hand shook and I felt so weak I couldn't open the letter immediately. All sorts of thoughts filled my head—Vladimir, the fake diamond, my father's face raised up to me out of the mob in the Finland Station.

Finally, I took a deep breath and tore open the envelope. I had passed. I was licensed—official documents would follow. I was a doctor in Switzerland.

My first thought was to run and tell Vladimir, but of course he wasn't in Zurich, and still no one knew where he was. There were all sorts of rumors—he was in Germany, organizing a counterrevolution, he'd been seen in Warsaw, in Prague, in Paris, and even in the United States. But the Russians in Zurich lived on rumors and gossip. The truth was that none of them knew where he had gone or what he was up to.

And then one morning at the end of summer, while I was at work with the children in their room, a message arrived for me: Vladimir was in Zurich. Could I meet him at the Café Odeon?

I was stunned. I hadn't realized how I had missed him, or how passionate my feelings for him had become. The Roykovs let me go, and I took the first tram. But on the way, I resolved to act coolly, to treat him civilly. I even planned to greet him by shaking hands.

But the first sight of him in the Odeon changed all that. I forgot everything and ran across the room to him, and in front of a dozen startled Swiss, I threw my arms around him and kissed him. I was so relieved to have him back safely, and overjoyed to be with him again.

Because I feared that love would interfere with the free and adventurous life I planned, I had decided not to fall in love. But my love for Vladimir was involuntary and took me by surprise. I had hidden that love from myself until I saw him again, and then it overwhelmed me.

It was much the same with Vladimir. In spite of himself, unknown to himself, he had begun to love me. Perhaps he had; I think he had.

He had brought me a present, a small gold cross on a chain, and to further shock the Swiss—the way with us Russians was to shock the Swiss—he ceremoniously hung the cross around my neck, kissed my cheek, and called me *Lybimaya*, dearest. Neither of us had previously used so affectionate a term, and with Russians of our generation such words were not spoken lightly.

"It's the Cross of St. Sampson," I said. "That little shop on the Karla Marksa near the church, it used to sell them."

"It still does."

"You've been in St. Petersburg?"

"Yes. And the little shop, it's still there."

I saw the street with the Church of St. Sampson, and the little shop. I saw the rooms in the house I had grown up in; all of it had grown smaller and more distant, and I feared that I would eventually forget it all, that it would cease to exist, and it would never have existed.

Vladimir was also an exile, who understood what I felt; he took my hand, and trusted me enough to lead me into the secret part of his life. Since Lenin's death he had been traveling all through Russia, using disguises and false papers, meeting in secret with friends there, people who were disillusioned with the Communists, and some of them had become agents, providing us with information.

Vladimir had tried to find my mother and father. "They're not at your old address," he said. "I asked the neighbors, but no one knows, or would say. We'll keep looking, and maybe one day they'll turn up."

How many times in those days did I hear "maybe one day they'll turn up"? I pretended to believe it would happen, and kept in mind those rare times when, after years, people did turn up.

But now it was time for good news. I quickly told Vladimir about passing the medical boards.

"That is good news," he said.

"Are you proud of me?"

"Immensely proud."

"They need doctors here, particularly pediatricians, which is what I want to specialize in. I've already got a work permit, and a part-time job in the hospital. Mostly I'm on duty on Saturday night and Sunday, when none of the other doctors wants to stay in the wards. The chief of pediatrics likes my work and has promised me a full internship at the end of the year."

Later on, as we were walking together along the lake, I took Vladimir's arm. "There's something else," I said. "A surprise. Let me show you."

"I'm nervous about surprises."

"You'll like this one, I promise."

I had saved something from my wages every month, and from the translations, and had used the money to rent the little attic room to which Vladimir had brought me that first night in Zurich. I had even bought a bedspread of my own, and hung curtains and a watercolor of the grotto in St. Catherine Park in St. Petersburg, which I had found in the flea market.

My own room, a place of my own at last, that was my surprise, and Vladimir was my first visitor.

"It's a beautiful room," he said. "And I'm proud of what you've done." He was gazing at the watercolor of the grotto, and I stood close by, so that we brushed against each other. He repeated the words, "I'm proud of what you've done." And again he spoke to me lovingly, and called me *Lybimaya*.

I said, "You told me you knew the Catherine Park, and the grotto, and one day I saw the watercolor. It cost only two marks fifty, because the artist isn't known, and there is a stain there on the corner."

"I used to walk around in that park," he said. "And in good weather sit on a bench. Always the same bench."

"Were you at school then?"

"Yes, when I was a boy. Later, my father decided I was to go to the cavalry school in Moscow, although I didn't want to go. My father was a good sport, and he wouldn't have forced me to go. But I didn't know what I wanted out of life, and so I went, and that was that."

"Did you like the school?"

"Not at first, but I got used to it. Then the war started, and we all went off to join the army and fight the Kaiser."

This wasn't one of his tall tales. He was telling me the truth, but only a little bit and short on details, a fragment of his life before I knew him, and precious to me because of that. He sat in the one chair; I had bought cigarettes, the kind he always smoked, and even lit one for him, and sat on a rug at his feet. I was so young then, and earnestly in love with Vladimir. That love was independent of me, like the sun or the rain, and was as natural as the sun or the rain, and I understood nothing of what I felt, and cared nothing for understanding. Understanding was far off. Disappointment was far off. Now it's come around, and I'm an old woman and that innocent girl in the attic room is far off. I envy her and I love her; my eyes fill when I remember her. I even forgive her when she offers Vladimir one of the cigarettes she's bought for him, and lights it, and then rests her cheek adoringly on the bony knee of that big ox.

I had decided to seduce Vladimir. He knew it, and it made him uneasy. I wore my hair long then and let it come a bit undone and brush against his leg. I looked into his eyes. My eyes are blue, not as blue as the Crimean sky, nothing so fancy. I had wished for eyes that captivate men; they are called bewitching eyes, and I wanted mine to be green. Well, I looked at Vladimir with my decent blue eyes, which had been called frank and honest, and frankly and honestly told him that I wanted him to make love to me.

Vladimir was breathing hard and was aroused, but when I put my professional ear against his chest, I heard a skipped beat or two, and a hiss of conscience. In a hoarse whisper he said something about a confession, but I put my finger to his lips. The time was past for confessions, for caution, or for me to listen like a doctor to his heart.

I reached out my arms to him, and he swept me up and carried me to the bed and there again I looked out at the rooftops of Zurich, at the smoke rising from the chimneys, at the sky, and in each other's arms we passed a time that was perfect. No secrets, no failures or disappointments, no sorrow or regrets—nothing spoiled our happiness. It was perfect. I remember that it was perfect, and still shiver when I think of it.

# three

☭ VLADIMIR WAS A WONDERFUL LOVER, BUT NOT A MAN TO stay around long. To save money, he had given up his own room and moved into mine. I was there only weekends, when I worked at the hospital, and returned only to sleep. We had Saturday nights together, although I didn't get off duty until midnight, and an hour or two on Sunday morning before I had to leave for the hospital, and again before I caught the tram to the Roykovs.

It seemed we were always greeting each other and embracing, hurrying to make love, and then lying in each other's arms, and saying nothing, and saying those intimate things that mean nothing and meant everything to us.

He was my first lover, and I adored him, and wasn't in the least shy or awkward with him. I had waited so long for the act of love, and hoped for so much—for there is a romantic side to me, although I keep it hidden—and in loving Vladimir I felt what I had hoped to feel, and more, and was satisfied that I had felt all that was possible for me to feel.

But there was something else, something that I held back. I loved, I trembled with love, and yet somewhere a clock went on ticking. I loved, but on duty in the hospital wards I was the same, and in the tram returning to the Roykovs' on Sunday night I was the same; for all I loved, there was a part of me that love never touched.

All told, we had half a dozen weekends together before Vladimir was again packing his bags.

"I may be gone a long while this time, dearest." I'd been teaching Vladimir English, and he said, "Irina, my dearest. Is it correct?"

"Yes, dearest."

"I'm correct, but you're laughing at me."

"Dearest is—it's too formal."

"Then what do I call you?"

"Darling is very nice," I said. "You can call me either darling or dearest."

"And you call me darling, too. No masculine or feminine." And

20

then in Russian, "You are my most darling, and I'll miss you. I'm going again to Russia."

"Will it be dangerous?"

"Not at all. I have many friends there, and a German passport. I'm a German salesman of textiles. Tell me, don't I look like a proper German salesman from Munich?"

"You look like an actor, or a magician." And he did, with his soft black hat and cape. "You could be an anarchist, or a spy. That's what you look like most—a spy."

"Is that what you think I am?"

"I wouldn't be surprised at anything," I said. "At the Roykovs' they say you were an officer in the Guards, loyal to the Czar, and when the army mutinied, you joined the Whites, and were twice wounded."

"Tall tales," he said. "Exiles sit around and tell each other tall tales. I'm an exile myself, and have done the same thing."

"But you have been wounded."

"Nonsense."

"But *darling*"—I was able to flirt; at least I had learned that much—"I've seen your scars," I said.

"What else do they say about me?"

"That you're a secret agent, a spy."

"Who do they say I spy for?"

"Everyone has a different opinion, but nobody knows. Some think you spy for the Germans, or the French. There's talk you're secretly a Bolshevik. But only I know the truth." I took one of Vladimir's cigarettes and lit it for myself, as I had seen it done by a notorious countess, and blew the smoke out through my nostrils. At home I had been forbidden to smoke, and now I smoked, and had a lover, and a job and a room of my own, where I entertained my lover. "I know you spy on the Bolsheviks," I said. "And that you work for the Americans."

He was thoughtful a moment and then said, "Have you told anybody about the translations, or seeing me with Andrew Winters?"

"Not a word to anyone."

"In time, my *darling dearest*," he said. "In time you'll be a good spy yourself."

That Sunday night Vladimir took me to a café—Richter's it was called—a romantic place, the only one we knew of in Zurich, with a band and sweet wine served in green bottles with long, graceful necks. We drank so much of the wine that even Vladimir got tipsy, and we wound up back in my room, where we made love all night, and I missed the last tram.

It was still dark the next morning when I woke up and started to dress. Vladimir heard me and got out of bed with the quilt wrapped around him, and began hopping and doing a foolish dance, slapping the freezing wooden floor with his huge bare feet.

I had always gone alone to the tram station, but that morning Vladimir wanted to go with me. When the station buffet opened, he bought me coffee, and when he looked at me I saw that he loved me and had also been happy in the attic room, that it meant as much to him as to me. So we were in love. It came clear, as it always does, at the moment of parting.

Yet he told me nothing about his mission. I asked no questions. We were émigrés, who accepted such separations.

Finally the tram came and I got on board. Vladimir reached up to embrace me, and we kissed, and I squeezed his hand. I remember how large it seemed, how smooth and cold in the morning air. He waited while the tram started, and went on waiting alone in the gray light of the early morning, huddled in his cape and black hat, looking after me. Long afterward, I saw him there and saw the loving and unhappy expression in his eyes.

Next Saturday, when I returned to my attic room, he was gone. There was no note, and he had left nothing of his behind. I searched the room, but found no trace of him. I pulled myself together and went off to the hospital. I was able to concentrate on my work there, and over the next few months, I thought often of Vladimir, but each day it was with less unhappiness.

All my spare time was spent in the children's ward, and the following year the resident pediatrician offered me the post of assistant resident. The Roykov family was happy for me, and gave me a farewell party, and even bought me a doctor's bag with my initials in gold.

I was proud of that bag, but also embarrassed to carry it, and never took it with me to the hospital. I felt humble as a doctor, conscious of how little I knew, how often I failed to cure the sick, and how terrible it was when one of the children died. I remember praying for those I had failed to cure, yet I don't recall thinking in those days of God, only of the mystery of life, and why humans are able to be compassionate but in the order of things there is no compassion.

A year passed. I lived alone and thought often of Vladimir, and wondered where he was, and if he were safe. I continued to love him, but not like the innocent girl who had sat at his feet and lit his cigarette. I wanted to hear from him, but no letter came, no message of any kind. I was angry at him, and other times, often at night, alone in that attic room, I imagined him moving over me, and making love to me. As the time passed, I began to notice other men and daydream about them, but I wasn't ready to begin another affair, although I was sometimes tempted, and perhaps took a lover or two. I can't remember, and can't see how it matters one way or another.

I had some friends among the émigrés, and we got together for Easter, and at Christmas I was invited to the Roykovs' and spoke English with the children. Once a month I went to a concert or a play, and the rest of the time I was at the hospital, learning to be a doctor. An orderly and solitary life, to which I became resigned and which after a time seemed quite natural.

One day I received a letter with a Berlin postmark; it was for Vladimir, but in my care, and to my address. It was a bulky envelope, apparently with several sheets of paper folded inside, and on the back flap the name of a hotel—the Central—and a room number: 211.

The handwriting was unusual—spiky and slanting to the left. I was, of course, curious about the contents, imagining all sorts of things. Vladimir must have given someone my address, although he left without saying anything about a letter. It raised my hopes that he might be coming back soon. I put the unopened letter in a safe place.

A few days later my landlady told me I'd had a visitor, a gentleman, who wanted to know if I still worked at the hospital.

"A gentleman?" I said. "What did he look like? Was he Russian?"

"I don't think so. He spoke German, I had a boarder once from Vienna, and he spoke a similar German. Also he had a dog with him that did a lot of barking. What do you call those dogs, they look like sausages?"

"Dachshunds."

"He had one of those."

"Did the gentleman give you his name?"

"No."

"Or tell you what he wanted?"

"He said he'd come again."

I knew no gentleman with a dachshund, and couldn't imagine who it could be or what he wanted. Something told me it had to do with the letter from the Hotel Central in Berlin, and that my visitor had to do also with the mysterious comings and goings of Vladimir.

That Sunday, I walked from my room along the Bahnhofstrasse to the Café Odeon, where I treated myself to a pastry.

I was in the Odeon only a few minutes when I began to feel that I was being watched. I glanced around, but saw no one I knew; all around were couples or families on a Sunday outing, busy with one another. I took a small mouthful of whipped cream and let it dissolve on my tongue, drawing out my weekly pleasure. Again, I felt a pair of eyes on me. As a child I'd used a magnifying glass to concentrate the rays of the sun and burn a hole in a leaf. Those eyes watching me felt like that, like the concentrated rays of the sun, burning a hole in the back of my neck.

Just then I saw a small brown dog, a dachshund, and a man holding him on a lead. The man smiled and raised his hat, a green hat of loden cloth. There's no accounting for the details one remembers: the green hat of loden cloth, and the man's light red hair. It was Andrew Winters, the American I'd seen in the park with Vladimir.

He stood at my table, the green hat in one hand and the dog's lead in the other. We chatted as if we were old friends, surprised to run into each other in Zurich. Andrew Winters spoke in German, excellent German, with a Viennese accent, as my landlady had said, but a German that nobody at the tables nearby would notice or remember.

When I invited him to sit down, he pulled his chair close to mine and whispered in English, "Regards from Moscow. Your dear friend asks especially to be remembered to you."

"Is he well?" I tried to show Andrew Winters nothing of what I felt; the pounding of my heart was my own affair. "I hope he's well," I said.

"Well. And actually enjoying himself." He signaled the waiter, and whispered again in English, "It agrees with him, the spy's life." Waiting for the waiter, he studied the menu card. "What shall we have? A nice pastry?"

"I've just had one."

"Have another."

"Two pastries?"

"Why not?"

"An éclair this time," I said.

Andrew Winters knew that I had been born in St. Petersburg. He knew the date, and the address of the house I lived in; he knew the story of the diamond my father had given me. He knew I was a doctor. I had the uneasy feeling that Andrew Winters in some way knew me intimately. I was put off by him, yet attracted to him. In those days Winters was an amusing, graceful man whose attentions to a woman were subtly flattering. But I began to sense that he was a bit too graceful, too attentive. I thought it was because women were allowed to slip

24

too easily in and out of his life and because none of them mattered very much. I wondered what did matter to Andrew Winters. I wondered if he had been married, and the kind of love affairs he'd had. Vladimir had told me of one affair with an Obelensky princess, who took her life when she learned of the murder by the Bolsheviks of her family. Years later, when I asked Winters about the Obelensky princess, he told me there had been a princess, although not an Obelensky, and not a tragic heroine. Winters' princess was working as a saleswoman for Cartier in Paris. She had kept contacts inside of Russia, and he'd cultivated her only to learn what he could. The spying had come before the princess.

But he talked of other things that afternoon on the terrace. The dachshund, Freddie, begged for whipped cream, and Winters spooned some into a saucer and put it under the table for him.

"Freddie belongs to my sister," Winters said. "She's a patient at the Meir Clinic. Do you know anything about that sort of thing? Psychiatry, I mean."

"I've read some, not much."

"I'm bewildered by it," Winters said.

"How long has she been at Meir?"

"Nearly a year."

"Is she better?"

"It's hard to tell," Winters said. "She's not as unhappy. *Depressed* is the word they use. She used to be very lively, very popular, and always ready for a good time. And she was quite a beauty—still is, as a matter of fact. She expected everything to go along smoothly. She expected everyone to be kind, because she grew up around kind people. She trusted everyone, but when she couldn't have the one man she ever wanted—" Winters cut himself off in midsentence. He hadn't meant to tell me all that about his sister, but it had been building up inside of him.

"They say Lenin used to come here," he said. "To the Odeon."

"Is it true, do you think?"

"A man I know used to meet him here all the time," he said. "That table by the window. Lenin used to drink his coffee and make plans. In 1916 all he controlled was that little table, my friend told me, but the next year he had all of Russia."

I said, "Are you alone in Zurich?"

"Yes. I came only to see my sister," he said. "And to see you, too. I wanted to meet you because Vladimir had spoken so highly of you."

"And to give me his message."

"Yes, of course. The message that he's well."

25

"Do you live in Europe?"

"Yes. In Paris."

"Did you come from there directly?" I said. "Or did you go first to Berlin?"

"And did I stay at the Hotel Central? Is that your next question?"

"The letter to Vladimir in my care, you sent it from there. But why?"

"Have you opened it?"

"I was tempted."

"It's nothing," Winters said. "Blank pages."

"You sent it to test me, to see if I'd put my nose in where it didn't belong."

"And you didn't."

"And what if I had opened it?"

"I wouldn't offer you a job."

"You mean to work for you?" I said. "To do what Vladimir does?"

"More or less, except you wouldn't have to leave Zurich."

"How do you know I want to work for you?"

"I think you'd enjoy the work, because it would suit you," he said. "Vladimir thinks you're a natural for the trade."

"The spy trade?"

"Living Memory," Andrew Winters said, "that's my name for the organization." Freddie, the dachshund, was back for more whipped cream, but this time he was ignored. At the tables near us, the Swiss ate their Sunday pastry and drank their sweetened chocolate.

"Spies must lie," I said. "And they must be expert at it, at lying."

"But we believe in truth," Andrew said. "We believe it's hidden."

"Is that why Vladimir is a spy," I said, "to learn the truth?" I laughed and added, "He doesn't give a damn for truth. He lies effortlessly, as one spreads butter on bread."

"It doesn't bother you?"

"I take him as he is." I was being much the woman of the world, the notorious countess. I said, "Vladimir is my lover."

"Then I'm sure you know he's no liar," Andrew said. "He's more an artist, one of those who creates himself. He tells tales, and acts a part, that's what makes him a top-notch spy." He was looking closely at me, at the dissolute countess, but from the corner of skeptically narrowed eyes. I was no countess, and Winters no fool. "Are you an actor, too?" he said finally.

"Not so good as Vladimir."

"But with the same love of theater?"

26

"Yes."

"Would you like to be a spy?" Little Freddie, with his soulful eyes, pleaded for more cream, and Andrew Winters couldn't resist. "What do you say, Irina, will you be a spy?"

"Will it be exciting?"

"I'm sure it will."

"That's what I want," I said, "an exciting life."

# four

☭ SO I BECAME A SPY, A PART-TIME SPY, PAID THIRTY FRANCS A
month; but it was not exciting, not at first. I got one or two letters a
week with a Berlin postmark, all addressed to me, and on each envelope the handwriting was different and on none was there a return
address. After a few months, letters began arriving from Paris, then
Vienna, Brussels, Budapest, Prague, and Warsaw. Eventually, I was
getting letters from all over Europe, and on each envelope the handwriting was different. I realized that a network existed with agents
all over Europe, and that I was a letter drop for that network, a network whose center was that courteous soft-spoken American, Andrew
Winters.

I saw him on the average of every four or six weeks, but never with
any regularity. From things he said, I had the impression that he was
on the go, continually traveling among the cities of Europe, and now
and then as far away as America.

He'd collect the accumulated mail, pay me what was owed, and
leave a book or two for me to translate from Russian to English, paying
extra for that. He volunteered no information about Living Memory,
and I knew to ask no questions. Once I gave him a parcel of warm
clothing and tins of food, in the hope they could be delivered to my
parents. Winters said he'd try, and I have no doubt that he did, but I
never knew if they received it.

Vladimir never wrote me. There were rumors that he had been
seen in Kiev, and then that he was traveling in the Ukraine. But these
were only rumors, the kind of thing heard in coffee shops; nothing was
confirmed, and then for months nothing was heard from him at all.

Winters spoke often of his sister, and one Sunday he asked me to
go along with him to visit her at the Meir Clinic. It was in the mountains on a lake, and she had a cottage to herself, a short walk from the
main building. Meir was a sanatorium, its founder a psychiatrist who
had studied with Freud and later with Carl Jung. Yet it had the reputation of being less a hospital than a refuge for the wealthy.

Julia Winters was a surprise to me, although I don't know what I
was expecting. When I met her, she had been at Meir in a private

cottage for nearly two years. Many of the furnishings in the cottage were hers; it had become her home. Although she was young, she made me think of a person living in retirement, a widow. Yet she was only thirty-five or thirty-six, the same as Andrew Winters. He had told me they were twins, although they didn't look alike. She was taller than he, slimmer, with dark hair and eyes, and a delicate oval face. Her voice was pitched low, and seemed to me more American than Andrew's. She joked about that; the family was from Virginia, but Andrew had been to school in Massachusetts and lived for years in England. She teased him about his English clothes and accent. I sensed the adored child, the pampered daughter who had grown into a woman who expected to be adored by all men.

I wondered what had happened to drive Julia to the Meir Clinic. She had grown up anticipating only kindness, and to get whatever she wanted—so Andrew had told me. "And when she couldn't have the one man she ever really wanted . . ."

Julia wanted to show me the grounds and to go for a walk around the lake. Andrew needed to write some letters, so he stayed in the cottage.

As we walked, Julia told me she got up every morning at first light to watch the birds in the woods and marshes around the lake. She pointed out different kinds, described their habits, and even showed me where some of them nested.

"Parts of Virginia are like this," she said. "And New England has similar lakes and mountains. Have you ever lived in America?"

"No, I've not yet been."

"But you speak very good English."

"I have a terrible accent."

"It's charming."

"Will you be going back to America soon?"

"I want to." She had become serious, and looked straight ahead, so that I saw her in profile. It was late afternoon, the winter sun was low, its rays directly behind her. Her nose and mouth were well shaped and her skin pale and flawless; her eyes, when she turned them on me, were dark, greenish, and introspective. She seemed delicate and insubstantial, and I instinctively spoke to her in a lowered voice, soothingly.

"Andrew told me you're studying here," she said.

"Yes, in Zurich."

"And that you're a doctor."

"Yes."

"What sort?" I saw her lower lip tremble. "What sort of doctor are you?"

"I'm going to be a pediatrician."

"You're not a psychiatrist?"

"No."

"Truly?"

"I don't know the first thing about psychiatry."

"And don't care about it?"

"Not in the least."

"Good, neither do I."

She was relieved and happily put her arm through mine. We were to be friends. I thought: She wants to go on trusting everyone, relying on everyone. I smiled and squeezed her arm.

"I would have liked to have been a doctor or a teacher," she said. "Somebody who works with children. I've always wanted to be someone useful."

"You're still young enough to do what you want," I said.

"Did Andrew tell you anything about me?"

"Only that you were twins."

"That always surprises people," she said. "Did he tell you anything else? Did he tell you why I've been staying here?"

"No."

I felt her grip tighten on my arm; I had been partly right about her, she wanted to trust me, but to trust anyone had become difficult for her. I tried to guess who had betrayed her. She was deciding if we really could be friends, and if she could confide in me.

But just then something happened that broke the mood of intimacy. It was something trivial, even silly—a flight of honking geese. I don't like the sound they make. They bay like hunting dogs; they are ominous. A flock of them were flying like arrows against a threatening sky.

But they didn't have that effect on Julia. She was fascinated and full of information about the migratory instinct. Because of the geese, she didn't tell me why she was at Meir—not then, anyway—and since I had sensed a mystery, a secret, I regretted that the opportunity was lost.

But Julia had a secret of another sort, which she was eager to confide in me. She took my arm and drew me close, and even though we were in the woods with no one in sight, she still whispered: "I have a friend here, a wonderful woman. We work together."

"What sort of work?"

"She's teaching me to—" She laughed, but suddenly became serious and squeezed my arm. "Promise not to tell the doctors or Andrew. Particularly Andrew."

She led me around the lake to another cottage, from the outside very much like hers, but closer to the main building of the clinic. As we approached, I heard voices from inside the cottage. One of the voices belonged to a man. An argument was going on, and I thought I heard Russian, but I wasn't sure.

"Perhaps we should come another time," I said.

But Julia stubbornly shook her head, and before I could stop her, she rapped on the door; the voices stopped at once. I heard a man's heavy step and the lighter tread of a woman. The door opened; it was Claire Balaban.

Julia certainly hadn't been expected, and Balaban wasn't pleased to see us. She was flustered, but she invited us in. It was an awkward moment all around.

The cottage had been done over as a painter's studio; there were a pair of easels and a long table with pots of brushes and jars of turpentine and paint. The only piece of furniture was a couch, and seated on it was a young man, who politely rose as we came in.

He was a stranger to Julia, who didn't like the idea of his being there.

"I'm sorry, Claire," she said. There was a jealous side to Julia, a side that hated to share friends. "We seem to be interrupting something."

"Not at all," Balaban said. "Interrupting something? But what? I want you to meet someone." She motioned to the young man, who stepped forward.

"No, we must leave."

Balaban took Julia's hand in both of hers, and gazed directly into her eyes. It was to calm her, the gesture of a therapist. It worked, and Julia quieted down.

With her eyes still on Julia, Balaban said, "Irina, how nice to see you again. You see we're friends, all of us are friends." Balaban was speaking French, holding tightly to Julia's hands, calming her further with her steady gaze.

The young man stood watching it all. I don't know what he was thinking, for I hardly looked at him, and he made no impression on me. I was more interested in Balaban's ability to calm and even control Julia. Finally, the young man was introduced. I didn't quite catch his name, yet he made an impression on me.

31

He wasn't tall but I don't remember him as being particularly short either. I noticed his hair, which was black, black as a crow, slick and parted in the middle.

He was supposed to be a student, a cousin of Balaban's.

I thought: On her father's side.

Why did I think that? I had remembered that her father was Russian. Had I guessed that young man was Russian, or was it something I added much later on, when I learned more about him? What is it psychiatrists call it—a screen memory? He called himself by a common French name, which I've forgotten. It doesn't matter what he called himself that afternoon.

Balaban had been teaching Julia to paint and showed off one of her oils, which stood on the smaller of the two easels.

It was a self-portrait, done in vivid colors, and it seemed to me very good.

"It is good," Balaban said, narrowing her eyes and standing back to look at it critically. Behind me, the young man murmured a word or two of praise, and I had a whiff of his scent, his hair oil.

"Julia puts so much of herself into her work," Balaban said.

I thought: It's a game they've gotten up between them, Balaban and this fellow.

We were offered tea. Balaban went to put a kettle on the gas ring. But it was late. I had to get back to Zurich.

"Irina was employed at the Roykovs'," Balaban said. "Isn't that so?"

I hadn't told her that; I wondered who had, and who Balaban had been questioning about me.

The young man stepped in. "I'm sorry that we haven't had a chance to talk." His French was fluent. "Perhaps another time. I've not had the pleasure of meeting the Roykovs. I'm told they have a remarkable circle of friends, and that discussions there are most lively."

"Yes, there are some very clever people."

"Too much politics," Balaban said, making a face.

"It really is late," I said, and we shook hands at the door.

Julia and I left Balaban's cottage and walked back around the lake toward Julia's cottage.

"Why must your friendship with Madame Balaban be kept secret?" I said. "If she's only teaching you to paint hair . . ."

"She's not supposed to teach me to paint," Julia said. "It excites me too much. The doctors think it's not good for my recovery."

We walked on for a bit and finally I said, "It's Balaban who wants your friendship kept secret, isn't it?"

"Yes."

"But why?"

Julia shook her head. "She just wants to be my friend."

"And you pay her nothing?"

"Oh, no. She won't take money. I offered it to her, but she became offended."

We turned away from the lake and walked along a path, coming out of the woods in sight of Julia's cottage. Andrew stood in the doorway, his hands jammed into his pockets, a worried look on his face.

"Where have you been?" he said.

"We had a long walk," she said, "all around the lake. There was a flight of geese. It was beautiful, Andrew. You should have come."

Julia, I noticed, was an excellent liar.

Andrew had built a fire in the grate and put a kettle on the ring for tea. We were cold and hungry after our walk, and it was delightful around the fire. But when Julia brought around a tray of sandwiches, I noticed something odd.

On the mantel had been a framed photograph of an athletic-looking man in a striped sailor's shirt at the tiller of a boat. There was something familiar about him: I'd seen his face or a photograph of him before. I couldn't remember where. Julia had seen me looking at the photograph, and I had had the feeling she wanted to tell me about him. It was the same feeling I'd had on our walk, just before she'd been distracted by the geese. She wanted to confide her secret. I was sure of it.

But a sudden glance from Andrew had put her off. It was a hard glance, a warning of some sort, which frightened her; she blanched, turned away, and told me nothing.

Now I noticed that the photograph was gone. I looked over at the mantel, and the space was empty. While we were out, Andrew had taken the picture down and put it away.

On the train back to town, Andrew began to talk about Julia's past. "She was married to a friend of mine," he said. "Ray Dean and I were roommates at school and in 1917 we enlisted in the Air Corps together. He was a wonderful pilot, much better than I, and after the war he designed a plane and started a company to build it. I put some money in with him, all his friends did. We were sure he was going to succeed because he always had."

"With Julia, too?"

"Yes, at first. I see what you mean. All the young men were after Julia, and Ray won her. They started out an ideal couple, and I think they were happy for a while. But Ray started to have trouble with the aircraft factory, and that took all his time. Julia isn't a woman you can leave alone. She began to give herself a bad time, and there was a divorce."

"Does Julia still love him?"

"I don't think so. She never talks about him."

"Who was the man in the photograph?"

"What photograph was that?"

"In the sailing shirt, on the mantel."

"I saw no photograph," Andrew said. "There was no photograph."

I didn't press it with him, but his hiding the photograph and then lying about it only made me more curious.

Before he left Zurich, Andrew gave me a manuscript written by a Soviet defector, a former assistant of Stalin's, to translate into English. The writer used a lot of slang and I had to consult the English shelves at the Zentral Bibliothek. In my spare time, I began to read the English and American newspapers.

One day in the *New York Times*, I saw a photograph of a man I thought I recognized. I'd seen his face before, but just where I couldn't say. In the article he was described as a well-known American politician, photographed at his desk behind a battery of microphones. Finally it came to me where I'd seen his face. He was heavier and older, he was dressed differently, and he wore glasses; but I was sure he was the man in the striped sailor's shirt in the photo Julia Winters had kept on her mantel, the same photo Andrew claimed never existed. I read the caption under the photograph, and for the first time learned his name: *Franklin D. Roosevelt*. I must admit at the time it didn't mean a thing to me.

I didn't get to see Julia for several months. In the spring she wrote me at the hospital, saying she was coming to Zurich, and asked if we could meet for dinner.

I found her changed, more relaxed, more lively and confident. I wondered if the doctors at the Meir Clinic had helped her, or if her improvement had to do with being free of Andrew, who had been away for nearly three months.

"I'm going home," she said, "back to America. The doctors told me I'm well. Cured of melancholy," she said, laughing. "I'll bet I'm the only person you know who has had her melancholy removed."

After dinner we went back to her hotel and talked until it was so late that the trams had stopped running, and Julia insisted I sleep there. The two beds in the room were both made up, and they looked so cozy and inviting, and I was too tired to walk across town to my room.

Julia gave me a nightgown made of Chinese silk that she'd bought in Paris, and I'd never felt anything so fine against my skin. She ordered up cognac, a whole bottle and two big goblets, and we smoked American cigarettes, which were delicious. We turned out the lights, drank the cognac, and smoked our cigarettes, lying side by side on twin beds, and she began to tell me about herself and her marriage, and finally she began to talk about Franklin Roosevelt.

"I've known him most of my life," she said. "My mother's family is from New York, the Hudson Valley, where the Roosevelts live. When I was a child, I was taken to visit my grandmother in summer; Franklin was always around, although he was already grown up. I fell in love with him, but not with the kind of schoolgirl's crush that you get over. I grew up, met other men, and married Ray, but I loved Franklin and only pretended to love the others, even my husband."

We drank more cognac, smoked more American cigarettes. Through the spaces between the drawn curtains, I saw the first light of morning.

"After my divorce," Julia said, "I took an apartment in New York, so that Franklin could visit me there. This was before he got polio, but he was already married with five children and with a public career, so there could be no scandal. We never met outside my apartment, and never slept a whole night together. Our love was secret, illicit." She laughed and said, "I didn't mind at all."

"Were you discovered?"

"Not for a long time," she said. "But Franklin has enemies, every powerful man does. And his enemies have spies, and the spies found out about us . . ." She was silent; I waited. "There are things between Franklin and me that I've never told anyone, not even the doctors at Meir." She took a deep breath. "They know I took pills, and nearly died. But they don't know that Franklin found me, called Andrew, and then disappeared. Andrew was left to pick up the pieces, and look after me. Franklin was kept clear of it, and Andrew arranged for me to be whisked off to Meir." She turned and raised her head, and supported it on her arm. "There's another secret, one that even Andrew doesn't know. I've heard from Franklin, a long letter. He loves me, and can't live without me, and has rented an apartment for us." And she said, "Andrew is a guardian of Franklin's career. If he knew that I was going back to Franklin, he'd stop me. You must promise not to tell him. I've trusted you because I had to tell someone. I'm so happy. But it must be our secret. You must promise."

I promised to keep Julia's secret. When Andrew returned to Zurich, I said nothing of her letter from Franklin Roosevelt.

Julia returned to America a few days after we met, and Andrew soon followed. The translations and letters to be passed on from Living Memory became less frequent, and after a time stopped altogether.

Andrew had been unable to tell me anything about the fate of my parents. My contacts among the Russians in Zurich produced nothing. Like so many others in those days, my mother and father had vanished without a trace.

But there was word of Vladimir. He had been arrested and sent to a camp in Siberia. He was alive. The news was brought by Claire Balaban. How she learned it, or why she told me, I never found out.

I had heard what the prison camps were like, so I tried to put Vladimir's fate out of my mind. How else can one live, knowing that a person one loves is a slave in such a brutal place? I tried not to think of his suffering, or to see him cold and starving. But I did see him. And still I believed that he would survive, and I knew that he would survive.

Years passed—three years, four—and nothing was heard of him. Then a former prisoner came out of Russia who claimed to have known Vladimir in the camps, where they had become friends and had escaped together, although afterward each had gone his own way.

I'd known lots of such people, many with fascinating stories. Some were Stalin's spies, some were merely down and out, and others were swindlers. But there were also those who told the truth; to tell one from the others was hard, and I always feared turning my back on one who had suffered and needed help. Though I was suspicious of this fellow— his name was Pleshkov—I questioned him and then heard him out.

"Where did you see Vladimir last?" I said.

"On the Polish border, near Grodno," Pleshkov said. "I continued on the south road from there to Warsaw, where I had friends."

"And Vladimir?"

"He went west to Germany," Pleshkov said. "But I don't know if he made it."

Pleshkov told no tales of heroism or sacrifice. He said only that he had survived nine years in the camps. I believed him.

"What were you charged with?"

"I don't know."

"And how long was your sentence?"

"Indeterminate."

I gave him money for food, found him a place to live, and introduced him to people who could help with travel papers. One day I saw him staring at me in a strange way, and finally he said: "That gold chain around your neck—do you wear a cross inside your blouse?"

"Yes. The Cross of St. Sampson."

"He gave it to you," Pleshkov said. "Here in Zurich, when you were last together."

"It's true that you knew him," I said.

"I pray he's alive," Pleshkov said.

I was restless in Zurich, but stayed on in the hope that Vladimir would come. But in time hope began to fade. I was now a resident in pediatrics, but when a better job was offered me in Geneva, I left word where I could be reached, and went there.

I did my work, lived in a hotel, learned to drive a car, and had love affairs. These were brief, and left no trace, as if written in vapor on window glass; others survive as bits of conversation, erotic visions, men's voices, their rough skin. I see a room in which the bed is covered by a red-and-white patchwork quilt. I see restaurants, streets, a dance hall, its ceiling filled with colored lights.

In 1935, feeling restless again, I left Geneva for Paris, where I rented another attic room, this one on the Rue de Babylone in Montparnasse. I had made friends with a French doctor named Belloc, who had been studying in Geneva, and through him met other doctors and together we opened a small clinic on the Boulevard St. Marcel.

The neighborhood was a working-class one, and we kept the clinic open every day and most nights, collecting fees only from those patients who had jobs or money to pay. Most had nothing, but we got by. We chipped in for bread and milk and passed it out in the mornings to the children. Shopkeepers in the area heard what we were doing and began to help out, and we were given leftover food from a few local restaurants.

Mornings at seven, people were already on line waiting for treatment and something to eat. Much of the illness we saw came from malnutrition, from poor sanitation, from damp and unheated apartments. But we saw every kind of ailment, which much of the time we weren't able to cure. To see daily the misery of the poor made us frustrated and angry.

Many of the Communists around in those days were well intentioned. They believed—because they wanted to believe—that a new

37

world was on the way, led by the Soviet Union. "Things are different there"—that's what I heard all the time. "In Russia there's equality, and better times to look forward to." At first I'd argue, but there's no arguing with people who need something to believe in.

"The time wasn't right for the truth." That's what Andrew Winters had said, and he was right. So I kept my mouth shut, and tried not to think of the camps, of my parents, or of the millions who had perished. I worked all day in the clinic and did what I could. The other doctors were the same—Communist or not—and a loyal camaraderie grew up between us. At the end of a long day we'd go together for a drink and a meal, and on Saturday night we'd go to a dance hall, and once in a while I'd sleep with a fellow because he danced well, because he told a good story, because he or I needed cheering up, or for no reason other than that he took my fancy.

I heard occasionally from Andrew Winters, and saw him when he came through Paris. He rarely spoke to me about Julia, and her letters to me had stopped about the time Franklin Roosevelt was elected President. I never mentioned to Andrew that I knew of their affair. He had been seriously studying Russian, and we spoke it together. I did no translating for him—I was too busy at the clinic—but he was as active as ever with Living Memory, and friendly with every Russian in Paris.

Two years passed. In Paris it rained, or seemed to, most of the time. All winter long it was cold; one couldn't get warm. But it was a satisfying time because I felt useful, and at night I went to sleep so tired from my work at the clinic that I seldom dreamed of Vladimir, and when I did it was of the good times we'd had. I seldom dreamed of my mother and father, and when I did it was again of good times, of childhood when my father was prosperous and we were all happy.

One day in the street, thinking of something else, I was startled by a face I saw reflected in a shop window. The face was mine, although it took a second or two to realize it. There were shadows and lines in the face. It came as a surprise, a realization that my youth was past. I could look ahead, or back over my shoulder; I was in the middle of life, with the expectation that things would go on predictably, continuing as they were. That's what I expected, and perhaps even that's what I wanted.

But I was wrong. Things were not to continue as they were. Ahead were lots of surprises, and the first of these, and the very best, was the reappearance of my beloved Vladimir.

He didn't know where I lived, but he'd heard of the clinic through the Russian grapevine, and one morning he was there, one of the crowd huddled in front of the door. It had taken me a second or two to recognize myself reflected in the shop window, but I knew Vladimir right off. My heart leaped when I saw him, leaning against the wall and smiling weakly at me.

I said I knew he'd survive, and I'd prayed he'd survive, and he had survived. I was told I shouted his name, and that I ran to him, and took him in my arms, and covered him with kisses. I remember none of it. I remember only having him again in my arms.

His clothes were in tatters; he was filthy, smelled like a tramp, and had grown a beard and was weak from not eating. He had walked across France and Germany. He had managed somehow, without money or papers. It wasn't possible, but Vladimir had done it.

I took him home with me, fed and bathed him, and even shaved his beard. All of that before we could talk, although there was so much we had to tell each other. Then he fell asleep, and woke up, and ate again, and slept again, while I sat by the bed, stroking his face and kissing him.

As his strength returned, he began to joke and tease me, and there he was, the indestructible Vladimir, the great fool and genius I had never stopped loving.

# five

WE WERE HAPPY. WE HAD A WARM ROOM OF OUR OWN TO love in, and enough money for food, the delicious food of Paris. We even went out to bistros, to movies, particularly American ones, which we both adored, and to places where we could dance. In short, we began to live like other people.

In order to do that, Vladimir had to be decently dressed. He had arrived only with the clothes on his back, and those were in rags. In the past, with his floppy black hat and cape, he had been something of a dandy. And because I liked him as a dandy, I took him to the shops and fitted him up in dashing clothes. While I was at work in the clinic, he went around Paris, seeing the sights and frequenting the cafés on the Boulevard St. Germain. For that he needed pocket money, which I gave him willingly.

I feared that giving him money would be awkward, and that he'd make a fuss; but not at all. He liked being dressed up by me, and being made much of, and spending his days sightseeing and chatting up the other émigrés. He'd been through hell, and he told me that to find himself alive and with me in Paris, to be free, idle, warm, loved, and well fed, was a miracle. And I wanted the miracle to go on. I wanted to go on slipping money in his pocket when I left for the clinic in the morning, taking care to tiptoe around so as not to wake him, and I wanted to go on buying him dinner and taking him to movies, and I wanted to go on loving him.

But the years had changed us. In Zurich I had idolized and adored him, while he took me, I think, too lightly. No longer. I still adored him, but without illusions. In Paris we uncovered the stamina and endurance of our love. Speaking Russian, we confessed everything to each other, and yet I can't say we told all of the truth. Lovers are not made to talk plain truth to each other.

"Tell me why you went back to Russia," I said.

"Lenin died."

"That was the first time. I'm talking about the second time. Andrew Winters told me there was an order out for your arrest," I said. "But you went back anyway, and your motives weren't political."

"Not political?"

"Why did you go back?"

He had been stroking my hair, but stopped and went for a cigarette, and went through the business of lighting it, pacing back and forth in the little room, and came back to bed and dug under the quilt for my bare foot. When we were alone and talking, he needed to hold on to some part of me—my foot or my hand, sometimes my leg. And he liked to kiss whatever he had hold of. Eventually, he'd rest with his cheek and mustache against my bare stomach, and most nights we went off to sleep that way.

He settled down that night in the same way, but I was persistent, wanting to know why he had gone back to Russia. "It's a woman, isn't it?" I said. "A woman you went back for, a woman you risked your neck for."

"I'm going to tell you the whole story," Vladimir said. And he stroked my foot, and kissed my foot, and kissed one toe after another, and said, "It's a long story, my darling dearest . . ." But he didn't tell me a thing, just went on kissing my foot. I have small feet, and am vain about them and was pleased to have Vladimir kiss them.

"In Zurich, you were also about to tell me a story," I said finally. "You were on the verge, on the verge . . ."

"On the verge of what?"

"Of telling the truth."

"The truth . . ." Again, he kissed my foot. That was Vladimir's truth, this fussing over my foot, which made me feel a little foolish, but meant a lot to him and did no harm. So I let him hold my foot, and let him kiss it to his heart's content.

He said, "I'll open my heart to you."

"Just tell me why you went back to Russia," I said.

"It's a romantic story," he said.

"I'm ready."

"And an adventure story."

There was no hurrying Vladimir, so I settled in for a long story, and knowing Vladimir I settled in for a good story. The time was just past midnight, and outside it was cold and the wind was rattling the windows, and of course it was raining; we heard the rain tapping on the tin roof. But there was a cozy gas fire. The quilt on the double bed was stuffed with goose feathers, and I'd bought a bottle of cognac.

The tale I heard eventually became the centerpiece of the auto-biography that Vladimir was one day to write, a story that would sell hundreds of thousands of copies in twenty languages and make Vladimir rich and famous. He was right that it was a romantic story and an adventure story, and parts of it may even have been true.

Vladimir told me he had been married in Russia to a beautiful princess. He described their wedding, which took place in secret, at the home of the old prince, the bride's father. This was in Moscow, where the Revolution had spread from Petrograd, and during the ceremony there were riots and the sound of shooting in the streets.

Vladimir and his bride spent a single night together.

"Tell me about it. Was it a night of bliss?" I interrupted him. I couldn't resist, and the great fool squeezed my foot and said nothing.

He lowered a curtain on his one night with the beautiful princess. Instead he spoke of hurried embraces and tearful good-bys, of break-neck gallops through the night, of the riots of the workers and the peasants, of how the old prince was murdered and his house burned to the ground.

But the beautiful princess escaped to a remote village east of the Urals. While in Zurich, Vladimir learned that she was alive, and so he returned to Russia, a wanted man, to rescue her.

Quite a story, and Vladimir told it well. I was enthralled, and the gas fire hissed, the cognac went down, and the rain rattled on the tin roof.

I urged Vladimir to go on with his story.

He told me how he used forged documents to cross the border and make his way across Russia, how he swam rivers and trudged through miles of deep snow. He was betrayed to the Cheka and discovered and chased by a band of Red Cavalry, and survived all sorts of adventures, including being attacked by an enraged bear. He told me of shooting a deserter from the Whites, whom he found looting a monastery, and was himself wounded and nursed back to health by an old monk.

He finally arrived at the hut of an old peasant woman, a hut where his wife, the princess, was hiding. He found her dying of pneumonia, with little food and no medicine. They had only a few hours together, she was so near death. She opened her eyes only to see him, to recognize him, and to press her lips to his. She died in his arms and he buried her himself, under a single poplar tree.

He finished the story whispering her name. I think it was Natasha, but perhaps I'm confusing her with that other Natasha, Tolstoy's Natasha.

As I said, a romantic story, and what does it matter if it's true or not? I know how much of the faker there was in Vladimir, and how much of the reckless romantic, but with all his posturing and idling in cafés, and the business with the Czarist foot kissing, he had many fine traits. If he found a deserter looting a monastery, he'd shoot him. If they locked him up in Siberia, he wouldn't lose courage, but would pass on his courage to others and find a way to escape. If he had a wife left behind in Russia, or behind the gates of hell, Vladimir would go back for her, and he'd find her, and take her in his arms, and if she were dying she'd look up at the last moment and see his face and at least know that he had come for her, and loved her.

It was nearly dawn when he finished his story. The cognac was gone, the rain had stopped, and Vladimir was grieving for the beautiful princess, his Natasha or Tolstoy's Natasha, and real tears were rolling down his cheeks. At the same time he was telling me how he loved me, always loved me, and was kissing my hand, my foot, and every part of me, and pleading with me to forgive him.

I think I forgave him—he was always pleading and I was always forgiving—but I had drunk such a lot of cognac, and was so exhausted, that I'm not sure what happened. I know we fell asleep, and probably we made love, although I'm not sure of that either. But in Paris we were making love and falling asleep all the time. Vladimir could have had a wife, or three wives, it wouldn't have mattered. He was a rascal and a faker and a wonderful man, and I wish he were with me now. I wish he were here in the next room, so he could hold my foot, and I could tell him I forgive him—for whatever he was up to—and tell him how I missed him when he wasn't around, and always loved him.

# six

☭ SERGE DOLIN, THE YOUNG MAN IN CLAIRE BALABAN'S STUDIO in the Meir Clinic, was an agent of the Soviet secret service, traveling to Berlin and Prague, to Warsaw and Budapest; in his travels he spent time in every major capital of Eastern Europe. His cover was as a journalist, accredited to *Maintenant*, a Paris weekly of the militant left. These were the days in which the European Comintern was being built, and Serge Dolin's job was to tighten the bolts, to recruit and secure new agents and eliminate those who strayed.

Over the years he earned a reputation for intelligence and dedication. He was known to be worldly and widely read, at home with the artists and intellectuals of the left; a ladies' man. In Moscow he was praised for his skills as an organizer and valued for his connections, but most of all for his loyalty and ruthlessness, the qualities that in Stalin's court ranked above everything else.

In 1932 he was promoted to major, and returned to Paris, where he was made resident of the Baur network, outside of Germany, the most important in Europe.

Claire Balaban was then living in Paris, a member of the Baur network, and he contacted her and arranged to meet her in a café in the Gare du Nord.

Her first words were to congratulate him on his promotion, at the same time casting a flattering eye over the way he had matured as well as prospered. Balaban was an old friend, a family friend, free to joke in Russian with the new major. She commented on his continuing interest in fine tailoring and judged his changed hairstyle more becoming. He had grown a mustache and she admired that.

"It's to make me look older," he said.

"These days in Germany every fellow is wearing a mustache," Balaban said, "as a tribute to Herr Hitler."

Serge acknowledged the joke. "By next year Hitler could be in power," he said. "That's what Otto Weiner thinks. Hitler will take power, Hitler and his ridiculous mustache."

"Where does that leave us?"

"He'll try to crush the party in Germany."

The café waiter interrupted to take their order. When he had gone, Serge said: "In America things are a little better. There they may turn to Roosevelt."

Balaban nodded, lit one Gaulois with the end of another; they were getting down to business, to the purpose for their meeting.

"You want to know about Julia Winters," Balaban said. "She writes long letters, endless letters full of her thoughts about life—her philosophy." Balaban dismissed Julia's letters with a wave of her work-man's hands. "Schoolgirl prattle."

"Does she have any politics?"

"She thinks people ought to get along better with one another," Balaban said. "She prays for universal peace."

"What about gossip?"

"Some, not much. Poor Julia, she lacks malice."

"Does she see Roosevelt?"

"Whenever it can be arranged. He adores her. She's taken an apartment in Manhattan, and he visits her there."

"Are they lovers?"

"Intimate friends." Balaban shrugged. "Lovers or not, Julia is dis-creet on the subject, and I don't know precisely."

"But emotionally, they are deeply involved?"

"That's a good way to put it," Balaban said.

Dolin had ordered coffee, Balaban her usual Pernod. After it was served, she said, "She's invited me to New York, even to stay with her."

"I'd like you to do that."

"For a visit, do you mean?"

"Permanently."

"I'm settled here," Balaban said. "I have a home, my career is here."

"The party has great influence in the New York art world," Serge said. "Party members, sympathizers. They'll see your work is well ex-hibited and reviewed. There'll be commissions."

"I don't speak a dozen words of English."

"For a clever woman, English is nothing to learn," Serge said. "And I'm told Americans are charmed by an accent."

"And I'm to get to know Roosevelt? Is it that important?"

"A direct line to Franklin Roosevelt? Nothing could be more im-portant for us. In New York you'll operate outside the network. Resign from the party. Speak out against Stalin's excesses. Above all, have nothing to do with the network. Your only contact will be through me.

45

I'll set up a mail drop, a private one, and we'll write each other confidential letters."

"Like lovers?"

"Exactly like lovers."

"I'm old enough to be your mother," she said. "Or at least your aunt, your Tante Claire." When Serge Dolin chose to spread his charm, to unroll it like a red carpet, she was unable to resist him. "Just now you look much like your mother."

He took her hand; it wasn't to coax her or to persuade her. She needed no persuasion. He pressed her hand to his lips.

"My hands are ugly," she said.

"My mother called you her best friend."

"I adored her, Larisa Sergeyevna." Balaban made a deep sigh and left her hand in Serge's. "I adored your mother."

"The portrait you did of her, the one that hung in our house in Moscow," he said. "Did you ever find out what became of it?"

"No."

"I'd like to find it one day. I'm always looking in shops," he said. "It's become an obsession."

"Last it was in the hands of your father."

"What did he do with it?"

"He was angry with her. He never forgave her."

"For what?"

"I don't know."

"Tell me."

"They say she had a lover, but I don't believe it. Your father was a purist, a loyal Bolshevik and also ambitious for himself. In all of that he and your mother didn't see eye to eye."

"Did he have her arrested?"

"I don't know."

"Do you think so?"

"She disappeared," Balaban said. "Some say she went abroad, or that she died. But nobody knows for sure."

"He knows."

"There are rumors he's ill."

"I've heard them."

Balaban had opened her handbag and was searching inside of it. All the while she mumbled, "A strange man, your father. Tormented, brilliant." She found what she was looking for, a plain envelope, which she handed to Serge.

In it was a photograph of his mother, taken in some country place.

She stood in front of a hedge, a bunch of flowers in her hands, a spaniel lying at her feet.

"I was packing up some things and found it."

"She's very young here."

"It must have been taken just after you were born."

Dolin studied the photograph. "How did they meet?" he said.

"Larisa and your father? At a concert, I think."

"My father at a concert?"

"Perhaps it was a party. There was a family connection of some sort, a distant one. It's such a long time ago. Your father was a student, newly arrived in Moscow."

"And my mother dazzled him?"

"She dazzled everyone."

"Did he love her?"

"Of course."

"And later on he let her be taken away?"

Balaban shook her head, for a moment unable to think of an answer. Finally, she said, "One can't limit one's commitment to the party. It's all or nothing—an absolute."

"It's true." Dolin looked away, and then said, "The party must be an absolute."

"You resemble her," Balaban said, "but you want to be like him."

"With his commitment."

"Be careful, Serge. You don't know what they'll finally demand of you."

Dolin kept the photograph of his mother. He had rented an apartment in Paris, on the Rue Dauphine, and settled down to write a series of interviews and articles for *Maintenant*. His name began to be known. In Moscow his star continued to rise; he was not only the son of a famous and influential father, but the protégé of Stalin himself.

But with all this before him, Serge Dolin was often distracted and at times found it difficult to concentrate on his work. He lacked the single-mindedness of his father; he began, secretly, to doubt himself, and even the Soviet state.

In order to sort out his thoughts and get things off his chest, he began to write a private journal. But this was a dangerous matter. Secret agents do not keep private journals. Dolin destoryed his, and began it again. It was the only outlet he had. Eventually he found a solution. Every night he wrote a couple of pages—clearing his soul, he called it—and in the morning he tore everything up and burned the scraps of paper in an ashtray.

Toward the end of 1932, Otto Weiner, the head of the Comintern in Germany, arrived in Paris from Moscow. The day after his arrival Dolin met him in the garden of the Louvre.

Weiner was then fifty-three and traveled with a woman thirty years younger, whom he'd taken off the Berlin streets as a child, and then fallen in love with. Now it turned out he'd married her. "An unexpected burst of bourgeois respectability," Weiner called it.

She was a singer, popular in the political cabarets of Berlin. "She uses the name Roth," Weiner said. "It's her real name, Mitzi Roth. She's Jewish."

"Have you brought her to Paris?"

"With Hitler's bunch in the streets, I wouldn't leave her alone in Berlin."

Weiner was tall and heavily built. In his youth he'd been a sailor and worked on the Hamburg docks, where he'd been known for his physical strength and courage. There were stories of heroic battles against the Kaiser's police, and later on against the National Socialist Brown Shirts. To Dolin he seemed worn out, a towering ruin lumbering alongside him in the Louvre garden, gasping for breath.

"Come on, I've got to sit down," Weiner said. "I can't breathe." He took a pill from a small box in his coat pocket, put it on the back of his tongue, and swallowed it. "Nitro," he said. "I've got a bum ticker."

"You've got to go back to Berlin," Dolin said.

"You're giving me orders then?"

"You were told the same thing in Moscow," Dolin said. "Instead you came here."

"I want Mitzi safe."

"It's a crucial time in Germany," Dolin said. "Hitler will try to destroy the party. It's already becoming disorganized. With your influence you can bring them back together. Convince them to hold fast."

"Against Hitler?"

"Yes, of course."

"In Moscow there's talk of a deal with Hitler," Weiner said. "Moscow is going to shake hands with the Austrian corporal and sell out the German comrades."

"If you go back, you can salvage the underground."

"And if I don't go back?"

"Then you'll be alone."

"And you'd have me killed."

"It wouldn't be up to me."

"I want Mitzi to stay here, where the Austrian corporal can't get his mitts on her." Weiner took a deep breath, like a diver coming up for air. The day was cool, but he was sweating. "In a café she once insulted him, that shit of an Austrian corporal."

"We can look after her here."

"She won't stay without me," Weiner said. "That's the trouble. Because I'm sick, she won't let me go alone. Mitzi's tough, a tough little yid, you know what I mean?"

Dolin said, "If Moscow makes a deal with Hitler, it's to give us time. It's to protect the party, for the good of the party."

"You believe that crap?"

"I believe in the future."

Weiner tapped his chest. "A good thing I won't be around to see it." He rose slowly to his feet. The nitro pill had helped; he breathed easier and a little color had returned to his face. "I got news of your father, Stenoviev, the great prince of the Revolution. Are you as tough as he? I hear you are. Fancy clothes, a gentleman's education, but under the silk shirt is the heart of a Moscow thug."

"It's because you've got to go back to Berlin," Dolin said. "I don't blame you for being bitter."

"I'm not bitter."

"It's because Moscow will make a deal with Hitler. That's making you bitter."

He turned on Serge, seizing the lapels of his jacket; his fists were huge and heavy, like a pair of clubs. "I'm going to close up shop in Berlin, and send Mitzi out. If something happens to me, I want your promise to look after her."

"She'll be protected."

"See she goes to the States."

"If that's what she wants."

Weiner let Serge go. "I'm sorry. I'm glad you didn't get sore. The news is your father is in London."

"What?"

"He's also got a bum ticker," Weiner said. "A private hospital in Hammersmith called the Pembroke Clinic. I was told to deliver the message. He wants to see you."

Dolin didn't go directly to London. An agent planted in the Quai d'Orsey had picked up word of a senior Soviet diplomat in Amsterdam who had approached the French with the idea of defecting. Dolin had to interview the agent, write his report, code it, and transmit it to Moscow. Then he had to sit tight, awaiting Moscow's word on how the diplomat in Amsterdam should be handled. Finally, Dolin was dis-

49

patched to Amsterdam to have a look. The diplomat was to return to Moscow. If he refused, Dolin was to see that he went.

His orders on that score were explicit; on no account was the diplomat to be allowed to defect. Nor was he to be killed. Moscow wanted an opportunity to interrogate.

In Amsterdam, Dolin passed the word to the diplomat. But he refused to go home. When he ran, Dolin was waiting. There was a brawl. The diplomat was taken to a safe house in Harlingen on the North Sea, while local people calmed the Dutch police.

One night, the diplomat was put aboard a fishing boat with Dutch registration, and four miles off the coast he was transferred to a Soviet freighter, the *Luxembourg*.

The Dutch police, however, were stirred up, some thought by French Counterintelligence. The press got wind of it, and Dolin had to stay on in Amsterdam, covering the tracks left by other Soviet agents. A French comrade working for Dolin knew a Dutch comrade in the Ministry of Justice, and the diplomat's file was edited and found its way to the dead archives. Sometime later it was misplaced, then it vanished altogether.

By that time Dolin was back in Paris.

In Moscow, it was said, Stalin heard of the resolution of the Amsterdam case as he was going to dinner; he was so pleased that he ate a second bowl of potato soup and drank another bottle of his favorite Georgian wine.

Now that he had time, Dolin began to think again of his father. He had few personal memories of him, and none that could be called loving, even affectionate. He had been in Europe, taking the name Dolin, living an underground life, since the age of twenty. Of his father, he could recall only a remote, uncompromising presence, a figure carved in stone. Yet he was prominent in Dolin's ephemeral journals, and figured in his reflections on himself; Stenoviev cast a shadow across the passionate memory Dolin had of his mother.

He decided to travel to London under a different name, and got hold of a Belgian passport, one cool enough to pass the keen British immigration officers. England wasn't the Continent, where spies soared like hawks across the frontiers. Dolin knew of several who had been treated roughly by British Counterintelligence. The name on the Belgian passport was Albert Baum, a traveler for the firm of Friedrich & Gentes, manufacturers of maritime navigational equipment.

Dolin checked into a hotel near Victoria Station, contacted a jittery agent on the London *Times*, and spent three days making sure he wasn't watched, while he enjoyed the sights of London.

On the morning of his fourth day, just as he was growing edgy and wondering what was going on, the jittery agent called with the news that Stenoviev had been moved to a private clinic in Brighton, a place called the Royal Essex, where he was registered under the name of Joseph Brown.

Dolin spent a cautious day in Brighton, having a look around. In the car park behind the Royal Essex, he spotted a black Riley Saloon with diplomatic registration. Later he saw two blocks cut from the same slab of Russian granite, both in blue suits that didn't fit, both with Moscow Center written all over them.

Dolin took a deep breath and went through the front door of the Royal Essex. He asked to see Mr. Joseph Brown. He was directed to a staircase that led to the second floor—room 6. He expected the corridor to be littered with blocks of Moscow granite.

There wasn't a single one in sight. There wasn't a doctor, an orderly, or a nurse. The corridor was empty. Dolin knocked softly on the door of room 6. There was no answer. He tried the door. It was open. He tiptoed in.

Stenoviev was in a deep chair, dressed in a collar and tie and a woolen dressing gown, his legs wrapped in a blanket. He had dozed off while reading, the book open on his chest. He wore, as he always had, steel-wire pince-nez.

He woke when he heard Dolin. His eyes, behind the lenses, were blue—Dolin remembered them being brown—and he stared at his son without recognition, with alarm, an expresssion of fear.

Dolin expected to hear him call for help. He thinks I'm an assassin, Dolin thought.

A second or two passed in which neither man spoke. The fright went out of Stenoviev's eyes. Dolin saw a glimmer of recognition.

"Is it you?"

"Yes."

He pinched the bridge of his glasses and lifted them from his nose. "They hurt, you know. But I've grown used to them." He rubbed the bridge of his nose and sipped a bit of water from a glass on a table at his side. "Would you have known me?" he said.

"No."

"Nor I you."

"You recognized me."

51

"I've had word of you."

"A deduction then," Dolin said.

Stenoviev put his glasses back on for a better look at his son. "There's a chair there. Please bring it and sit near me."

"You don't look ill," Dolin said.

"The doctors say I'm going to live. No smoking, one glass of vodka a day."

"Did you ever take more than one glass?"

"Not even that," Stenoviev said. "I hear your work for the most part is good."

"For the most part."

"Yes, there is criticism. It's said you have been known to enter into friendships outside the party. There are stories of women."

Dolin gazed steadily at his father; there was no judgment in his look, nothing angry or even cold. But neither was there love in it, not a bit of love.

Stenoviev understood that look, and returned it without flinching.

"Let me give you a warning," he said. "It concerns Balabanovna. Claire Balaban."

"Mother's old friend."

"I don't know about that," Stenoviev said impatiently. "I'm speaking of her work for us. That's all that concerns me. At home there are some who have their eyes on her. Her access to Roosevelt has impressed them, and given them big ideas."

"What sorts of ideas?"

"I'm only warning you."

"What sorts of ideas?"

"In due course you'll hear the code name Archangel," Stenoviev said. "It has to do with intelligence about Roosevelt acquired from Balabanovna. But more than that . . ."

"More than that?"

"A plan to influence policy in America," Stenoviev said. "In my view it could be dangerous, highly so."

"Is that why you asked to see me?"

"Yes, to warn you."

"Are you going home soon?"

"In a fortnight."

"I've got something to show you." It was the photograph of Larisa Sergeyevna, Serge's mother, which he now showed to Stenoviev.

"Have you had this all the while you've been abroad?"

"Yes. She gave it to me," Dolin said. "Before she disappeared."

"I don't remember this picture," Stenoviev said. "It must have been taken before we were married."

"She told me it was after. After I was born."

"No, it's before."

"Are you sure?"

"No, I'm not sure at all. It could have been before, it could have been after." He shook his head slowly and sat with his shoulders slumped forward, looking suddenly old and exhausted. "May I keep the picture?"

"Yes."

"You resemble her," Stenoviev said. "A great resemblance, except that her hair was a bit lighter. When you came in, because you resemble her, I recognized you."

"Then it wasn't a deduction."

"No."

It was time to go. Dolin stood and held out his hand. Again their eyes met and Dolin saw something in his father's eyes that he had not seen before. It was nothing that he understood. It might have been affection, a fleeting memory, a moment of regret. Perhaps it was only something Dolin imagined.

Quickly there were goodbys, and Dolin went out, certain that he would never see his father again, and wondering what would become of the photograph of Larisa Sergeyevna.

# seven

☭ MY LIFE IN PARIS WITH VLADIMIR HAD SETTLED INTO A ROU-
tine, which suited me, but not him. He wasn't the kind to hang his hat
long in one place. He had no work permit, and even though I was
perfectly satisfied to go on giving him the money he needed, the novelty of that for him had worn off.

"It's possible to get a work permit," I said. "There are jobs around,
things you can do."

"Yes, by all means. I know of a Russian restaurant near the Etoile.
They are looking for a doorman; he must speak Russian, and he must
be tall. It's essential that he be tall, so that when he's dressed up like a
cossack, he'll be impressive. Do you think I can dress up like a cossack
and be impressive?"

"There are better jobs."

"Of course. For example, in the same restaurant one can strum the
balalaika while brandishing shashlik on a flaming sword."

"There are other jobs," I said. "Some that are worthwhile."

"I've been offered one," Vladimir said. "The work is interesting,
the pay isn't much, but there's an opportunity for travel. Do you want
to hear about it?"

"I can guess." I'd given him Andrew Winters' address in New
York, and there had been letters back and forth.

"Are you going to work for Winters?"

"Yes."

"And going to America?"

"Both of us," Vladimir said. "Dearest darling . . ." He began prat-
tling in his terrible English. "My name is Vladimir, so glad to meet
you. Thank you. Good-by. Hello." And then in French, "Andrew
wants us both to go to work for him. He's got Roosevelt's ear, and has
been given money to build up Living Memory."

"I'm not going to America," I said.

"But Winters wants you."

"Does he? Winters wants me to go, and you want me to go, and so
it's settled." I was shouting, furious at Vladimir, and at Andrew. "I
suppose you've negotiated a salary for me, and maybe a place to live,

and all of it accomplished without a word to me. Winters offers you a job for me, and you accept for me . . ."

"But why are you angry?" Vladimir said. "Dearest darling . . ."

"Enough! If I hear darling or dearest once more, I'll hit you with this lamp." I actually had the lamp in my hand, and held it like a club.

"I have a job here, a life here," I shouted. "I've worked years to build up my practice at the clinic. You think that's nothing? And what about the doctors I work with? We're a team, we rely on one another. I have a responsibility to them."

"But I thought you liked Winters."

"What has that to do with it?"

"And working with Living Memory, I thought you liked that, too."

"But I'm not a professional spy," I said. "I'm not an adventurer, and I'm not a romantic. I'm not a beautiful princess, or a tragic heroine, or any kind of heroine. I try to see the world as it is, and myself as I am. I'm a woman thirty-eight years old, a doctor. Now and then I take out an appendix, or treat a case of measles or pneumonia. It's not much, a drop in the bucket, but at least once in a while it does a little good."

Vladimir listened to all of this without a word; he listened with his chin on his chest. He listened and nodded, and let me go on, and finally said in a soft voice, "It's true. You have a place, a real place, but I don't. As it is now I'm an idler; I sit in cafés and chew the fat with other idlers. I watch them borrow money from one another, brag to one another, and tell one another cock-and-bull stories."

Poor Vladimir. He looked so downcast that my anger vanished as suddenly as it had come. In our first days togther, he'd seemed a hero, and I now regretted the harsh things I'd just said.

"You're not like the others in the cafés," I said. "They talk, but haven't done a thing. You've been a soldier, you've risked your neck, and you've starved in the camps."

"But none of that matters," he said. "What can I do besides odd jobs? I've no skills to sell. My only real use is to a man like Winters. If he wants to build up Living Memory, I can help him do that. I've been in the White Guards, in Lenin's prison, and Stalin's too. Living Memory will talk to me. I'm one of them and we understand one another."

For once Vladimir spoke simply and directly. He didn't strut or try to charm me or win me over. He didn't reach under the covers for my foot, or try any monkey business at all. He only told me truthfully what was on his mind, and I merely listened, and that brought us even closer together than we had been before.

It was several weeks before Vladimir left. Winters had to complete arrangements—an American visa, French travel documents, a ticket on the *Normandy*. A courier would be sent from New York to meet us on the dock in Le Havre.

"Why send a courier from New York?" I said. "Andrew can use Roosevelt's name. The papers could be sent in the diplomatic pouch."

"He doesn't work that way. Living Memory is his. He won't share it with the American Department of State. He doesn't trust them, not as far as Living Memory is concerned."

"Perhaps it's us he doesn't trust," I said. "That's why he's arranged for the travel documents and visa to be given only at the last minute. The war could start anytime, and Paris is full of people who would pay a fortune for a set of papers."

Vladimir said, "There'll be two sets of papers. I told Winters you were coming."

"You still think I'll change my mind?"

"One way or another, you'll have the papers," Vladimir said. "If you don't come, put them away. But I have a hunch—call it a hope— that you'll change your mind at the last minute, and we'll go to New York together."

Vladimir was right. I nearly did change my mind. I thought of giving up the clinic and going with him to America; I thought of going, and decided to go with him, and resolutely decided to go with him, and woke in the middle of the night frightened that he had already gone, and clung to him; but in the morning, hurrying to open the clinic, I was determined to stay, and keep on with the life I had made.

When the day came for Vladimir to leave, I was still vacillating. Only on the boat train, crowded in with the others who were leaving, among the refugees, did I decide finally to stay in Paris. I had a room of my own, and in it were furniture of my own, books of my own, and one or two pictures on the wall. I belonged in Paris, and not among the refugees, fleeing with their pale and frightened faces, their suitcases and overflowing cartons.

Vladimir was thrilled at going to America. When we arrived at the dock, in the center of all that hubbub, the shouted good-bys and the hustle and bustle of the porters, the tears of the refugees, I sensed his eagerness to be gone.

I resented that, and had to fight to hold back my tears, and fight even harder to make sure he saw none of what I felt; I wouldn't try to keep him with me in Paris. I wouldn't cling to him. I had been alone before he came, and was ready to be alone again, and if I missed him, and if my heart ached for him, it was something to be kept to myself, my own affair.

In the meantime we were on the lookout for Winters' courier, who was to meet us with the travel papers.

"How are we to recognize him?" I said.

"He'll be carrying a copy of the *Herald Tribune,*" Vladimir said. "His name is Willi."

"Willi Koder. Willi the Mouse," I said. "Andrew used him as a mailman in Zurich."

It was getting close to time for final boarding. Vladimir had begun to worry that he'd missed Willi or there had been a mix-up, and he'd gone to Cherbourg to meet the *Queen Mary,* which was sailing the same day. Finally, I picked Willi the Mouse out of the crowd; he was a big man, not as tall as Vladimir, but twenty pounds heavier. He wasn't timid, and as I was to learn, there was nothing particularly furtive about him, nothing of the mouse. He didn't steal other people's cheese, and he wasn't one to scamper for his hole when the lights came on. He was called the Mouse because he'd worked as a cartoonist in Vienna, where he'd stayed alive pirating Walt Disney characters. I remember him signing his name with a little sketch of Mickey Mouse. I thought him oddly conspicuous for a spy, but he was clever, a staunch friend and fearless. It was his reckless courage that finally did him in, but that was a few years off, and of course I didn't know that on the dock in Le Havre.

He saw me at about the same time I saw him, and shouldered his way toward us through the crowd. He nodded to Vladimir and kissed my hand, which took me by surprise. He really was an amusing and likable man, although I hadn't learned to take him seriously.

He took hold of both our arms, apologizing for being late, making jokes about the weather on the Atlantic in winter, handing out seasick pills, and all the while firmly leading us to the buffet at the end of the dock, where he handed us each an envelope drawn from inside his coat.

"All the documents you need are there," he said. "Priceless these days, priceless. Put them in a safe place. Good luck. Bon voyage. Don't forget to take your pills."

Vladimir put his envelope inside the pocket of his coat, but I held mine, not quite sure what to do with it. Willi was sharp, and immediately sensed that something was wrong. "You really must put that in a safe place," he said.

I started to speak; I was going to tell Willi that I wasn't going. I was going to return the documents, but Vladimir cut me off. He quickly shook hands with Willi, and took him aside. I heard him say something about friends here to see us off. Somehow he got rid of Willi. I was left with the envelope of travel documents.

"You know I'm not going with you," I said to Vladimir.

"I know. You didn't bring any luggage," he said. "There's going to be war. What then?"

"I'm staying in Paris."

"At least hold on to the American visa."

"Good-by, Vladimir."

"Wait."

I kissed and held him, and pulled away. I feared I'd never see him again. I was convinced of it. I turned and walked quickly away. There was a blast from the ship's whistle, and lots of shouting men and women tearfully clinging to one another and porters dashing with luggage, and cries that it was time to board. I broke into a run, half expecting Vladimir to run after me, hoping that he would. I thought I heard his voice above the noise of the boarding. I thought I heard him shouting my name, but I'm not sure.

# eight

☭ I TOOK THE PARIS TRAIN LATER THAT SAME AFTERNOON. FEW people were returning, and I had a compartment to myself. I'd brought a book and read for a while, and looked out at the countryside. The morning rain had left a heavy mist in the air, blurring things and making them seem out of focus. My thoughts were of Vladimir, who had reentered my life, filled it, and then gone away. The miles passed. I read, dozed off, and was awakened when the conductor came around for my ticket.

I was hungry and thirsty, and after a wash I walked to the dining car, where there were only a few people and where I was shown to an empty table. I ordered dinner and drank some wine. I'd brought my book, and when I looked up from it, a man was standing over my table. I wasn't really surprised to see Willi Koder.

"We're both alone," he said. "May I join you?"

"Yes, of course."

"I had the feeling you weren't going to America," he said.

I offered no explanation, and Willi didn't pursue it. He acted as if it were no concern of his whether I used my visa or not. We talked about dinner, what I had ordered, what he was going to order. He noticed the book I was reading. We talked about books; we talked about movies. Willi loved movies, and he told me that he intended to go to California and get a job in Hollywood.

"I want to work for Walt Disney." He had a broad smile that showed the metal in his teeth. "I sent him a portfolio of my sketches, but so far I've had no luck. Last Christmas, I got a job in Macy's, doing sketches of people for a dollar." Willi the Mouse knew how to get by in hard times, and how to keep his spirits up by making a joke of it. "Macy and me, we were partners. Fifty cents for him, fifty cents for me. Sometimes I got a quarter tip. The women are the tippers, you know. But I think it's because I make them look like movie stars."

Willi had stories about the goings-on in Macy's, and other stories about New York. He was an amusing man, good to have dinner with, and he was a sport. I'd been drinking carafe wine, and he ordered a bottle of champagne.

59

"It's cold in New York, isn't it?" I said. "But warm in California."

"It's heaven," he said. "Absolute heaven, Los Angeles is. And the houses, the mansions." He clapped his hands. "God in heaven, the mansions."

"You've been there?"

"Not yet," he said.

We drank the champagne and Willi ordered a second bottle. "I send the bill to Andrew Winters," he said. "I can only guess who he sends it to."

With the champagne, I was feeling gayer; I was determined to be gay, and not go around mooning for Vladimir. I even flirted with Willi the Mouse. "If you had to, you'd pay for the champagne yourself," I said. "You're the kind to spread his money around."

"Sure, if the company is good. And it's true Winters watches every penny," Willi said. "I do a lot of his odd jobs."

Conversation had gone along easily, but suddenly there was a long-ish pause. I saw the wheels turn slowly in Willi's mind. Certainly he'd followed me from the dock, contrived to join me in the dining car, and was now getting down to the reason for it all.

It wasn't that he had his eye on me; it wasn't to be lust. There's a pity, I thought, although Willi was no beauty. But with the wine in me, with Vladimir again come and gone, I did crave a man's warmth, a man's weight.

"I've heard you run a dispensary in Paris," Willi said finally. "And that you help out people in trouble."

"Who have you heard that from?"

"People talk," he said. He had been sitting back from the table with his legs crossed and the right side of his face toward me. Just then he shifted and turned and I noticed a swelling and discoloration on his left cheek, a bruise that he'd tried to conceal with powder.

"I've got a friend in Paris," he said. "A kid, really, the daughter of a man I used to know. She wrote me in New York, but I didn't get the letter for months. You understand, I've got to move around a lot." He noticed my glance move to the bruise on his cheek. "I got into a scrape," he said.

"People talk . . . I got into a scrape . . ." I had to laugh. "Are you as mysterious as all that, Willi?"

"It was a woman," he said. "Not the kid in Paris. Nothing to do with the kid in Paris," he said, touching the bruise. "This one got into a jealous fit."

"And she socked you in the eye?"

"Later on, we made up," he said. "Life is short, after all. I watched him pour another glass of champagne and watched the froth rise in the narrow glass.

"On the dock I was wearing a hat," he said. "Did you happen to notice it? Gray, with a little green feather."

"I certainly noticed your hat, Willi."

"It's a Borsalino," he said. "A Borsalino like that costs twenty dollars. She bought me it to make up."

"It's begun to rain again," I said.

"Now the kid in Paris," he said. "That's a different story."

I said, "Does the boat dock in New York, or is there a boat train?"

"Right in Manhattan. The pier is there, and they park the boat like a car."

"Five days across," I said, and suddenly was about to cry. What a damn fool, I thought; yet it took all I had to keep back the tears.

"Drink up," Willi said. "Go on, you'll see him again. It's not the end of things, not by a long shot. You've got your own entry permit. Follow up if you want."

"Tell me about the girl in Paris," I said. "Your friend's daughter."

"Her father was a good friend of mine," Willi said. "He published a newspaper and I worked for him. He was a good guy, and I owe him a lot of favors. As for the daughter, well I used to bounce little Magda on my knee. She's still a kid," he said. "She never was a sweetie of mine. You see, I got out of Vienna a step ahead of the Nazis, and it was Magda's father who loaned me the money. He stuck around a day too long, and they snuffed him out. Magda was in Paris, in school, but now she's got no money, and her papers have run out." He took an envelope out of his pocket and laid it on the table under my plate. "Working for Winters keeps me hopping," he said. "So I'll only be changing trains in Paris. You see, there's a fellow I got to have a few words with in Amsterdam. Could you put the envelope in your bag?"

"What's in it?"

"Four hundred American dollars, and Magda's address," he said.

"Why don't you give her the money yourself?"

"I told you, I've got to be in Amsterdam."

"Tell me the real reason," I said. "You want me to help, tell me the truth. Has it to do with Andrew Winters?"

"No, nothing like that."

"Then what?"

"It's personal," he said. "Magda's a funny kid. She's up against it—

no papers, no money. But if I brought the money around she might throw it in my face."

I took the envelope and put it in my bag.

"Maybe she'll tell you the story—it's up to her," he said.

And that was all he said. When we ate dinner, we talked of other things, and said good-by in the Gare du Nord. I went directly to the clinic, where I knew there would be people waiting, some who were sick and some who needed only an aspirin and a kind word. It was past nine o'clock by the time I left. According to Willi, Magda Renner lived on the Rue Hebrod, an alley off the Place du Maroc, in a place called the Hotel Morocco. It took me an hour to find it, and when I arrived the old crone of a concierge complained of the lateness of the hour and directed me to the top of four flights of stairs, which reeked of cabbage and bad plumbing. I knew lots of places like the Hotel Morocco, with walls that were cold and clammy to the touch, with hallways that were alive with roaches and mice, and where all night long one heard the deadly coughing and crying of hungry and sick children.

I came at last to the top floor of the Hotel Morocco, and knocked on Magda's door. There was no response.

I knocked again. There was a muffled sound, a woman's voice, a soft groan. I tried the door. It was unlocked and I went in.

The room was dark and cold, that particular penetrating chill of an unheated building. As my eyes adapted to the dark, I made out a bed in the corner, and someone lying on it. The electric lights didn't work. I parted the curtain and let in a little light from the street. The figure on the bed was a woman, her dark hair spread out on the pillow. She stirred and took a deep breath, although her eyes remained closed.

"Magda Renner?" I said. "Can you hear me? Willi Koder sent me. I'm a doctor. Do you have pain anywhere?"

Her eyes flickered, opened, and closed, and she parted her lips as if to speak, but only shook her head.

I could see she was running a fever, and when I took her pulse, it was rapid, but regular. I'd come from the clinic with my medical bag, and took her temperature and read it in the light from the street; it was 102 degrees. I palpated her abdomen, looking for tenderness in the liver or spleen. There was no pain when I pressed the abdominal wall, no sign of peritonitis. I found a water tap, rinsed a glass, dissolved two aspirins, and raised and held her head so that she could drink the mixture.

Because she was sweating and shivering simultaneously, I took off my coat and wrapped it around her.

"I'm going to call a friend of mine with a car," I said. "We're going to my place. It's warm, and I can look after you there." Her eyes were open and fixed on me; I saw in them the dull indifference of the sick and undernourished. "I'll telephone and be right back," I said.

I had to wake the concierge, and pay her to use the phone. I called one of the doctors from the clinic at home, and he promised to come for us in his car. He said it would be less than half an hour.

The concierge was grumbling about being awakened again, and then asked for money. "She hasn't paid me in two weeks," she said.

"How much?"

"Twenty francs."

"For that pigsty? There's no heat, and the lights don't even work."

"I have my costs," she said, "And I'm paid to look the other way. She has no card. I run a risk."

I gave her the twenty francs and told her to pack Magda's things, that I'd be back for them in a day or two. When I returned to Magda's room, I found her dozing, but she woke when she heard me. I thought her temperature was a little lower.

I sat next to her on the bed, and took hold of her hand. Her fingers were long, and the palm was calloused; her hand was limp now, but I realized that she wasn't frail, that when she was well she was certainly strong.

"The car will be here any minute," I said. "Do you think you can walk?"

She nodded her head. I helped her up and put my arm around her waist, and together we made it down the stairs. In a few minutes the car arrived, and I helped her in and we drove to my place, where I put her to bed, warmed some clear soup, and fed it to her along with two more aspirins.

When she was asleep, I made a bed for myself on the couch. I was tired enough to fall asleep almost at once, but I suddenly woke up and was wide awake. Either I'd dreamed it or I'd heard a groan. I ran to the bed and looked down at Magda; she was sleeping peacefully. Her skin was dry and her fever was gone. I turned on the bed lamp, and for the first time saw her face clearly. She was beautiful, and very young, like a child asleep, pale and perfect.

I slept myself, a good night's sleep, and when I opened my eyes, she was already awake, her brown eyes watching me.

"Are you feeling better?"

"Yes."

"My name is Irina Markova. I went to your room and brought you here to my apartment. Do you remember that?"

"Some of it. Why have you helped me out?"

"I'm a friend of Willi Koder."

"Yes, I remember." She had no reaction to Willi's name. I watched her carefully, but there was none. She only repeated it: "Willi Koder."

I wrapped her in my coat and helped her down the hall to the toilet. She was so weak that on the way back, she nearly collapsed. I put her back in bed, warmed more soup, and, after propping up her head with a second pillow, fed her a few spoonfuls. Her eyes had a look I couldn't quite fathom; because of the fever they had taken on an unnatural brilliance, and in her thin white face they seemed huge and compelling, staring back at me without wavering. I had seen the same expression in sick children, those who are frightened and bewildered because they don't quite understand where they are or what will happen to them.

"You're safe here," I said. "And you can stay as long as you want. I'm a doctor. I examined you a bit last night, but I'd like to have a better look at you today. It won't hurt, it'll take only a few minutes, and when I'm finished you can rest."

I got out my stethoscope and listened to her heart, and sounded her chest, which was clear. Her blood pressure was a little low, and from her color I thought she was probably anemic.

"How long since you've eaten?"

"I don't remember."

"Do you think you can swallow some toast?"

The expression in her eyes had changed. "I'm hungry," she said.

In the next two days, her health improved quickly. Her temperature returned to normal, and her color was better. I was able to leave her to go to the clinic. She spent those first few days sleeping, regaining her strength, and then later on, reading some of my books. I saw her reading Charles Dickens, and in that way I discovered that she knew English.

"I went twice to London with my father," she said.

"Willi told me he published a newspaper."

"And he wrote books, too," she said, "and some were published in England."

I waited, expecting her to tell me about herself, that now her story would begin, and I would learn all about her. Every refugee has a story, and with most of us you soon hear it. But not Magda. "I went twice to London with my father," she had said. "He published a newspaper and wrote books." The door had opened a crack, there was a glimpse of light, of cultured voices, of shadows moving on a polished floor. Willi Koder had told me her father was dead.

Her voice had a charming hoarseness, a Viennese voice, and when she spoke of her father she lowered her eyes, and when she raised them again they were moist. And I thought how beautiful she was, how very beautiful.

It was a shock, that beauty, and it sent a shiver through me. I wasn't jealous, only admiring. I wanted to reach out and stroke her hair. Beauty has always disturbed me, and near it, I feel uneasy, as some people are around cats or birds. They fear being scratched or bitten. With Magda, I felt the opposite; I loved and trusted her immediately, from those first days.

The next day I stopped by the Hotel Morocco for her things, and on the way home bought bread and a beefsteak and a bottle of wine. Magda had cooked a soup on the hot plate, and I smelled it all the way up the stairs. While we ate I told her about Willi and gave her the money he'd given me to give her.

"Four hundred dollars," she said. "A fortune. Do you know, for two-fifty you can buy passage to the States."

"Is that where you want to go?"

"America? Sure, why not?"

"Have you family there?"

"No, but I've none here either," she said. "What about you? You're not French. Are you going to stay on?"

"For the time being."

"Are you Jewish?"

"No."

"Even so. The war's coming here—Jewish or not, it's best to pack up."

Once she had recovered, she was eager to get out of the room. All her clothes were worn out, and she hadn't even a decent pair of shoes or a warm coat. We went shopping together across the Seine in Samaritaine. We got on well together, like old friends, and had fun looking for bargains. Magda got what she needed and persuaded me to buy myself new shoes and a warm sweater, and she bought me a present of a blue-and-yellow scarf. There was no talking about the hard times she'd been through, and no more talk about the war. She made me talk about myself; she wanted to know all about my work at the clinic. She was eager to see it, and to make herself useful there. She was a clever girl and learned things quickly. In no time at all, she knew where everything in the clinic was, and how to take a patient's medical history and to fill out the medical forms for the government. She was popular with the patients, and trusted by them, and by the other doctors as well.

There was a café I used to go to—I think it was on the Boulevard St. Michel—a big hall where they sometimes held political rallies, but on Saturday night there were barrels of new wine, and a band with one man playing the accordion, and a brother and sister who sang and thumped out popular songs on the piano. When I brought Magda there, she became the hit of the place; all the men wanted to dance with her. She made me get up and dance, but I was soon out of breath, and she came and sat next to me, and took both my hands, and looked straight into my eyes.

"You're my best friend," she said. Her face was flushed from the dancing, her eyes looked black and sparkling. "We're happy now," she said, as if it were a miracle. "Are you happy, too?"

"Yes."

"And your new scarf is very chic."

And suddenly she kissed me. It startled us both, and for a second or two nothing was said and neither of us moved. Then a fellow with a cigarette in the corner of his mouth came along, a soldier with his tunic unbuttoned and draped nonchalantly over his shoulders, his shirtsleeves rolled up over a tattoo, and he led Magda away for a dance.

There were a few nights like that, but lots more days of work, with refugees pouring into the quarter. We kept the clinic open until nine or ten o'clock and ate our dinner together in the room, and we knew that the war was near, that the war was certain to begin at any moment.

Germany attacked Poland, and France and England declared war. We waited in Paris, but nothing happened. We went to the hall on the Boulevard St. Michel and drank plenty of wine, although the soldiers were all at the front, and there were none left to dance with. We waited for the war to begin. We held our breath, but nothing happened; Paris felt as if all the air had been sucked out of it.

I had made up my mind to stay in Paris as long as I could, and to keep the clinic open as long as I could. But it was clear that Magda had to leave. I showed her the travel documents Andrew Winters had sent through Willi, and took her to a man who could lift and seal and replace my photograph with hers.

But Magda had changed her mind about America, and now didn't want to go. "Why should you stay?" she said. "And why should I leave?"

I gave her all the reasons: She was a Jew; her father had been on the Gestapo list. She had no papers.

"You're not even in France legally," I said.

"And with a forged visa, will I be in America legally?"

"Does it matter? You'll be in America, you'll be safe. And that's all that counts."

"Safe? Safe to starve to death." And then she said, "I have no friends. Willi is nobody to count on."

"He paid back what he owed."

"And that's the end of it," she said.

"I have the feeling he adores you."

"Adores me? That's a laugh."

"He told me he used to bounce you on his knee."

"Sure he did, any time he could get his hands on me," she said. "And he'd like to have another go at it." And then, "You think it's funny? Is that why you're laughing?"

"Willi told me he wasn't your sweetie."

"That's because I was a kid," she said. "And he was scared of my father. But when nobody was looking he still used to pat me on the ass."

"How old were you?"

"When?"

"When Willi used to pat your ass?"

"I told you. I was a kid," she said. "The last time I was about sixteen."

"Why didn't you tell your father?"

"Never mind. I shouldn't have brought it up," she said. "Willi used to pat my ass, and you want to throw me out and send me to America. I'm scared to go alone. It's a huge place, full of gangsters and red Indians. And I'll be in the middle of it, and with no money."

By this time she was laughing, too; at the same time she was near tears. "I feel safe here with you," she said. "I was thinking I could keep up the work at the clinic. I make myself useful, and at least earn my keep."

"And what if the Germans come?" I said.

She shrugged and said, "Damn the Krauts . . ."

She was talking tough, but I could see she was scared. "I know I get in your hair," she said. "Your apartment is small, and you spend a lot of money on me. I can't blame you for wanting to kick me out."

"You talk a lot of shit," I said.

"It's true," she said.

"What's true is that you're my friend," I said. "I know what it is to be without a place of your own. At least in America you'll be safe, and you can make yourself a place."

She listened to what I had to say, but she wasn't convinced. I couldn't blame her. My own words sounded false to me. She was a refugee in France, and she'd be a refugee in America. She had been down and out here, and she was scared of being down and out there. Once Willi's money ran out in America, she'd have no place. That's how it looked to Magda; it looked like a dead end; I couldn't blame her for being scared.

But the next day she went with me to have the papers altered. It wasn't as simple as we thought, and took a couple of weeks, and most of my money. I never told her about the money, because she wouldn't have let me pay it. To the end she felt I'd betrayed her, that I'd kicked her out; that's how she saw things. Because in the past she had been abused and humiliated, because she was a refugee with no place of her own. That's how she saw things.

Finally, the day came when Magda was to leave. She had booked passage on an Argentinian freighter leaving Le Havre for Buenos Aires, with stops in New York and along the South American coast. One of the doctors at the clinic had also decided to pack up and go. He had a small car and just room enough to squeeze in Magda and her one suitcase for the drive to Le Havre. We arranged to meet at the clinic, early on the morning they were to leave.

The other doctors from the clinic came to say good-by, and friends from the quarter, patients we had treated, and relatives of some we had treated, and even relatives of some we had buried—all came to say good-by. It had become an everyday thing, this packing up and leaving, and yet a crowd always showed up, and lent a hand, and stood shivering in the cold and rain. Be sure it was cold and the rain was pouring down. And be sure the car was old, and on its last legs, and be sure that the motor sounded like a coffee grinder, and that the doctor and his family, their cat, and Magda, and all their suitcases wouldn't fit. Bags had to be opened and repacked, and some bags had to be left behind.

When it was all done, the remaining bags were stuffed into the trunk and piled on the roof of the old car; there were hugs and handshakes and kisses. There were packages of food, and a French flag on a stick tied to the roof.

Finally, everybody squeezed into the car, Magda in the back on the driver's side with the doctor's cat in a box on her lap.

She rolled down the window, and I leaned in and said, "We'll see each other again."

And she said, "Sure, why not?"

"Good luck."

"You too."

The car was started, and stalled, and wouldn't start; the hood was raised, and there was a lot of fiddling with wires, and water poured into the radiator. The motor was started again, and now they were on their way, exhaust pouring from the tail pipe, and as they turned the corner, the doctor tooted the horn, and last thing I saw was the tricolor fluttering above the bags piled on the roof of the car.

After they had gone, I drank a cup of coffee and a marc, and opened the clinic. More than ever I concentrated on my work, keeping the clinic open until late at night. Work kept me from thinking about the war, the danger to me and to others, and my fears of becoming a refugee again.

There were plenty of sick people to be treated. Political refugees from the east were pouring into Paris, and some days we treated as many as a hundred people; at night, we'd close the clinic in order to go around to places like the Hotel Morocco, to treat those too sick to come to the clinic. But there were too many to visit and often we'd send volunteers from the quarter, who carried medicine and shared their food with the refugees. There was much kindness in those days. Of course, there was greed and selfishness too, and a lot of cheating of the refugees; one expects that and is never surprised when one person profits from another's misery. That's no surprise. Goodness is the surprise. Well, now and then there was ordinary goodness, and I even saw it from people who you'd expect to pick your pocket.

But as the war went on, and as the Germans at last began their offensive, a panic swept through Paris. Another of the doctors packed up and left. Now the only one remaining with me was a surgeon named Perles. He was a bachelor, older than the rest of us, who kept to himself and never joined us for a drink or a meal. A nasty scar ran from his temple down one side of his face, and he walked with a limp. He had served in the Spanish War on the loyalist side and had been wounded. Somehow we knew this much of his history, although not from Perles, who never spoke of himself.

One day, he took me aside and told me he was getting out.

"I'm sorry to run out on you, Irina," he said. "I know you can't keep the clinic open yourself, but I've stayed on as long as I can. The Gestapo has me on one list and the GPU on another. Hitler or Stalin, one way or another, my head is in a noose."

"Do you think the Germans will get to Paris?"

"There's nothing to stop them."

"And then what?"

"You know the answer to that," he said. "They round up the Russians, and the ones they can use they put to work in the factories. The others . . ." He shook his head. "They stick you in a camp, or ship you back to Stalin for him to do the job. If you want my advice, pack up and clear out."

"I've got a residence card."

"It won't protect you from the Germans."

"I don't want to clear out. I want to live in a place, and not keep moving around."

"That's what we all want," he said. "You know, you're a good sort. And also you're a handsome woman. A handsome Russian woman."

"What do you know about Russian women?"

"Not much, but I'm willing to learn."

We bought a couple of bottles of wine and went to Perles' room. Perhaps we were an unlikely couple, but the Germans were at the Maginot line, and it seemed that Perles and I were the last two people left in Paris, and neither of us could bear to be alone.

I'd heard that Perles, the refugee, kept two suitcases packed and ready in his room. It was true. It was also true that the room hadn't been cleaned since Perles moved in. He apologized for the state of things, and when he politely went to the bathroom down the hall for a wash, I turned the sheets on his bed and made myself comfortable under the covers.

He came back carrying his clothes and wearing only his overcoat, which came only as far as his knees, and revealed his skinny legs and tiny white feet. My taste has always been for men with big hands and feet, and while Perles was small in every way—he told me that in Spain they called him the Runt—he was ardent, and clean after his bath, and his skin was smooth, and with the Germans a couple of hundred miles away, it was good to sleep with my arms wrapped around him.

In the morning, he gave me a valuable present: a blank immigration card to Cuba. He also gave me the name of a forger, who would validate it for a thousand francs.

"But you've got to promise me to use it," he said. "Promise me you'll get out."

"I will."

We had coffee and a marc for breakfast. Perles carried his two suitcases, and I asked him where he was headed for this time.

"To Peru."

"I hear it's beautiful there," I said.

"We'll see."

"And good to foreigners."

"We'll see about that, too," he said.

We were reluctant to say good-by, and had another coffee and a croissant, and then drank another marc.

"Is Cuba a long way from Peru?"

"I think so."

"Maybe we'll see each other again anyway."

It was time for Perles to leave. We kissed each other and said so long, and when he had gone, I went to the bank and took out all my money, and from there went to the forger and paid him to validate my Cuban immigration card. It took a couple of days, and by that time the boulevards were full of trucks taking soldiers to the front, and trucks and ambulances coming back with the wounded.

When I was packed and ready, I joined the mob at the Gare du Nord waiting for a train to Le Havre. In the faces of those around me I saw the same pinched and frightened look I remembered from the station in Petrograd. At least now I was leaving nobody behind, and so I shed no tears. I wasn't a kid anymore, clutching a fake diamond and ready to jump off a bridge if things went wrong.

But I didn't know what to expect in Havana, and I didn't want to hang around there. My destination was New York, even if it meant going back into the spy trade. Before I left France, I wrote Andrew Winters, and when I walked down the gangplank in Havana there was a familiar face to meet me, a burly man in a white suit and a Panama hat with a green band. He stepped forward and handed me a bouquet of flowers. It was Willi Koder, Willi the Mouse. Winters had sent him with a U.S. entry permit in my name, tickets on the Key West ferry, and a connecting ticket on the bus to Miami and a sleeper to New York—all of it neatly arranged and inside a manila envelope.

"As easy as that?" I said.

"If you've got the right business connections," Willi said.

# nine

⚒ FROM THE POINT OF VIEW OF THE SPY TRADE, MY FIRST
years in New York were uneventful. Winters had a friend in the district
attorney's office, and through him I was able to get a job as an assistant
pathologist in the medical examiner's office.

I was assigned to the Manhattan morgue, which was still in the
basement of the Caledonia Hospital in lower Manhattan. The hospital
had been built to care for the wounded of the Union Army, and later
on for prisoners from the city jails, and there were still bars on most of
the windows. It was a grim red stone building, still more of a jail than a
hospital, close enough to the Hudson River so that on a foggy night, as
the mist rolled in, one heard the moan of ship's horns, an appropri-
ately gloomy setting in which to practice pathology.

I saw Julia Winters occasionally, and a couple of times dined with
her and Claire Balaban. Julia's painting had fallen off, but Balaban
was now teaching her Russian. Julia wasn't a bad student, and was
happier than I'd ever seen her. Whatever had been troubling her in
Zurich seemed to have passed.

The newspapers never published anything connecting her to FDR,
but from certain things she said, comments about trips to Washington
and Georgia, where the President vacationed in Warm Springs, I concluded that she saw him regularly, and that Balaban had made herself
part of that circle.

Vladimir was in New York and had gotten a job with a marginal
publisher of travel books who occupied a dingy office overlooking
Union Square. The publisher claimed to have risen with the rebellious
sailors at Kronstadt, claimed an intimacy with Trotsky, and in and out
of his dreary office trooped old Bolsheviks and opera singers, head-
waiters and former Moscow cabdrivers, modernist painters, por-
traitists, cavalry officers, and priests of the Eastern Church.

Vladimir complained how little he was paid, but he flourished in
this backbiting spy's nest above Union Square. He dined out every
night and enriched those literary and social events at which, during the
war, Russians were so in demand. I was jealous of his many love affairs, and flew into rages, and told him he had made an ass of himself,

and swore not to see him again, and kept my word, and gave in to him when he called, and loved him and ached with loneliness and settled down to a life of my own.

I passed the state examination, which qualified me to practice medicine on the living, left the morgue, and started over again in St. Monica's Hospital as an assistant resident in pediatrics.

Andrew Winters told me that President Roosevelt had lost interest in Living Memory. The Soviets were our allies, and brave comrades, and all of American intelligence was aimed at the Germans and the Japanese. As in the 1930s, Living Memory was bureaucratically neglected while Andrew Winters did all he could to keep it alive. He arranged for the publication of books by members of Living Memory, although none was remotely profitable. He managed to get programs of Russian studies started in a few universities and arranged the funding. Many of Andrew's friends were rich and others were prescient; they knew that eventually the war would end and who the postwar adversary would be. He put the prescient beside the educatable rich and explained the dangers of the postwar world and the need to keep an eye on the Soviets. The rich funded Russian studies, and the universities hired members of Living Memory, and paid them peanuts, but Living Memory hung on, tenacious and sure that when the war ended, their time would begin.

They were right. By the close of 1944, with the end of the war in Europe in sight, the Soviet Union was again seen as a danger, and word came to take the wraps off Living Memory. Winters called me back to work, and I admit I went eagerly. It gets in the blood, the spy trade.

Winters had learned that the Soviets had sent an agent to New York. I said there was nothing new about that; their agents came and went regularly through their embassies, their Munitions Procurement Board, and Amtorg, the Soviet trading company.

"This one isn't run of the mill," Winters said. "He's one of their dark man. What was it Lenin called them? *Phantomas.* My *Phantomas.*"

"Do you know his name?"

"No."

"Or what he looks like? Anything at all?"

"I've heard his passport is French."

"Why is he here?"

Andrew needed to tell me something of what he knew, to confide something. But how hard it was for him. "There's a Polish political leader, a key figure in the postwar scheme of things," he said. "In London they tried to kill him. It was decided to bring him here. Churchill and FDR decided. I was told to hide him."

"Why do they want to kill him?"

"It doesn't matter," Andrew said. "I need you to find out who the *Phantoma* is. I need a name, maybe a face. Is he here to kill the Pole? Use Willi. He's tight with the French comrades."

"Willi is having a hard time," I said. "He'll want some money."

Andrew gave me two hundred dollars, but said, "Give him only a hundred at a time. Willi needs to be kept on a short lead."

The one number I had for Willi, on West 57th Street, was supposed to be his office, although he was never in it. I had to call around to get hold of him, but I finally did and we met in Riverside Park.

Willi had grown more secretive in the last years, a bit fatter and seedier. Something had worn down the brashness and breezy charm of Paris and Havana.

I told him what Andrew Winters wanted, and he said, "A package from Moscow. Is that what Andrew is looking for, a *Starke?*"

"Andrew doesn't know what he's looking for."

"I'm to tell him, is that it?"

"He's heard a rumor from Living Memory," I said. "A warning. It's made him nervous."

"What's he got to protect?"

"Protect?"

"From the *Starke*. Irina, my dear old friend, Andrew has a china egg wrapped in cotton wool. Now he hears there's a *Starke*. We both know that much. We ought to confide more in each other. I could tell you stories."

"For example."

"Nothing. I'm only teasing. Pretending I know a lot more than I do. I'm a fraud, Irina, but you know that already."

We had met at a predetermined bench on a path that ran along the Hudson River. It was shielded from the rest of the park by a row of trees, a secluded place even in winter, when the branches were bare. "A lovely trysting place for spies," Willi called it, and as we walked I noticed that there was ice on the river, not solid, but in sheets, and in places only a film on the surface of the water. It was late afternoon, just growing dark, and suddenly the street lamps in the park came on, all of them at once. I glanced at my watch: five-thirty. There had been a click, like the fall of the shutter in a camera, and the lights had come on.

I said, "The man Andrew wants, it's likely he traveled with a French passport."

"Very likely," Willi said, with a breath of his old jaunty manner. "A Russian *Starke* with a French passport, French credentials, a French history." He took my arm to draw me close, to drip confidence into my ear. "I know the man, and I even have a way to snuggle up to him." I felt Willi's warm breath against my ear. "A way to snuggle up to the *Starke*," he said. "Do you think I'm teasing?"

"If you're serious, Andrew will want to hear."

"He took me off the payroll. Three months without a nickel. Tight, that Andrew, tight as a rat's ass."

I gave Willi the two hundred dollars, all of it, and said, "He told me to put you on a short lead."

"Tight as a rat's ass."

"You said you had an idea who he was," I said. "And a way to get at him."

"I do," he said, and when he said it, I thought of Magda. Her name came suddenly to mind, and I saw her face. "A way at him." I'm not sure how or why I made the connection between Magda and the man with the French passport. But it was clear to me, as if Willi had said her name.

"Is Magda in New York?" I said.

"Magda Renner? She's been out west."

"But is she back?"

"In a couple of days," he said. "I'll call you with news of the *Starke*."

"Wait! Has Magda anything to do with this?"

"A couple of days," he said. "I'll call and explain everything."

He turned and walked quickly away, along the path beside the river, casting a shadow under the street lights.

I hadn't seen Magda since Paris, but I'd had word from her—a letter from Los Angeles, another from San Francisco, and a postcard from Cheyenne, Wyoming. But she'd never included a return address. Willi didn't know where she was. He didn't know what she was doing. He knew nothing about her—that's what he said. What was she up to in California, or in Wyoming for that matter? Who was she with, and who was paying her bills? She seemed deliberately to have dropped out of sight and then covered her tracks. Yet she knew how to reach me, and she'd written. The letters were affectionate, nostalgic; she wrote about the good times we'd had in Paris, about our friendship and the permanent bond between us.

The more I thought of it, the more certain I was that Willi was in touch with Magda, and that she was involved in Willi's schemes. A week passed without a word from him. Andrew pressed me, but I told him that I needed to run Willi my own way, and that way was to leave him alone. Yet I began to suspect that something was wrong. It worried me at work, and eventually I could think of little else. I had edged back into the spy trade. What worried me was Andrew's urgency, and the danger I sensed for Willi, and also for Magda; the danger came from the man with the French passport, Willi's *Starke*.

Ten days passed before Willi called, but then it was with good news. He'd located our man. "A rare bottle from France," he said. "Prewar vintage, one of their best. Lovely color and nose."

We were talking on the telephone, and Willi didn't like telephones, didn't trust them, never knew who was listening, he said, and so he made word games and spoke in riddles. "Magnificent bouquet," he said. "One can smell it across the room."

"Come down, Willi. Let me know what you have."

"Andrew hasn't been forthright."

"Meaning what?"

"The wine, such a rare and costly bottle."

"Damn it, Willi. In plain English, tell me what you know."

"I've got Andrew's man. He's not an ordinary *Starke*. This is a prince, sent by Uncle Joe. Do you know who I'm talking about?"

"Stalin."

"The same."

"You watch yourself, Willi."

"Tell Andrew I'm to go back on the payroll."

"Tonight in the park. I must see you."

"Tomorrow at five," Willi said. "Me and the *Starke*, we got a big date tonight." That's what Willi said, "We got a big date tonight."

The next day I arranged to leave the hospital early and went by subway to Grand Central, changing there to the Times Square shuttle and the Broadway local uptown. I was in Riverside Park a minute or two before five o'clock. There was no sign of Willi, no sign of him at five-thirty or at six. Snow had come down in flurries most of the afternoon, but while I waited for Willi it began to fall heavily, the thick flakes settling with a hush; in no time the paths of the park, the grounds, and the slats on the empty benches were white. A shepherd dog bounded happily along, his paws leaving perfect tracks in the fresh snow. The park lights came on as they had the night I last met Willi. The shepherd galloped after a stick and carried it through the falling snow in triumph to his master. On the train from Le Havre to Paris, Willi had touched the bruise on his cheek, and said, "I got into a scrape." I shivered, certain that Willi was again in trouble.

At five past six I gave up and left the park for a club on 86th Street, run by a Hungarian. From there I telephoned Willi, but got no answer. To warm up from the long wait in the cold, I ordered tea with rum, and drank it while trying to decide what to do next.

There was entertainment on a tiny raised stage, which served at the moment as a dance floor on which four couples swayed to recorded music. The men were younger than the women, slick, dolled-up young men who held the women as if wearing rubber gloves. I took a second look and saw that two of them weren't men at all, but women dressed as men.

It was Willi's sort of place, an intriguer's sort of place, disreputable in an old-fashioned way, reeking of cologne and cigarette smoke. When the music ended and the dance floor cleared, two women came out from behind a curtain on the little stage. They were sisters, with identical gowns and with their hair waved and set identically; one sister played the piano and the other the violin. They concentrated on the music, although no one in the audience did, and what they played sounded familiar to me and I thought they probably played well. They were certainly serious about it, as if they had been trained to perform in a concert hall and not in a club.

I tried telephoning Willi again, but there was still no answer. I really hadn't expected one. I had a friend with the New York police named Francis Keogh. We'd met when I worked for the medical examiner, and we'd done each other favors and gotten on. Francis had a son, who'd been reported missing in action in Europe, and then there was a second, unconfirmed report that he'd been taken prisoner. I asked Andrew Winters to check with the Red Cross through intelligence contacts of his in Geneva, and Francis' son was found, alive and well.

I had to call around to find Francis, but when I did it turned out he'd been trying to get hold of me. There was news of Willi. "Bad news, I'm afraid," Francis said.

From the phone booth I could see the sisters with their identically waved hair and gowns, I could hear the music, and just then one of the young men who had been dancing with an older woman came out of the men's room and passed close enough for me to smell his cologne and to notice the shadow with which he darkened the bottoms of his eyes, the left a trifle more than the right, giving him an unbalanced look.

Over the phone, Francis said, "In the men's room at Grand Central Station."

"What?"

"Your friend Willi Koder. His body was found in the men's room."

Francis could supply no details, except that Willi's body had been taken to the morgue, and first thing next morning we met there, in the basement laboratory, with its specimen jars of preserved human organs and photographs of notorious corpses. Willi's body had been wheeled in and lay before us on a steel dissection table, covered by a sheet.

"I suppose you're used to autopsies." Francis was a sympathetic and reflective policeman, the kind who with a second turn of the wheel could have been a priest. "You're a doctor and you worked a couple of years in this place," he said.

"And you're a cop, Francis."

"It gives me the creeps," he said.

"It does me, too."

There was nothing to do but pull back the sheet and have a look at Willi. I sometimes believe in the immortal soul, and never more than when I look at the inconsequential husk that remains after death. I examined the body, but found no wounds—a bit of dried blood from the left ear, which wasn't unusual and proved to be nothing. Willy had had surgery for a right inguinal hernia. He suffered from varicosity of the legs and feet.

"There don't seem to be any wounds," I said. "Not even a bruise."

"He was found by a porter yesterday morning," Francis said. "The porter called a patrolman in the station, and he called an ambulance. Someone from the medical examiner's office has already had a look and concluded he died of natural causes, heart attack probably."

"No autopsy?"

"Not so far."

"You don't think he died naturally?"

"He was wearing a tuxedo," Francis said. "And he was in a closed toilet in Grand Central Station."

"Perhaps he took the subway home from a party and didn't feel well," I said. "Willi went to a lot of parties, and he liked to dress up."

"I suppose he did. The tux was made for him by a London tailor in March of 1931. That's the date sewn inside the breast pocket. The lining has been patched, not very well either."

"Willi probably did it himself," I said. "He was short of money. He

78

told me he'd even learned to repair his own shoes. He said there was nothing to it."

"Did he own an overcoat?"

"Yes, a blue one. Smart, but well worn, like the dinner suit."

"No overcoat was found," Francis said. "His wallet was in his jacket, no overcoat, and he had four dollars and a door key."

Willi's jaws were gaping open, and I bent close enough to smell the contents of his mouth. I used a cotton swab to collect mucus from inside his nostrils and looked under a magnifying glass at what I had found.

From under the brim of his gray hat, Francis watched me closely. "I suppose I can smoke in here," he said.

"It's not a church, Francis."

"What did you smell?"

"Something like peaches," I said. "But sweeter, as if the fruit were rotten."

"Cyanide?"

"In one form or another. It was vaporized, and he was made to inhale it," I said. "There's dried blood inside both nostrils, and tiny fragments of glass. I think a vial of the stuff was exploded in his face."

"How do you know that?"

"It's been done before. I've heard of it."

"And if we do a full autopsy?"

"I'm not sure what we'd find. Cyanide poisoning can cause pulmonary edema or heart failure. It can look like either of those, but if you look further—. What's the difference, Francis? Either way he's just as dead."

"Tell me what happens if you look further," Francis said. "How do you tell if it's cyanide?"

"Cyanide prohibits tissue utilization of oxygen," I said. "Because oxygen can't be used, the venous blood is bright red. The oxygen is still in it."

I pulled the sheet up and Francis rang for the attendant. We were both anxious to get away from the specimen jars, the photographs, and Willi's remains. Francis knew of a café on the docks near the wholesale fish market. It was a couple of blocks away and we walked without speaking, huddled against the icy wind off the river. Earlier the snow had stopped, and now it began again, flurries whipped by the wind.

In the café we ordered breakfast and warmed up with mugs of coffee.

"You were supposed to meet Willi, but he didn't show up," Francis said. "That's why you called me. What was the meeting about?"

"We've been looking for somebody. A Russian with a French passport. Willi was going to tell me about him."

"Do you suspect the Russian killed him?"

"I don't know."

"But you do want it kept quiet," Francis said. "Nothing in the papers, nothing to scare off the Russian."

"It's a big favor," I said.

"It is that all right." Francis caught my eye and held it; there was a long silence, meditative, judgmental; I waited, and squirmed, and bowed my head under Francis Keogh's cold blue gaze. Finally, he said, "Andrew Winters is in this, I suppose?"

"He'll want it kept quiet."

Breakfast had come, a pair of fried eggs staring up at Francis from his plate. He didn't touch them. Francis knew how to break the rules when he had to, he knew how to dirty his hands, but he needed to be sure it was done for good reason. We're still friends, Francis Keogh and I; when his son was freed from the German camp and came home, I was at the party for him, and a couple of years later I was at the boy's wedding, and the christening of Francis' first grandchild. When his wife died, I went to the funeral. I've visited him in Florida, where he's retired. But whenever I think of Francis Keogh, it's that bitter cold morning in the café on the docks of lower Manhattan, after we'd been to the morgue and examined Willi's body, and Francis was making up his mind if it was right for him to break the rules for a friend.

"What if you find the Russian?" he said. "And what if it turns out he killed Willi?"

"It'd be Andrew's decision," I said. "It'd be up to him what we do."

A pair of men came into the café, burly men in watch caps and rubber boots, bringing with them a blast of cold air and the smell of fish. Francis' pale eyes flicked up and down, measuring both men, identifying both. He said, "You mean the Russian could get away with it?"

"Sure he could."

"That'd be a hell of a thing," Francis said.

I ate buttered toast, and Francis picked at the white of his fried eggs, working his way slowly toward the yoke, instinctively saving the best for last. He'd had a bleak childhood, an orphan raised in a home for Catholic boys. I don't remember if I knew that then or learned it later. But I did know that his morality was of the uncompromising sort.

I'd always known that, and I wondered how it would be to love a man like Francis Keogh. I imagined his hands were cold, and I thought: With Francis a woman must never lapse. She dare not.

Francis said, "Did Willi have any relatives?"

"None I know of."

"Was he Jewish?"

"He never let me know one way or another," I said. "Probably he was."

"As a rule, the Jews are opposed to cremation."

"I don't think Willi held strong views on the subject."

"Good luck with the Russian," Francis said. "Let me know if you get him in a corner."

# ten

I NEEDED TO KNOW IF WILLIE HAD LEFT SOMETHING BEHIND, a clue as to who the Russian was or how to get hold of him.

I had never been to Willi's office, but a latchkey had been found in his pocket, and Francis Keogh let me use it. The building was on 57th Street, two blocks west of Carnegie Hall, near Ninth Avenue, and of course there was no elevator, and of course Willi's office was on the top floor. His name was in gilt on the door, and as on the card he'd given me, he was described as an artist's representative, although I had no idea what sort of artists they were and how Willi represented them.

I'd waited until Saturday morning, in the hope of meeting nobody on the staircase or in the halls. One of Willi's neighbors imported books in Arabic, and the other manufactured dentures. Both doors were locked; I saw no light from either, and heard no sound. In the gloomy corridor, with its stained carpet and flaking walls, a single yellowish bulb glowed day and night.

Willi's office was a single, narrow room with a desk, file cabinet, and couch. There was a hot plate, and he'd set a bottle of milk outside the window, where it had frozen and burst. In the file cabinet I found a can of coffee, a saucepan, and half a loaf of stale bread. Mail had collected inside the door, under the slot. These were mostly telephone and electric bills—Willie was a couple of months behind in both— and a postcard from an actor on a USO tour of the South Pacific. Were actors, entertainers, the artists Willi represented? This one also sang, but complained of laryngitis and diarrhea.

Another drawer in the file cabinet held Willy's spare shirts, a suit of underwear, and darned socks. There was a closet, and in it hung a lounge suit with the label of the same English tailor who had made his evening clothes. It was true that Willi's flag had flown on balmier days. I came on a cigar box stuffed with letters from different women. Most were written in German, some in French, and a few in English. They went back over many years, and it was fitting that these letters, fragile and crumbling as dead leaves, should be prized by Willi and kept by him in his meager baggage. I put the box of letters in my bag, to read another time.

Other drawers held odds and ends: a pipe with a chipped bowl and a tin of tobacco collected from cigarette ends, a refugee's trick or a prisoner's. I dug deeper into the drawer and found another box; this contained a folded prayer shawl, a black skullcap, and a leatherbound Old Testament, printed in Hebrew. On the inside cover a date had been written—June 11, 1908—and a name: Mendel Kollerwitz.

I reckoned Willi to have been about fifty. He'd have been thirteen in 1908, and the bible could have been a gift on his bar mitzvah. And the name Mendel Kollerwitz, was it Willi's real name? I wondered about Willi, about the dark corners of his life, which of his secrets I'd learn, which I'd never know.

I was still poking around his office when I heard a door slam and footsteps in the hall outside. Somebody was whistling. My grandmother had taught me that whistling brought bad luck, and if she heard someone at it, she crossed herself.

The silhouette of a man passed before the glass panel of the closed office door. The metal plate over the mail slot was lifted and an 11″ × 14″ envelope fell just inside the door. I waited until the mailman passed to the end of the corridor, until the stairway door slammed and the whistling stopped.

The envelope was addressed to Willi and contained a photograph, an 8″ × 10″ glossy taken in a nightclub. But the photo was of a couple I'd never seen, a man and a woman, grinning into the lens. The odd thing was that they were out of focus, and for a moment I thought there had been some mistake. I had to look a second time before I realized what had been done.

In the left background of the photo, in sharp focus, was another table, another pair of faces; it was Willi, in evening clothes, holding a match to the cigarette of a second man.

I didn't recognize the second man. He was looking away, and the camera had caught him in profile: an attractive man, even handsome, with a strong, aggressive chin, straight nose, and what seemed to be dark hair brushed back from a high forehead. He wore evening clothes as well, and studying his features I began to wonder if there wasn't something familiar about him. Yet I was sure that if I'd seen him before, I'd have remembered; it was a face one noticed, a face of some distinction.

I believed I was looking at a photograph of the Russian with the French passport, the man Moscow had sent. It was their *Phantoma*, I was certain of it, and I thought: Bless Willi, he managed to pass on another of his secrets.

The logical thing was to show the photograph to Vladimir and see if he could identify the man with Willi. But Vladimir and I had been going through one of our difficult times. He had gotten himself appointed to a committee to raise money for Russian war relief, and on the same committee was a beautiful society divorcée—that's what the *Daily News* called her—and the *New York Times* printed a photograph of her and Vladimir, she looking up adoringly at him and he grinning at her with that great horse face of his.

Vladimir assured me the committee was all part of his work for Andrew Winters. He told me that he loved me, and only me, and to ignore the beautiful society divorcée. But I couldn't ignore her. Ten or fifteen years before I might have managed. But the older I got, the more vulnerable I became and the more jealous.

But what was I to do? I missed him. I worked extra shifts at the hospital. I read and took long, exhausting walks, but as soon as I was alone, and if for only a minute or two I had nothing else on my mind, my thoughts would turn to Vladimir, and it would take all my will-power not to pick up the phone and call him.

Now I could give myself an excuse to call him. "Where are you?" he said. "Come up. Come up at once."

"Are you alone?"

"Alone? Of course, I'm alone. I was asleep, and dreaming of you, my dearest—"

"Don't talk to me in Russian," I said. "It'll do you no good. And no sweet talk in any language. I want to see you on business."

"Very well," he said, in English. "Quite so. I'm all business. But I've not had breakfast." Vladimir lived on Third Avenue, in a single room that he never cleaned. Nearby was a magnificient bakery, Greenberg's, and I knew what he was driving at. "Crullers from Greenberg's," he said. "A sign that you forgive me."

"I don't forgive you."

"In any case, the crullers," he said. "Later, I'll beg, and perhaps you'll forgive."

It was typical of Vladimir. He was overjoyed to hear from me. He loved me and had been dreaming of me, and could I bring crullers from Greenberg's? And what can be said of me? Just as typically, I brought the crullers, in a box tied with a red ribbon.

I gave him his crullers, but didn't offer to make him coffee. Instead, I let him make a pot for us both, which was undrinkable and had to be thrown out, and I wound up making coffee after all.

I tried to talk to him about Willi and the *Phantoma*, but he

84

wouldn't let me. "I first have to get something off my chest," he said. "I need to be honest, and tell you right off that I love you, only you, and I never want to make you unhappy again."

"The sugar," I said. "Where is it kept in this pigsty?"

"Can you believe that I'm sincere?" he said. "A man has only a few women in his life. Those he's born with—his mother, perhaps a sister—and then a single love that lasts all his life. It doesn't matter if he's separated from her, or even if her life goes in a different direction. He thinks of her and in that way she's with him permanently."

"What about your wife?" I said. "Didn't you love her in that way?"

"God rest her soul," he said. "I rarely think of her."

He had spoken in Russian. He was sincere, and he was also saying what he knew I wanted to hear, and was trying to win me back. I knew that I ought not to be won back; there are some lives that need order and ought not to be lived with passion, and perhaps mine was one of those. But he had hold of my hand, and kissed me, and because I loved him there was no thought of happiness or unhappiness, no thought of what was wise or unwise, and no thought of what would come later.

We made up, as we always did, with tender embraces, with Russian endearments, and finally with that passion which I both feared and craved, which disrupted my life and fulfilled it.

Much later on—it was already dark—I told him about Willi's death, and showed him the photograph of Willi and the *Phantoma*. "It's cleverly done," he said. "Willi would have had to explain it to the photographer." Vladimir had lately begun wearing reading glasses, and he put them on to study the photograph. "What about the place—do you know it?" he said.

"No."

"And our friend, the *Phantoma*? Is he familiar?"

"Not really, yet there's something about him. I might have seen him somewhere."

"Is it a Russian face, do you think?"

"That wasn't my first impression."

"And now?"

"Yes, a Russian face."

Vladimir took a scissors and trimmed the photograph so that it fit in his pocket. "We need to put a name to our *Phantoma*," he said. "For that our best bet is Mitzi Roth."

Mitzi Roth was an old friend of Vladimir's, and at one time they had been lovers. Vladimir admitted it. I was jealous, but I couldn't hold it against Mitzi, who was a good sort, a veteran of Living Memory who had known everyone in prewar Berlin, in Paris, and now in New York. She was a volunteer for the USO, and every night, after eleven o'clock when the shows broke, she could be found in the Backstage Ballroom, a favorite hangout for servicemen of all the Allied countries.

Admission to the Ballroom was free, and food and coffee were on the house, but only for enlisted men; officers had to go somewhere else.

"Officers can pay the prices in New York," Mitzi had said when she started the Ballroom, which was on 44th Street west of Broadway and had at one time been a dance hall and later on a rollerskating rink. After eleven o'clock, the band was made up of musicians from the shows on Broadway, and there was plenty of food sent over from Reuben's, Sardi's, and Leo Lindy's. Lots of people famous in the theater dropped in to serve, and stars in town from Hollywood had their pictures taken washing dishes. There were always beautiful girls from the shows to talk to the men and dance with them. Mitzi turned up French women to talk to the Free French, and found Polish, Czech, Dutch, Australian, and English women. Even the famous Foo sisters from Shanghai took to dropping in. It was the gayest continuing party in New York, really the spot to be in the winter of 1944.

We found Mitzi on stage at the Ballroom, in the middle of a German song, in spite of the war. "I like the German songs," she said, "and no one will mistake me for a Nazi."

It was like Mitzi to say and do as she pleased. She had nerve and intelligence, a woman who had been knocking around on her own since the age of twelve. She claimed to have been illegitimate, a foundling, but then she told stories about her father, who she said was a composer killed in the 1914 war. Her mother was an actress, a renowned beauty. She produced pictures of her mother, and faded newspaper clippings. Perhaps it was so. Mitzi was another of those refugees for whom truth and fiction were the same. It was true that she had been a street singer in Berlin. There were a few who remembered her early days, witnesses to it; and she had had a career in German films—also true. The Museum of Modern Art occasionally ran one or two of her movies. The story of her encounter with Hitler in 1929 in the Café Jahland in Hamburg, of throwing a drink in his face—that is probably fiction, a legend; although there are some—Willi Koder was one—who claimed to have been in the Jahland that night, and swore they saw Mitzi throw the drink, a glass of champagne, and saw it run down Hitler's face.

Another fact, for which there exists ample documentation, is her love affair with and marriage to the head of the German Comintern, Carl Weiner. During her years with Weiner she owned the most popular cabaret in Berlin, known for the latest in political satire and popular music. When Hitler came in, it was closed down, and his storm troopers smashed it to pieces.

Mitzi got out of Germany with the Rumanian State Opera Company, posing as a man. "A tenor," she said, and built upon the story, claiming to have become the lover of a noted soprano, although she never made clear how she managed it. In New York she produced plays, but only those written by the more serious of the European playwrights, experimental, politically controversial works that other producers were afraid to touch. And usually she made money. That was another of Mitzi's talents: She knew how to make money, and she made it effortlessly, on her own terms, as she made friends, or caused men to fall in love with her. She hadn't gone far in school, and I never saw her with a book, but she was a women who knew everything she needed to know.

When she finished her song, she joined us at a table, carrying a bottle of champagne, held by the neck like a chicken.

"It's good to see you two together," she said, and hugged and kissed us both. She poured wine for us, and tried to get us to eat something.

We tried to talk, but a crew of Free French sailors had arrived and catching sight of Mitzi, insisted she sing for them. She refused, pretending she was tired. But of course everybody knew Mitzi was never too tired to sing, particularly for a crew of French sailors. She said there were better singers in the room—this one from Hollywood, that one from the Metropolitan Opera. But the Frenchmen insisted on Mitzi, the incomparable Mitzi.

Finally, they lifted her onto their shoulders and carried her to the stage, and she went happily, triumphantly, still carrying the champagne bottle by its neck.

She knew all the sidewalk songs, and the ones from the Paris music halls. Her voice was thin and not very strong, but had a little curl at the end, a plume of smoke. She sang and looked people square in the eye. She also had her own way with clothes; that night she wore a chemise held up by thin straps that left her chest and arms bare and was made of some material that glittered under the stage lights. I couldn't even imagine myself in such a dress. I hadn't the nerve. But Mitzi had the nerve. You had to hand it to her, she had nerve enough to do as she wanted and live as she wanted.

We left the Ballroom around two o'clock and went by taxi to Mitzi's apartment on Central Park West, on a high floor with a view of the park facing east. The rooms were large and the ceilings high, and Mitzi had decorated the apartment in a style that was elegant, but comfortable, and not in the slightest bit pretentious. There was a piano by the window overlooking Central Park, and the walls were covered with extraordinary paintings by German Expressionists and some of the early Cubists, most of whom were friends of Mitzi's. Somehow she had managed to get them out of Europe, and later on some of them became very valuable. But she refused ever to sell them, even near the end of her life, when things became very difficult for her.

Vladimir started off by showing her the photograph of Willi with the *Phantoma*. She took it and immediately said, "Yes, I know him. At one time we were good friends."

She went on studying the photograph without speaking, drawing us closer with a faint smile, and with an ambiguous glow in her expressive eyes. She was an actress and we were her audience. Patiently, Vladimir said, "The man in the photo with Willi, tell us his name."

"He calls himself Dolin," she said. "Serge Dolin."

Vladimir and I exchanged a glance, a deep sigh of relief. We had a name.

"Is he Russian, Mitzi?"

"Yes. With French papers. I knew him last in Paris, where he worked as a journalist. But he's from Moscow."

"Is he a strong-arm man?"

"Serge? Oh, no."

So he was not a strong-arm man, not a *Starke* as Willi had said. But then she shrugged and said, "I suppose he has done his share of strong-arm stuff, but he's not at all that type. A clever man, and complex. Do you want to hear stories of Serge Dolin?" She laughed and clapped her hands. "We can stay up all night."

But first there had to be coffee and a plate of warm pastries. Wake Mitzi in the middle of the night, give her five minutes, and she'd produce fresh coffee and a plate of delicious pastries.

"I met Serge Dolin in France, in Paris," she said. "Weiner pointed him out to me." She had tucked herself into a corner of a long couch, kicked off her shoes, and drawn her legs up under her. Her toes were bare, and she had tiny feet, like a child's, her toenails painted bright red. She liked to pamper herself with pedicures and massages, exotic exercises and mud baths, and to be rubbed and patted, and she emitted a constant sexual beam, a beacon, which swept the room indiscriminately, lighting me as well as Vladimir.

"Weiner had gone to Paris to attend a secret meeting of the Comintern," she said. "And he took me with him. This was in 1931, so I was still a kid. It was my first time in Paris. My first time out of Germany."

Vladimir said, "Weiner could do that? He could take you with him?"

"Weiner did what he wanted. The German party was the biggest in Europe, and the underground the most effective. He was a big shot, with more brains in one finger than Stalin and all the rest of those *patzers* in the Kremlin."

"How did you meet Dolin?"

"I was with Weiner on the terrace of a café," she said. "And Serge passed. He was alone, just passing by, and didn't see us. Weiner pointed him out, and he made an impression—the way he looked and the way he walked, the way he held himself. He was cocky, but watchful at the same time, with his head lowered and one shoulder forward, like a battering ram. I tell you he made an impression. Weiner said that was bad for an agent, to stand out like that. And he was too smartly dressed—that was a weakness of his, expensive clothes. I can see him with a soft black hat with the brim pulled over one eye. I tell you, he was the type women looked at a second time. A classy guy, but in some way menacing, a man to be feared."

"Did Weiner tell you what he was doing in Paris?"

"He was there as a journalist, writing for the popular front press. But that was only his cover. In fact he was a political officer, and his job was to keep the French left in line."

"You say he had French papers?"

"That's right. But he came and went, sometimes legally, sometimes not."

"Did you get to know him?"

"Not right away. He hadn't seen us, and Weiner didn't call him over. Later on, after the conferences had finished, he came around— to pay his respects to Weiner—and we went out to dinner."

I'd noticed that Mitzi always called her late husband Weiner, as if to draw attention to his role as a figure in history, a personage, like a statue in a public park. At first I thought of it as affected and self-serving, but as I got to know her better, and to appreciate her loyalty, I saw that it was meant sincerely, as homage to her late husband.

"Serge carried the Moscow line," she said. "And later on Moscow called the tune. But in 1931 the national parties still had a say, and there was a lot of jockeying still going on. Let me tell you something else—when Weiner talked, Serge listened. In those days, there was no doubt who had the power."

Mitzi began to talk about Weiner; the popular front was a creation of his. He was responsible for the seduction of the European intellectuals. On she went about the brilliant work Weiner had done. We gave her time to eulogize him, listening attentively, still the audience.

When she paused for breath, Vladimir brought her back to Serge Dolin. "Tell us when you got to know him. Was it in 1931?"

"Not then. Not that first time in Paris," she said. "There was trouble with the party in Berlin. Stalin suspected that Weiner was growing too powerful and he tried to replace him. So we had to return to Berlin."

"And Weiner died there?"

"Hitler had him shot. But he wouldn't have dared if Stalin hadn't first turned against him."

Vladimir was at the coffee table, refilling his cup. "When did you finally get to know Dolin?" he said. "When was that?"

"A few years later, early in 1935," Mitzi said. "After the Nazis busted up my place in Berlin, I cleared out and went to Paris, and got a job singing in a club. One night Dolin came in, and bought me a drink."

"Let me see. You first met in Paris in 1931, and when you returned in 1935 Dolin was there. Had he been in Paris those three years?"

"I don't think so, at least not the whole time," she said. "There was talk he'd been to the States, and I know he'd learned English. But there was no way to pin him down. He was a Comintern agent, a shadow on the wall."

"In 1935," Vladimir said. "Were you still in the party?"

"I was never in the party. I was Weiner's wife. I was a Communist only as long as he was. But they did as Stalin told them, that was the Communist party, and don't forget it was Stalin who had Weiner shot."

"So you left the party out of loyalty to Weiner."

"What else?"

"And Dolin, did he know you were out of the party?"

"He didn't care."

"But he was one of them."

"One of them, but his own man. A rare bird. There's not another like Serge."

I watched her light one cigarette with another, and drink cognac. She had trouble sleeping and was always after me to write prescriptions for sleeping pills. She was afraid of the dark, and never went to sleep before dawn.

"I was happy to see Serge walk into that club in Paris," she said. "I was really down on my luck, drinking too much, and even playing around with the white stuff. There was a pimp hanging around who wanted to turn me out. That was an *espèce de merde*, that pimp. I cried on Serge's shoulder, and he said not to worry, that he'd take care of it. That pimp was a tough guy, but Serge took him aside—you know what I mean? One day the pimp was there, the next he wasn't. I was broke, and missed Weiner, and Serge helped me out."

"Did you have a love affair?"

"A love affair?" Mitzi turned the question over in her mind. "We slept together a couple of times. But a love affair? No, we never got started on that." She was thoughtful a moment and then said, "Serge could surprise you. I thought I knew him, but one time we were in a place, and we'd had a lot to drink, and there was a piano. Serge went over and began to play. He played well, and concentrated on the music. He must have played for an hour."

"Did he tell you where he learned to play?"

"No. He shrugged it off. He wouldn't talk about it. But it meant a lot to him, the music. It was another part of his life, one he wouldn't talk about."

I had been listening and watching Mitzi, encouraging Vladimir to ask the questions. Finally I said, "Have you seen him in New York?"

"Until you showed me the photo, I didn't know he was here."

"Could you get in touch with him?" I said. "If he were here legally, with French papers. Could you reach him through friends, people who knew Weiner?"

"I could try. But it would take a while," Mitzi said. "A better bet is the place the photograph was taken. It's called the Danube, on West 86th Street. The guy who owns it is named Phil. I know him. He borrows money from a pal of mine."

Now we had a name for the *Phantoma*—Serge Dolin—and also the place he had been to with Willi—the Danube.

Mitzi and I went there the next evening, around six o'clock, when I had finished my work in the hospital. I was eager to go, and all day at work I thought of nothing else.

I kept thinking back to my first meeting with Willi on the train from Le Harve to Paris, when he had given me money to pass on to Magda. He had claimed it was to pay back an old debt to her father, but even then I had suspected there was something more. Willie cared for Magda, perhaps he loved her. She denied any feelings for him. She didn't trust him, didn't even like him. "He's nobody you can count on," she had said.

In Cuba Willi had denied seeing Magda after she came to America, or even knowing where she was. I'd asked him about her several times over the last few years, and always he'd shrug and say, "I never hear from her. If it wasn't for the letters she wrote you, I wouldn't even know she was in California."

I hadn't believed him. I believed Magda was one of Willi's secrets.

Phil, the owner of the Danube, claimed to know nothing. "Willi Koder used to come here once in a while," he said. "He was a customer, not a bad one, but a customer, nothing more."

"And the man he was with?" I said. "The man in the photograph?"

"I never saw him before."

"Or since?"

"You mean has he been in again? No, he came in with Willi. That's all I know."

I said, "What about the photographer who took the picture?"

"She's not here."

"When will she be in?"

"She doesn't work here," he said. "She quit. I was going to let her go, and she quit."

"Why were you going to let her go?"

"Why so many questions? What is it all about?"

"Come on, Phil," Mitzi said. "You run a popular place. I've heard it's a lot of fun. I heard the food is good. People say you're a nice guy, maybe slow paying the bills, but a nice guy."

"I'm a terrific guy," Phil said.

"The girl quit or you kicked her out?"

"I had to let her go."

"That means he couldn't get in her pants," Mitzi said.

"She was a fresh kid."

"And what else?"

"She was a friend of Willi's," Phil said. "I don't talk against the dead. Let him rest in peace, he had a heavy hand. He came to me with this girl. She needs a job, but she's got no papers, so it has to be off the books. I don't need her, but Willi's got a heavy hand. So I give the girl a job, and I let her alone, out of friendship for Willi."

"Where does she live?"

"In the forties someplace, near the river. I can look it up."

"Tell me her name."

"Magda Renner."

I wasn't surprised. I hadn't expected the photographer to turn out to be Magda, but there was a satisfying click when I heard her name, a sense of one part fitting precisely into another. After we left the Danube, I told Mitzi that Magda was an old friend who would talk more freely to me in private.

I said that because I wanted to see Magda alone, In spite of letters she'd written, I was uncertain she'd be happy to see me. Perhaps she still resented my sending her away in Paris. But she must have long realized that I did it only to save her life. It was childish to think otherwise. Yet in our friendship there had from the beginning been something in her actions of the child, the adored child. I was as much responsible for that as she. If Magda wanted to be adored, I wanted to adore her.

I was afraid only that having learned of Willi's death, she'd run off. But run where, and to whom? The address I'd been given for her was on 44th Street, near Ninth Avenue. I hurried there.

It turned out to be a brownstone with an entrance through a little garden off the street. The owner was a woman named Rafferty, and the building was divided into apartments of one room, each with a little bath. These were clean and well kept up, and with apartments hard to come by in New York, I knew they had to be expensive, and wondered where Magda's money came from.

"She lived here about six months," Mrs. Rafferty said. "Such a nice girl, well brought up, very pretty. I liked having her around, and used to miss her when she traveled."

"Did she travel a lot?"

"Now and then."

"Do you know where she went?"

"She didn't talk about her trips. She wasn't a chatterer. Some people bore you to death with their trips, what a dandy time they had while you stayed home, and even make you look through stacks of dull photographs."

"Madga didn't show you any photographs?"

"I told you, she wasn't a chatterer."

93

"Is she traveling now?"

"She moved out."

"When was that?"

"Last week. Saturday morning."

Magda had left the day after Willi's death. "A forwarding address," I asked Mrs. Rafferty, "did she leave one?"

"No. She just packed up and went." It was said reproachfully. Magda had bruised Mrs. Rafferty's feelings. She was a woman of about sixty, with pale delicate skin and neat white hair, a look of purpose and order about her. She wore a starched housecoat, and I imagined her laundering and ironing, putting things in order.

"I liked Magda," she said. "We got to be friends, at least I thought so."

We stood in the open door of her apartment, and from behind her, from the kitchen, I heard the trill of a canary, and on the radio, the voice of an announcer reading the hourly news.

I said, "Magda and I met in France."

"She rarely talked about her life in Europe," Mrs. Rafferty said. "I suppose she had a bad time of it."

The news broadcast stopped in midsentence, the dial turned, and the sound of a woman sighing followed. Mrs. Rafferty wasn't alone.

"And she left no address at all?"

"Not with me."

"Perhaps with someone else."

Mrs. Rafferty looked at me a second time. Her eyes were an odd amber color, with much yellow in them, and not at all innocent; she was, after all, a landlady, and had seen all types come and go. She called over her shoulder into the hallway leading to the apartment. "Tom, can you come a minute?"

Tom was her son, a brawny man in a sweater, whose step fell heavily on the uncarpeted wooden floor. He walked along the hallway chewing some of his dinner, a paper napkin fluttering from his waist. The resemblance between mother and son was strong, although his eyes were an ordinary and guileless brown.

"When Magda left, I tried to explain about her leaving to my mother," Tom said.

"It was very sudden," Mrs. Rafferty said.

"She was upset because of her uncle. His dying, it was unexpected."

"Her uncle," I said. "Did you know him?"

"He used to come around."

"Was his name Koder? Willi Koder?"

"Uncle Willi is right," Tom said. "I think his last name was Koder, something like that. I'm not so hot with names. But he used to help her out with the rent. She told me that, and with him gone she couldn't afford the apartment."

"We were already giving her a break," Mrs. Rafferty said. "We couldn't do any better."

Tom said, "She had made up her mind to leave."

He glanced at his mother, and it was she who said, "We've answered a lot of your questions."

"Magda is an old friend," I said. "I only want to find her and help her."

"After the uncle died, some fellow came around," Mrs. Rafferty said. "I never heard his name. My guess is she knew him from the other side. I could tell he was foreign."

"French?"

"I don't know what kind."

"Foreign."

"I didn't like the look of him," Tom said.

"Magda is a beautiful girl," Mrs. Rafferty said, glancing at her son.

"Help me find her," I said. "We really are old friends."

Mrs. Rafferty said, "That foreign fellow was on to monkey business."

"She moved only a couple of blocks from here," Tom said. "Over to 48th Street, number 411. I've a cart in the basement, and I carried her bags over."

I walked to 48th Street and found 411, a far less attractive house than Mrs. Rafferty's, and was directed to Magda's room—number 10—on the third floor by a landlady far less cordial even than Mrs. Rafferty. I climbed the stairs and searched in the unlit, gloomy landing for number 10, and found it at last, knocked softly on the door, and had to knock a second time before I heard Magda's voice, which was just as I remembered it. She opened the door, but there was no light; she had been asleep.

"Magda, is it you?" I reached out for her, but felt her stiffen and draw back. I couldn't make out her expression, and didn't know if she was happy to see me. With Magda one was always unsure.

"It was difficult finding you," I said.

"I've been with Willi. Do you understand? I didn't want you to know."

"But why? What difference does it make?" I reached out for her again, and this time when we embraced she clung to me, and I felt her tremble and a sob start deep in her throat.

"I've missed you," she said. "I've needed a friend, that's why I wrote you, but I made Willi promise not to tell you where I was." She clung to me. "I don't believe he's dead," she said. "Poor Willi. In his way, he was good."

"He loved you," I said.

She stepped back. "You don't know a thing about it," she said. "You don't know the truth about Willi and me."

She stepped aside and I passed into her room. She switched on the light. In Paris she had looked like a child, but she was no longer that. Her figure was fuller, yet the bones of her face were more pronounced, the watchful eyes more deeply set, which gave her a brooding and exotic look. If anything she was more beautiful; certainly she was more striking.

She put the water to boil on an electric ring, the same kind of electric ring that I had, that all refugees had and clung to, and that we carried like an icon from one furnished room to another.

"What do you think?" she said, looking around. "Buckingham Palace." She caught my eye, and said affectionately, "But not so bad as that rat trap in Paris. What was it called?"

"The Hotel Morocco."

"If you hadn't come that time, I'd have died there."

"It was Willi who sent me."

She shook her head; she didn't want to talk about Willi, or even to think about him. "I heard you're working at a hospital in town," she said. "And you're doing okay."

"Not bad."

"You look good."

"Couple of years older."

"Not so one can tell."

The water in the kettle on the electric ring had begun to boil. "Do you want a cup of tea?" she said.

"Not really."

"It really is a dump, this place," she said.

"Mrs. Rafferty and her son were unhappy that you moved."

"Tom is a city fireman," she said. "His photograph was in the *Daily News*, on a ladder carrying a woman out of a burning building."

"There was a fireman you used to dance with at the St. Denis," I said. "The one who said he owned a boat and docked it under the Pont Neuf."

"Pepe. That was his name."

"He was crazy about you."

"I don't think he was really a fireman," Magda said. "And he didn't own a boat."

"I heard he went into the army and was taken prisoner."

"When I wrote to you, I didn't put a return address on my letters because I didn't want you to find out how it was with me."

"How it was with you?" I said. "If you were living with Willi, what would it matter?"

"I only lived with him part of the time."

"Willi or some other guy," I said. "Men, or anything else you did to get by. Would it matter to me? How could you think it would matter? I'm not your conscience."

She had stopped listening. She paced the little room, touching things and rearranging them idiosyncratically. I heard my own words, sounding pompous and silly.

She said, "Willi must have shown you the photograph I took at the Danube."

"He died before he could. But it was mailed to his office."

"I mailed it."

"What do you know about the man with him?"

"Serge Dolin? He's a big shot."

"How do you know?"

"Because Willi kissed his ass."

"Can we go for a walk?" I said.

"A long one," she said. "I can't breathe in this dump."

We walked east, in the direction of Broadway above Times Square. The lights were dimmed for the blackout, and the smoke machine above the Camel cigarette billboard blew great smoke rings, which held only briefly before disintegrating in gusts of cold wind. Broadway was filled with servicemen, sailors tanned from duty in the Pacific, and marines, disdainful of the cold, wearing only a trim dark green tunic, campaign ribbons displayed over the left breast. They traveled in pairs or in threes or fours, some with girls who were gaily dressed and made up and who laughed and flirted, holding tight to their warriors' arms and clutching at the hems of their skirts, which the wind kept lifting.

While we walked, Magda described her first difficult days in New York. Her money ran out shortly after she arrived, and the only person she knew was Willi. She had an address for him, but refused to use it. She had made up her mind to stay clear of Willi. She wouldn't tell me

97

why, and when I pressed her, she shook her head and said only, "I didn't want to be involved with him again."

"But eventually you got involved."

"Yes, eventually." And then she quickly said, "Only when I could no longer scrape by on my own."

She began to talk about that, about scraping by. Early one Saturday morning she took the subway to the Bronx, where she'd heard of a job in a movie theater as an usher—usherette, they called it. There were usually several people hoping to land the same job, but on this Saturday it was raining so heavily that nobody else showed up. She was given a flashlight and a uniform with a little round cap, like a pet monkey's. There was a time when having to wear such a cap would have humiliated her, and there was even a time, long ago, when she would have refused to do it. Now she was only happy to get the job, twelve hours at sixty-five cents an hour.

"I'd have worn a little collar and chain around my neck," she said. "For a couple of bucks, I'd have done a dance naked, like a monkey."

But when she came around to be paid, they cheated her. "The boss's wife did the paying off," Magda said, "and she told me I'd stained my uniform and she had to take out for the dry cleaning. It wasn't true, it was crooked, and I wouldn't let the old bitch cheat me.

"I asked to see the uniform, to see if it was stained. She said she'd already sent it to the cleaners—sent it to the cleaners, midnight on Saturday!

"It got to be awful. She said I must be having my period, that's how I'd stained it. She tried to humiliate me, but it didn't work, not that time. I tried to stand up to her, but she was a big fat bitch, and she slapped me around, and threw me out of the place without a cent. Twelve hours in that monkey hat and not a cent for it. Everybody having a pinch and a pat at me, and not a cent for it. But what could I do? I'm an illegal, I shouldn't be working at all, so I've got no rights.

"On the subway to Manhattan, I wanted to jump under a train. When you've been kicked around and humiliated, the one you hate is yourself."

We walked on; the streets were dark and nearly deserted. We crossed 14th Street, and in Greenwich Village it was lively again, the bars full of people having a good time. We walked east and uptown, and Magda went on with her story.

She told me about a girl she'd met coming over on the boat from France. The girl had been to America before, where she'd learned how to get by. She took Magda to a dance hall where men came in, bought

98

tickets, and danced with the girls. Some of the girls met the men afterward, some didn't. There Magda met a man named Klein who spoke
to her in French, and then in German.

"Klein bought a bunch of tickets," Magda said, and told the manager he wanted to reserve me. So I was reserved for Herr Klein, and
after we danced a while, and chatted in German, Klein questioned
me, and learned that I was from Vienna, a Jewish girl of good family
who had fallen on hard times. I also learned about him: Herr Klein
was a street peddler's son who dreamed of Jewish girls of good family,
but was, of course, never permitted near them.

"After half a dozen dances, Herr Klein got down to business. 'How
much is your rent?' he said.

"'Forty-six dollars a month,' I said.

"'Do you have hot water?'

"'No hot water.'

"'For forty-six dollars you should have hot water,' he said. 'How
much does it cost you a month for food?'

"'I don't know. Maybe another forty.'

"'Makes eighty-six,' Klein said. 'Carfare, cigarettes, lipstick. Now
and then an article of clothing. Would you say another twenty would
do?'

"'How should I know?'

"'Of course you should know. A person in your difficult position
should know where every dime goes.'

"'Two hundred dollars,' I said. 'That's what I need a month.'

"'Two hundred dollars. That's a lot of money.'

"Herr Klein had his own way of pronouncing the word *money*, of
reaching out for money as it slipped by, of touching it and holding it
up to the light.

"I said to him, 'Another thing you ought to know is that I don't
have a decent dress. I need a new one. And a coat, Herr Klein, a warm
coat.'

"'A warm coat?'

"'Do you want to reserve me or not?'

"'Is a warm coat necessarily a fur coat?'

"'Necessarily a fur coat,' I said. 'Absolutely a fur coat.'

"'It costs a lot of *money*, a fur coat. Are you worth it?'

"'Of course, I'm worth it,' I said. "I'm a Jewish girl of good family.'

"We had been dancing all this time, but now Herr Klein stopped,
took a step back, and stared at me. He had dark, unhappy eyes with
droopy lids, and in his eyes was an expression I didn't understand. But

it was only that he was looking at me affectionately. From Klein in that dance hall affection was the last thing I expected. But there it was, like a diamond glittering on the dusty floor, Herr Klein's hesitant and timid affection.

"We got along, Klein and I; he turned out to be a grateful lover who made few demands. He liked to talk about how he had suffered, particularly as a child. How he'd gone to sleep hungry, and how he'd been mistreated. He was so young when his mother died that he scarcely remembered her. His father beat him. Poor little Herr Klein, how he needed my sympathy, the sympathy of a young woman. For him, love was mostly that, lying against my breast and telling me how he had been made to suffer."

Magda laughed and said, "Now and then there came a little poke from Herr Klein, but such a little poke."

"What about the fur coat?" I said. "Did you get it, finally?"

"I got it," she said. "And I wore it one winter. But later on I had to sell it."

We walked on, and Magda continued with her story.

"It troubled Herr Klein that he was distrusted by the other refugees and that they all disliked him. He owned an art gallery on 57th Street and made a lot of money. He claimed the other refugees were jealous of him. He had fled Germany for America in the first days after Hitler came to power. 'I saw the handwriting on the wall' was one of Herr Klein's sayings. Another saying was, 'If a Jew doesn't help himself, who's to help him?'

"Others had fled in time and taken their money with them, but Herr Klein was hated. Once in a restaurant a man came up to our table, and without a word yanked poor Klein to his feet and slapped his face. Smack! And everything stopped. There wasn't a sound, and everybody was staring at Herr Klein. His face turned bright red. He almost died of shame. To this day, I don't know why he was slapped. It was believed that Herr Klein traded for the Nazis, selling the art they stole from the Jews and depositing the money in hidden bank accounts.

"I don't know if it was true. I think Herr Klein was capable of it— 'If a Jew doesn't help himself . . . ,' and so forth. Poor Herr Klein. I should have despised him. If his money came from the Nazis, then the money he gave me also came from the Nazis, then my fur coat came from the Nazis. Instead of taking his money, I should have thrown it in his face. I should have slapped him, like the man in the restaurant. But I didn't. I took his money, and his fur coat, and slept with him, and listened to his endless and sad stories. So we were the same, me and Herr Klein, both refugees, both Jews, and 'If a Jew doesn't help himself . . .' Do you see how it was, Irina? Do you see?"

We had walked for blocks, across Manhattan, and had come to the wooden piers at the edge of the East River, where the United Nations now stands. Then there was nothing so grand, only a row of tenements, a warehouse used by a meat packer, and a restaurant, in the style of a Dublin saloon, called Jerry's, although Jerry was long dead and the place was run by his daughter, a woman with a startling laugh and red hair. There was a passageway from the cellar of Jerry's to that of the meat packer, and it was said that the best of his prime steaks were carried to Jerry's kitchen. Certainly they were delicious. Magda and I drank a whiskey after our long walk in the cold, and I ordered a double steak and French fries, and Jerry's red-haired daughter sat with us long enough to tell us a joke and be sure we were comfortable—two unescorted women in a saloon—and bought us a second whiskey.

The steaks were brought and served, and while we ate, Magda went on with her story.

"Klein had clients in Los Angeles and went there regularly. After a while, he began taking me with him. He loved Southern California," she said. "They were made for each other, Herr Klein and Beverly Hills. There was lots of cash out there, made God knows how, and Klein showed them a way to take the cash safely out of their deposit boxes, where nobody could admire it, and hang it on the wall, where everybody could."

"Time for a brandy, ladies." It was Jerry's red-haired daughter. "I got a bottle here that goes down like silk."

She filled our glasses and left the bottle, and Magda returned to her life with Herr Klein.

"Klein was greedy and got himself in hot water," she said. "The hows and whys I never found out. He had to pack up fast and beat it to Mexico. He had taken me to a lawyer to see about a residency permit, but after he left for Mexico the FBI came around, and I got scared and packed up myself and cleared out for New York. I had enough money for bus fare and a couple of weeks at Mrs. Rafferty's. Just before it ran out, Willi knocked on my door."

"How did he know where to find you?"

"Klein told him," Magda said. "I'd told Klein about Willi. It turned out he knew Willi, although he never told me. Willi steered Klein clients for a small cut. Willi told me that later." She made a little shrug, a gesture to convince me that none of it mattered, and she said, "Klein had told Willi to keep an eye on me."

"Meaning what?"

"He'd turned me over to Willi."

I said, "And it was Willi who got you the job at the Danube?"

"My Uncle Willi," she said. "I was broke, no papers, nothing at all. Willi took over for Klein, paying the rent. My Uncle Willi. The FBI was out looking for Klein."

"What did he want you to do at the Danube?"

"Take a lot of pictures, and keep my eyes and ears open," she said. "It's a popular place, the Danube. Plenty of journalists and refugees hang out there, most of them peddling something or other."

Asleep at the end of the bar was an elderly man with a harmonica on a chain around his neck. The others called him Uncle Jimmy. He slept with his head on his arm, which rested on the bar, and his fingers curled around the handle of an empty beer stein. A pal of his, signaling the others to be still, delicately stole away the empty stein and replaced it with a full one; in his sleep Uncle Jimmy closed his fingers around the handle.

"Serge Dolin," I said. "Did you meet him at the Danube?"

"He started coming in a couple of weeks ago."

"And you noticed him, and told Willi about him?"

"He's attractive, but I don't like the type."

"What type is that?"

"Cocky. Sure of himself. Plenty of money."

"Did you go out with him?"

"No." She repeated it. "I wouldn't go out with Serge Dolin."

Uncle Jimmy opened his eyes, wondering at the full stein, gazing at it as if it were a miracle.

I said, "Did Serge ask you to go out?"

"Sure, he asked."

"And even came looking for you at Mrs. Rafferty's."

"I told you, he's a cocky guy, not one to take no for an answer," she said. "Willi gave him my address. Your pal Willi. Two of a kind, Willi and Herr Klein. Willi tried to hand me over to Serge."

"Did you move from Mrs. Rafferty's to get away from Serge?"

"That's part of it," she said. "Also the money. I got fired from the Danube."

"But you're afraid of Serge?"

She shrugged and shook her head.

I said. "What did Willi say to make you afraid of Serge Dolin?"

"Not much."

"But enough. You did move, and you are scared of him."

"Serge speaks native French," Magda said. "He says he's French, but he's not. He's Russian."

"He's Russian. What else, Magda? What did Willi tell you?"

"A name. He mentioned a name, a man Serge needed to find. Willi promised to help him. He had contacts. He was stringing Serge along. But Serge caught on, and they had a fight. After that, I don't know what happened."

"The man Serge was looking for," I said. "The name Willi mentioned, you remember it?"

"He's a Pole."

"And the name?"

"Godinsky."

I'd heard the name before, from Andrew Winters. "Did you meet this Godinsky?"

"No."

"Where does he live? What does he do?"

"I don't know."

"Why does Serge need to find him?"

"I don't know."

"Why, Magda?"

"He was sent here to find him."

"Why?"

"To kill him."

From the bar came requests for "The White Cliffs of Dover," and Uncle Jimmy took up his harmonica. Magda said, "Willi told me Serge was sent from Moscow to kill a man named Godinsky."

# eleven

WAS IT TRUE? HAD SERGE DOLIN BEEN SENT BY MOSCOW TO kill a man named Godinsky? All that was known of Godinsky was that he was Polish, a patriot. But why was he to be killed? Winters had mentioned him, but only once, dangling the name for a moment in front of me, and then snatching it away.

After being with Magda, I went to see Vladimir and told him what I had learned. We agreed to find out all we could about Godinsky from Andrew Winters.

Vladimir said, "Godinsky is the key."

I remember him saying that, and then urgently trying to get hold of Winters. But Winters didn't return our calls. We were told he wasn't in, he was traveling. Where he was traveling we never learned. It now seems clear that he was avoiding us. Did he know that we had made the connection between Godinsky and Serge Dolin? But why try to hide Godinsky from us?

Vladimir concluded that Godinsky was Andrew Winters' secret, and he wasn't going to share it. It is sometimes true of spies that they come to adore their secrets and are jealous of them, guarding them like lovers.

But if Godinsky's presence in New York was a grave secret, perhaps Winters was correct to keep it to himself. Even FDR, who had ordered Godinsky's transfer to America, wasn't told where he was. Winters suspected White House leaks to Moscow. He knew to be wary of the FBI, and to distrust the circle that had closed around the President.

But looking back—knowing all the tragic story—I see that more than secrecy was involved: A duel had begun between Winters and Serge Dolin. Godinsky, a solitary Polish exile, was the first of the prizes. There were to be others, even more significant.

In the meantime, Vladimir and I went about learning what we could about Serge Dolin. He had arrived in New York on October 11, 1944, a passenger on a ship called the *Gripsholm*, chartered by the Swedish Red Cross. He traveled with a French passport that gave his date and place of birth as April 9, 1906, in Astrakhan on the Volga River.

He checked into a small hotel called the Earle, just off Washington Square, and stayed there until October 14, when he moved into a furnished apartment sublet from a man using the name Barret Martin Fisher.

Fisher remained a shadowy figure, whose real identity was never established. It is likely that he was an agent of the Russian secret service, Thirteenth Department, slipped into America illegally and reporting directly to Colonel Borodinov, head of that department in Moscow.

The real Barret Martin Fisher was born in New Orleans on June 3, 1894, attended Tulane University, and served with the American Expeditionary Force, the 69th Division, in France. He was wounded, recovered, and was discharged honorably in 1919. He lived for a time in New York City, at the YMCA on West 34th Street, and worked as an electrical engineer. He sat for the civil service examination in March of 1920 and scored well enough to be given a job as an assistant inspector of subways. He was fired when he tried to organize his fellow workers into an illegal union of municipal employees; he was remembered as a "red," and as an enthusiastic supporter of the Bolshevik revolution. Sometime around the spring of 1922, Fisher went to California, and nothing much was heard of him until the following year, when he wrote his sister that he was going to the Soviet Union. She next heard from him in 1924, through a letter from Vorograd, where he had been working in a truck plant. He wasn't well, and wanted to come home. He asked for money. She sent four hundred dollars—which was every cent she had—but she heard nothing more from him, although the bank draft was cashed.

Over the next few years, she wrote to the Soviet government to find out what had become of her brother, but received no reply. She wrote again, for the last time, in 1934, after the United States had established diplomatic relations with the Soviets. She was informed that her brother was dead of cholera and that, consistent with health and sanitary regulations, his body had been cremated.

As for the second Barret Martin Fisher—the one living in New York in 1944—he had entered the United States in March of 1932 using a valid passport, made out in that name, and was able through Russian contacts in New York, former students at the Maly Theater in Petrograd, to get a job as a rehearsal pianist with the American Ballet and then the Metropolitan Opera, where he was employed for nine years.

He traveled in artistic and intellectual circles, and made many friends, particularly among the American left. Though his salary was low, he managed to buy a small house in Montauk, at the eastern end of Long Island. In it he installed a Hallicrafter shortwave radio, able to contact Russian ships cruising in international waters.

In April of 1945, Fisher disappeared. It's not known where he went or what he did. A woman cellist formerly with the Metropolitan Opera, touring the Soviet Union in 1957, claimed to have seen him on the Moscow subway. The cellist knew Fisher well. They had had a love affair. When she called to the man she thought was Fisher, he looked up but didn't acknowledge her. She was certain he recognized her, but he fled, disappearing into the subway crowd.

But this encounter has never been corroborated, and the final whereabouts of the second Fisher are uncertain.

In New York, the apartment Fisher rented was in a row house on 76th Street just off Riverside Drive, facing a rear courtyard with no view of the Hudson River, a single room with a tiny kitchen that looked as if neither Fisher nor Dolin ever used it. No pots or pans, not even a knife or fork, were ever found, and the only water glass was in the bathroom and held the toothbrush. It was a place deliberately kept barren and impersonal, like a room in a hotel near a railroad station. There were no books or magazines, no pencils or scraps of paper, not a used cake of soap or razor blade, not a cigarette or a book of matches, although both Fisher and Dolin smoked. The only wall decoration was a 1944 calendar next to the bathroom mirror, the days neatly crossed off, as if by a prisoner in his cell, the last on October 14, the day the apartment was taken over by Dolin.

Dolin hadn't been in New York since before the war, and spent the final week of October refamiliarizing himself with the city. He bought a street map and bus and subway guides, and explored the museums and city parks and the main reading room of the library on 42nd Street, where he had spent much of his time on earlier visits, taking the advice of Lenin, who recommended the libraries of the West, which he found not only free but brilliantly organized and, above all, heated in winter.

Dolin also attended concerts—everyone who knew him agreed that he loved music—and he went frequently to the movies, particularly the big places on Broadway above Times Square. He went late in the afternoon, when there were no crowds and he could sit in an empty row, in the dark, and be alone with his thoughts. I've tried to imagine what he thought on those afternoons, traveling on the subway, or sitting in the library or the park, and particularly those afternoons in the movies around Times Square. I always liked the movies, and whenever I could, whenever I wanted to give myself a special treat, I'd sneak away to see one alone. So I understood Dolin, and even went to the library and looked up back issues of the *New York Times* in order to find out the movies he'd probably seen. *A Tree Grows in Brooklyn* was playing then and *Laura*, as well as *Anchors Aweigh*. I've seen all of them, and can visualize him watching them and afterward walking on Broadway, and stopping somewhere for a meal. Moscow had supplied him with enough money to live well, but he preferred modest self-service restaurants. New York had lots of cafeterias in 1944, and Dolin ate mostly in those. He knew where all the Horn & Hardart restaurants were—Magda later told me that—and he had a sweet tooth, and used to go to Lindy's or the Turf for Danish pastry and cheesecake.

At that time there was still no woman in his life. Wandering around the city, he certainly met some. He was attractive and had plenty of money. If he had affairs, they were brief, probably casual and unemotional. There are no names, no woman who remembers him. He took on the habits of a solitary man, of a *Phantoma*. Yet he was not one of them, not a shadow on the wall. There was to him a third dimension, as there is to more ordinary men, and that dimension was a fervent past. It turned out he was passionate and romantic; I think of his desire for Magda, and of how he came eventually to risk everything for her, even his life.

Sometime around the beginning of November, Dolin made his first contact with the Russian embassy in Washington, using as his recognition signal an ordinary postcard on which he'd written a religious message ending with a quotation from the Book of Judges, about an angel appearing to Manoah's wife.

The day following its delivery to the embassy, Dolin received a phone call at the Fisher apartment from a man with an unfamiliar voice and an accent that was difficult to place. He wanted someone named Fitzgerald. The name was repeated. It was necessary to speak at once to Mr. Fitzgerald.

The following morning Dolin bought a *New York Times* from a dealer on the corner of Broadway and 79th Street. It was a clear, cold morning, and Dolin decided he needed a cup of coffee before beginning his search of the classified ads in the *Times*.

He had gotten into the habit of having breakfast in a coffee shop on Broadway just up from the newsstand. The place is there still. I've been to it, and have sat at the counter, perhaps the same stool Dolin occupied. It's been done over and given a Greek name, and on the walls are posters advertising travel to the islands of the Aegean. There are also color photographs of skewered meats, and one photo of a whole grilled fish. In 1944 the place was owned by Jews, a husband and wife, who had immigrated from Morocco.

It was the wife who remembered Dolin. She naturally thought he was French, and somehow got it into her head that he was an actor. It was the way he spoke, his perfect French. In Morocco, her father had been a tailor and she noticed that Dolin's clothes were stylish and well made. He reminded her of another actor, a popular one, although she couldn't remember his name.

"Most of the time he played the he-man," she said, "a rugged type, but still in the end he was the one who got the girl."

But this quality of being remembered was a danger, a flaw in Dolin's talent as a *Phantoma*. He was unable to fade into the background. He was attractive, but that could have been concealed. Dolin was noticed and remembered because he wanted to be, because he needed to be. The *Phantoma* is not an actor, able to change identities; the *Phantoma* is best invisible, without identity. This Dolin couldn't manage. The intuition of the woman in the coffee shop was correct: Dolin was theatrical, an actor.

With his second cup of coffee, Dolin opened the *New York Times*. In the classified ads, under merchandise offered, he found a list of musical instruments: violins were plentiful, pianos a glut on the market. Several people offered flutes, one a Haynes for $300. There was a harp, a piccolo, and finally a used German Gordet English horn, its condition excellent, its price $290.

The code was known to Dolin: The first digit was the date of the meeting, November 2. The second digit was the place, number 9, a drop prearranged on a map of New York City. The third digit was the time: 10 o'clock.

The meeting place, drop number 9, was in the Lower East Side of Manhattan. Dolin went by bus, through Central Park at 66th Street, and downtown on Second Avenue to Delancey Street. From there he walked east past secondhand clothing stalls, kosher delicatessens, and a storefront scribe who wrote letters in Hebrew, English, Polish, German, and Greek, all for a fee. There was a secondhand bookstore— Dolin browsed there—another shop selling Hebrew religious articles, a bank in the style of a Greek temple.

Dolin came to a cobblestone street, narrow as an alley, which ran beside the Williamsburg Bridge to Brooklyn. At the end of this street was a live poultry market, the birds kept in stacks of wooden crates, their heads poking through the slats. It was four minutes past ten. Inside the market were more crates of chickens, ducks, geese, and turkeys. There were even pigeons, white ones, with brilliant black eyes. The stench was of blood and bird droppings, the wooden floor thick with sawdust and feathers. There were vats of boiling water into which the slaughtered birds were dipped so that their feathers could be more easily plucked. The language of trade was Yiddish, although Polish and Russian were heard as well.

Dolin saw Mr. Gray first. It had been nearly six years, and though he was thinner—his collar stood away from his neck and the flesh there was loose—Mr. Gray looked much the same. He wore a dark coat and hat, a proper tie and crisp collar, as he always had; Dolin could imagine him dressed no other way. And there was about him the same reserve, the same sturdy competence, the taut and watchful intelligence.

They shook hands. Dolin looked into Mr. Gray's pale blue eyes, enlarged by the lenses of his glasses, and said, "The great rise and fall, only Mr. Gray endures."

"*Endures* is the word," Mr. Gray said. "But only just endures." He had spoken first in English and then switched to Russian. "Barely endures, by the skin of the teeth." He stepped back for a better look at Dolin. "On the other hand, Sergei Dimitrovich, you're looking marvelously well. Very prosperous, a star on the rise; one hears nothing but praise for you."

"But you, my old comrade, for years one heard nothing at all of you."

"As if I were dead and buried."

"Yes, I feared that."

"Well, almost, almost dead. Certainly I was buried, in the deepest and darkest prison cell."

"A Fascist cell or one of ours? In whose jail were you?"

"Does it matter? All jails have the same stink." He had taken out a spotless handkerchief and held it to his nose. Mr. Gray's linen had always been immaculate. He was said to be of aristocratic birth, although he denied that emphatically. Dolin imagined him in a rented room, caring for his laundry, sewing and darning his socks, polishing his shoes while listening dreamily to Italian opera. Mr. Gray liked Italian opera. He had served for years in the north of Italy, organizing the underground party under the nose of the Fascists.

"It stinks in jail," he said. "And it stinks the same in here." He began walking toward the door of the market, his arm under Dolin's. "My jail was called Misery," he said. "That's the name we convicts gave it. I was in Misery for two years, and I was dead and forgotten and without any hope at all. Have you ever been in such a state?"

"I've not been in jail."

"Or without hope?"

Serge answered gravely, "I don't know what you mean."

"Of course not, Sergei Dimitrovich," Mr. Gray said. "You're a man of hope, a man of history, a man of the future."

They stopped before a wooden crate that held several white pigeons, and Mr. Gray poked between the slats with his finger and stroked the birds. He called them doves, innocent creatures, and said, "We could buy them, and set them free. In Asia, they do that before starting out on a trip, or any risky adventure. It's to bring luck, to earn credit with the gods."

"It's true, they're pretty," Dolin said. "A shame, such a shame." But he walked on, and they went out of the market, and Mr. Gray spoke again of the prison, of Misery, where he had spent two years. "It's an odd state," he said, "to be dead, and still stumbling around. Dead and buried, and trying to scratch up somthing to eat."

"But you found something to eat," Dolin said. "You didn't starve, and you didn't freeze. You survived. You survived the wars, the purges, the prisons. All of those who were with you in 1917 are long dead."

"Dead in a great cause."

"Only Mr. Gray survives."

"Survives, but how?" He squeezed Dolin's arm. "Survives as a ghost." They walked on, arm in arm, in the Russian style, and Mr. Gray said, "It would be pleasant to spend a little time in gossip, and telling stories, the kind that go best over a cup of tea. I miss that part of life. Do you, Sergei Dimitrovich?"

"Drinking a cup of tea with an old friend?"

"Well, intimacy. Do you miss intimacy?"

They were in the shadow of the Williamsburg Bridge, on the quay beside the East River. Mr. Gray had turned his eyes on Dolin; there was something modest in his glance, something shy, demure; but of course with those pale eyes, which had seen so much and told so little, with that masked intelligence, it was impossible to know what Mr. Gray thought, or if he were serious or merely teasing.

"For example," he said, "if there were time for a cup of tea, I'd talk about your father, that remarkable man. An intellectual, but fond of horseback riding. I remember a favorite horse of his, a little mare, with a flash of white between the eyes. People said he was ruthless, a heartless man. Do you think your father was ruthless, Sergei Dimitrovich?"

"He was an idealist," Dolin said.

"An idealist, yes. An idealist." Mr. Gray's lips closed around the word; Dolin thought of certain plants, flesh eaters, that lured their prey by scent or color, and whose inviting petals then snapped shut. "An idealist," Mr. Gray repeated. "Also he had human feelings. He loved that little mare of his, but in the winter of 1919, when so many were hungry, he had her slaughtered and the meat distributed to the people. It broke his heart. He wept. I was there, and saw it. Those tears on the idealist's cheeks seemed to me a miracle, like a statue weeping."

"He is a statue," Dolin said. "You can see him on his pedestal on Borovitskaya."

"Is that how you think of your father—as a statue?"

"I rarely think of him at all."

Dolin had spoken in English, as if to separate himself from these reflections and put them at a distance; he looked away, his eye following the parabolic curve of the bridge and the broad back of a bus lumbering to Brooklyn.

"Godinsky is hidden in Brooklyn," Dolin said. "That much we know."

"Why so much trouble to find this man?" Mr. Gray said. "He's not much, you know. As far as I can see, he's not much at all."

"He's the one Pole the others have agreed on," Dolin said. "After the war, if there's to be an independent Poland, he will be head of state."

"But there's to be no independent Poland."

"Of course not," Dolin said. "Our man will be put in, and it'll be our Poland, a buffer land between us and Germany."

Mr. Gray turned up his collar and shivered; he hated the cold, the damp, and dimly lit rooms. His dreams were of lying in the sun, of warmth and the smell of flowers.

Dolin said, "The winters here are nearly as cold as in Moscow." He'd been watching Mr. Gray closely. "Nearly as cold."

"Very nearly."

"But not so much snow."

"Not so much."

"And here places are heated," Dolin said. "One can warm one's bones."

Mr. Gray distrusted chitchat carried on in the open. Comparisons between New York and Moscow were not innocent. He said, "Regarding your shopping list, it was at first rather a problem. A print of a French motion picture made in 1932, a creaky old farce called *La Princesse*."

"I'm told it was popular."

"No one knew it," Mr. Gray said. "And I had a devil of a time getting hold of it. Now the actress in it, what was her name?"

"Nadine Berne."

"I've a Hungarian in Hollywood, and he's heard of Nadine Berne," Mr. Gray said. "This Hungarian made pictures in Paris all during the 1920s and 1930s, and he knew her well. He'd even been to her wedding."

"Her wedding?"

"It's a small world, isn't it?" Mr. Gray said. "Nadine Berne was married to Karl Godinsky."

A train sped across the bridge on the upper level, its weight sending vibrations through the supporting steel and causing flakes of paint and bits of dirt to rain down. They walked from the quay and turned into one of the narrow streets that ran north from Delancey; these were paved with cobblestones and lined on both sides with stalls and bins heaped with goods. They had a cramped, sunless look. Some of the bins were filled with clothing, men's and women's, and shoes tied together by their laces and strung up on lines, like fruit on a tree; other bins were filled with nuts and bolts, tools and lead pipe, and bars of soap, socks, and cheap woolen sweaters.

"Commonplace things," Dolin said. "Everyday things, things for the people."

"It makes one think of home."

"Do you miss home?"

Mr. Gray didn't answer. Dolin recalled hearing that his wife and infant daughter had died in the civil war. He noticed that Mr. Gray was taller than he remembered, and that his nose was somewhat longer and red at the tip. While they walked, he gave Dolin a key to a numbered locker in Grand Central Station. "I'm coming down with a cold," Mr. Gray said. "In the locker, you'll find what you asked for—the print of *La Princesse* and two other films from the same period, enough for a little show."

"You've done a good job."

"Perhaps it's the flu," Mr. Gray said. "I'll need to go to bed for a couple of days."

Dolin said, "Did your Hungarian know Godinsky?"

"He thought he wrote books. A mousy little man. Nobody could figure out what Nadine Berne saw in him." Mr. Gray unfolded his immaculate handkerchief and blew his nose into the center of it. He was eager to be off. "I was told Godinsky adored Nadine Berne," he said.

Dolin stood for a moment after Mr. Gray had walked off; he watched him blend into the people poking in the stalls along the street. It was uncanny, like a trick by a magician, but there was no magic word, no puff of smoke. Mr. Gray was there, and the next moment he wasn't. He simply had vanished.

# twelve

☭ DOLIN WENT TO THE LOCKER IN GRAND CENTRAL STATION and collected the parcel of film Mr. Gray had left. The parcel was rather a large one, and he felt conspicuous carrying it. He knew of a warehouse on the far West Side of Manhattan with secure space for rent, and took the parcel there and locked it away.

Dolin was in America legally, and didn't think he was under surveillance, but he was cautious nevertheless. He had been trained to live underground, as a hunted man, and during the four years of German occupation of France, he had done just that. It had become natural for him, a way of life, and living in the open made him uneasy; like a soldier or a prisoner, Dolin needed to look both ways, to be sure the light wasn't at his back.

Before the war began, in August of 1939, he had taken control of a small Communist weekly called *Les Engagés* when its editor, who had broken with Moscow over the Nazi pact, was shot to death in the street outside his apartment on the Rue Christine.

The assassin was never identified and no link between Dolin and the murder was ever established. But the next day he was at the editor's desk. Some of the staff protested, but Dolin calmed them and persuaded them to go along with him. The surprise was how, under his direction, the editorial policies of *Les Engagés* moved away from the narrow Moscow line. The magazine was still of the left, but of a more broad-based, independent left. So it seemed, and people stopped thinking of Serge Dolin as a Communist.

After the war began, even as the Germans approached Paris, Dolin stayed on. Moscow had created escape routes and provided travel documents for all its important agents in France. But Dolin, now operating in secret, was ordered to go underground, to infiltrate the French Resistance and establish a Comintern link to the Gaullists. It was risky and took great courage. The Gestapo was efficient as well as ruthless, and not likely to believe Dolin had broken with Moscow.

Certainly he was in danger. He knew the escape routes, and could have gotten out by way of Sweden, Portugal, or even Switzerland. He had the money and the contacts. But Dolin obeyed Moscow's orders and stayed on, living underground during the four years of the German occupation of France.

That he survived was a miracle. The Gestapo hunted everywhere for him. They took hostages, and tortured all those able to give information. Dolin had several close calls, but always managed to get away. He was a master at living underground, and of course he was lucky. He took half a dozen identities, and there are reports of his being seen in different parts of France at the same time. Some say he wasn't in France at all, but spent most of the occupation in England, and returned only with the Allied armies. As with much of the history of the French Resistance, it's impossible to separate truth from myth. There are survivors of the Resistance, men and women of the right and the left, who swear Serge Dolin was the bravest and most resourceful of their comrades. At the same time there are stories of his being an informer, and betraying non-Communist members of the Resistance to the Gestapo. In these stories he's portrayed as a Communist agent—first and last—a ruthless man, obedient only to Moscow, whose sole purpose was to purge the Resistance of those who were not so obedient.

Dolin himself never spoke of what he did, not even years later to Magda. He denied nothing, affirmed nothing, defended nothing. He wrote in his journal at night, and in the morning he tore the pages up. The rest of us need to take someone we love aside and say, "Here I was good, here I failed, and here I came through. This one I loved and this one I hated." We have a need to pass on our lives to others. But not Dolin. He trained himself to live secretly, keeping contact only with others in the Communist underground. One by one they were killed or captured and tortured to death. The network grew smaller, the ring closing around Dolin; but he continued to transmit to Moscow, and occasionally he received word—his messages were getting through.

During those years he learned to kill dispassionately, and to think dispassionately of his own death. The story was started that he was dead. Good, he'd build on that. If Serge Dolin was dead, his memory was gone; he could pull a sheet over his past. He fought the Germans, but was dead. He wrote no more in his journal.

In the summer of 1944, Dolin was hiding northwest of Paris, operating a resistance cell near Nantes. When the American Third Army under George Patton passed, heading due east for Paris, Dolin separated from his comrades and slipped alone into Paris. He was there when LeClerc and the Americans arrived.

Three days after the liberation, a party of Soviet military officials flew in—a Red Army captain and two GPU officers, the ranking one a major named Ryabov. The party went directly to the Soviet embassy, but found Dolin already there, occupying the empty building.

"How the devil did you get in?" Major Ryabov said.

"Through the front door," Dolin said. "It was wide open."

"Our orders were to learn if you were alive and to find you," Major Ryabov said. "Personally, I didn't think it possible you'd survived."

"It's not possible," said the captain, slapping Dolin on the back. "How did you manage it?"

Dolin had no answer. He looked from one Russian face to another. He couldn't believe that they were speaking Russian, and he was answering in Russian. He asked for news of the war in the east. He was told that the Red Army had crossed into Germany. Victory was certain. It was incredible; all of it was incredible.

That night there was a victory celebration. There was no vodka, but Dolin knew where to get his hands on red wine and cognac. Someone else rounded up a few French girls. The party in the embassy went on all night, and the next morning one of the army officers found more wine; the girls had passed out, and even the Russians slept a bit, woke up, and slept again. Only on the third day did Major Ryabov and the Red Army captain take Dolin aside for a confidential talk.

"Very few of your messages got through, you know," Ryabov said. "But those that did made an impression. The one reporting the Allied landing in Normandy, that one comrade Stalin saw himself." He was still drinking brandy, glass after glass, without it having any effect on him. "A firsthand report, comrade. Not bad at all." He raised his glass by way of salute. "Stalin trusts first of all his spies," he said. "Second his own diplomats, and last of all his allies."

"Stalin himself set us to find you," the captain said. "You know, I still think it's a miracle you're alive."

"Yes, a miracle."

"Perhaps you're an impostor," the captain said. "Maybe the real Serge Dolin is dead, and you're a spy."

"They'll know in Moscow."

Dolin had been standing with arms folded, taking it all in. Partly it was chatter, drunken talk, and partly genuine suspicion.

"Are you Dolin or not?"

"Look for yourself."

"They'll know in Moscow."

"What's this talk of Moscow?"

"You're to go home," Ryabov said. "They'll give you a medal, a new assignment."

"A medal or a bullet," the captain said. "When you get home, you'll find out."

"There's talk comrade Stalin himself wants to see you."

"Hush-hush. Big stuff," the captain said. "Is there any more cognac?"

"It's like piss, that wine."

"You fly out the day after tomorrow, to Italy, and then to a British base in Cairo."

"In the meantime you stay here," the captain said. "Stick close, comrade. And then go home and get your medal—or your bullet."

The Red Air Force had requisitioned an abandoned Luftwaffe base south of Paris, near Fontainbleau, and from there Dolin flew by C-47 to an American base on the Adriatic, and from there, after a two-day stopover, to an RAF field in Cairo.

He was going home—for the first time in eight years. He wasn't afraid of the reception he'd receive—he hadn't even adjusted to the idea of being alive; as he got closer to Moscow, the past returned in sudden and disconnected images, as if he were recovering from a prolonged state of amnesia.

From Cairo he flew to Turkey, and his first night there, sleeping in his overcoat on the floor of an unused hangar, he woke in a panic, covered with sweat. He'd dreamed of his father, who was warning him of something, his father in a chair with a blanket wrapped around his legs as he'd seen him in the clinic in England. And his mother, Larisa Sergeyevna, was also in the dream, an elusive, ghostlike figure.

But his father's presence was real, and his father's voice spoke out clearly: "Stalin trusts first of all his spies."

In the morning Dolin continued the long trip to Moscow, arriving there eight days later.

He hadn't been in Russia since 1936. His father was dead. There was no brother or sister, no relatives at all. The friends he'd made as a boy were dead or scattered by the war. He was shocked by the poverty and suffering of the ordinary people. In Moscow he searched for the house he'd lived in as a boy, and when he finally located it, it was so changed he didn't recognize it. He had to check the address twice. The grand apartment that once belonged to Commissar of the People Stenoviev had been broken up and was now occupied by a dozen or more families, their sleeping rolls, laundry, and personal possessions everywhere. The old furniture had long ago been carted off or cut up and burned for firewood. The chandeliers, mirrors, even the moldings—everything had been stripped and carried away.

Even so there were corners that were familiar, and things that he remembered. But that only confused him. He had lived so long as Serge Dolin that Sergei Stenoviev had become a different person, and it was that person whose childhood had been spent in this apartment, and that person to whom the memories belonged.

He stood in the center of the large room, once the Stenoviev parlor. It was quiet, unnaturally so, the air still, with motes suspended in the rays of pale sunlight coming through the tall, old-fashioned windows. Seconds passed while he held his breath and waited, and listened.

Much later he described the scene to Magda: "My life had come to a stop," he said. "A pause in life. Do you know what that is?"

"I think so."

"A full stop, there in the old apartment in Moscow. I listened to hear if it would start up again. And how would it start up again—as Stenoviev or as Serge Dolin?"

"And how did it start up?" she said.

"It started—I walked to the window, the tall window from the floor to the ceiling, climbing over heaps of clothes and a mattress on which somebody slept. I went to the window and looked out on the street, which was just as I remembered it. My mother's piano had stood by the window, and then I saw her exactly as she had been, her head bent over the music and the sun on her neck, the light making her dark hair shine. I thought I had forgotten her, or rather I had taught myself not to think of her. I was twelve when she disappeared. I loved her, but it was necessary to bury all feelings for her. I thought they were gone, those feelings, but by the window they came back with a rush, strong as ever, overwhelming."

"Your mother at the piano," Magda said. "The pause in your life. And when it was over, were you Stenoviev?"

"Yes. But I couldn't allow it. I had to bury those feelings again. I had been summoned to Moscow by Stalin. I was to meet Stalin, to be given an assignment as Serge Dolin."


Dolin's stay in Moscow was brief, only long enough to receive his new assignment and prepare for it. It was given to him personally by Stalin, in his office in the Kremlin.

Stalin told Dolin that the service he was being asked to perform was of the greatest importance; in order to protect Russia from Germany and the West, Poland was needed as a buffer, a dependent state.

"That is our primary foreign policy objective," Stalin said. "A man named Godinsky, now living in New York. He's an inconsequential man, historically a nobody—except that events have brought him to the center of the stage—the only man the different Polish factions can agree on. So we have to eliminate Godinsky in order to put our own man in Warsaw. And we back our man with the Red Army." Stalin gripped Dolin's shoulders. "The Red Army," he said, with that little smile of his, Stalin's smile. "The Red Army and that's that."

Stalin then kissed Dolin on both cheeks and on the lips and pinned a medal on his chest.

Later that same night, in the rooms below Stalin's office, there was a party given by Colonel Borodinov of the GPU, head of the Thirteenth Department, the assassination bureau.

The guest of honor at this party was Serge Dolin.

It was a special party—there was talk that Stalin himself might come. Everyone stayed sober and hid the girls. Colonel Borodinov was nervous and didn't know what to do with himself. It was like a funeral, everyone waiting for the corpse to arrive.

Finally, about midnight, Stalin showed up. He was in good humor and told a joke about a pigeon that laid an ostrich egg. No one understood the joke, but everyone laughed. Stalin wore an old sweater and carpet slippers, and to Dolin he appeared benevolent, like a kindly grandfather. He smoked a cigarette and let the ash fall on his chest. He had a drink, possibly two, before going upstairs to his apartment. As soon as he was gone, somebody sent for the girls—actresses and dancers from the Moscow theaters.

Stalin had singled out Dolin and so a great fuss was made over him. The girls called him "the Frenchman" and wouldn't leave him alone. They wanted to know if he had learned any special sexual techniques in France.

But Dolin didn't bother with the girls. He had other things on his mind. He took Colonel Borodinov aside and asked if it all came down to one man.

And Borodinov put his arm around him and said, "Yes, one man." Borodinov was drunk, at that dangerous stage when the drunkard feels he's in control and is confident of his cunning. He said, "One man, one man at a time. Godinsky may be the final one, and then there may be another after him. Another assignment, even more daring. The most daring assignment of all." Both his arms were around Dolin, and he hugged him, and then took a swig straight from the bottle of vodka.

"You remember your old friend, your agent in New York?"

"Who do you mean?"

"From before the war. The old friend of your mother."

"Balabanovna."

"We've been in touch with her."

"Who has?"

"Our resident in New York."

"But she was to be left alone," Dolin said. "She was not to be approached, under any circumstances—"

"Except by you."

"Exactly."

"But you were in France. You could even have been dead. Balabanovna was a sleeping agent. We had to wake her."

"Why?"

"Because of FDR. Through Julia Winters, Balabanovna is now in the inner circle. Through her we know something of FDR's state of mind, certain of his attitudes, even the truth about his health, which isn't so bad as is rumored. He could actually live for years."

It was a hint, one of those made and not made. "Roosevelt could live quite a few more years."

"What of it?"

"We have an operation named Archangel. In due course, you'll learn more of it."

"Does it concern Roosevelt?"

"Yes."

"His health?"

"In due course, comrade."

The morning after the party, Dolin went to work researching the Godinsky file. The most recent confirmed intelligence was that Godinsky had left England early in April of 1944, and was flown to America in a Boeing B-17 bomber. His escort was an American intelligence agent using the code name Konrad.

Dolin cross-checked Konrad and found it first mentioned by a Comintern agent operating in Switzerland in 1926. Konrad was the American contact for two early Central Committee defectors.

Mention was made of a second agent, resident in Zurich during the same period and known as the Russian Woman. But no file existed for her, and who she was or what she did—the Russian Woman—or what became of her appeared nowhere in the central Moscow files.

Dolin read further in the files of the defectors themselves. One had died in Bern, apparently of natural causes, shortly after he came out, but the other had been resettled in the United States under a different name and was teaching Russian language and literature at Blair College in Connecticut. He'd been recommended for the job by a trustee of Blair, and now, for the first time, Dolin came upon the name Andrew Winters.

He wasn't surprised to find a file for Andrew Winters, or to marvel at its revelations. Andrew Winters was the brother of a woman known to be the intimate friend of Franklin Roosevelt. He was the trustee of two colleges and universities besides Blair, and had placed Soviet refugees and defectors on the faculty of each of them.

He was thought to be well off but not rich, and he served as financial patron for three small New York publishing houses; it was likely that he raised some of the money and served as a conduit for more. One of the publishers specialized in bilingual texts of Soviet works, another did inexpensive art books, and the third reprinted mechanical and electrical training manuals. The three were unprofitable, but their editorial and production departments were made up of émigrés who had fled the Soviet Union, part of a loosely knit organization known as Living Memory and controlled by Andrew Winters.

Reading on, Dolin found that Winters had been in and out of Zurich in 1926, ostensibly to visit his sister, who was recuperating in a psychiatric sanatorium—but that his real purpose was to create the intelligence network that served as the basis for Living Memory.

And then, in one of those rare revelatory flashes, it all came together. A Soviet agent used to penetrate Living Memory had in his report flagged the code name Konrad. Konrad was Living Memory control. Konrad was Andrew Winters; and Konrad had flown Godinsky to America.

Dolin returned to the Godinsky file, looking for hobbies, idiosyncracies, something in his character that would help locate him. At first Dolin saw nothing, at least nothing obvious. Godinsky was described as a solitary man, reflective, living among books, going out occasionally to the theater or movies. His tastes were intellectual; he had come late in life to politics. He wasn't motivated by personal ambition, and certainly not by dreams of glory. He was a man others trusted, a man of moderation, not particularly cunning or with outstanding intellectual gifts, but a man on whom the fractious Poles could agree. That was Godinsky's great value, and it was that which made him unique.

The Soviet agent in the British postal service, who had helped locate Godinsky in London, reported that he had left England immediately after an attack on his life, had left owing his landlady fifteen pounds. Three weeks later, an American bank draft in that amount arrived for her. It had been drawn on the Corn Exchange Bank, written at its branch on Eastern Parkway and Utica Avenue in Brooklyn.

From the first Dolin was convinced that the draft had not gone through Andrew Winters, but had been sent personally and artlessly by Godinsky, without Winters knowing about it. It placed Godinsky in Brooklyn, near Eastern Parkway, an area Dolin had explored on an earlier visit to New York. It was European in flavor, the population mostly refugees and first-generation Jews. Godinsky would be inconspicuous there. He'd be safe. Dolin remembered the excellent free library, the small movie houses that showed prewar European films, the shops, coffee houses, and little restaurants. Around Eastern Parkway, Godinsky would fit in and have all he'd need.

The next question was how to find him there. Dolin went back over the thick biographical file in the section covering Godinsky's years in France, looking for something that had earlier caught his eye.

Godinsky had lived in Paris more than ten years, and spoke French as well as Polish. It was in France that Godinsky's eclipse had passed, and that the obscure side of him had turned slowly toward the light. It was in France that he'd met Nadine Berne.

When he read the name, Dolin's heart jumped; he copied it down, but was disappointed to find nothing more in the Godinsky file about her. Instinct told him there ought to be more, a good deal more; Dolin had been looking for the intimate in Godinsky's life, the person he loved, the soft spot, and the way to get at him. Dolin thought he had found it in Nadine Berne. But the Godinsky file held nothing more about her, and there was no individual file for her, and nothing in the cross-reference.

But the name tantalized him. Dolin had heard it before—Nadine Berne—at least he thought he'd heard it. He tried everything he could to remember, but it was no use. The old newspaper files for France were incomplete, crumbling away to dust, and without a name index.

With the pressure growing, it was a frustrating couple of days. Then a surprising thing happened, one of those psychological mysteries for which there is no explanation: A tune began to run through Dolin's mind, and he began to hum a little song popular in France in the early 1930s. It was called "Toujours Aimer," a ditty about loving and remembering, with a banal lyric that went around in Dolin's head until he suddenly realized what it meant: "Toujours Aimer" was from a movie of that name, and appearing in the movie was a young actress in a secondary role; the actress's name was Nadine Berne.

It was nearly two o'clock in the morning when Dolin remembered her. He had the duty officer call the director of the Moscow Film Institute—the director had been a filmmaker himself and had worked in London, Paris, and Hollywood. Dolin sent a car for him, had him pulled out of bed, and ordered him to open the archives, which hadn't been opened since before the war, and together they spent the rest of the morning and most of the afternoon going through cartons and stacks of newspaper clippings, some of them eaten by mice. But finally Dolin had what he was looking for—a thick envelope, fairly well preserved, and stuffed with articles and publicity releases dealing with Nadine Berne.

She was French, born in Lyon in May 1904, and had worked in several provincial touring companies before appearing and enjoying a modest success on the Paris stage. There were bit parts in films, the featured role in *Toujours Aimer*. Her only leading role was in a film called *La Princesse*, made in 1934.

Dolin carefully handled the brittle, yellowing newspaper clippings. They had been put into the envelope in chronological order, and Dolin read slowly, moving patiently through Nadine Berne's life. She had traveled with the smart set; in one picture she was in an open motor car with an English aristrocrat, Lord Hood, and in another she was at a ball dancing with Charlie Chaplin. There were photographs with Coco Chanel and Josephine Baker, and with society people and others of evanescent celebrity whose names meant nothing to Dolin.

Dolin anticipated the appearance, in Nadine Berne's life, of Godinsky. When, at last, he came on, it was pure gold, a photograph of the two of them, at the head of an article about their engagement. The photograph wasn't an ordinary snapshot, but there was no photographer's credit, and Dolin thought it had been done by one of the news services.

It was a full-length shot of both of them and they were walking across what looked to be a formal garden. Dolin thought it might be the Tuileries, since both were dressed for the city, Godinsky in a smart striped suit with a handkerchief showing in the breast pocket of his coat. It was the handkerchief that caught Dolin's eye, the particular way it was folded, with three points showing like a star; he was certain Nadine Berne had folded it and arranged it lovingly in the pocket of her fiancé's coat. Dolin held the photograph under a lamp and studied the expressions on their faces: the unsmiling, composed, and dignified Godinsky, a shy and reclusive man, a gifted writer who had begun as a mathematician. A man who had spent his time in lecture halls and libraries, a man of abstractions, with little passion in his life. And then in middle age he had met Nadine Berne, the beautiful French actress, who admired his intelligence and learning, and who loved him. In the photograph she clung to his arm, the beginning of a smile in her eyes and around her mouth. She wore flat heels so as not to appear taller than Godinsky, and she had folded the handkerchief and arranged it in his pocket just so.

The marriage took place in Lyon, in January of 1933, at the home of Nadine's widowed mother. The wedding was a small one, attended only by the bride's family and a few intimate friends. Later the same year, Godinsky published a novel about the South Seas, a romance that was translated into English and sold to Hollywood. He and Nadine crossed to America on the *Mauritania*, and there was a clipping from the *New York Mirror* dated December 21, 1934, in which Godinsky is described as a Rumanian writer, and Nadine is photographed seated on a steamer trunk with her legs crossed and her skirt above her knees, adorable in a mink coat and matching hat, her hands deep in a muff.

Dolin stopped reading, put down the clipping, and tried to imagine Godinsky's reaction to it. Had it annoyed him to be called a Rumanian writer? Dolin thought not. More than anything it had probably struck him funny, a story to be told over dinner. What wasn't funny was the photograph of Nadine Berne, his adored wife, with her skirt above her knees. Dolin's Karl Godinsky was a man of firm and uncompromising standards. The readers of the *Daily Mirror* were free to believe him to be Rumanian or Chinese, but they were not to gape at his wife's legs. That Godinsky would not permit. No doubt he took Nadine aside and explained his feelings to her, for no more provocative photographs of her were found in the file.

From New York they went by train across the continent to California. In Hollywood they hobnobbed with Douglas Fairbanks and Mary Pickford, and there is even a photograph of them around a grand piano with the Marx Brothers. They stayed on in Southern California, and Godinsky published another novel, this one set at the time of the American Revolution, its hero a Polish aristocrat who, after killing a man in a duel in Warsaw, flees to Virginia, where he joins the colonial army, is wounded at Yorktown, and falls in love with the lady who nurses him back to health.

After that, there was a year or two of silence, with no pictures in the newspapers, no hijinks in Hollywood, no more popular novels.

They returned to France, and Nadine Berne entered a sanatorium in Geneva in 1937. She died there of leukemia the same year.

An introverted, intellectual man, Godinsky had fallen in love with a fascinating and beautiful woman, who had come to love him. For three years he had lived in her glamorous world and was adored by her, and went around with a handkerchief folded in the breast of his coat. And then it was over, brutally snatched away. Nadine Berne was buried in Lyon, and Godinsky went home to Poland.

His books and earlier articles had established his reputation, and he plunged into political life. He spoke out against the Fascists, detesting Hitler, but at the same time warning against the threat to Poland from Russia. He had no illusions about Stalin, and predicted the Nazi-Soviet pact in May of 1939, three months before it was signed.

Here the file on Godinsky filled out. There were clippings from the Polish papers describing socialist worker rallies at which he spoke, copies of his articles calling for an independent socialist Poland, the Russian translations pinned to the yellowing newspaper cuttings.

The first attempt on his life was made by the Gestapo in July of 1939, one month before the pact was signed. A car in which he was supposed to be riding was machine-gunned. Two men were killed, but Godinsky was in another car. That same night, he stood on the roof of a sound truck outside the Warsaw Electrical Workers Hall and fearlessly denounced the Nazis.

He was in Warsaw in September of 1939, when the German panzers crossed the border. Somehow he escaped and made his way to Paris, where another attempt was made on his life. In 1941 he surfaced in London, as head of a group known as the Free Polish Union—the FPU—which was dedicated to an independent and socialist-democratic postwar Polish state.

In March of 1944, a third attempt was made on his life, this time by Soviet agents: A car in which he was riding with two other men was machine-gunned; both of his companions were killed, but Godinsky walked off without a scratch.

Across the bottom of the report of that incident, someone had scrawled in Russian: "A charmed life, the lucky bastard."

The following month Godinsky flew to America with Andrew Winters.

Dolin put away the files. He'd found what he needed, breathed enough dust from the archives. His next stop would be in the film library itself, and he sent word to the director requesting a meeting later that morning.

In the billet provided by Colonel Borodinov there was hot water for half an hour in the morning—not much water and not very hot, but enough for a sponge bath and a shave. After that Dolin slept for a bit, had a cup of tea, and started out for the film library, which was separate from the archives, located in the basement of the old Golovkin Palace. Near it was the Borovitskaya Circle, and just off that, by itself in a small park, was the statue of Dolin's father.

He saw it only at a distance, and hadn't time for a closer look. At the western end of the Borovitskaya, Dolin lost sight of the statue; it was obscured by the morning mists from the river and the leafless branches of the trees that grew in the little park.

By the time Dolin arrived at the film library, the director was in his office, or rather in a tiny room off his office, where there was a fireplace with a couple of sticks burning in it and a worn sofa with a blanket thrown over it. The director slept there. He kept water boiling on a small gas stove, and Dolin accepted a mug of tea.

"I've no biscuits," the director said. "I had a piece of sugar somewhere."

Dolin warmed himself with the tea, which was bitter, as if it had been made of boiled grass. "I need the print of a French film made in 1934," he said.

"What's it called?"

"*La Princesse.*"

"Hartmann directed it. One of his flops, I'm sorry to say."

"Do you have it?"

"We don't have any films."

The director had been going through the drawers of his desk, finally locating the missing sugar, which he'd stashed in an empty matchbox, a tiny piece from which one end had been bitten and from which he picked bits of thread and dust. When Dolin declined the sugar, the director fixed it behind his front teeth and sucked the tea through it. "We've no films at the institute," he said. "Just after the start of the war, a truck came and carried them all off."

"Where to?"

"Hollywood. Foreign exchange was needed. I suppose they fetched a good price. They were sold to a man named Kepler."

Dolin's request for *La Princesse* was sent in that day's diplomatic pouch to Soviet embassy officials in Washington. They passed it on to Mr. Gray, whose agent in California approached Mr. Kepler. Some money changed hands—not much—Kepler had done well distributing Soviet films in America and was eager to start up his business again after the war. A well-preserved print of *La Princesse* was located and hand-carried east—the courier was the Soviet press attaché Oleg Mosevnin, and he gave the print personally to Mr. Gray.

Dolin was restless during his last days in Moscow. He was confident that his plan to find Godinsky would work, and eager to put it into operation in New York. But before he could leave, he had to pay a call on Colonel Borodinov at the Thirteenth Department. In the laboratory he was shown a steel tube seven inches long and half an inch in diameter, outfitted with a spring trigger that detonated a small charge, which in turn pulverized a glass ampule spraying vaporized prussic acid. He was trained in aiming and using the device, and was given an antidote pill to take before discharging the prussic acid vapor and another pill to take just after.

Dolin was taken to the woods outside of Moscow, where the device was tested on a dog. The dog was large and playful, but when the ampule was exploded in its face, it fell over at once, went into convulsion, and was dead in less than a minute.

Colonel Borodinov explained that the vaporized prussic acid contracted the blood vessels, simulating cardiac arrest and causing death within seconds.

"Can those ampules be fitted to accept a small hypodermic syringe?"

"We have some already."

"And will it work as well?"

"Yes, it's the same. Even more effective."

Dolin was then given a blank rental agreement and signature card, acquired by an agent in Manhattan, that gave him access to a safe deposit box in a bank on Park Avenue at 20th Street. He filled out and signed both. They were sent by diplomatic pouch to the agent in New York, who then rented the box in Dolin's name. Colonel Borodinov assured him that all the equipment, along with a pistol, twenty thousand dollars in American twenty-dollar bills, and a valid Canadian passport would be inside the safe deposit box rented under his signature.

"What about the key to the box?" Dolin said.

"The main post office in Pennsylvania Station. Do you know it?"

"Yes."

"There'll be a registered letter for you," the colonel said. "In the envelope, together with the key, there'll be the address of the Fisher apartment and directions for a newspaper code."

"In New York, who'll be my contact?"

"An old friend. A ghost risen from the past."

"Mr. Gray?"

"A miracle, isn't it?"

Dolin left Moscow that same night, returning to Europe by a different route. He flew to Novgorod, and the next morning to Tallinn in Estonia on the Baltic Sea. From there he went by steamer to Stockholm. In Stockholm he secretly contacted a lawyer named Jean-Marc Zauderer, who was highly respected and without political affiliations. Dolin was careful to see that he was not observed by Soviet intelligence, which was to learn nothing of his meeting with Zauderer.

Dolin retained Zauderer, paid him a fee, and explained that he'd be sending him confidential documents, which were to be kept by Zauderer until instructions for their use arrived from Dolin.

Zauderer agreed, and on September 29 Dolin sailed for New York on the Swedish liner *Gripsholm*.

# thirteen

☭ IN NEW YORK, VLADIMIR AND I, CALLING ON SOURCES IN LIV-
ing Memory, located a man named Yakov who was reputed to have
known Serge Dolin as a boy in Moscow.

This Yakov lived in a remote part of western Pennsylvania, where
there was no train service, but Vladimir got Winters to give him a car
and gas ration stamps, and even a small expense account. It was done
informally: The car, an old Dodge coupe, actually belonged to Winters—at least it was registered in his name. Probably the expense account money came straight out of Winters' pocket. Despite the interest
shown by FDR, Winters continued to run Living Memory like a
small, family-owned business; all the paperwork was handled by two
elderly women at steel desks in Winters' outer office in the Chrysler
Building. Both of them were seen only in pleated skirts, sensible shoes,
and cardigan sweaters, their blue-gray hair carefully coiffed; one was
Winters' maiden cousin, and the other the widow of the former pastor
of the Episcopal church on 89th Street and Madison Avenue that
Winters belonged to but attended irregularly.

Vladimir took charge of the old Dodge, which had been up on
blocks, and put it in good running order. He liked cars and was handy
with them, and after the war, when he made a lot of money with his
autobiography, he was always buying new ones; every time I saw Vladimir, he had a new car. And like his mistresses—with success and
money Vladimir took mistresses, while I remained the woman in his
life, as he said, "the fixed point"—the mistresses came and went, and
so did the fancy cars, the nationalities of one as varied as that of the
other.

When Vladimir was satisfied with the Dodge, we drove to Pennsylvania to talk to Yakov, a tough former soldier with one leg, a veteran of
the first Soviet of Workers' and Soldiers' Deputies, who boasted of
having been with the heroes waiting to welcome Lenin at the Belo-
Ostrov Station on his return to Russia. Yakov had shaken Lenin's
hand, swallowing his disappointment at finding it "soft and small, like
that of a countess."

Yet he joined the escort accompanying Lenin to the Finland Station and across the Alexander Bridge along Shalernaya Street to Bolshevik headquarters. Yakov stood with his comrades in the cold and sang the "International." He lent a hand to lift Lenin onto the turret of an armed car, and saw the searchlights play on his face, and trembled at the hoarse voice declaring that at long last the worldwide socialist revolution had begun.

"When I heard those words," Yakov said, "and saw the face of Vladimir Ilich lit up by searchlights, I was certain that I had lived to see the beginning of a new order of things. I believed that justice, true democracy, and equality had come into the world at last."

At this point Yakov went on to describe how he had fought against the White Guards and lost a leg, and how, while he was fighting, his wife and child disappeared and probably starved to death.

He had told the story of his wife and child to Winters and repeated it to Vladimir and me when we met. He probably told it to everyone. All those in Living Memory had such stories. In time I got used to them, and even stopped listening, and had to remind myself that these were true stories, that the suffering described was real, and the deaths were of real people; I had to remind myself that every life lost in the wars, in prison, or through famine—every life snuffed out—had begun full of hope.

Yakov came through it all and somehow wound up in Pennsylvania, working as a porter in the town hall of a place called Blairville, and it was here that Winters tracked him down, and Vladimir and I went to speak to him.

It was nearly dark when we arrived in Blairville, and parked across from the town hall. It was a gloomy place, built in the last century, constructed of stone, like a prison. The deer-hunting season had been extended because of the wartime meat shortage, and for the last hour or so, driving through the hills to Blairville, we had heard the crack of rifle fire and the deeper blast of shotguns. I hated the sound, and the wet brown-gray hills all around, and was grateful for a good swig of vodka from the bottle Vladimir had brought for old Yakov.

Just then he came out of the town hall, hobbling on his wooden leg, and began to haul down the America flag at the top of the pole in front of the building. A light at the end of the street went on. With the motor and heater off, it was cold in the car, and a light rain had begun to fall. Yakov unhooked the flag, carefully folded it and tucked it under his arm, and limped back into the building. It was now quite dark.

He lived in one room in the cellar with a black dog. Because it was near the boiler, the room was warm, and smelled of the dog. The furniture was castoff odds and ends, but Yakov had made the room cozy and human, with a bubbling samovar, lots of books, and a radio big as a refrigerator, on which he claimed to pick up Russian language broadcasts from a station in Montreal.

Yakov was a great talker, a self-taught man, and, I suppose, a lonely one, eager to speak Russian. His English was poor, and he had no friends in the town. He was at least sixty at the time, but healthy and vigorous in spite of his missing leg. I wondered why he hadn't found a woman in America, why he hadn't married again. I guessed that the heartbreak of his early years had been too great. Is that perhaps too sentimental? I wonder at the secrets of people who live most of their lives alone—I was one myself.

As for Yakov, I saw no family photographs in his single room, no mementos at all. There were the books, the radio, the old refrigerator, and the friendly black dog.

As I said, he was a great talker, and with the first glass of vodka he began to tell us a story about how Lenin gave out tickets to the lavatory on the sealed train that took him and the other Bolsheviks through Germany to the Finland Station. It seems most of the old Bolsheviks smoked cigarettes one after the other, and since the windows of the train were nailed shut and Lenin hated cigarette smoke, he gave orders that smoking was permitted only in the lavotory. Since there was only one lavatory on the train, the Bolsheviks began to argue over who could use it. The arguments became loud and fierce, which disturbed and angered Lenin and caused him to take the matter into his own hands. He gave power over the lavatory to one person, a nonsmoker, and this person, this "Commissar of Lenin's Toilet," as Yakov called him, "had absolute power over who went in, either to smoke or to take a piss."

Yakov held out his glass for another vodka. "And so while still on the train," he said, "before he had even set foot on Russian soil, Lenin had appointed his first commissar."

Vladimir filled his own glass. He could drink with the best of Living Memory, and never got drunk. "Now tell me, Pavel Pavlovich, what was the first act of the first commissar?" he said.

"He put a guard at the door of the toilet."

"A guard at the door." Vladimir spoke as if addressing a vast audience, a rally of a million or so in Red Square. "Comrade Pavel Pavlovich has testified that the first official act of the first commissar was to put a guard at the door of Lenin's piss house."

"That was the first act."

"And the second?"

"To appoint a deputy to assist him," Yakov said. "And his job—can you guess what the deputy's first job was?"

"Tell us," I said, pouring a glass for myself. "The job of the first deputy commissar."

"To catch any smoking going on in secret," Yakov said. "The deputy spied on the others." He polished off his vodka, and went on. "And there you have the beginning of everything. Cops everywhere, the Cheka. And it all began with Lenin's piss house." He held out his empty glass. "We should have known what was in store for us," he said.

Yakov was now talking freely, and Vladimir brought the conversation around to the years in Moscow after the civil war.

"About 1924," Vladimir said, "perhaps a year or two later. You were in Moscow then?"

"I was wounded in 1921," Yakov said. "And it took eighteen months before they found me a wooden leg. And then it was only a stump, so I went hobbling around like a pirate."

"But by 1924, were you in Moscow?"

"Yes, but only at the end of the year. It was winter, near Christmas. It was bitter cold in Moscow, the Christmas of 1924."

The black dog had settled near Yakov's chair, on a worn spot in the carpet. It was the dog's place, and as we talked Yakov reached down and idly stroked his head. "When I got out of the hospital in Petrograd," Yakov said, "I slept under a bridge on the Karpovka Canal. I had nothing, and I was starving. So I wrote for help to my old friend, who had been commander of the Petrograd Soviet and had become a big shot in Moscow."

It was clear to me that Vladimir was eager to hear about this "big shot in Moscow," and that he had sought out Yakov to learn about him. But Yakov began to ramble, and tell his story in his own way, describing his adventures during the Revolution and the civil war, and reminiscing about his wife and child and the short time they had lived together.

He held out his glass for more vodka, and stroked the dog's head, and remembered his wife; Vladimir listened sympathetically, slowly nodding his head. I admired how well he understood and got on with Yakov, and with others like him, the older Russians, those whose past had been taken from them. They sought out Vladimir, who always had time to listen to their stories. He helped them get jobs, put them in touch with friends and relatives, and when he got rich he gave them money.

After listening for a while to Yakov, Vladimir said, "Tell me something about those years in Moscow. You got a job, isn't it so? A job and a place to live."

"It was through my big shot," Yakov said. "My comrade commander, that's what we called them in those days. But he was a good sort, and later sat on the Council of Commissars. He remembered me, and lent me a helping hand because I was an old soldier." Yakov waited until the vodka had been passed; Vladimir was pouring slowly now, enough to satisfy Yakov, but not enough to make him drunk before he told his story.

"You're also an old soldier," he said to Vladimir. "Even though you're not so old, and we fought on opposite sides. I don't hold that against you. Do you hold it against me?"

"No."

"I believed in what I fought for. Did you believe in your side?"

"No. I only wanted to stay alive and find my wife."

"To find your wife," Yakov said, nodding his head. "Yes, that's what matters." He unlaced the boot on his one foot and politely asked permission from me to remove it. "It's in order to air my foot," he said, and pulled off the boot with a deep sigh of pleasure.

Vladimir said, "We'd like to learn more about your experiences in Moscow. Your former comrade commander sent for you and gave you a job. What was his name?"

"It was Stenoviev." He looked at me and patted his breast with pride. "Yes, Stenoviev," he said. "I fought under the famous Stenoviev."

"And in Moscow," Vladimir said, "what kind of job did he get you?"

"A janitor, the same as here. I worked in the house on Sadovoye in which Stenoviev lived."

"And you got to know the family?"

Yakov glanced sideways at Vladimir, a cunning look in his eyes. I'd heard the expression "peasant cunning," and there it was, old Yakov with his vodka, airing his foot in a torn sock and resting it on the back of his sleeping dog. "Stenoviev is dead," he said. "It's the family you've come to see me about."

Vladimir spoke softly, and urged him on. "Tell me first about the wife," he said. "What do you remember of Madame Stenoviev?"

133

"It's her you want to know about?" Yakov laughed, and winked at me, and gently scratched the sleeping dog with the nail of his toe, which stuck out of the hole in his sock. "You want to hear gossip of the comrade commissar's wife? Is that it?" Again he winked at me, and the look of peasant cunning again came into his face. "Or is there somebody else you've come to talk about? Is it another member of the Stenoviev family? Is it their son you want to hear about? Have you come because of him?"

Vladimir said, "I've seen a photograph of Stenoviev; he seems to have been a tall man."

"He was short."

"And with a beard."

"A mustache only."

"The photograph I saw," Vladimir said, "was in Stenoviev's biography, an official one published in Moscow. In it no family is mentioned, no wife or son. They are officially forgotten."

"Officially forgotten," Yakov said, "but not forgotten by me."

"Stenoviev came once to inspect the medical school in Moscow," I said. "And afterward he gave a speech. He was a fine speaker."

"A damn sight better than Trotsky," Yakov said. "Better even than Lenin."

"What sort of woman was it that he married?" I said. "I'd be very interested to hear about her."

Vladimir said smoothly, "As I say, she has been officially forgotten, and ceased to exist."

"But she did exist; and I knew her, and the son as well. I knew them both, and I remember them."

"Then please tell us what you remember," I said. "Particularly about the wife. What do you remember about her?"

"First, she put on no airs," he said quickly. "I was the janitor, and her husband was the great Stenoviev, but she treated me fairly. She treated everyone the same—fairly." He looked directly at me, hoping that I would understand. "She lived with her husband in a splendid suite of rooms, and I was in the cellar next to the coal bin. That's the way things are. She's not to be blamed for her splendid suite of rooms, any more than I am for my place next to the coal bin. She was a good person, refined and polite. Some said she was Jewish, but I don't know about that. She had fair hair and light eyes, and kept none of their holidays, so I don't know how the Jewish business got started or if there's any truth to it." Vladimir refilled his glass, but Yakov ignored the vodka and slowly shook his head as if clearing it. "Officially forgot-

134

ten. Think of it!" he said. "She was pretty and younger than Stenoviev, and more cultured. It's true he adored her. How could one keep from adoring her? Once he bought her a piano, a beautiful thing that had belonged to some prince. I had to haul it up the stairs, and believe me it weighed a ton. But it was a pleasure to do it for her." Then he drank the vodka, and held out the empty glass to be refilled; I saw there were tears in his eyes. All that he had drunk made him sentimental; no doubt he had been in love with Madame Stenoviev, a one-legged soldier, dreaming about her from his place next to the coal bin.

"She played the piano all day long," he said. "It was lovely the way she played, and one could hear it anywhere in the house. One Christmas she gave me two eggs, which in those hard times was a precious gift. But she wasn't a happy woman. She had no friends, and sometimes she would talk to me, out of loneliness, I think."

I said, "What happened to her?"

"I don't know. It was said she went to her family in Tbilisi, and then I heard she went abroad, to Germany. But then I heard she was dead. I don't know what happened to the poor woman, or what the truth is."

"Do you mean that she was taken away? Arrested?"

"I mean that she was there one day, and not there the next. But so were lots of others."

"But Stenoviev was on the Central Committee, and she was his wife," Vladimir said. "How is it that she just—disappeared?"

"She never got along with the other wives. There was the talk of her being a Jew. But if you ask me it was that she was a lady, better than the others, so there was a lot of jealousy."

I said, "Did Stenoviev send her away?"

"He loved her, but he was ambitious, and with him that came first."

"He sent her away? He had her arrested?"

"She was arrested," Yakov said. "I myself saw them come for her."

"And Stenoviev?"

"He did nothing."

Yakov paused, deep in his own thoughts, remembering that apartment in Moscow, and the woman in it who played the piano. The rain was heavier; there was the splatter of drops against the window, the racket made by the wind, and the low rumble of thunder. The dog woke, yawned, stretched out his front legs, and got stiffly to his feet. "It's time for his dinner," Yakov said. "I feed him every day at the same time, and he always knows to the minute."

He went to the refrigerator and began filling a bowl with scraps; the dog came and stood beside him, looking up and slowly wagging his heavy tail.

"What's his name?" Vladimir said.

"Yakov."

"The same as you?"

"Well, he's my dog."

After Yakov the dog had been fed, the bottle of vodka was found to be empty, and Vladimir offered to take the dog for a walk, and buy another bottle. He glanced at me, meaning that he would take his time coming back, so that I would be alone with Yakov, and get him to talk. Vladimir and I sensed that he had more to tell us, and would talk more easily alone with me.

"Is it true," he said, after Vladimir and the dog had gone, "in the book about Stenoviev, the official biography, there is no mention of the wife?"

"I haven't read it."

"What is it Vladimir said? 'Officially forgotten.' Can they do that, do you think? Make it so that there was no such woman?"

"No. There was such a woman. You heard her play the piano."

He liked that. His eyes were watery and a little bloodshot, probably from the vodka. But he was very keen. "I remember Stenoviev's son, too," he said, "although apparently there's no mention of him in the biography either."

"Tell me what you remember about him."

"He was like the mother, in that he didn't bother putting on airs. Once I came into their apartment, it must have been a holiday because he was home from school, and the two of them were at the piano. They played together, the mother and son, next to each other on the piano bench. I stayed quiet and listened, enjoying the music. They looked very much alike, although she was fair and he was dark, and I could see that they loved each other."

"And then his mother disappeared?"

"Not long after. The boy was away at school. When he came home, he was told that his mother had been sick, and later that she had died. His father was the one who told him. He was brokenhearted, and confused. After all, he was still very young."

"And you became his friend?"

"He used to come to my place in the cellar of the house in Moscow. His father had no time for him, and also he was very strict and demanded a lot from the boy, a great man's son who always had to be first in his class. So he'd sneak down to my room, and I'd tell him stories about the war, and when he got older we'd even have a nip or two of vodka to drink. And later on, later on—"

Yakov had started to say something, but caught himself. I could see that he was afraid.

"What happened later on?" I said.

"Nothing happened."

"Did you see him again? After Moscow, did you see Stenoviev's son again?"

"See him again?" He nodded his head, and said under his breath, "Officially forgotten." He looked up and caught my eye. "Later on, I saw him again."

"Where?"

"Here. In this room. He sat where you are."

"Stenoviev's son?"

"He was grown then."

I had brought a copy of the photograph Magda had taken of Dolin, and showed it to Yakov.

"There he's older," he said. "And his hair is different. But there's no doubt."

"It's the same man?"

"Yes, the same."

"When was it that he came?"

"Before the war, 1937. I think it was 1937."

"How did he find you?"

"I had a sister, dead now, rest her soul, but she used to write me from Petrograd. They say the Cheka keeps track of all such letters and so he would have known."

"He was in America, and he came to see you," I said slowly. "What did he want?"

"To talk to a friend," Yakov said. "He was alone and suffering from grief. He needed to talk in Russian to an old friend about certain things in his past."

"What things?"

"His father. He had just learned that his father had died."

I thought a moment and then said, "Was it in the American papers, about his father's death?"

"No. Stalin had made it a secret, and so it wasn't in the papers, or on the Russian-language radio from Canada. But somehow he found out. He was told his father had died."

"Told? Who told him?"

"He talked a lot," Yakov said. "He was beside himself, and we had a lot to drink. He got drunk and we talked all night. It was a Russian who told him about his father. I remember, a Russian he called the 'Old Man' told him."

"Did he mention a name? The Old Man, do you know his name?"

"He called him Mr. Gray," Yakov said. "But it's a joke, I think. An old man named Mr. Gray."

"Did he tell you anything else?"

"I told you we were drunk and we babbled all night."

"Nothing about what he was doing in America?"

"No. He talked about his mother and father, and finally we both passed out. When I woke in the morning, he was gone."

"That's all, he was gone?"

"Yes, and not a trace of him left behind," Yakov said. "It was like a dream, but it wasn't a dream. He had been here, Stenoviev's son."

For several seconds neither of us spoke. I tried to picture Dolin and Yakov together in the cellar room in Pennsylvania, the black dog, the vodka passing back and forth. I closed my eyes and saw an earlier scene, the boy at the piano beside his mother; I saw it vividly and even heard the music, as if I had been there.

Yakov interrupted my reverie. He leaned forward and said, "He came again."

I held my breath; the rain flew against the window and there was a crack of thunder. Yakov repeated what he had said, "He came again."

"When?"

"Two weeks ago."

"Why? Why this time?"

"Because he was afraid."

"Of what?"

"Of what he had been sent to do."

"What was it? Did he tell you?"

"No."

"The name Godinsky, have you ever heard it?"

"It means nothing to me."

"Your visitor, Stenoviev's son, he calls himself Serge Dolin. Did you know that?"

"We used familiar names with each other, the same as in Moscow."

"And no mention of Godinsky?"

"None."

"But he confided in you?"

"And so it ends there," Yakov said.

"It's not a question of betraying him."

"Of what then?" Yakov said. "He tells me in confidence, and I tell you, and you say it's not betrayal."

I argued with him and tried to persuade him to tell me what he had learned of Godinsky. "Another victim, another of Stalin's crimes," I said.

"It won't be on my conscience," Yakov said. "Stenoviev helped me and saved me from starving. The son was my friend."

And that was it. He'd say no more.

Vladimir returned, rain dripping from his hat, a bottle of vodka in a bag under his coat. The dog, Yakov, shook himself and stood with his head hanging until his master brought out a towel and rubbed him dry, filled his bowl with water, and gave him a biscuit.

After that, Yakov had another drink, closed his eyes, and with his foot in its torn sock resting on the dog and the vodka bottle in his lap, the one-legged soldier, his conscience clear, went off to sleep.

# fourteen

DOLIN CROSSED THE ATLANTIC ON THE SWEDISH LINER *Gripsholm* in thirteen days. Although repeated attempts had been made to sweep the North Atlantic of German submarines, the threat of sudden attack persisted. Red Cross ships had been sunk before. All passengers were instructed to carry their life jackets with them everywhere, and boat drills were called unexpectedly, sometimes in the dead of night. It seemed a daring crossing, vivid to those on board.

Meals were taken at communal tables, and Dolin usually came with a book and kept to himself. He was remembered by an American woman, a consular official, returning from Stockholm. She thought him polite, but not particularly friendly. She noticed that the book changed regularly, and that he spent hours on a deck chair, wrapped in a blanket, reading or staring out at the North Atlantic.

During his hours in the deck chair, Dolin turned over the details of his plan; and the day following his arrival in New York, even before he contacted Barret Martin Fisher or checked the contents of the safe deposit box that had been rented in his name, he took the IRT subway to Utica Avenue in Brooklyn and had a look around the bank from which the draft had been sent to Godinsky's landlady in London. He spent an hour poking in the small shops on Utica Avenue. In one he bought a soft hat, its color dark gray, and let the shopkeeper stamp the initials "SD" in gilt on the inside band. One moved so easily in New York, with so little need for caution. Through the open door, he looked out into the street, half expecting to see Godinsky's face in the crowd. At the cobbler's he had his heels replaced and his shoes shined. Next door an elderly barber cut his hair while listening to a radio recording of *Traviata*, singing along softly to himself, his warm breath on Dolin's neck, smelling of black Napoli cigars. In the window of the shop was a service flag with five stars—five sons, each with his photograph in uniform in a frame alongside the mirror opposite the chair. Dolin went for lunch to a kosher restaurant where no meat was served, and where many of the male patrons wore skullcaps. He wondered how much Godinsky had changed from the man with the handkerchief folded like a star in his pocket, the man walking across the garden of the Tuileries with Nadine Berne on his arm.

Dolin ate blini and sour cream, and when he had finished with his lunch he walked along Eastern Parkway until he came to an imposing building, the public library.

Dolin went in and had a look at the racks of newspapers and magazines, and wandered between rows of books until he located the section on twentieth-century European history. Godinsky was a man uprooted and put down in a strange place, an intellectual, without friends and with time on his hands. He'd go straight to the library, and it was a good bet he'd read books about his own area—Germany, the Soviet Union, Poland. Dolin noticed a three-volume history of Poland.

Though there was nothing in the Moscow files about Godinsky knowing English, he did speak other languages, and he had spent time in California and had lived in England. Dolin took down the first volume of the history of Poland.

Pasted to the inside front cover of the book was a small pocket envelope, and inside that was a filing card with the library card numbers, names, and addresses of those who had borrowed the book; beside each entry was the date it had been taken out and the date returned. Dolin moved methodically down the aisle, checking books on Poland after the 1914 war, all the books on the Soviet Union, and one in particular that caught his eye: *Russia Moves West—The Annexation of Poland.*

He spent the rest of the afternoon and part of the evening on the book cards, copying out names and addresses, and when the library closed at eight o'clock, he went across Eastern Parkway to a cafeteria for coffee and something to eat, while going over the names, noting those that began to appear regularly in books a week or so after Godinsky was flown out of England.

He was able to narrow the list down to four names, all giving neighborhood addresses. Two of them were listed in the Brooklyn phone directory, which hadn't been reprinted since the war and therefore couldn't contain a Godinsky alias. Dolin went that same night to see if he could get a look at the other two. One was a doctor, his name on a plate in front of his house; his phone either was unlisted or had been installed after the directory had been printed. The fourth name was Rosen, I. F. Rosen. The address given was 1489 Carroll Street, about half a mile from the library and only a couple of blocks from the doctor's. Dolin went for a look, and of course there was no 1489 Carroll Street. There was a 1487 and a 1491, but 1489 didn't exist.

But was Godinsky Rosen? I. F. Rosen. Dolin thought so, but wasn't sure, and never would be. Dolin believed Godinsky used half a dozen names, and I. F. Rosen was only one of them. Maybe so. But in October of 1944, Godinsky was in fact living in a room rented in a house on Montgomery Street, near Lincoln Terrace Park in the same section of Brooklyn. He probably did use the library, although no card, in any name, was later found among his effects.

Dolin returned to Manhattan and slept that night at the Hotel Earle off Washington Square, and shortly afterward contacted Barret Martin Fisher, among whose friends in the New York art world was a noted philanthropist and patron of the arts, a man whose family had once owned the land on which Commodore Vanderbilt had built Grand Central Station.

Fisher's friend was president of the Manhattan Chamber Music Society and the Vivaldi Society, and sat on the board of three New York museums, one the Brooklyn. Fisher knew him as an ardent supporter of the Soviet Union, and once Dolin had acquired from Mr. Gray the print of *La Princesse,* Fisher got his friend to use his considerable influence to arrange a retrospective of French film comedies of the 1930s, and to have them shown at the Brooklyn Museum.

The arrangements took a month, during which time Dolin was active in New York, going around to places like the Danube, making friends with men like Willi Koder. Finally, a date was agreed on for the retrospective at the Brooklyn Museum.

Money was spent to advertise it in the *New York Times,* on the radio, and on WNYC during its programs of cultural interest; a flyer was sent to everyone on the Brooklyn Museum's mailing list, and posters were put up in all the branches of the Brooklyn Public Library. On all of these, the name Nadine Berne was given special prominence.

Dolin was certain that Godinsky, a man of cultural interests, an avid reader of the newspapers, would learn of the show. But what would he think when he first saw the advertisements with Nadine Berne's name? It would certainly come as a shock, and then, after he had a moment to reflect, would it seem an odd coincidence, and would his suspicions be aroused? Dolin fretted over the advertisements, wondering if the billing given Nadine Berne was too prominent. She hadn't, after all, been a major actress.

But Godinsky had loved her, and his years with her were the happiest of his life. Dolin reasoned that if Godinsky had any suspicions, he would ignore them, and say nothing to Andrew Winters; nothing would stop him from seeing Nadine Berne again in *La Princesse*.

That's how Dolin reasoned; and of course he was right.

Godinsky wore his one good suit the night *La Princesse* was to be shown. He dined alone in a restaurant called the Esplanade, which was on Flatbush Avenue and was regarded as one of the best in Brooklyn. He drank half a bottle of claret and smoked a cigar.

He carried a rolled umbrella, a habit he'd picked up in England, and using it as a walking stick, he strolled across Eastern Parkway and along Prospect Park to the main entrance of the Brooklyn Museum. The night was cold, but he was dressed for it, in a tweed overcoat, a gray hat, and a woolen scarf knitted for him by his landlady, who'd taken a shine to him.

The movie was scheduled for eight o'clock in the first-floor auditorium; admission was fifty cents to visitors, free to staff and members of the museum. Between sixty and seventy people attended.

Dolin, who was unknown to Godinsky, came early and sat in the last row, from which he could observe everyone who arrived. He was on edge, waiting for Godinsky, and worried that he wouldn't show up. Perhaps Godinsky hadn't heard about the movie, or was out of town. Or had Andrew Winters also learned of Godinsky's marriage to Nadine Berne, seen the advertisement, put two and two together, and warned him off?

Dolin had dug into the files—that was his advantage, he'd done his homework. He feared only that Winters had done as much.

And just then Godinsky, loosening the scarf his landlady had knit, came into the auditorium and walked down the center aisle. Dolin knew him from the photograph taken in the Tuileries. He'd aged, he was thinner and had gone gray, a smaller man than Dolin thought, but there was no mistaking him. Dolin had guessed right; Godinsky couldn't stay away.

He took a seat in the sixth row, near the center of the auditorium, empty seats on both sides of him. The film was late starting. Godinsky still wore his overcoat, scarf, and hat, and now he stood and took them off, and Dolin watched him turn the coat inside out and fold it, and arrange his things neatly on the empty seat to his left. An orderly man, he thought, a man to make up his own bed and sew on his own buttons. A man able to go about his business and keep to himself what he knew and what he'd lost. *Stoical* was the word; Dolin understood Godinsky, saw him clearly, and sympathetically.

A man from the museum came out and gave a brief talk about *La*

*Princesse*. He'd prepared biographical notes on the principals, the director, screenwriter, and producer, and then said a few words about Nadine Berne. Dolin quickly realized that he had his facts wrong; he had her born in the wrong place at the wrong time, and he had gotten the names of her other films wrong.

Dolin listened, slumped in his seat, concentrating on the back of Godinsky's head. He idly wondered if he'd been to the barber with the five sons in the American service. Dolin remembered I. F. Rosen. Deep in his jacket pocket, Dolin's hand closed around the ampule of cyanide. When the lights went down and the picture began, he'd fit it into the steel tube hanging from a loop under his armpit.

Godinsky removed his eyeglasses and cleared the lenses with a pocket handkerchief. Dolin thought he must have been going through hell. He and Nadine had only just been married when she got the part in *La Princesse*, and during the filming they'd lived in Montparnasse in the Hotel Lisette; it's still there, unchanged, with a lovely garden in back with climbing roses, lilacs, and wooden tables where, in summer, breakfast is still served around a water fountain.

Finally, the lights dimmed and *La Princesse* began. Nadine was on screen from the first scene. She played a poor girl, a clerk in a little shop, who befriends an old man, without knowing he's rich. When he dies, she is left his money. The old man has a son, a notorious playboy, who is cut out of the will and who schemes to get his hands on the money by seducing Nadine and making her fall in love with him. He succeeds, but she finds out what he's been up to, and breaks off with him. By then, the tables have turned, and he's fallen in love with her and begins to pursue her in earnest and tries to persuade her that his love is genuine. In the end she reforms him, and they go off to live happily ever after. A silly movie, but certainly Nadine was funny and charming, and very beautiful.

The movie ended and the lights came up at 9:50. Refreshments were offered for sale and members of the audience were invited to write their comments about the film on little cards. Later on Andrew Winters found one written in Godinsky's neat script: "I want to thank the Brooklyn Museum for showing this very good film." And then, as an afterthought, he wrote: "Nadine Berne was born in Lyon on May 4, 1904, and died in Geneva on September 11, 1937."

Godinsky left the auditorium after writing his comments. He spoke to no one, and went out of the museum by way of Eastern Parkway, through the north door, the only one open at the time. In the subway

144

station two blocks farther along at Grand Army Plaza, he waited on the platform for the New Lots Avenue local.

Dolin followed him to the subway, but Godinsky never noticed. The train was scheduled to arrive at Grand Army Plaza at 10:12, and there is no record that night of any delay. Dolin and Godinsky entered the same car. Perhaps Godinsky recognized him from the museum, perhaps not; his thoughts were on the film and his years with Nadine Berne. If there were other passengers in the car, they haven't come forward. Godinsky's station was Utica Avenue, three stops from Grand Army Plaza, a trip of seven minutes.

Sometime during those seven minutes, Dolin acted; the antidote pill was kept in a Chiclets box, and he put one in his mouth and swallowed it, while pretending to chew. He stood and walked across the car to where Godinsky sat, just inside the center door. Dolin stood in front of the door, waiting for the train to pull into the next station and the door to open. He steadied himself by holding the overhead strap with his left hand. His right was inside his coat, gripping the steel tube fitted with the poison ampule.

Just as the train pulled into the station—Kingston Avenue—the one before Godinsky was to get off, Dolin drew the tube, thrust it into Godinsky's face, and before he had time to react, squeezed the firing device, paralyzing Godinsky with the poison spray.

Dolin swallowed the second antidote pill, the train door opened, and he stepped out onto the platform and ran up the station stairs two at a time to the street.

By that time, Godinsky had gone into convulsions on the floor of the subway car. He was dead before the train arrived at Utica Avenue, a matter of three minutes. He died as the dog had in the woods outside Moscow.

# fifteen

♪ IT WAS A FEW DAYS, PERHAPS AS MUCH AS A WEEK, BEFORE I learned of Godinsky's death. After going with Vladimir to see old Yakov, the janitor and former hero of Petrograd, I thought that my work with Living Memory was finished. Andrew Winters, because he was a spy who had fallen in love with his secrets, had kept Godinsky to himself. And as for Vladimir, my darling had begun another of his flirtations, this one also in high society, and was making a front-page ass of himself with a lady from Palm Beach.

I concentrated on my work at St. Monica's, on First Avenue on the Lower East Side, a neighborhood of laborers and poor immigrants, most of them from Eastern Europe. Few had money enough to pay for treatment. The wards were crowded, and we were understaffed, with so many doctors and nurses in military services.

Among my patients was a boy of twelve whose mother was Rumanian, probably a Jew. His father had died in a Nazi camp. The mother was ill, unable even to look after herself, and the boy was alone in the world. His name was Louis, a very intelligent child, with dark luminous eyes which every day became larger in his face. He was wasting away, dying of leukemia.

Doctors learn not to become attached to their patients, not to treat them as human beings, and above all not to love them. We do that to protect ourselves, to keep from falling to pieces each time a patient dies.

Louis was my patient, and also a child, who had been chosen to face death alone. How merciless that is, how wrong. So I stayed near him, drew the curtain around his bed, and waited under the light from his table lamp. I was nearly forty-five years old, and knew I'd never have children of my own. Perhaps Louis was a son to me, but I don't think it's as simple as that; there have been others, who could not have been sons, but touched my heart in the same way.

On the night that Louis died, Vladimir and Andrew Winters came to the hospital and asked to see me. Word was brought to me; it was urgent. They were waiting in the visitors' lounge and I was to go and see them at once. I refused and stayed with Louis. Winters had influence, and the hospital director was called at home, in the middle of the night. Word was brought to me a second time, but still I refused to leave. Winters and Vladimir had become nothing to me. Louis was everything, and I wouldn't leave him alone.

If life had been merciless to him, death was at least kind. One moment he was alive, able to breathe and to open his eyes and recognize me. I held tight to his cold hand, he turned his dark eyes on me, and he stopped breathing. He was alive and then he wasn't. That was it, he was no more.

He had died around four o'clock in the morning. I filled out the certificate, signed it, and left it with the duty nurse.

I saw Vladimir and Andrew Winters sometime after that, but my recollection of just where and when isn't entirely clear. We went to an all-night place for coffee and Winters told me about Godinsky's body being found on the subway. In the greenish light of the restaurant, Winters' skin had a waxy bloodless pallor, with dark patches under the eyes. He was more gaunt than ever. Vladimir bloomed beside him, richly fed and suntanned after his Palm Beach romance.

Winters said, "I need you to have an unofficial look at Godinsky's body. I need to be certain he was killed."

"The same as with Willi," Vladimir said.

"Talk to your friend, the policeman," Winters said. "Talk to Keogh and have a look at the body for us."

"I need to get a few hours sleep."

"Irina lost a patient tonight," Vladimir said.

"Nothing could be done," I said.

"A child," Vladimir said. "I heard he was a boy of twelve. What can one say about such a thing?" He reached over and draped my coat over my shoulders. "First Irina must get some sleep."

Unexpectedly, my eyes filled with tears, and I began to sob. I don't remember crying before or since, but I couldn't stop. I had lost all control. I felt a fool, a silly woman in front of these two men. They watched me without knowing what to do. I don't understand how it began, or what had come over me. Finally, Vladimir put his arm around me, half carried me out of the coffee shop, and took me to his apartment, where he gave me warm milk and a pill to help me sleep. I slept until midafternoon, and when I woke, Magda was there, beside the bed with a cup of tea.

"Vladimir called me," she said. "He thought you'd be needing something when you woke up."

"Where is he?"

"I don't know. He left you the apartment."

"Did he?"

"He's crazy about you," she said.

"Him and his lady from Palm Beach," I said.

"There was a man with him," she said. "An American. He gave me the fish eye. I didn't catch his name."

"Winters."

"He said you've got time off from the hospital. A month, if you want it."

"Winters arranged it?"

"I guess so."

"What about a doctor to take my place?"

"All arranged."

"All arranged."

"You could do with a change," Magda said. "Maybe a little sun."

"I've been trying to get hold of you," I said. "I left word with your landlady a couple of times."

Madga gave a shrug, followed by one of her long silences. They were adolescent, those silences of Magda, yet one could be harmed by them, by their sharp edge. "I go out," she said finally. "I come home. I do as I please."

"Sure, why not? Do as you please."

"You're not my conscience," she said, "although you're good and I'm not. You're on the up and up, and I'm a bit of a tramp."

"*Tu parle merde, ma chatte.*" I said. "What's true is that we're both refugees, both in the same boat."

"Except mine is sinking," she said. "That lousy boat has sprung a leak."

"Then get it plugged," I said. "But this time by the right guy."

She laughed and poured fresh tea in my cup, added sugar, and drank it down herself. "Willi gave me a song and dance about a friend of his," I said. "A friend who needed American papers. He wouldn't tell me the name. He was quite mysterious about it, as he was with most things. I didn't know you were with him, so I didn't think of you. I didn't put two and two together."

"The papers were for me," Magda said. "Willi actually tried to help. In spite of everything, he wasn't such a bad sort. A couple of times I was in hot water, and he helped me out." She used a spoon to eat the sugar that had collected at the bottom of the teacup. "I stole something one time—in a fancy shop. The guy who caught me was a real bastard. He slapped me around; him and his pals had a party.

They gave me a real going-over. Then he turned me over to the cops. I got hold of Willi, and he came and got me, and straightened things out."

"Not a bad sort, Willi."

"He had a sister in Canada," Magda said. "He got her and her husband out of Europe, and he set them up. Willi had his good side."

"The Russian in the photograph with him," I said. "Have you seen him since?"

She shook her head, a bit too quickly, a bit too emphatically. I said, "Serge Dolin, you haven't seen him?"

"No. Tell you the truth, I hardly remember what he looks like." And then she said, "Vladimir filled the fridge. What about a good breakfast? Bacon and eggs, and a pile of buttered toast."

"I can get you legitimate papers," I said.

"How?"

"From Winters. Remember, he arranges everything."

"He's not a type to do favors," she said. "He'll want me to do something in return."

"We'll see."

"Something with Serge Dolin?"

"And if it is with Dolin?"

"One way or another," she said. "I only want my papers."

After we had eaten, I bathed and dressed, and telephoned Francis Keogh, asking for permission to examine Godinsky's body. He wasn't happy—I heard that in his voice—but he'd been expecting my call, and agreed to meet me later that afternoon in the morgue in the basement of the Caledonia Hospital.

Godinsky's body had been kept in a refrigerated room, the corpse stiff with rigor mortis, and with no detectable odor of cyanide. There were no obvious traces of pulverized glass, as with Willi's body; I saw no bits buried in the skin of the face and neck. But I'd brought a magnifying glass, and with it was able to find tiny fragments, like grains of sand, clinging to the stubble of beard around his mouth and in the fine hairs lining his nostrils.

Keogh said, "It's like Willi, isn't it?"

"Yes."

"The same man do it, you think?"

"It's the same method."

"I'm to put a lid on it again," Francis said. "The Commissioner himself had me in and told me to keep it out of the medical examiner's office. He had a call from Washington, that's what the Commissioner told me."

"I see you don't like it, Francis."

"Four and a half years until I retire." Francis had bought a boat and a house in Fort Lauderdale, and spent his vacations relaxing on the water and fixing up the house. "Godinsky's landlady was the one who reported him missing," he said. "And she's asked to have his body released so she can bury him." He put on half-glasses and read from a pad that he carried in his jacket pocket. "Her name is Berkowitz. Address 1411 Montgomery Street, Brooklyn, which is where Godinsky lived. She owns that house, and a women's clothing shop on Nostrand Avenue called Madame Berkowitz." I saw the trace of a smile on Francis's lips and a glint in his cool blue eyes. "She's a woman of property, Madame Berkowitz," he said.

I telephoned Andrew Winters and arranged to meet him later that day in his house on Sutton Place, where I told him what I'd discovered about Godinsky's death. Winters wasn't surprised; he'd been certain all along that Godinsky had been murdered, and knew of the interest of the landlady, Madame Berkowitz.

"She and Godinsky were friendly," he said. "They may even have been lovers, and he could have been indiscreet. He wasn't a conspirator born. Damn it, I don't know what he told what's-her-name."

"Madame Berkowitz."

"Would you go and talk to her?" Andrew said. "She'll be more likely to open up with you than me. Tell her you and Godinsky were pals in Paris. Give her any cock and bull. Madame Berkowitz." He closed his eyes and rolled his head, a way he had of easing the tension in the muscles of his neck. "Do you know anything about yoga?"

"No."

"People swear by it," he said. "Damn Serge Dolin. What's he up to? He was sent to kill Godinsky, and he's done it. He ought to be getting out. Hit and run, that's how it's done." He put a finger to his lips. "Shall I tell you something? I've got a man inside—he talks about something big in the works. Big and risky. So risky he's getting ready to run. The problem is Dolin has set up a line of communication outside established channels. He's got his own cipher, even his own transmitter. Our man was involved at the beginning of the Godinsky operation but not now. My guess is he knows more than he's told us, but probably not the whole picture."

I said, "What about the Fisher apartment? You've a microphone there."

150

"Dolin is always alone there. He doesn't talk to anyone, never uses the telephone." Winters was discouraged. "It's damn hard getting a handle on him," he said.

Godinsky's murder had shaken him. He saw it as a personal defeat, and beyond that loomed something more unsettling; he believed what he had been told, that the Godinsky murder was the first act of a larger and more sinister plot. He might have already heard of Archangel, even learned of it in connection with Serge Dolin. But who or what was Archangel? Winters didn't know. He couldn't have known then.

"It's a crucial time," he said. "A crisis. I want you to work full time for Living Memory."

"Give up my work at the hospital?"

"I've already arranged—"

"I know what you've arranged, Andrew. You arrange too much, too damn much, too fast."

"It's that I need you," he said. "I assure you, Irina. All of this is urgent. Urgent and crucial."

"What is it about? What's urgent and crucial?"

Winters didn't answer. He never would answer, not a direct question, never a direct question. "I want to know what Dolin is really up to," he said. "Stalin sent Dolin, Stalin himself. But why? Help me find out the truth, Irina. Stalin sent him personally. Stalin."

Then Winters flattered me; I'm an awkward woman and have often considered myself unattractive. Andrew flattered and fussed over me. "Are you feeling well?" he said. "At the hospital the other night you looked all in."

"I'm fine now."

"Is it cold in here?"

"Freezing."

"The boiler is always breaking down," he said. "It's almost as old as the house itself." He brought me a sweater from another room and poured stiff drinks for us both. Later on he built a fire. He told me about the house, which his grandfather had built with money he made selling brass fittings to the Union Army during the Civil War. It was a lovely house, with exquisite marble fireplaces and elaborate moldings along the ceiling and around the doors. Behind it had been a small meadow, and Winters remembered when sheep were allowed to graze along the banks of the East River. The house was sold a few years after the war, and eventually it was torn down and a high-rise was built on the spot.

Winters gave me a dinner; he had a butler who prepared and served

151

it on a table, which he set in front of the fire. We ate from Minton plates with English silver and there was a bottle of old burgundy to drink. It was all part of Winters' courting me, of his flattery. He wanted me, but not as a woman—I wouldn't have minded that, not with the old burgundy in front of the fire—he wanted me back at work as an agent of Living Memory.

Winters didn't have to court me for that; but he didn't know it, and I certainly didn't tell him. In fact, I played hard to get. He hadn't realized how much Louis' death had taken out of me, or how, at that moment, I craved the excitement, danger, and diversion of the spy trade.

I let him tell me a lot of tales about his family that night. We hadn't talked that openly since Zurich. He even talked about Julia, and her intimacy with Franklin Roosevelt. Andrew was with her one New Year's Eve—just the two of them in her apartment on Fifth Avenue—when the phone rang. She was busy and asked Andrew to pick it up. When he did, the voice on the other end turned out to be Roosevelt.

"I had known Franklin fairly well from school," Andrew told me. "He was a couple of years ahead of me, and I can't say I liked him in those days, although that changed later on."

The butler had cleared the table and gone to bed, and Andrew went into the kitchen for ice for our afterdinner drinks, and picked up the story when he came back.

"On the phone, I didn't tell Franklin who I was, and he didn't recognize my voice. In fact, I let him think I was a fellow spending the New Year with Julia. I must say he didn't like that one bit. Julia had to explain to him later on, and he questioned me about it when I saw him next. Under that affability, he's quite a suspicious man, and he's got a hell of a temper."

"Has he been told about Godinsky's death?"

"He has. Franklin can be slow to catch on to certain things," Andrew said. "Stalin was one of them. He liked to think Uncle Joe was a reasonable man. Some of the crew around Franklin went to great lengths to persuade him of that. But lately he's begun to see Soviet Russia clearly. He told me he's going to bring the Godinsky affair up with Stalin when they meet. After that there ought to be some housecleaning, and a tougher line."

We talked until it was quite late. The fire went down and Andrew brought more logs from the cellar. We had eaten well, and drunk a lot, and somehow the conversation turned to Magda Renner.

"We met only once," Andrew said. "And then for only a few minutes. I called her to be with you at Vladimir's apartment. She is bright, I think. Certainly she's attractive."

"Serge Dolin thought so."

"So I understand."

"Do you want to put her beside Dolin?"

"Something has to be done," Andrew said. "Dolin did make a big play for her."

"She'll need to be paid."

"Something can be arranged."

"And proper papers," I said. "A backdated certificate of entry. And a residence card. Later on, she can apply for citizenship."

"Hold on—"

"That's what she'd want to do the job," I said.

"I don't know about backdating a certificate of entry."

"Then send her up to Canada and bring her in legally," I said.

"Is she reliable?"

"In what way?"

"Is she tough enough? Cold-blooded enough?" Andrew said. "She's got to sleep with Dolin, gain his confidence, pretend to love him. After all that, she has to betray him. Can she do that?"

"I don't know."

"I dread Dolin," Andrew said. "Shall I tell you something? I'm afraid of him, the way he hunted down Godinsky."

"He's human. He has a past."

"What about her?"

"Magda has been through hell. She's a refugee. She'll do anything to get her papers."

"We've got to gamble on her," Andrew said. "We've no other choice."

I said, "Arrange things for Magda in Canada. She'll go, and in the meantime Vladimir can get Mitzi Roth to give a party for Dolin. Magda will be there."


When I went to Brooklyn to see Madame Berkowitz the next day, I asked Magda to come along, but said nothing of the plan Andrew and I had worked out.

The trip took half an hour on the subway. Magda was in one of her sulky moods and sat beside me with her arms folded across her chest, refusing to say a word; she made me think of a sleepy child on Monday

153

morning, hating to go to school. She hadn't bothered to put on makeup, and only ran a comb through her dark hair. But she wasn't a child anymore—she had to be twenty-three or twenty-four, although she certainly didn't look it. When she got into one of those moods in Paris, I used to play to her and try to coax her out of it, but I left her alone now as the train rattled on to Brooklyn, and by the time we got off she was in better spirits. She hadn't had breakfast, and wondered if we could stop for some.

We both brightened up, walking through the Brooklyn streets, which were a lot prettier than we had expected. Most of the houses were small, built for one or two families, and well kept up, with front porches and small gardens, the streets lined with old trees. Montgomery Street, where Godinsky had lived, had a Catholic church on one corner and a new elementary school directly across the street.

Andrew had told me that Godinsky had used the name Braun, and I'd telephoned Madame Berkowitz, introducing myself as an old friend of Mr. Braun's from Paris, who had heard of his death. She was cordial, even friendly, and was waiting for us at the house. I put her age at about forty-five, my age, or a day or two older, and attractive—an animated and sexual woman, I thought, with hair a shade darker than Magda's and lively eyes that were nearly black. I guessed right off there had been something between her and Godinsky. It seemed inevitable, the moody, lonely foreign gentleman and the lively matron.

She gave us tea and little cakes, which she'd baked herself and which resembled the cakes I'd eaten as a child in Moscow and hadn't eaten since; and even though Magda and I had eaten breakfast, it was impossible to pass up Madame Berkowitz's cakes. She was a generous woman, that was certain, and it seemed to me a kindness of fate that Godinsky's last few months had been spent with her.

Her English was fluent, with hardly any accent, and over tea we soon heard the beginning of the story of her life. She'd been born in Berlin, although her mother was from Latvia, an opera singer from Riga. "A lyric soprano in the grand tradition," she said. After her parents divorced, she traveled with her mother all over the world. "An exciting life, a wonderful life, although more often than not we were down on our luck and did what we could to get by." She winked and laughed, and shook her shoulders when she laughed; the gold bangles at her throat and around her wrists tinkled like temple bells. "After my mother drowned in Shanghai—a terrible story, which I'll tell you sometime—well, I was on my own, and without a dime in Shanghai, and there was nothing for it but to marry Mr. Berkowitz." She poured

out more tea and passed around the delicious cakes. "He was a busi-
nessman, in textiles, twenty-two years older than me and, when we
met, already a widower. A generous man, with a good sense of humor,
but lacking—how shall I say it? We're women of the world, and expect
in our men a certain something."

"Finesse," Magda said.

"Exactly." Again she laughed, and shook her shoulders, and the
temple bells tinkled. "Your friend Godinsky—don't be surprised, he
told me his real name—now he had finesse. To the tips of his fingers,
a man with finesse."

She sighed and slowly shook her head, and said his death had been
a great shock, and that even though she had known him only a short
time, they had been close friends. "You might even say we were intimate," she said.

Although furnished rooms were in great demand, she hadn't adver-
tised his or made any attempt to rent it. She couldn't bring herself to
do it, but left it as it was the day he died, and later took us to see it,
climbing three flights to the top floor; it was a snug, airy room with a
pitched ceiling that reminded me of my place in Paris. From Magda's
glance, I could see that she had the same thought.

"Godinsky was a neat man, very tidy," Madame Berkowitz said.
"All of his things just so."

In his closet were two suits and an odd pair of trousers, which
looked to have just come from the cleaners; his shoes were freshly
polished and lined up on the floor of the closet next to a pair of worn
house slippers. His underwear and socks and spare shirts were all precisely folded away, and Madame Berkowitz went around opening the
closet and drawers, fondly touching and straightening the things that
had belonged to him. I heard a hiss of steam from the wall radiator,
but otherwise the room seemed unnaturally still, a ray of winter sunlight coming through the window. On the top of the bureau was a box
of tea bags and another of sugar cubes, and farther along a kettle and
an electric ring, the refugee's electric ring.

"He was free to use the kitchen whenever he wanted," Madame
Berkowitz said. "But he was a very early riser, so as not to disturb me,
he made his own tea." She looked over at Magda. "Such a thoughtful
man," she said.

"Did he work in this room?"

"At that desk."

There was a typewriter, a Remington noiseless, the kind Winters had in his office, and next to it a stack of blank paper, a two-volume history of the United States, and an English-Polish dictionary.

"He told you his real name," I said. "He trusted you. He must have confided in you."

"He told me about his wife," Madame Berkowitz said. "And he invited me to the movie at the museum, but I didn't want to stick my nose in. It wasn't right. 'Let him go alone, let him remember and even enjoy a good cry.' That's what I said to myself."

Magda was at the window, looking down at the garden below. "Is that a cherry tree?" she said.

"Not the sweet cherries, the sour. I use them to make pies."

"Did he tell you anything else about himself?" I said.

"That he was a writer."

"Nothing else."

"He said he was involved in politics in Poland, and that the less I knew the better. He didn't want me to get involved."

"All right."

"And I don't want to be involved."

"You won't be."

"I know I talk too much. I should have told you he was just a boarder. I should learn to keep my mouth shut."

"You're not to worry. We were friends of his, and you won't be involved."

"He was working on a book, a manuscript in Polish. He gave me the address in London and told me if something happened to him I was to mail it there." She looked over at Magda at the window, and said, "It looks like nothing, that cherry tree. Come around in May and it's gorgeous."

I said, "Did you mail the manuscript?"

"Sure. To an address in Knightsbridge." Again she glanced over at Magda. "It was what he wanted," she said.

Later that afternoon she drove us to the subway, pointing out first the Brooklyn Museum and then her clothing shop on Nostrand Avenue. On the spur of the moment, I told her that since Godinsky's room wasn't spoken for, I wanted to rent it myself. She was happy with the idea, and said I could have it for fifteen dollars a week, which was more than fair, and the next day Magda helped me pack up my things—I had been living in an awful room near the hospital—and Madame Berkowitz volunteered to pick us up in her car.

I'd taken a liking to her, and she to Magda and me. She'd prepared the room, changing the bedspread and arranging a vase with fresh flowers. She even cooked us dinner, and we drank a lot of wine, and the three of us sat around swapping stories and getting to know one another in the kitchen.

It got to be too late for Magda to go back to Manhattan, so she spent the night on a couch in the parlor, and after coffee in the morning, I walked her to the subway.

"I think I've got a way for you to get your papers," I said.

She grabbed hold of my arm and stopped in the street. "Are you serious? In my name?"

"You'll have to go up to Canada for a day or so," I said. "The American consulate in Toronto will issue an entry permit and the residency card."

"Just like that?"

"Yes. But that's not the end of it. Afterward, you've got to do a job."

"I don't care. Whatever your friends want."

"It's about Serge Dolin. You have to understand."

"What's there to understand?" she said. "I'm to screw him."

She tucked her arm under mine, and we walked on, past a group of boys playing hockey on roller skates in the street. "It's no big thing," Magda said. "You don't have to make such a face. Just tell me what it's all about."

"It's not just the sex."

"Am I to try to make him fall in love with me?"

"You're to get him to talk."

"And tell you what I find out. Is that it?"

"We want to know what he's up to."

"I'm to be a professional spy?"

"Yes. You'll be paid."

"Like Willi?" she said. "A spy like Willi?"

"It's too dangerous," I said. "I'll try to get your residency card another way."

"Another way? You can't."

"Dolin is dangerous," I said. "He's a killer, and very clever."

"And very attractive," Magda said. "Don't forget how attractive he is."

"You want to do it," I said. "It appeals to you."

"I only want my papers," she said.

After Magda left, I telephoned Winters from a public phone and told him that Magda had accepted our offer.

157

"I want her to leave tomorrow for Canada," I said. "And I want her protected."

"I'll handle the arrangements with immigration and the consulate in Toronto."

"Did you hear what I said, Andrew? She's to be protected. We both know what Dolin is, the kind of man he is."

"She'll cross from Buffalo. There's a bus that leaves for there every morning."

"Andrew . . ."

"Something is breaking. A message from your relatives." His voice rose. "Do you understand? A message from your hometown, from Uncle Joe." He caught hold of himself. I heard him take a deep breath, and then he said, "Godinsky was step one, Archangel is two."

It was the first time Andrew had mentioned Archangel, the first time I'd heard it from him. "Is it a second assassination?" I said. "But who?"

"That's what we need to know. Magda is our only chance."

"She'll need directions," I said. "Who to see at the border in Canada and at the consulate. Some money."

"At the hospital, have you a box, a place you get messages?"

"Yes."

"I'll leave an envelope for you tonight." He started to ring off, and then said, "Get hold of Mitzi and set up a party. Tell her I'll pay for it."

"Vladimir was supposed to call her."

"Make sure he does it. Christ. One of you call her and get it done fast."

I checked at the hospital that night, and the envelope was there. I turned it over to Magda, who caught the bus that night to Buffalo, arriving there late the next afternoon. She spent the night in Buffalo, in a hotel called the Niagara, room 312, which had been booked in advance. The room was large, and though she couldn't see the falls, she could hear it. She crossed the border in the morning and went along the western shore of Lake Ontario up to Toronto. The bus was due to arrive at ten-thirty, but a tire blew out, and it didn't pull into the terminal until nearly twelve. By the time she got to the consulate, the visa office was closed and the official she was to see had gone to lunch.

That day in Toronto the temperature was 11 degrees and it was snowing. She shivered outside the locked gate in front of the visa section until a Marine guard invited her into the guardhouse on the consulate grounds, where she was able to warm up in front of a coal-burning stove, and there was even coffee, a tin pot kept hot on the lid of the stove.

She got her documents from the visa section that afternoon—permission to enter the United States, and a permanent residency card, both made out to Magda Renner. There was even a photographer, so she wouldn't have to go around finding someone to take her picture. Orders had been given to waive the visa fee. Everything had been worked out in advance. Andrew Winters had made his call to the White House, and from there a long arm had reached out, and everything was arranged. After her years in France, after six years in New York, Magda Renner was able legally to enter the United States and reside there.

And all of that, the paperwork, took less than half an hour; at two-thirty she walked out of the consulate. The marine at the gate was just going off duty, and asked Magda to have a drink with him. She declined, saying she had to catch the bus to Buffalo. He offered to drive her to the terminal, but she refused that too.

The bus to Buffalo left at four o'clock, but Magda wasn't on it. Andrew had arranged for an officer at the border to keep an eye out for Magda, and to call when she crossed. No call came. Magda didn't reenter the United States by way of Buffalo. She didn't call me, and I had no idea where she was. No one did.

In the meantime, Vladimir had spoken to Mitzi, who'd begun arrangements for the party. Serge Dolin had been invited, and accepted. Three days passed with no sign of Magda, not a word. Andrew Winters was beside himself. There'd been an increase in Soviet cable traffic, and he hinted at an intercept, even a break in the Soviet code. There were tantalizing allusions to Archangel.

"Damn it, what does it mean?" he said.

"Maybe, after all, it has nothing to do with Dolin."

"But he's still around. Godinsky is dead, and the bastard is still here."

"In the Fisher apartment," I said. "Is the microphone in working order?"

"Fat lot of good it does."

"Give Magda a chance."

"Chance? We don't even know where the little bitch is."

"She'll be here for Mitzi's party."

"She damn well better be."

I went around to Magda's room, and left a note giving her Mitzi's address and the time and date of the party.

Vladimir had broken off with the most recent of his society widows, and swore an oath to reform. Not for a minute did I believe him. But I had missed him, and took him back, as I always did.

"As you always will," said Madame Berkowitz, who had met Vladimir and was, of course, charmed by him. "A rascal," she said, "but with finesse."

When he came to pick me up on the night of Mitzi's party, I noticed he and Madame Berkowitz exchanging glances, and even whispering together when they thought I wasn't around. They were up to something, and I had the feeling it concerned me.

Vladimir had dressed himself up like a prince, with a Borsalino hat and a dashing silk scarf. As soon as we were alone in the old Dodge, even before he started the motor, he began teasing me about the way I never bought new clothes.

"You refuse to dress yourself up," he said. "it's a matter of principle with you. 'Take me as I am, or not at all.' That's what you say."

"And what about you? Dressed up like a prince."

He ignored that. "Look at your coat," he said. "For two years in Paris, you slept in the poor old thing."

"My coat is my business, and it's good enough for Mitzi's crowd."

"You're going to meet important persons tonight. Important persons, and in such a coat."

"Important persons? Let them stand under my window, your important persons, and keep their hands in their pockets while I empty my piss pot."

I said it in Russian, the good old Russian of the last century, which made Vladimir laugh until he had to wipe his eyes with that silk scarf of his. I pretended to admire the scarf and took it from around his neck to have a better look. The label was from a shop in Palm Beach.

"Your friend the widow, a present from her?"

"A small token," he said. "If you like, I'll return it to her."

"There's no need for you to bother," I said. "And you might even offend the lady." I rolled down the car window, balled up the scarf, and happily threw it out the window.

"The hat was also a gift." He handed it to me, and I skimmed it out the window after the scarf. "Later on," Vladimir said, "after the party, we can go back to my place. It'll be just like in Paris, when you saved my skin." He reached out to touch my face, and then kissed me, and when his eyes rested on me I saw, incredibly, that they were brimming with tears. "It's time we got married and finally had a good life together," he said. "We ought to get married. We will. See if we don't."

160

Vladimir spoke in an offhand way, playfully, like the prank of giving me his hat to throw out the window. But it wasn't a prank. It was only that he was unable to speak seriously about what was closest to us both. I understood him, and pretended to go along with his joking manner, because I was also unable to be serious. Yet at that moment I realized—perhaps for the first time—that Vladimir and I would marry one day, that it was inevitable. And I silently wished for it to happen, and because I'm a superstitious woman, I crossed my fingers and prayed for a little luck.

But I didn't say anything. Happiness was there in front of me, but I didn't reach out to take it. I said, "We better get going, or we'll miss the party."

We still hadn't moved from in front of Madame Berkowitz's door. "I have something to do first," Vladimir said, and reaching behind him and stretching his long arm over the backseat of the Dodge, he lifting out a large box with a label from Madame Berkowitz's shop. I recalled how she and Vladimir had been whispering together, and I wondered if it had been about a coat I'd admired and asked her to put aside until I'd saved enough money. I quickly opened the box and under the tissue paper there it was—the coat I wanted. Madame Berkowitz had told Vladimir and he had bought it for me, a beautiful thing with a mink collar and a silk lining, the finest coat I ever owned.

I couldn't say a word, not even thank you. I was overcome. Years later, when the coat was old and falling to pieces, Vladimir teased me because I refused to throw it away. He also claimed that as soon as I got my hands on it, I got out of the car and put it on, and danced around in it, showing myself off in the light from the street lamp, while Madame Berkowitz peeped out at us from her bedroom window.

That's how Vladimir told the story, although I don't remember that part of it, and I don't actually believe Vladimir, who was always teasing me.

When we arrived at Mitzi's party at about eight o'clock, it was already in full swing. Magda hadn't arrived, and there was no word from her. But Dolin was there, moving easily among the other guests. Although I recognized him from the photograph Magda had taken of him with Willi, he looked younger in the flesh, and shorter than I expected, hardly taller than I, and so broad through the shoulders as to make him seem even shorter. I noticed the fine black hair on the backs of his hands, which were square and looked very strong. Vladimir thought he had a Russian face, but I would have taken him for Italian or French, one of those menacing Corsicans I'd known in Paris.

161

By nine o'clock Magda still hadn't arrived, and Vladimir was getting nervous. "Will she come?" he said.

"I think so." I thought a moment and said, "Yes, I'm sure of it. She'll come because of Dolin."

"In spite of what he is?"

"Because of it."

Magda had actually arrived from Canada earlier that same day and had seen the note I'd slipped under the door of her room. She had spent a couple of hours deciding whether or not to come, and even sat on a bench in Central Park just across from Mitzi's apartment, trying to get her nerves under control. She had spoken lightly to me of Dolin, but in fact she was afraid of him, although she never thought that he'd harm her.

She had seen something in Dolin that the rest of us had not; or perhaps it was something in herself that she saw. I had been right about Magda; she was attracted to Dolin, even fascinated by him, and it was the intensity of her own feelings that frightened her.

But finally she screwed up her courage, crossed Central Park West, and at 9:15 rang Mitzi's door bell. Through the closed door she heard the sound of voices, of music and people having a good time. A maid in uniform let her in and took away her coat. She stepped into the apartment, and stood with her face composed and with her hands folded, as she'd been taught as a girl. A butler passed with a tray of drinks, and she hesitated, not sure whether to take one or not. She was unsure and ill at ease. But then she gathered her courage, and joined a group around the piano, singing in French, songs she remembered from the dance halls around St. Germain. Soon she began to sing, but in a low voice, only to herself.

There were several beautiful women in the room—there always were at Mitzi's parties—but these were models and the kinds of actresses who relied on their beauty and allowed themselves to be defined by it. Magda's beauty was of a different sort. It was unassertive, without glitter, and didn't stop the eye. One glanced at Magda, and then looked more critically, not quite believing the marvel one had seen.

I watched her from a corner of the large room, without her seeing me. Her hair was pulled back from her face, her dress was plain, she wore no jewelry—she owned none—and her only makeup was lipstick from Woolworth's.

When she looked up from the piano, she saw me and nodded, as if we knew each other only slightly. She was a good actress. There was a sudden flurry of activity off to one side and the sound of Mitzi's bril-

liant laugh, carrying above the piano and the singing. The expression
in Magda's eyes deepened and signaled something to me intimate and
elusive. Mitzi came into sight, Serge Dolin with her.

And what was it, just then, I had seen in Magda's expression? I
thought: She's lost her nerve. It lasted only a second or two, that intimate signal. Mitzi called her name, and Magda turned toward her.
She was about to be offered to Dolin. I was puzzled by what I had seen
in Magda's eyes. It was an enigma then. It still is.

"My darling, you look lovely," Mitzi said to Magda. "But why so
late? I was afraid you'd changed your mind." She held Dolin's elbow
and gave him a little push forward. "But I think you two have already
met," she said, and then carefully introduced them. Dolin made a
dignified bow and bent over Magda's hand to kiss it.

It was done like a prince at the czar's court, and seemed a bit out of
place. But Mitzi was delighted. "You see how gallant he is," she said,
"gallant and heroic. Serge has the Cross of Lorraine, the Order of the
Liberation."

"Mitzi, my dearest," Dolin said. "I don't know what you're talking
about."

Magda was now solidly on her own feet, looking squarely at Serge
Dolin. And Mitzi repeated, "The Cross of Lorraine."

"As if for Joan of Arc," Magda said.

"But he has a medal," Mitzi said. "And De Gaulle himself pinned
it on him."

"No. It wasn't so important a medal."

"But it must be so," Mitzi said. "Because I've told everybody that
De Gaulle himself gave you your medal. Please, Serge let it be so."

"So you want it to be so?"

"Yes. I want to be the friend of a great hero."

"Well, then it's so." Dolin said, not taking his eyes from Magda.

Mitzi let herself go, and stepped back, clapping her hands. It was a
triumph, but at the same time she glanced at Magda as if to say: "Here
he is. I give him to you. Now make the most of it. Don't be a fool."

The first words Serge and Magda spoke were in English, but then
they switched to French. No mention was made of his approaches to
her at the Danube. He was ashamed of that, and now seemed reserved,
even shy, and that appealed to her. He was nearly forty then and
had known many women, but his shyness was genuine. Magda had
touched something in him, something long buried away, emotions
and distant images that he thought he had forgotten.

As for Magda—she believed he had changed from the man she

remembered; she thought him simpler, less vain, without arrogance, and more attractive. She was certain she could control her feelings. She had regained her confidence. Her purpose wasn't to love him, but to deceive him. He plucked two glasses of wine from a tray carried by a passing waiter. She sipped the wine, smiling at him over the rim of the glass. Deception seemed to her the easiest thing in the world.

They went to the buffet and filled plates with smoked salmon and sturgeon, cheese and cold meats. Magda was hungry and couldn't remember when she'd eaten such delicious food. She drank a glass of vodka, and led Dolin back to the piano, where both of them began to sing and have a good time. The pianist played Russian songs, and then, to the surprise of everyone, Serge Dolin began to sing in Russian. The pianist played one Russian song after another, and Serge knew the words to them all and sang out in a rich baritone. Then the pianist joined him, and when they sang together all conversation stopped and everyone at the party crowded around the piano. I heard Vladimir singing along, and I joined in with the rest of the Russians.

Magda was next to Serge Dolin, part of it all, singing a word here and there, looking happy and quite at ease. At that moment, I caught Vladimir's eyes, and he gave me a delighted wink. The singing went on, the songs became more spirited, and in the end everyone applauded and called for more.

Afterward there were toasts—"To victory in the war." And a French army officer raised his glass, and said: "To President Franklin Roosevelt." And I remember Serge Dolin raising his glass and draining it in one gulp.

The party went on a bit after that. Dolin and Magda stayed together. They made a handsome and intriguing couple, and it was noticed and commented upon when, around midnight, they quietly left together.

They walked downtown alongside the park, on Central Park West. He wanted to know how she had learned Russian.

"I speak only a few words," she said. "I learned it from my father, and later on from a friend."

"Your friend, is it a man?"

"No." And she said, "The songs I learned from my father."

"Is he Russian?"

"Austrian, but he knew a lot of languages, my father. He particularly liked to sing in Russian, and play the guitar."

"And he taught you. You were his pet?"

"He's dead now," Magda said.

They walked on; after the music and excitement of the party, and the emotions both had felt on meeting, there was a letdown, and conversation was difficult.

Eventually, Magda said, "I know that you're Russian, although you live in France. Willi told me that."

"He told me he was your uncle."

"My uncle, yes. That's what he told people," she said. "An uncle who was also—" She groped for the right words. "Also an intimate friend."

"Willi was the kind to tell a lot of stories," Serge said. "What else did he tell you about me?"

"That you were a journalist, and a big shot. He wanted me to be nice to you."

"Nice to me?"

"Yes, to sleep with you."

"And you told him to go to hell."

"That's why I was rude to you."

"I'm not a big shot," he said.

"What does it matter?" she said. "Big shot or not."

"Willi should have kept his mouth shut."

"Don't bother yourself. Willi was like that, an opportunist who thought others were like himself."

They came to Columbus Circle and, despite the cold, there was a festive air around the monument, with lots of soldiers and sailors on leave, some of whom had found girls and others who were merely tipsy.

Two Australian soldiers had met a pair of girls, one pretty and one plain, and were courting them, singing and playing the harmonica; the effect was comic, for the girls were tall and the Australians short, but lively, and they pranced like fauns around the girls.

"Everybody is celebrating," Magda said. "Everywhere you go."

"It's the war coming to an end."

"Will you go back to France?"

"Not yet."

A third Australian came out of the crowd that was cheering the revelers, and passed a whiskey bottle to Dolin. "Here you are, mate," he said. And after Dolin tipped the bottle, the Australian saluted, touching his fingertip to his forage cap, and said, "See your beautiful lady gets her nip."

Magda smiled her thanks, tipped the bottle, and licked her lips.

After they had walked on, Serge Dolin said, "I'll have to travel soon. How long I don't know. Have you ever been to Mexico?"

"Is that where you are going?"

"Mexico, or South America."

"For your work?" she said.

"Yes, a business trip."

She felt that he wasn't suspicious of her, and she decided: This will be easier than I thought. "I've heard Mexico is fascinating," she said.

"Would you like to go there?"

"Sure. Who wouldn't?"

"Perhaps you can."

"With you? You don't even know me. You're kidding me along, making fun of me."

"I'm not making fun of you."

"Even if you're not. What if it turns out we don't like each other? We'll be in Mexico, and we'll find out we don't like each other."

"All right, we won't go to Mexico yet. Tonight we'll only go for a drink. Over on Fifth Avenue, the Plaza, we can go there."

"I've had too much to drink."

"If you're not cold, we can walk for a while."

"I don't live far," Magda said.

On the way to her place, they passed an old woman selling flowers, and Dolin bought Magda a bunch of violets, and a bag of peanuts from an all-night shop on Broadway. It was quite late when they finally got to her building and took off their shoes to climb the stairs to her room. On the way over, she had been deciding whether or not to let him in and go to bed with him. The decision had been going back and forth in her mind. When he bought her flowers, she thought: I'll sleep with him. But by the time they got to her house, she thought: No, I won't. Climbing ahead of him on the stairs, she felt a seductive warmth rise in her, and she changed her mind again. But there was more to come, more shifts of mood. She thought of holding herself back from him, of tempting him, of touching and pulling away, of keeping the power of love in her hands.

In front of her door, she raised her face to dismiss him with a single goodnight kiss. But he only touched his lips to hers and put his cheek for a second against her hair, then took her hand and bent over it with a formal bow. It was something he had been taught, or more likely read in a book. It was romantic, even foolish. But with his head bent over her hand, under the flickering yellow bulb in the gloomy hallway, as his lips touched her hand, the game ended, and Magda began simply to love Serge.

After Mitzi's party, I couldn't get Magda alone for nearly a week. She was with Serge the whole time. When finally she was able to call me, we arranged to meet. But she was reluctant to talk about Serge or about her feelings for him.

"From the first, I began to love him," she said. "It's a surprise, what I feel. Yet it was there all the time, a surprise waiting to be discovered. I expected to love Serge."

"You said you were afraid of him."

"Afraid? Yes, of what I would feel—afraid of love itself. But not now," she said. "When he took me home from the party, I opened my door, and he followed me inside and closed the door. We were alone, Serge and I, in that lousy little room. You know the room, eh?"

"I know it."

"A lousy room with green wallpaper, and cold as hell."

"What are you trying to tell me?"

"That it's my lousy room. Mine and Serge's." It was said with her chin out, defiantly. "Our lousy room, and our squeaky bed, and what happened there is between us, and nobody else's business."

I agreed with her. I let her get it all off her chest, and then I said, "Your feelings are your own, but if later on something were said— For example, did he give you a hint about his plans? Since Godinsky is dead, there must be another reason for his staying on."

"He says it's for me," she said. "Because he loves me."

I laughed and said, "So soon?"

"From the first night. Even before that, at the Danube." I'd gotten her to ease up. "A week is plenty of time. We didn't speak to anyone else, the whole time, not a soul. Serge bought food, and we cooked in the room."

"On the electric ring."

"He's used to it," she said. "He's also a refugee."

After Magda called, we arranged to meet at the first place I thought of, in Riverside Park, where I had waited for Willi. Events had come full circle—even the bench was the same. I looked for the shepherd dog that had left tracks in the snow the time I'd found out Willi was dead.

"Serge talks about going away," Magda said. "He talks about Mexico. He's been there, and he likes it. He's got friends in Mexico, that's what he says; Mexico is beautiful, and you can get lost there."

"Get lost?"

"Disappear. He wants to disappear. I think he's been working something out in his mind. When I wake up in the middle of the night, he's usually sitting by the window, smoking and looking out at nothing. He doesn't know I'm watching him. I pretend I'm asleep. One time, I got up and stood beside him. The damn room was freezing, and I made him get back into bed, It was late, almost morning. I saw the light at the window. I held him tight, we held each other. He was trembling. Maybe it was only the cold—whatever it was, Serge was trembling."

"Is that when he talked about Mexico?" I said. "About disappearing there?"

"He wanted to know if I had a passport. I told him no, only a residence card. He said he could arrange a passport. Is it true—can he arrange such things?"

"He's a magician," I said.

"He sleeps with one eye open," she said. "Like a soldier. On the outside he seems confident and unafraid. But it's not so. He's afraid, although I don't know of what."

I had watched Vladimir coax the truth from members of Living Memory—for example, from Yakov, the janitor and former hero of the Petrograd Soviet. Vladimir's technique consisted of asking questions without appearing to do so. "Invisible questions" he called them.

"Tell me, Magda," I said. "Do you miss him now?"

"At this minute?"

"Yes, right now."

"I know I'll see him soon."

"But if he weren't there . . ."

"He will be."

"You said he was like a soldier. What if he gets marching orders?"

"He's already gotten orders," she said. "He has a job to do. Something important and dangerous. That's what wakes him up in the middle of the night, and when he stares out the window, it's the orders that he's thinking about."

I decided to take a risk; it was like holding a card, a hidden card, and suddenly throwing it down in the middle of the table. "Archangel," I said. "He's awake thinking of Archangel."

"He won't talk to me about it."

I said, "Is it after Archangel that he escapes to Mexico?"

"We both do."

"When do you go?"

"He told me to be ready," she said. "It could be any time. Tomorrow, next week. I'm to be ready."

"Where does he think you are now?"

"I told him I had to go to the doctor, and the pharmacy," Magda said. "I told him I didn't want to get pregnant."

"And where is he?"

"He had some business," she said. "And there was something about a car. He had to borrow a car."

"Fisher has a car."

"Yes. Fisher is the one with the car," she said. "Serge has to drive to Long Island, all the way to the end."

"Montauk."

"Fisher also owns a house there," she said. "And Serge has to go. I don't know what it's all about." Abruptly, she stood up. "What time is it?"

"Quarter to five."

"I'm late now." She started to walk off, but she turned back and took hold of me and kissed me. "I'm all right," she said. "I'm safe. Even if he knew we were meeting, he wouldn't hurt me. He'd never hurt me," she said, and again started away. "Serge would never hurt me."

Unhappily I watched her hurry along the path to Riverside Drive. It was the middle of March, with no sign of spring. Rain fell, stopped, and a cold mist filled the air. I turned up the collar of my coat—I'd worn the old one—and went out of the park by a different route from the one Magda had taken. I thought again of Willi, of the afternoon I'd waited for him. By putting Magda and Serge Dolin together, I had arrogantly begun something that was impossible to control and that might end tragically. I feared for Magda, as one fears for a child; and I wanted her near me, protected, as one does a child.

But she was gone, and I didn't see her again until the first week in April.

In the meantime Winters induced Francis Keogh to take two months accumulated leave from the police department, and to drive out to Montauk, where he searched the tax records until he located the house owned by the mysterious Barret Martin Fisher. Winters stayed clear of the FBI but trusted Keogh, whom he knew to be loyal, close-mouthed, and competent. Keogh found the Fisher house, and one moonless night near the end of March, he and Andrew Winters entered it surreptitiously.

It was a single-room shack set back a hundred yards through tall

dune grass along a path off the Montauk Highway. The grass and sloping dune hid it from the highway, so that even in daylight it was difficult to locate. Fisher had bought it in May of 1943, paying $3,200
dollars in cash. Taxes were $48 a year. There was no running water,
no plumbing.

The windows were bolted and there was a padlock on the door, but
Keogh picked the lock in a matter of minutes. Inside were two folded
sleeping bags, a tin basin containing a towel and worn bar of soap, the remains of a fire in the grate, a bottle of drinking water, a half-empty jar
of peanut butter, and a box of crackers. The only furniture was an old
wicker chair and a picnic table, and on that stood a quarter-horsepower
generator and a Hallicrafter shortwave radio with earphones.

The radio had been placed at the window facing the beach, with
no building between it and the ocean.

"Do you think there's a Russian out there?" Keogh said. "A sub-
marine?"

"I think there was."

"And Dolin?"

"He's come and gone. He got the message he came for."

Dolin had his orders; Magda had confirmed that. "He told me to
be ready," she had said. "It could be next week. It could be
tomorrow."

On the drive back from Montauk, Keogh recommended putting
Dolin under surveillance; he had a few reliable and skillful men, retired cops—gumshoes and shadow artists is what he called them.

"Your fellow won't know he's being watched," Keogh said.

"He'll know."

"Maybe, maybe not. If they make him nervous, he takes the long
way around or bungles the job. Even better, he runs and doesn't do it
at all."

Winters agreed, and Keogh's gumshoes went on the job round the
clock. Dolin saw them, Winters was certain of it, but he ignored them.
Winters' respect for Dolin was great. In dreams he saw him as a card-
sharp, a sorcerer who made others disappear and in the end himself
vanished in a melodramatic puff of smoke.

Keogh was more matter of fact. "He's clever, but so are the fellows
I put to watch him."

"He sees them," Winters said. "He wants us to know where he is.
We are to believe his hands are clean."

"He goes everywhere with the Renner girl," Keogh said. "Billing
and cooing, a pair of lovebirds."

170

"We are to believe his hands are clean," repeated Winters.

"He likes throwing around his money," Keogh said.

There was no doubt of that. Nearly every night for two weeks Dolin took Magda to a different club. They went to the Oval Room at the Ritz Carlton, which then stood at the corner of Madison and 46th Street. They went to the St. Regis, the Iridium Room, and the Blue Angel on East 55th Street, to Billy Rose's Diamond Horseshoe, Leon and Eddie's, the Four Hundred Club, and the fabled El Morocco. Dolin liked eating and drinking well and rubbing shoulders with what was known then as café society. I saw in him more of the czarist prince than the Marxist, and I suspect he saw himself more that way also. He was dashing as a prince, courting Magda with flowers and champagne and drives in horsedrawn cabs through Central Park at dawn.

I saw them together once during those two weeks, at a rally held by an organization called the Committee Against Fascism and War at the St. Nicholas Arena, an old boxing club on West 66th Street. Posters advertising the rally were put up in local colleges and union halls, and outside subway stations in Greenwich Village and around Union Square. The posters were exciting and dramatic, designed by the Mexican artist David Sequieros, and I got hold of one and kept it. The date of the rally was March 29, 1945, and listed among the principal speakers was Serge Dolin, who was identified as "an internationally known journalist and hero of the French Resistance."

There were perhaps fifteen hundred or two thousand people there —the *Times* the next morning put the figure at just under two thousand. The Communist *Daily Worker* claimed a capacity crowd of six thousand, but it was nowhere near that.

The FBI had worked one or two agents into the committee and sent several more to the rally, where they mingled with the many celebrated people, mostly from the arts, who attended. Whatever information the bureau collected it kept to itself, sharing nothing with Andrew or anyone else. My guess is the agents didn't come up with much. They were simply too easy to spot, even in a crowd that size.

"They stood out," Vladimir said, "like ducks in a chicken coop."

There were lots of speeches that night, boring for the most part, full of Communist party tub thumping. Vladimir and I were a distance from the speakers' platform, secure in the anonymity of the crowd, watching the goings-on through opera glasses. Dolin sat on the speakers' platform and Magda was in the first row, gazing up at him.

He was to be the final speaker, following a playwriting lady who had been to Stalingrad. She touched on the misery and destruction

171

she'd seen, but only touched on it, before getting down to her meeting with Stalin and the inspiration of his firm handshake, the affectionate intelligence in his dark gaze, and the warmth of the greeting she carried from him to all American comrades.

So it went. Magda clapped politely—I was sure she hadn't heard a word—and through Vladimir's opera glasses, I saw that she never took her eyes from Dolin.

Now the crowd grew restless. People shouted for Serge Dolin, hero of the Resistance. The lights around the arena dimmed, and the brilliant arcs above the platform went on. Vladimir said, "Now comes the main event," a phrase I didn't understand, and when he translated it into Russian, the boxing expression lost all meaning. By that time Dolin had been introduced and was on his feet. There was much applause and cheering, and above the noise a hearty voice broke into the "International," which was quickly taken up by nearly everyone in the hall.

Through it all, I watched Magda. From her expression I knew she had fallen in love with Serge Dolin. The singing and the applause went on, and he held out both his hands, opening his arms in the way of politicians and actors, as if to embrace the audience, and only after the tumult died down did he begin to speak.

His voice was surprisingly low, and somewhat hoarse, yet even without a microphone it carried to the last row of the arena. It was an actor's voice, and Dolin was an actor, poised and utterly sure of himself. He said nothing memorable, speaking only of the need to continue the war against fascism "and to forge an iron brotherhood of workers." He told the people exactly what they had come to hear, wanted to hear, and what they had heard dozens of times before from other speakers.

But it didn't matter what he said. The words spoken by his actor's voice didn't matter. All that mattered was Dolin himself, the party's anointed hero of the French Resistance.

After his speech, he was surrounded by well-wishers, shaking hands and even signing autographs, like a movie star. Magda stood apart. I went up and stood beside her. "Don't be startled," I said. "Don't look around."

But she was startled. She had been looking adoringly at Dolin in a circle of his admirers, and I had plunged unexpectedly into her thoughts.

"I don't want him to see us together," she said.

"Meet me tomorrow in the park. Three o'clock."

"I'm not sure I can."

"Try. If not, I'll meet you the day after, same time."

She glanced over at Dolin, who was still caught up by the crowd and hadn't noticed us. "I don't want him to see us," Magda said, and went to join him.

I went to the park the next day and waited almost an hour, occupying a bench near an old man with a small dog whose anxious black eyes never strayed from his master. The old man wore a baseball cap and had brought a chair of his own, one of those that fold and can be carried like a walking stick.

Magda didn't show up. She didn't appear the next day either. I realized she'd fallen in love with Dolin and wouldn't betray him. We had lost our gamble. I understood Magda and was sympathetic to her. But waiting in the park, I hoped she'd come and explain it to me. I'd have been on her side. She'd not betray Dolin and I'd not betray her. She should have realized that.

I told Vladimir what had happened, and we went to break the news to Andrew Winters.

"We've got to be careful," I said. "She may tell him about us."

"She already has," Andrew said. "She's betrayed us to Serge Dolin."

"Betrayed us?" I said. "Or chosen not to betray her lover? It depends how you look at it."

"Let me tell you how I look at it," Andrew said. "Dolin is an assassin, the probable killer of two men, and now he's gunning for a third. He's not Romeo, any more than your Renner is Juliet."

We were in Andrew's house on Sutton Place. He had built a fire, but we'd let it run down, and now Vladimir had taken up a poker and was trying to get it going again. "Have they been living at the Fisher apartment?" he said.

"For nearly two weeks," Winters said.

Vladimir had built up the fire in the grate and added a pair of logs, arranging them to catch the draft; he did so with precision, as he did most things. "In the Fisher apartment, there was a microphone," he said. "And the recording wire, did that stuff work at all?"

"You can judge for yourself."

Winters had arranged to meet the man who lived above the Fisher apartment, an unemployed actor, and offered him a job in an army training film in production in Florida. In return Winters was given the use of the actor's apartment. He installed the wire recorder and Keogh was able to plant two microphones, one in each of Fisher's ceiling light fixtures. Electronic surveillance was in its infancy then, so Dolin hadn't searched for a microphone, or if he did he never found one.

Keogh's men had recorded two reels of tape and Winters now fitted them to the sprockets on a machine the size of a large suitcase, a machine so heavy Vladimir had to help him set it on a table in front of the fireplace.

The recording wire was the thickness of fishing line, and when Winters started the reels turning, one of the wires snapped and had to be knotted. The machine was restarted, the wheels of tape turned, there was several seconds of background noise, a prolonged vibrating hum, and then a woman's voice; I recognized it as Magda's, by the accent as much as anything else.

Winters said, "Can you make out what she said?"

"Something about a telephone," I said. "She's speaking French. It's something between them." I didn't like eavesdropping on Magda. "She doesn't know she's being recorded," I said. "She should have been warned."

Serge was speaking, calling her by a pet name, and then he spoke in Russian, calling her *Dorogaya*. Darling. In Russian, she was *Dorogaya*.

"It's between them," I said. "Quite private between a man and woman, and none of our business."

We heard them whispering together, but couldn't make out what they said. We heard Magda laugh, a laugh that I remembered from the Rue de Babylone and that made my heart ache.

My instinct was to turn off the machine. It would have been the right thing to do, but I needed to know what had passed between them; I needed to know the truth of things, and that held me back. I heard their voices, but most of what they said was impossible to make out. I heard some Russian and English, but mostly they spoke in French. Andrew frequently stopped the machine, rewound, and played parts over. We listened to words of endearment, to sounds of passion, and to interludes in which nothing was said, when the reels turned and the only sound was the monotonous hum from the recording wire.

Suddenly, Magda began to sing. The song was in Russian, a lullaby, the kind sung at bedtime to children. She sang it well, in a pure, thin voice. When she finished, Dolin applauded and called her *Dorogaya*, and afterward everything was quiet.

There was a second reel of wire, one Winters hadn't heard.

"Magda went out," Winters said. "Serge was alone and Fisher paid a visit. He brought a parcel."

Winters put on the second reel, threaded the wire, turned it on, and sat hunched over the machine, listening intently.

There were words of greeting; I had expected to hear Russian, but they spoke English, Fisher with an American accent. I felt the tension between them, and the terseness of their conversation, as if both wanted the meeting over quickly so as not to be caught with each other.

Fisher said, "Max knows what he's to do. I've spoken to him. He knows exactly what he's to do and . . ." His next few words were lost in what sounded like the scraping of a chair leg across the floor. "Max needs more money," I heard him say.

Dolin said, "Why didn't you give him the equipment yourself?"

"He insists—"

"Who the hell is he to insist? Max isn't . . ." The next words were unclear and Winters rewound the wire and played it again. ". . . giving orders." That was it. "Max isn't giving orders."

"It's the money," Fisher said. "He wants part of it before. From you. I don't have it. Also, the equipment should be with you in case it could be used against us. What if in the end Max doesn't agree?"

"He already has agreed."

"He's afraid. He's begun to think about what's involved, and to brood on the consequences . . . the consequences . . ." Fisher's voice trailed off; he had moved away from the microphone. But then he returned, for his voice was clear. "The consequences worry Max. The risk."

"We've arranged to get him out of the country."

"He's not afraid for himself. He's afraid of the risk of a new war. The suffering of the *Narodya*. Max is haunted by how the *Narodya* would suffer."

Winters stopped the machine.

Vladimir said, "The *Narodya* are the people, the simple people, the ordinary folk."

"Those who suffer most in a war," I said.

"And Max is afraid of another war."

"Of causing it himself."

Winters turned on the machine; the reels began to turn. We heard Dolin clearly: "Max afraid for the suffering of the *Narodya*?" he said. "I never trust such sentiments. Max is afraid for himself."

"You'll have to persuade him. You'll have to twist his arm."

"What do you mean?"

"Tell him about the money," Fisher said. "Then show him the letter from his sister."

"Twist his arm," Dolin said. "Yes, of course."

"Max wants money," Fisher said. "And even more he wants his mother and sister across . . ." Winters stopped the machine. The last word was unclear. It sounded like *gull* or *golf*, but neither made sense. Max wants his mother and sister across the gull? Across the gulf?

"What sort of gulf are we talking about?" Winters spoke rhetorically, and turned the machine back on.

Dolin said, "Max's sister. Have we found her?"

"We have a letter," Fisher said, "a letter from her to Max. And a photograph. Both are in the parcel."

There was a rustling of stiff paper, and after a moment Dolin said, "Everything is here but the antidote pills."

"They won't be needed. Max can inject Archangel in the foot, between the toes."

Nothing more was said. The reels went on turning, and we sat mesmerized watching them turn, but heard nothing. It's true that every silence has a character of its own, and during that particular silence I tried to see Dolin and Fisher, and to place them in the room in which they had met and spoken, and to imagine what was going on in their minds.

The wire had run out; Winters turned off the machine. "How do we find Max?" he asked of the motionless reels. "How do we find him?"

Vladimir stepped in easily. "We haven't much to go on," he said. "Max wants his mother and sister across the gulf, but we don't know which gulf. He's close enough to Archangel to inject him in the foot, but of course we don't know who Archangel is. One thing is certain. Max has been paid money."

"Moscow keeps good books," I said.

"They watch every damn ruble," Andrew said.

"That's a lucky thing," Vladimir said. "How do you call it in English—paybook? Stalin keeps a good paybook, and somewhere in it is Max."

"Every damn ruble," Andrew said.

"Do we have the paybook?" I said.

"Maybe the next best thing." Vladimir nodded and shook his finger, like a schoolteacher, then stood and stretched, rubbing the small of his back, as if it pained him. He asked for a glass of water, and when it was brought he ignored it. "I'm thinking maybe we have somebody who saw the paybook. Andrew, do we have somebody like that?"

Andrew raised his eyes, and I thought how worn he looked, how weary. The defector was his secret and he was reluctant to share it with us. He said to me, "I told you I had somebody inside—a defector. That's what Vladimir is talking about. He wants to talk to my defector."

"Is he with the embassy?" Vladimir said.

"No."

"An illegal?"

"Yes. He was a Soviet resident here. He ran the apparat."

"If he ran the apparat, then he certainly saw the paybook," Vladimir said, and finally took a sip of the water that had been brought to him.

"I've questioned him about personnel," Andrew said. "He's reluctant to identify people. He's not a traitor or a stool pigeon."

"But he has defected," Vladimir said.

"To save himself, not to put someone else's neck in a noose."

"The matter of Max is urgent."

"I told you I've questioned him about personnel."

"But not about Max," Vladimir said. "You've only just heard of Max."

Andrew started to answer, to argue, but wound up shrugging and saying nothing. Vladimir was right and Andrew knew it. He had been holding his cards against his chest, but the time had come to lay them on the table. How reluctant he was, how it pained him. Yet secrets are heavy, and grow heavier with each step. Poor Andrew took a deep, exhausted breath and in a confidential tone began his story.

"After the defector made up his mind to come over, he followed me around in order to learn my routine. He's very good at it. I never saw him—he's able to make himself invisible. When I'm in New York, I go every Tuesday and Thursday morning to my club for a swim. One Tuesday after a swim I came back to the closet where I hang my clothes, and inside my jacket was an envelope giving me directions for a meeting."

"And you followed the directions, and went to the meeting?"

"He was a professional," Andrew said. "He knew to bait the hook."

"How did he do that?"

"He included a photograph."

"A photograph," Vladimir said. "A photograph. Could we see this photograph?"

Confident that the victory was his, Vladimir had warmed his voice and I watched him turn a coaxing smile on Andrew, and Andrew gave in. He pushed aside a bookcase, revealing a wall safe. He spun the combination dial and then opened the door of the safe. From inside he brought out an unmarked yellow envelope. In the envelope was a photograph, three inches square. It was of a diplomatic cable; Winters even supplied a magnifying glass for us to read it.

Vladimir read it, then passed it with the glass to me.

NO. 706 PERSONAL AND TOP SECRET. FEBRUARY 27, 1945

PRIME MINISTER TO PRESIDENT ROOSEVELT
SUBJECT: POLISH GOVERNMENT IN EXILE

WE HAVE CONTACTED POLISH ARMED FORCES AND THEY, TOGETHER WITH ALL OTHER FACTIONS, HAVE AGREED TO ACCEPT GODINSKY AS HEAD OF STATE, FOLLOWING END OF WAR. AGREEMENT FOLLOWS DIF-FICULT NEGOTIATIONS, AND WHILE THERE ARE RESERVATIONS ABOUT GODINSKY, AT THE MOMENT HE IS THE ONLY PERSON ACCEPTABLE TO ALL.

WE ARE CERTAIN STALIN WILL OPPOSE GODINSKY IN ORDER TO FRUS-TRATE ALL ATTEMPTS TO CREATE AN INDEPENDENT POLAND, AND DO ALL IN HIS POWER TO ESTABLISH A PUPPET GOVERNMENT IN POLAND.

AS PREVIOUSLY AGREED, I SUPPORT YOU, EVEN INCLUDING THE USE OF FORCE IF NECESSARY TO REPEL ANY SUCH MOVE BY STALIN.

CHURCHILL

I returned the cable to Andrew, who put it back in the safe and began to describe his meeting with the defector. "As I say, a profes-sional. He'd clipped a movie advertisement from the newspaper and circled the time the show started in a theater just off Times Square, one of the sleazy ones, where the concrete floor is sticky, littered with food and peanut shells, like the bottoms of the cages of the monkey house in the zoo.

"The man I was to meet knew me by sight, although I couldn't recognize him. I'd heard of him, but by different names, in Europe as well as here. He's old Bolshevik, a passenger on Lenin's sealed train, in and out of favor, and it thrilled me to think of all he'd seen, all he knew, all his memory held.

"He'd come to make a deal. I questioned him about people in his apparat—names, methods of communicating, the nuts and bolts. He

178

hated to talk, and I had to pick and gather tiny bits of information from him, pluck them like threads from his coat.

"He told me what he wanted: a new name, and the documents to back it up. He wanted money, enough to buy a place in Florida. He said he wanted to buy a boat."

A boat? I couldn't imagine a crony of Lenin's with a boat.

"'I've always wanted to be a sailor,' he said.

"I think it was meant as a joke, a way of teasing me. He did smile enigmatically. It was odd, as if he were flirting with me. We were still in that vile theater, the last row of the orchestra, and the light wasn't good. I noticed he wheezed when he breathed, and his shirt collar was a couple of sizes too large."

Vladimir and I had been listening attentively. Now Vladimir said, "The cable he left in your jacket, it's the same one we just read?"

"Yes."

"It's marked top secret. How did he get hold of it?"

"A copy was made in the White House."

"By an agent in his apparat?"

"Yes. But since he had already decided to defect, as part of his preparations, as a way of accumulating capital before retirement . . ."

"He made a second copy for himself."

"Exactly."

"And what other documents has he copied?"

"I don't know," Andrew said. "He's hinted at others, even more startling, but he holds tight to them." Andrew turned to me. "Perhaps a native Russian, a woman, would have better luck with him."

Vladimir was following his own line of thought. He said, "The first copy of the cable, the one he got from his agent in the White House, did he forward that to Moscow?"

"By air pouch on August third. It was in Stalin's hands by the sixth, no later. Dolin was pulled out of France and was in Moscow by the end of the month. Stalin then gave him the order to kill Godinsky."

"And also Archangel?"

"Archangel came later. It was in the works, in Stalin's mind, but Dolin wasn't told much about it in Moscow."

"And when he was finally told about it?"

"He didn't like it. He'd killed Godinsky, that was his job and it was risky enough. He expected to be pulled out."

"But he was given Max," I said. "Why was that?"

"Because my man came over," Andrew said. "Archangel scared

the pants off him. He dropped the cable copy in my jacket, and asked to be put in a safe place."

Vladimir thought a moment and said, "You told FDR of Godinsky's murder?"

"He was furious."

"At Stalin?"

"At Stalin. Finally, at Stalin. He swore to drive him and the Red Army out of Poland."

The telephone rang, startling us. Andrew didn't answer it at once. The implications of what he had said hung in the air, vibrating like the note struck on a tuning fork.

It was Francis Keogh calling. He'd been given Andrew's unlisted number to call in the event of an emergency. Andrew held the receiver to his ear, listening without expression to Francis while I idly plucked the dead leaves from a neglected plant and used the bar pitcher to water the soil around it. I heard Andrew give Francis a telephone number with instructions to call at regular intervals. It had to do with Dolin; Magda was involved. It was urgent.

"We must know where they are," Andrew said before he hung up. "Dolin has left the Fisher apartment." He turned to me. "He and your little Renner. Both lovebirds. They packed their bags in the dead of night and fled in Fisher's car."

"She may try to reach us."

"Lovebirds," Winters said.

"What about Keogh's surveillance?" Vladimir said.

"He's stayed with them," Andrew said. "They left the city and took the Sunrise Highway east. When they stopped for gas, Keogh's man called in."

"What was the number you gave Keogh?"

"The tower at Floyd Bennett Field," Andrew said. "My defector's in Virginia. We're going to fly there."

"I've never been in an airplane," I said.

Andrew said to me, "The defector will open up to you, a Russian woman. Also he's not feeling well, and he doesn't trust our doctors."

Andrew telephoned to arrange for a car to pick us up, for a plane to be gassed and ready at Floyd Bennett Field, and for a medical bag to be put on board. He gave orders and those at the other end obeyed. Power had settled on Andrew; one felt its tap on the shoulder.

"I'm thinking of Archangel." Vladimir had taken me aside and spoke in Russian, whispering in my ear. "*Lybimaya*, I'm thinking who Archangel is. Who he must be." I saw the worry in Vladimir's eyes, the disbelief and fright. "Dolin is still here," he said. "The murder artist is still here. And Max, why is a creature named Max required for the murder to be done?"

"An injection between the toes," I said. "The others were killed by cyanide gas."

"An injection between the toes," Vladimir whispered. "Who would have the opportunity? Only a doctor or nurse, someone of that sort. Between the toes, the needle mark wouldn't be noticed at once. But it would hurt. Archangel would cry out."

"Not if he had no feeling in his legs."

"Is it possible?" Vladimir whispered. "Is it possible?"

Andrew turned back from the phone. The car was on its way, and would be at the door in minutes.

"In the medical kit," he said, "will you need anything out of the ordinary?"

"Tell me his symptoms."

"Shortness of breath. Palpitations."

"Any pain?"

"In the chest."

"Nitroglycerin. I'll need tablets, 6.5 mg."

We went out to wait for the car and left as soon as it arrived, Andrew seated next to the driver and Vladimir and I in back.

"We're to fly in a bomber," Andrew said. "It's not very comfortable, but it's fast. A B-25, the kind that first bombed Tokyo."

"Is that what we're going to do?"

I made the joke to break the tension, and because I was so frightened. "I've never been in an airplane," I said to Vladimir.

"There's nothing to flying." He had his arm around me. "Except I also have never in my life been in an airplane."

The driver pressed on the gas pedal and without another car in sight we sped over the Manhattan Bridge and through Brooklyn along Flatbush Avenue. When I'd been on emergency duty at the hospital and gone out on ambulance calls, I'd felt the same breathless excitement, racing through traffic lights with the siren screaming. We had no siren, but Andrew's driver took turns on two wheels and ignored traffic lights. As in an ambulance, there was a sense of urgency, of a race between life and death.

It was still dark when we arrived at Floyd Bennett Field, just off Jamaica Bay on the southern end of Brooklyn. We were passed through a guarded gate onto the field itself, and drove around to the front of one of the hangars, where a two-engine plane was being fueled and serviced. There was activity everywhere, jeeps and fuel trucks coming and going, and the steady throb of airplane engines overhead. I stood close to Vladimir, determined not to shiver from cold and fear, and watched a two-engine plane identical to ours bank and turn and wobble in for a heavy landing on the next runway, its undercarriage spraying sparks along the tarmac.

I was given a pair of coveralls and shown a place to put them on, and then we all gathered under the wing of our plane. Its undercarriage was covered with scratches and dents, and even patches of rust; I had previously seen airplanes only at a distance or in photographs, and consequently thought of them as sleek and perfect. But the one we were about to risk our necks in was only a battered and worn machine. I looked over at Vladimir, who smiled and squeezed my hand. He was as frightened as I was, but having him there reassured me. My life, my life as a woman, had begun with him, and I was confident it would end with him, and confident too that the ending was a long way off.

"Don't be afraid," he said.

"You, too."

The hatch under the plane's fuselage opened and Andrew hoisted himself up and on board. I was next and, reaching over my head, took a firm grip on a pair of handles inside the bay and to either side of the open hatch: I used all my strength to lift myself, at the same time swinging my legs up and inside the plane. Another great heave and I was on board, scrambling on the floor of the plane. Vladimir followed, and we were strapped and buckled into parachutes, although I couldn't imagine what I would do if I had to use mine.

The hatch was closed and locked, and the plane began to taxi slowly toward the runway. Because there were no benches or seats, we sat on the folded parachutes, with our legs drawn up. I looked over at Vladimir and pressed his hand again, and just then I felt the plane turn and begin to pick up speed, the engines roaring and the walls around us vibrating and then shaking as if the plane were going to fall apart. I looked out of the window at the ground racing by in a blur. The roar of the engines was deafening, and the plane lifted—incredibly it began to rise from the runway—and when I looked out the window again, the earth was rapidly falling away and the landing gear lifted and locked in place with a terrifying bump.

I had to swallow hard to clear my ears; chewing gum was handed around by one of the Air Force crew, a lovely boy of about nineteen with silver bars on the collar of his shirt, wearing a battered leather jacket and a crushed cap with a hard peak. He politely called me ma'am, and showed me where the toilet was—he called it the head, although he quickly corrected himself: It was the lavatory. He led me by the hand into a gun turret—the machine gun had been removed—and for the first time I looked down on the sea coast of North America from the air.

It was a clear night, perfect for flying, he said, and assured me it would stay that way. I thought he was the handsomest boy I had ever seen.

After a while I came down from the turret and sat on my parachute next to Vladimir. Sandwiches and a Thermos of steaming coffee were passed around.

"What do you know of the defector?" I said.

"Only what Andrew told us," Vladimir said, "and that he's called Mr. Gray."

Andrew had been up front with the pilot and radio operator, and just then left their cabin and made his way half the length of the plane to us. His expression was grave. "Mr. Gray knows who Max is," he said. "We've got to dig it out of him."

Vladimir said, "It's Dolin, isn't it?" He turned to me. "Keogh's man lost him."

"Dolin is a magician," Andrew said. "He's gone up in smoke."

"And Magda?"

"Gone with him," Andrew said.

"To the Fisher house in Montauk?"

"Keogh's man called from there. No sign of them, no warm ashes in the damn grate, no sign of them anywhere," Andrew said.

The plane rolled suddenly, caught in a crosscurrent of air, its nose sailing and then dipping like a ship in heavy sea. I waited for it to steady and listened for the reassuring and unvarying drone of its two engines.

"Dolin has gone to meet Max," Andrew said. "He's gone to wind him up and point him at Archangel."

# sixteen

ONCE HE HAD LOST KEOGH'S MAN ON THE SUNRISE HIGHWAY to Eastern Long Island, Dolin doubled back, keeping to the side streets, and crossed the Queensboro Bridge into Manhattan.

He drove Magda to an all-night movie near Times Square and left her with instructions to meet him under the marquee in an hour.

"I don't want to be left," she said. "Let me come with you."

"One hour," he said. "I'll be back for you."

He drove over to Fifth Avenue and from a pay phone called Claire Balaban, arranging to meet her in Washington Square Park.

"You have a dog, don't you?" he said.

"Yes."

"In ten minutes take him for a walk around the park."

"Is there trouble? You sound worried. What is it?"

"Ten minutes."

Dolin drove down Fifth Avenue to Washington Square and waited on the north side of the park. It was seven minutes since he had hung up on Balaban. In five minutes she walked out of her building near Waverly Place. Ahead of her, tugging on his lead, was a red-and-white cocker spaniel.

Dolin thought: The dog in the photograph of my mother; the dog had belonged to Balaban.

He started the car, cruised slowly until he was next to her, then reached over and opened the passenger door. Balaban lifted the dog and climbed in.

"His name is Valentino," Balaban said.

"I've only got a couple of minutes."

"What is it, Serge? What's the trouble?"

"I want you to stay clear of Julia Winters."

"What do you mean?"

"For the next few days, a week or so, stay clear of her."

"But I'm going away with her. It's all set. I'm supposed to meet her in a couple of hours."

"And go to Warm Springs?"

"How did you know?"

184

"That doesn't matter," Dolin said. "Stay clear of her. Didn't you tell me you weren't feeling well, that you might need an operation?"

"My gall bladder," she said. "It sometimes bothers me, but it's not serious."

"Today is a good day for a gall bladder attack," he said. "Call your doctor. Tell him you're not feeling well. Describe the symptoms for gall bladder. Get him to check you into the hospital."

"An alibi," she said.

"Just so."

"But I promised Julia I'd go with her to Warm Springs. She's arranged for me to do a portrait of FDR, a commission I've been trying to get for years. If I don't show up—"

"Please don't argue," Dolin said, reaching across her to work the latch on the passenger door. "Have a gall bladder attack today. Call your doctor."

"What does it mean, Serge?"

"Good-by." He squeezed her hand. "Good-by, Tante Claire."

"If I'm Tante Claire, then give me an explanation"

"You know that can't be done."

"What are they up to, those devils in Moscow? What now, Serge?"

"Go on," he said. "Stay away from Warm Springs. Look after yourself."

"Are you part of it? Are you one of them still?" She looked at him closely, her narrow eyes touching each of his features, as if memorizing them. Slowly she shook her head, touched his shoulder, and finally turned away, climbing out of the car with Valentino.

She watched Dolin drive off, and continued her walk, completing the circumference of Washington Square Park.

She had been waiting two years for a chance to do a portrait of President Roosevelt. It was an opportunity not to be missed.

But what of Serge's warning? She had been in America a long time, and in spite of her contacts, Moscow seemed a long way off. She had long ago stopped believing in them and was no longer afraid of them. She was too old to be afraid of anyone.

"Well what about it, Valentino? Should I go to Warm Springs or have a gall bladder?"

It's nothing for an old lady to talk to her dog, Balaban thought, the danger is when the dog answers. But the good Valentino only sniffed at the curb and left Balaban to make up her own mind.

Julia is my friend, she thought, exactly as Serge's mother was. I couldn't help her, my darling Larisa Sergeyevna, but at least I can stick close to Julia.

And to Valentino she said, "Damn those devils in Moscow. Damn them."


When Dolin returned to the theater on Times Square, Magda was waiting for him under the marquee. They drove west and left Manhattan by way of the Lincoln Tunnel. From there they drove south along the New Jersey shore in the direction of Atlantic City.

About an hour out of New York, they pulled off the road and stopped at a diner for breakfast. Next to the diner was a service station where Dolin had the tires and oil checked; and while the gas tank was filling, thanks to ration stamps provided by Fisher, he took a roadmap of the northeastern United States from a rack near the register and spread it on the hood of the car for a careful look. Magda stood beside him, nearly as tall as he, with her hand on his shoulder. She whispered something to him and smoothed his hair with the palm of her free hand. He spoke to her directly and earnestly, not taking his eyes from hers. He was persuading her of something. But she shook her head and her lips formed the word *no*. When he went on she looked away, and when she looked back and raised her eyes there were tears in them, and a soft radiance in her face, and she nodded, allowing herself to be persuaded.

Another car pulled into the station, the driver touching his horn for service. A scruffy dog raised his head, stretched, yawned, and ambled stiff-legged from the service bay.

"I should have kept it to myself," Magda said. "The responsibility isn't yours, it's mine."

"It's not so. You can't believe that."

"I shouldn't have told you," she said. "I swore I wouldn't, and even had a plan worked out. I was going to let you go to Mexico alone, and if later on, when you were safe, you got in touch with me, I'd have met you someplace."

"And what would you have done in the meantime?"

"Stayed with friends in Canada," she said. "They're the kind to ask no questions and to keep things to themselves. Another thing—where they live it's remote."

"And what about money?"

"I have a little," she said. "And my friends would look after me."

"I won't be able to get in touch with you for a few months, maybe a

186

year," he said. "There may be a lot of trouble, and you'll hear all sorts of stories. But if I don't do my job, if I run now, they'll send somebody after me. Then we won't have a chance."

"So you have to be on your way," she said. "Why not say good-by here? There must be a bus station north . . ."

"I'm going to drive you to Canada."

"It's too far," she said. "There's not enough time."

"I don't want to say good-by here. Not yet."

"The longer you wait, the greater the risk," she said. "You told me that yourself."

"I'm going to drive you to the border," he said. "That way, we can have a couple of days—you and I."

"A couple of days together?" she said. "Is it really possible, Serge?"

"Sure, why not?" he said.

"I know a place to go. It's on the way to Canada, and quite romantic, near Niagara Falls."

She folded the map and waited in the car while he changed two dollars into silver and made a long distance phone call. He spoke briefly, only a couple of words, and hung up. Almost immediately, the pay phone rang. This time he spoke a bit longer.

When he had finished, he bought a package of cigarettes and a Coca-Cola for Magda, and they pulled out of the station, heading northwest.

They drove steadily the rest of the morning, stopping only for gas—Fisher had supplied plenty of ration stamps—and sometime in the early afternoon arrived in Scranton, Pennsylvania.

Fisher earlier had rented a deposit box in the vault of the First Farmers' Bank of Scranton. The box was in his name, but Dolin was authorized to enter it, and his was one of the signatures on the rental agreement. The box contained five thousand dollars in twenty-dollar bills, a .38 Smith and Wesson revolver, and a valid Canadian passport, with Dolin's picture, made out in the name of Etienne Terrelle. While Magda shopped for food to eat in the car, Dolin emptied the box, and within half an hour they were back on the road, heading toward Buffalo, New York.

They ate lunch in the car and spoke little as the hours on the road passed. Magda slept. When she awakened, she watched him without him knowing. She studied the details of his face, his profile as he drove, and it was as if she had never seen him before; two days more together was all they had, and she realized that after she left him this time she might never see him again. There was nothing but to live every moment intensely, to remember every detail, and in that way make the two days last all her life.

She closed her eyes again, and a Russian tune came into her mind—something he had taught her, and she began unconsciously to hum it. When he heard her, he smiled and held out his hand, which she pressed to her lips.

"I stayed in a nice hotel near the falls," she said. "An old place called the Niagara."

"Shall we stay there tonight?"

"Yes."

"I'll call ahead for a room."

"There's no need. It was nearly empty."

"The secret you told me," he said, *"the great secret* you told me. Is it true?"

"I think so."

"But you're not sure?"

"Not sure," she said coyly. "But a little bit sure."

"Before I leave, I want to be positive."

Magda said, "I've been thinking of Irina. If it's definite, I want her to know. And if I need help, I can count on her."

"I don't know about her," Serge said.

"She's my friend, and also she's a doctor. I may need her, you know."

"Wait until you're safely in Canada," Serge said. "A month, maybe two. Get yourself settled in with your friends there. What's their name?"

"Heller."

"And you'll be safe there?"

"They can be counted on," she said.

"Are you tired?"

"No, I had a good nap."

"I'm told you sleep a lot, particularly the first few months."

"Do you want a boy or a girl?"

"I don't know. I can't quite imagine it."

"Neither can I," she said. "But perhaps I will later on."

"I pray it's not hard for you," he said. "And I regret that I can't be with you."

It was nearly dark when they arrived in Buffalo, and had to ask the way to the Niagara. By the time they found it and checked in, they were worn out, but the room was what they hoped it would be and what they needed for the two days they had together. There was hot water for baths after the long drive and a canopied bed with a down quilt set before a fireplace. The central heating had broken down, but they were given plenty of split hardwood logs, all cut to the same length and stacked on the fireplace apron. There was venison for dinner and red wine that was cool, as if drawn from a cask in the cellar; it was served in a bottle without a label, but tasted of fruit, like new burgundy.

Dolin discovered a phonograph in a room just off the lobby, and very good records. He called it a treasure: Josep Hofmann playing the *Waldstein Sonata*, and Rachmaninoff, the master, playing Liszt. There was a blazing fire and glasses of cognac to drink while the north wind howled and rattled the windows.

They saw no other guests, no one at all but the waitress at dinner. Magda claimed the Niagara was enchanted. In their bedroom, the fire had been laid, needing only a match to set it blazing.

"It was done by an invisible hand," Magda said. "Could it be a ghost?"

"I think so," Dolin said. "I think a ghost for sure."

They spent the night under the down quilt in each other's arms, and in the morning the ashes from the hardwood logs were still warm, and the ghost who laid the fire also knocked on the door with the morning tea. When Magda opened the door, there was no one there, and when she peered along the hallway of the old building, its leaning walls covered with Dutch blue paper, there was no one; from around the corner at the far end, she heard a footstep on the polished floor, a shadow for an instant on the wall, and the hurried slam of a door.

"The tea cart is here," she said. "But not the person who brought it."

"Is it the ghost again?"

"The tea is hot," she said.

She pushed the cart into the room and prepared a cup with no cream and lots of sugar, and served it to him in bed.

"Aren't you having a cup?"

"I'll share yours."

"You said I take too much sugar."

"I love you, Serge."

"Just now? Have you just made up your mind? Love isn't a fact, you know."

"Of course it's a fact."

"It's an emotion, like any other. It comes and goes."

"It doesn't come and go with me," she said. "All night I was thinking that I'm with Serge and I love Serge. When I was asleep it was the same—I'm with Serge and I love Serge."

"And no thought of what comes later?"

"No." She had left the bed and was standing with her back to him, looking out the window at the partially frozen, brownish lawn which still showed traces of snow. "I don't think at all of what comes later," she said.

After breakfast, Magda looked up the address of an obstetrician and was able to get an appointment that morning. He examined her and confirmed that she was pregnant.

Dolin had driven her to the doctor's office, but parked at the end of the street and waited there.

"When did he say to expect it?" he said, after she had joined him in the car.

"The middle of December."

"A long way yet."

"I want to have the baby, Serge."

"And your friends in Canada, you're sure they'll understand?"

"I'm sure." Her voice rose. "I'm absolutely sure."

"And not ask a lot of questions?"

"I told you, they mind their own business. They won't ask who the father is, and I won't tell them. You've nothing to worry about." The tension had been building in her all morning. "I told you, you've not a damn thing to worry about," she said.

He started up the car motor, but let it idle. He turned so as to face her and extended his arm along the top of the seat. "I don't blame you for being angry," he said. "We can talk about love all day long, but the hard truth is you're going to have a baby and go off alone on the bus."

"And what about you?" she said. "You have an assignment. A soldier, isn't that what you said? You sleep with one eye open, like a soldier."

Slowly, he said, "I have no choice."

"No choice? If you have no choice, then go now. I don't need you to put me on a bus or to hold my hand. I don't need you at all. You're a soldier, and I'm a refugee who knows very well how to get by on her own."

"I'm not a soldier out of zeal," he said. "Or even out of loyalty, and not out of ambition either. One time yes, but not now, not for a long time."

"You've told me all of it before," she said. "If you back out now, they'll try to kill you."

"And you too," he said. "They'll come looking for you in order to find out what I've confided in you." He moved his hand from the back of the seat to her shoulder. "I've money hidden, enough for us to live on for a while," he said. "A cold passport, one for me; I'll get another for you. When I settle in a safe place, I'll get word to you. At your friends' in Canada—"

"Take me back to the hotel," she said. "It was awful with that doctor poking around inside of me. Take me back, I want to sleep."

"What is it, that you don't believe me?"

"Yes, I believe you. You're going to get me a passport. You've got lots of money hidden, and we're going to have a terrific time. I can hardly wait." She turned in the seat, facing him. "You want to hear the truth, Serge. I don't believe any of it, not a word. When we say good-by, I'm going to try to forget you. You're one man, Serge. There'll be another, and after that another." He listened with his eyes lowered and without responding. He set his jaw and endured. He endured, stoically, as one does a whipping, her words falling like a lash across his back. She said, "You want to stay alive, you'll do what you have to do in order to stay alive. Well, so will I. Do you understand, Serge? I'm going to Canada to have the baby because I want him to have a chance. He must have a fair chance."

"Yes, he must." Serge managed to raise his eyes at Magda and with that loving, hopeful, and pathetic look to try again to win her over. "*He* must or *she* must," he said. "And we must also have our chance. Our chance, for love's sake—"

She interrupted him. "It's only an emotion, no different from any other. Isn't that what you said? Love comes and goes."

"One says a lot of things—all sorts of things, some true, some not. I don't want to leave you. Does that mean I love you? I think so. Yes, it must be so. I don't want to leave you and I love you, Magda."

"Do you know how we got started, you and I?" she said. "They promised me an American residency and told me to be at that party. Do you know that?"

"Yes."

"I agreed to spy on you."

"I know."

"You've known all along?"

"From the first."

"Then why have you taken me this far?"

"Because I couldn't leave you."

191

He took his hand from her shoulder and started up the car, driving toward the hotel. After a couple of blocks, he made a sudden turn.

"Where are we going?" she said.

"We haven't seen the falls."

"It's raining, and there's a heavy mist. We won't be able to see a thing."

"And besides," he said, "it's only a bloody lot of water."

She had to laugh; in spite of herself, Serge made her laugh. He drove her out to the falls, where there were gusts of wind so strong that the park rangers had put up a red warning flag and guard ropes to keep visitors back, allowing them to see the falls only from a distance.

Serge took her hand and they walked bent into the wind, the falls thundering around them. No other tourists had come out in the bad weather, and there was nothing to be seen in the rain and mist, not even trees or shrubs near the path leading to the falls; nothing stirred but the red warning flag tied to the guide ropes, left there to flap in the wind. They saw no one on the path or on the road, no one at all on the other side of the river, and farther along no one in the blue shadows at the edge of the woods. As in the Hotel Niagara, an air of enchantment hung over the place.

They didn't stay long; it was cold and wet, and soon they got into the car and drove back to town. Serge found a bar and ordered two double whiskeys and they watched a man play solitary billiards. He was an expert player with a specially made cue who had been playing in shirtsleeves and a scarlet waistcoat, but when Magda came in he respectfully put on his coat.

Magda smiled at him, and he bowed to her, and Serge asked if he could buy him a drink. He accepted, and then bought them drinks, and asked Serge if he played billiards.

"I'm not in your league," Serge said.

"We can knock the balls around."

Magda enjoyed drinking her whiskey and watching them play. Serge was good, but not nearly so good as the man with the scarlet waistcoat.

After a couple of games, he thanked Serge, unscrewed his cue, and packed it in a leather case with a scarlet lining, the same shade as his waistcoat.

When they were alone again, Serge ordered another drink. Magda said, "I liked watching you play, you and that classy gent."

"His name is Jimmy Little," the waitress said. "He's a professional. He gives exhibitions and plays all comers, but nobody ever beats him."

The waitress served fresh drinks, and when she had gone Magda said, "Watching men play billiards, that's what girlfriends do?"

"My darling girlfriend," he said.

"We could have met a long time ago," she said. "We could have had a nice romance. We were living in Paris at the same time, not far from each other. We could have met there."

"We could have met at a café," Serge said. "The Lily, or George's. Any one of them around St. Michel or Rue Dauphin."

"Or at a dance hall," she said. "I went often with Irina, and I was quite brazen there—in fact, a flirt—and made it my business to dance with the best-looking guys. I would have caught your eye. I can just see Serge, the tough guy, the man of mystery, looking over the girls." She was able to mimic him, to cock her head to the side as he did, and to imitate his voice and accent, and his hoarse rolling French. "Well, that's a nice-looking piece over there. I'll send her flowers, a bunch of red roses—that ought to knock the dopey kid off her feet." She poked him with her elbow and gave him a loud kiss. "Isn't it so, Serge? A good-looking piece, eh? That's what you thought at the Danube."

"That's what I thought."

"Maybe okay between the sheets, am I right?"

"That's what I thought."

"And now?"

"Now, I'm sure of it."

She gave him another poke with her elbow, and he kissed her and told her that he wished they had met in Paris, for he would have had a longer time to love her.

"Tomorrow, I'll go one way and you another," she said. "I've got a long ride, a lot of time to stare out the window of the bus. I'll be unhappy, and worried that I'll never see you again, but I don't regret loving you. And even getting pregnant, I don't regret that either. People say they love each other and want to live together forever, but mostly they talk a lot of crap."

"We don't talk a lot of crap," he said.

"Maybe after all, in the end, we'll wind up together."

"Six months," he said. "Maybe a year. But we'll make it."

"We'll keep our fingers crossed," she said.

"The kitchen closes in five minutes," the waitress said, "if you want something to eat."

But they wanted nothing to eat, and no more to drink. They wanted only to be alone and in private, and as soon as they were—in their room at the Niagara—they embraced and hurriedly undressed;

their actions were desperate, even frenzied. Lovemaking had been measured and sensual, with Serge skillful and Magda compliant. Now something unpremeditated was let loose. Love strained and came with a rush and then a pause as if they'd fainted; and they loved again, and slept awhile, a refreshing and contented sleep, and woke only after nightfall; the furniture in the dark room, those commonplace shapes, seemed strange and ominous.

They bathed, dressed, and went down to dinner. In the lobby Serge replayed the Rachmaninoff records, and when they returned to their room, again the grate had been swept and the fire laid, and still they saw no one.

Magda was exhausted and went off to sleep, dreaming of ice skating on a lake in the woods near the house she had grown up in. She was in the middle of the lake, which was so huge she couldn't see the shore, like an ocean frozen over. In the dream she was cold, although the sun was shining and her mother told her it was spring. Suddenly, she heard a crack like a pistol shot, but louder, much louder, and the ice moved under the blades of her skates. The ice had cracked, it was cracking all around her.

She woke up, sweating and terrified, and it took her a second or two to realize she had been dreaming and wasn't going to drown. But she was able to fall back to sleep, and when she finally awoke, it was morning and Serge was already up and dressing in the bathroom.

She lay in bed, collecting her thoughts. The light coming through the window was without promise or hope; it meant only that the day had come in which she was to be parted from Serge.

They drank coffee in the dining room, and while Serge checked out and paid the bill, a car pulled up and a couple with two children and a pet cat in a carrying box checked in. A porter came through a door half hidden by a Chinese screen; he was a dour old man with tattooed forearms, and Magda wondered if it were he who had brought the tea cart, cleaned out the grate, and laid the fire both nights in their room.

Serge brought the car around, put in their bags, and drove to the bus station. He bought her a ticket and gave her an envelope with a thousand dollars.

"There'll be more later on," he said. "I'll get it to you."

"I'll be all right," she said. "I don't need anything. I've been happy with you." She felt the tears rise, and fought to hold them back, but they came anyway. She clutched him and said, "Let me come with you."

"I can't."

"I don't want to leave you. I don't care about anything else. Nothing else matters. Nothing, Serge, but being with you."

The bus appeared at the end of the road. He said, "It's not the end of us."

She shook her head, as if to clear it, and dried her eyes with the back of her sleeve. She didn't remember saying good-by. She supposed they did; she supposed they kissed. She remembered getting out of the car and walking quickly across the road, carrying her own bag. She made it a point not to look back. She gave her ticket to the driver and found a seat on the bus. She didn't wave, and doubted that he could see her through the narrow window of the darkened bus. She reached up to put her bag in the rack above her seat, and when she next looked through the window, Serge was inside the car. When he started the engine, there was a puff of exhaust from the tailpipe, and she watched through the bus window as he drove away.

# seventeen

AFTER HE LEFT MAGDA IN THE BUS STATION AND WAS ON THE road south, Serge drove as fast as he could without attracting the attention of the highway patrol. He had arranged to meet Max at eight the next morning, eight hundred miles away in a town called Buchanan, just north of Lynchburg, Virginia.

He intended to drive the rest of the day and most of the night. Max was scared. He wouldn't stay long in Buchanan. If he arrived and Serge wasn't on hand to meet him, he'd bolt.

Serge had met Max only once before, in the lobby of the Astor Hotel on Broadway, near Times Square in New York City. Mr. Gray had brought him.

The lobby of the Astor had been filled with people coming and going, servicemen and women; it was a landmark and a meeting place known to most visitors to New York. Serge picked it because they wouldn't be noticed. But Max was uneasy; crowds made him nervous. Serge thought him high-strung and suspicious, a man of biting discontents, perhaps unstable. Mr. Gray moved deftly to calm him. He knew exactly how; in his long career, Mr. Gray had recruited many like Max, who stood with the despised and the humiliated.

Mr. Gray suggested they go to a place around the corner. Max would be more comfortable there. It turned out to be a Spanish bar with food so awful that few people came, and the room was so gloomy that those who did could hardly be seen.

But Mr. Gray was right, and Max relaxed in the awful Spanish bar. He ordered two quick drinks, and asked for a third. His fondness for drink was noted in his file; Serge had read it. Max drank too much, and had a risky preference for boys and very young men. He was Finnish, and had walked into the Soviet embassy in January of 1940 looking for information on the whereabouts of his mother and sister. During the Finnish-Soviet war, they had lived in a part of Finland overrun by the Red Army, and had been removed to the Soviet Union.

In the embassy, Max spoke first to a security guard, and then to a clerk, who copied down his real name, his address in Washington, and the names of his sister and mother. The clerk had been taught never to turn away a walk-in with ties in the Soviet Union, to start a file on everyone, and to ask two key questions.

"When did you first come to America?"

"1932."

"Are you an American citizen?"

Max's answer was yes; he was an American citizen, and he had strong ties in the Soviet Union. The next question wasn't asked: How could Max be used? The clerk turned Max over to the embassy political officer, who began by asking Max his profession.

"I'm a masseur. I work at the Metropolitan Club." It was said proudly. The Metropolitan was the most prestigious men's club in Washington, its members some of the most important men in business and government.

Until then, the political officer hadn't thought Max of much value, but with the mention of the Metropolitan Club he took a closer look. It had dawned on him that he might have turned up something rare and precious, something to further his career—a useful walk-in.

"Were you trained in Finland?"

"No. I was a seaman. I studied massage here."

"In Washington?"

"In Boston. I worked there for a while, but it wasn't so good, the pay. A friend recommended me to the manager of the Metropolitan, and I got the job."

"Do you make your living from massage?"

"What do you mean?" When suspicious, Max had a nasty squint; he was a fair, bony man with a long, somber face. The political officer thought he looked like a horse, and he had already picked up his homosexuality. Max said, "How else should I make my living?"

"I meant another kind of work. You seem to me an ambitious man. Intelligent."

"I want to do physical therapy," Max said slowly.

"That requires more training, doesn't it?"

"Yes. School is required, and a certificate. I want to go at night, but of course it costs plenty of money."

The political officer took all the personal information Max could supply about his sister and mother. A promise was given to investigate. The officer put a friendly arm on Max's shoulder. He had his valuable walk-in—a foot up in his career, he was sure of it.

That same afternoon, a report was sent to Moscow Central, and with it a request to follow up on Max. Two weeks passed. It is not known who in Moscow opened the file on Max, who read it, and how

197

much higher it went. It is said that eventually it was shown to Stalin himself. It is said that Stalin himself recognized Max's value. Earlier he had summoned Mr. Gray from his dungeon, earlier he had forgiven him, returned his medals and former rank, restored him to grace, and had him slipped back into the United States. Now Max was given to Mr. Gray.

Max's sister was located in Gorki, and Mr. Gray showed Max a letter from her. She was well; mother was ill, but recovering in a clinic. The Soviet state was looking after Max's dear old mother, providing the best of care. In addition, Max was given money—he demanded money—and was enrolled in school. In due course he got his certificate and was registered as a nurse and physiotherapist. A Soviet agent buried deep inside the White House was asked to help arrange a job for Max. It took time, it took skill, but it was done. Max replaced one of the four therapists who regularly treated President Roosevelt.

It was said that when Stalin heard the news of Max's success, he drank a toast to Mr. Gray. Deep inside the Kremlin, nothing stirred him but deceit; Stalin trusted only his spies: Truth was never given, he had learned, only stolen.


From the bus station in Buffalo near Niagara Falls, Dolin had driven all day, stopping only to gas and service the car and quench his thirst with bottles of Coca-Cola kept in chests of melting ice near the registers where he paid for the gas. The deeper into the night he drove, the farther south, the less ice and the warmer the Coke. Toward morning he pulled into an all-night truck stop for food. Stretching his legs in a booth, a mug of hot coffee between his hands, he closed his eyes and saw the road rushing toward him, the stunning glare of headlights from oncoming cars. He opened his burning eyes, closed them wearily, and heard Russian spoken. The waitress had said something to the only other patron, a trucker sucking his coffee from a mug with the spoon still in it.

But of course they hadn't spoken Russian; Dolin had imagined it, or perhaps had dozed off for a second or two and dreamed it.

He smiled guiltily at the waitress, who said, "Beats me why you boys kill yourselves driving all night."

Dolin ordered more coffee, bacon and fried eggs, a stack of pancakes. The waitress told him Buchanan was just a couple of miles down the road.

He was ahead of Max by a few hours.

He glanced at a large wall calendar. April 11. There was time to relax, enjoy his breakfast. He was hungry enough, but when it came, he couldn't eat it. The waitress looked insulted and wanted to know if anything was wrong.

"The eggs are good," she said. "Fresh laid."

Dolin nibbled at his breakfast, forced himself to swallow some of it. He was to do nothing out of the ordinary, nothing that would cause her to remember him.

There was only one hotel in Buchanan, the Hubbard House it was called, a handsome clapboard building with a wide porch and freshly painted rockers. Dolin smelled the fresh-mowed grass and noticed beads of moisture condensed on the cool metal screen of the door to the lobby.

Dolin rang for the clerk, who came out of the back room, his hair wet and freshly combed, his skin smelling of citronella. Dolin gave his name as Brown, asked for a room, and was given the key to number 8 on the second floor. He told the clerk he was expecting a visitor, and asked that he be sent up. Dolin had practiced the sentence "I'm expecting a visitor; please call me when he comes." He pronounced it like an American, one who had grown up in Virginia or possibly a little farther north. He wasn't to sound foreign or to stand too long under the clerk's gaze. The man who met Max in the Hubbard Hotel in Virginia on April 11 must not be remembered.

But there were complications, problems impossible to anticipate. "I can't call up, sir," the clerk said. "No telephones in the rooms." The clerk was young enough to be in the armed services, but one arm was shorter than the other, the hand deformed. He hid it well, and Dolin hadn't immediately noticed it. The clerk said, "There's one in the hall on the second floor. I can call you on that."

Dolin thanked him, already turning away, averting his face and carrying his bag across the lobby to the stairs. "It won't be necessary to call; just send him up, please."

"Give the dining room an hour," the clerk called after Dolin. "They're just setting up for breakfast."

The door of number 8 locked from the inside. Dolin unpacked his clothes and shaving gear. Fisher had given him a letter prepared in Moscow, written in Finnish by Max's sister, who was kept in a cell in Lubyanka. Dolin folded the letter and put it in his pocket and spread everything else on the bed and took inventory: the vials of hydrogen cyanide, each wrapped in cotton; the box of Swiss-made hollow needles and syringes—all of it untraceable, brought secretly into America by Fisher's apparat. There was also a folded canvas bag, which Dolin had bought for ninety-nine cents in Macy's, and four thousand dollars of the five thousand he'd taken from the bank in Scranton. He unloaded, cleaned, and reloaded the revolver. He examined the cold Canadian passport: Etienne Terrelle had been born in the town of St. Boniface in Manitoba Province on January 12, 1906. The photograph was of Dolin, but the history of Etienne Terrelle, his habits, quirks, and tastes, those waited to be invented. Etienne Terrelle was to be created, and he had to be a very different man from Serge Dolin. There were to be no links between the two. Dolin's history was to end in Buchanan, Virginia, on April 11, 1945. And Etienne Terrelle? His life would begin shortly, but in a different place, another man with another history.

Dolin lined the canvas bag with toilet tissue, packed it with the vials of hydrogen cyanide, the Swiss hollow needles and syringes, and a thousand dollars in cash, and closed the zipper. The Terrelle passport and the remaining three thousand dollars went into his large suitcase—the revolver he slipped into his jacket pocket.

It was six-thirty, an hour and a half before Max was due. Dolin showered, shaved, changed his clothes, and stretched out fully dressed on the bed. When he closed his eyes, his inner lids burned and he couldn't sleep. He tried not to think of Magda or of the room they had shared in the Niagara. He thought instead of the man in the scarlet waistcoat with whom he had played billiards; when Magda came into the bar, he had put on his coat. A gentleman, Dolin thought, and tried to retrieve the name, but instead glimpsed Magda's face in desolate profile through the bus window.

His thoughts trailed off then; he was in the country in winter outside of Moscow, crossing a frozen field near a peasant's hut, smoke curling from its chimney. As he fell asleep, he saw one-legged Yakov and the black dog asleep beside his chair.

There was a knock on the door. Dolin woke with a start: 8:06.

Max was as Dolin remembered him—tall, broad, fair-haired, with long, sinewy arms and immense hands dangling from the ends of bony wrists. He covered Dolin's hand with his own and wrung Dolin's awkwardly, as if it were a bell. He was unused to shaking hands, and grunted by way of greeting, then took away his heavy hand, his eyes darting nervously around the hotel room. Odd eyes they were, the irises translucent blue, the pupils enlarged, black, cautious.

He hardly spoke, managing a word at a time in his heavily accented English, and always with his eyes elsewhere. He wanted to know about his mother and sister. Dolin gave him the letter and he took it in his great hands; he stared at it for several seconds before opening it carefully, as if to preserve the envelope, and sat on the edge of the bed to read it. Dolin watched him from across the room. The letter had been composed in Moscow, written first in Russian, its contents approved by Colonel Borodinov, before being translated into Finnish and given to Max's sister to copy.

"I don't know about this," Max said. "It doesn't sound like Lisi, not so much."

"What does she say?"

"Mother is better. First pneumonia, but now in a sanatorium in Yalta. Lisi works in a truck factory in Gorki and has applied to a hairdressing school after the war."

"Isn't that what she wants?"

"It was her ambition," Max said. "When small, she was cutting pictures from magazines. It is a good profession, do you think?"

"It's very useful," Serge said.

"And good pay. Very good. I think after the war women will want to dress up and have hair that looks nice."

"Does she want to go back to Finland?"

"No. She and my mother promise to come to America, and Lisi then opens a shop."

Once Max had done his job, the sister would be heard from no more. The mother was already dead. Dolin stood before the window, his arms folded, the morning sun warming his back. The man with whom he'd played billiards was named Jimmy Little. The name had risen like a cork to the surface of his mind.

"It costs plenty of money," Max said. "Good plumbing, the hair dryers, and rent, all that costs money."

"A lot of money," Serge said.

"And the steamship tickets, also a lot of money."

"It'll be difficult."

"But after I do my job?" For the first time, the pale blue eyes fastened on Serge. "If I do my job?"

"I don't know. It'll be difficult to do. Your end of it, I mean."

"I can do it."

"If you do, we'll manage to bring her here."

"And my mother?"

"Yes, her too."

"And the money for a hairdressing shop?"

201

"All of it," Dolin said.

Dolin showed him the canvas bag from Macy's, the syringes and vials of hydrogen cyanide, and gave him the thousand dollars, which Max slowly counted.

"You know how to use the newspaper code," Dolin said. "We'll keep in touch through that."

"You'll be the one I meet?"

"Yes, of course."

"And the rest of the money?"

"Afterward."

"He's sick, you know," Max said. "Maybe dying. You only have to wait."

"We can't wait."

"I'm on duty tomorrow morning," Max said. "The twelfth."

"Do it tomorrow."

"I need ration stamps," Max said. "It took a lot of gas to get here, and now I have to drive back to Warm Springs."

Dolin had extra ration stamps. Max took them, and left with the money and the canvas bag. From the window of his room, Dolin watched him come out of the hotel and cross the main street of the town, the canvas bag like a toy dangling from the hooked fingers of his right hand. His car was an old coupe, dusty from the country roads, and he had to crank it by hand to start, and made a great racket driving out of town.

Dolin came away from the window. After he'd packed his things, he went over the room with a wad of paper torn from the toilet roll. Not a fingerprint, nothing of himself or Max, was to be left behind. Serge Dolin no longer existed. The sister in the cell in Lubyanka would be shot. By tomorrow Archangel would be dead. After Max responded to the newspaper advertisement, he'd be surprised by two of Stalin's gunmen. Dolin turned out the light and closed the room door. Nothing connected to Archangel would survive. Nothing.

# eighteen

WE HAD FLOWN FROM FLOYD BENNETT IN NEW YORK TO A military airport in Maryland, a hundred or so miles from the town of Buchanan, landing on the morning of April 11, at about the same time as Serge Dolin's meeting with Max.

The car that was supposed to meet our plane was late. Winters was furious, and started making phone calls. But we had to wait hours in an unheated Quonset hut before a car finally arrived, and then the driver didn't know the way to the mountain cabin in which Winters had hidden Mr. Gray. We got lost on back roads, some of which didn't appear on our map, and stopped repeatedly to ask directions. Vladimir and I exchanged glances over Andrew's head—the poor man had hidden Mr. Gray so well that he couldn't find him—but of course we kept quiet. The mood in the car was grim. We had lost track of Dolin—and as for Max, our only hope of locating him was through Mr. Gray.

We found the cabin finally, just before dark, and it seemed an attractive place, built of fieldstone and logs, with a cozy plume of wood smoke rising from a brick chimney. To get to it we had to pass through an electrically operated gate at the end of an unpaved road. Two cars were parked nearby in a clearing laid with gravel, and we were made to identify ourselves to a man who came out of the shadows on the front porch. He was cut from the same cloth as our driver, an American in a business suit and a fedora hat, a big fellow with a close-cropped military look to him.

There was just enough light to make out two more men, deeper in the woods behind the house, patrolling with rifles slung over their shoulders. With all that protection, it seemed odd that Mr. Gray would be alone in the house. But that was the way he wanted it. "Guards are a waste of time," he said. "All guards have guns that point both ways." Mr. Gray believed only in secrecy. It was his one weapon. "If I were to be given one wish," he said, "can you guess what it would be?" His greeting to Andrew Winters had been cold, even rude, and Vladimir had been ignored altogether. He repeated the question to me in Russian, and made it a challenge. "Are you able to guess what my wish is?"

"I can't guess."

"I was told about a Russian woman, a doctor, who passed messages and lived once in Zurich. Is it you?"

"Yes."

"Try to guess my one wish."

"Is it to know everyone's secret?"

"That's a doctor's wish," he said. "My profession is spy, and so my wish is to be invisible." He laughed, flashing false teeth. "A spy's wish is to see and not be seen." He had begun to cough, a bad cough from deep in his chest.

"Tell me about that cough," I said. "How long have you had it?"

"A couple of weeks, something like that."

"From the look of you, you're running a fever as well," I said. "Come in the other room, I'm going to examine you."

I was firm with Mr. Gray, authoritative, as I sometimes was with children in the wards.

"Come along," I said. "I'll see what's wrong, and make you feel better."

He did as he was told, and followed me meekly into a bedroom. When I closed the door behind us, he turned and took hold of my hand, looking straight into my eyes. "I want to trust you," he said. "But can I? Even though you are a good Russian woman—that's what I heard about you: 'Trust her, she's a good Russian woman.'" His hand was dry and hot and his eyes feverish. "I went to the Americans, to Winters. I went to tell them what I know, and they were to help me disappear, to become invisible. But now I have had second thoughts and have begun to hate what I've done."

"But before you went to the Americans, you must have thought about it," I said. "I'm sure it wasn't an easy decision. For what you've done, there must be a good reason."

"A good reason? Oh, yes, I have a good reason."

"What is it?" I said. "Will you tell me what it is?"

"My reason for defecting?" he said, turning it over in his mind. "I'm to tell that to a Russian, a sympathetic woman, a doctor."

"It's true," I said. "It was thought you'd talk more easily to me."

"Confide in you?"

"Yes."

He drew himself up and gathered the last of his pride and strength. "Why should I confide in you, in anybody?" he said.

"You have a secret; it's best to get it off your chest," I said. "I know how it is. You see Stalin and the rest of them clearly, you probably have for a long time. But they've been your life, the *idea* has been your life."

"The *idea* has been my life," he said bitterly. "The future. I've been a Communist from the beginning, from the first days. The *idea* was the Communist idea, and without it there was no future and no hope.

"I've closed my eyes to the crimes because they were necessary, and the lies and betrayals because they were necessary, and the murders—all necessary. So I closed my eyes, and made excuses, and kept on. But now, now . . ."

"And now?"

He looked up, his eyes red, as if with tears, and said, "Am I a traitor?"

"No."

"The *idea* isn't false," he said. "It still hasn't been proved false."

He shook his head and sat heavily on the edge of the bed. No doubt he also had been guilty of crimes, and had done his share of murders. But if now he was disgusted by what he had done, and what he had helped others do, if now his conscience tormented him, it was because there was some good in him.

"You'd better get into bed," I said. "Undress in the bathroom. Have you pajamas?"

"Yes, but they didn't give me a robe."

"I'll get you one."

"A wool robe," he said. "See it's a wool robe."

"After you're in bed, I'll examine you."

"I'm very tired."

"So am I. Come along."

I took his hand as if he were a child, and he followed me as far as the bathroom door; but something made him pause, and then stubbornly shake his head and refuse to take another step.

"What's today's date?" he said.

"April 11."

"It's too late," he said. "Nothing can be done."

"Too late?" I said. "Are you talking about Archangel?"

He jumped back; he acted as if I'd given him an electric shock. "What do you know about it?"

"Why is it too late? What's happened?"

"Dolin was to meet Max on the morning of the eleventh."

"Where? Who is Max? There's no time to lose. Tell me what you know."

Again he shook his head, and folded his arms, and refused to answer any of my questions. He complained of being tired; he was ill, cold, and hungry. He demanded something warm to eat. He demanded a wool robe. He turned away and went into the bathroom, firmly closing the door behind him.

Andrew waited for me outside the bedroom door, and he and Vladimir followed me into the kitchen.

"What has he told you?" Andrew said.

"Very little."

"You were with him nearly an hour," Andrew said. "Damn it, we don't know what's going on. I've been on the phone with Keogh, and there's no trace of Dolin—Fisher either. They've both disappeared."

"Andrew doesn't want to bring in the FBI," Vladimir said. "There are too many reasons to distrust them."

"I can't contact FDR either," Andrew said. "I won't have him thinking I've lost control."

I caught Vladimir's eye, and said, "Dolin and Max met this morning."

Andrew turned on me. "For God's sake, where?"

"I don't know."

"Mr. Gray knows."

"I need time with him."

"Cat and mouse," Vladimir said. "Let Irina handle Gray."

"There isn't time," Andrew shouted, his voice cracking. "Damn it, there's no time."

Vladimir laid a restraining hand on Andrew. We all felt the pressure, but Andrew most of all. Vladimir said, "You really have to give Irina a little time. She's our best chance."

"Does he want to bargain?" Andrew said. "Damn it, there's no time. No time at all."

Vladimir said, "What does he want?"

"A bathrobe," I said. "A wool one."

Vladimir said smoothly, "Andrew, have we a bathrobe?"

We did. It belonged to one of the guards, a warm robe, far too large for Mr. Gray, but he was happy with it, and after I presented it to him, he willingly let me examine him.

He had a fever of 101 degrees, and his throat was inflamed, but as far as I could tell with only the stethoscope, his heart was sound, his blood pressure was normal, and his lungs were clear. He'd been through plenty—"a lot of wear and tear," as he called it—but he was tough, a durable old man, Mr. Gray.

I brought him some soup, and was hungry myself so I joined him in a bowl, with a plate of buttered toast. As we ate, we talked. The clock ticked, like the meter of a taxi, but Mr. Gray took his time. He asked about Vladimir, if he was my lover, and if I had ever married, and then why I had never married, and where in Russia I had been born, and who my parents were, and if they were educated or if they were "simple folk," which was his archaic way of referring to the peasants.

Eventually, he began to talk about himself, about his parents, who *were* simple folk, the children of emancipated serfs, superstitious, illiterate, living in the misery and awful poverty of a Russian village. He was proud—his eyes lit up and he became animated when he spoke of the "revolutionary spark" that he was born with. It was a stubborn quality that refused to accept conditions as they were. He remembered the Revolution of 1905, and the murder of the people by the Czar's soldiers. He described how he fought in the trenches against the Germans in World War I, and how he joined in the soldiers' mutiny and marched at the head of a column to seize St. Petersburg in March of 1917. He described the glory and promise of those early days. It was a familiar story, an old story, but it thrilled me and I never tired of hearing it from those who had been part of it.

While he talked, I heard Andrew pacing back and forth outside the closed bedroom door. I heard the telephone ring, and muffled voices before the front door opened and closed. I heard a car engine start and the sound of tires turning on the gravel outside the bedroom window.

"It's time to talk about Archangel," I said.

"Not yet," Mr. Gray said.

"We must."

He sighed and shrugged.

I said, "Is it your plan, Archangel?"

"No."

"Then Dolin's?"

"It's Stalin's own work," Mr. Gray said. "Stalin's plan to hold on to Poland, and from Poland to grab everything in Eastern Europe."

"Roosevelt won't allow it."

"And so Stalin has ordered Roosevelt's murder," Mr. Gray said. "But you've already guessed that. I can see it from your face. You've known it all along, but couldn't face it. Roosevelt is to be murdered by his nurse, his physical therapist."

"Is that Max?"

"His real name is Hinoy," Mr. Gray said.

"And he's on the White House staff?"

"Yes."

I started for the door, but Mr. Gray jumped up and was able to move more quickly than I thought, and blocked my way. "There's more," he said. "Afterward, we were to kill Max. And after Max— after Max we were to kill Dolin."

"Kill Dolin too?"

"Kill the lot," Mr. Gray said. "Kill everyone connected with Archangel. Everyone who knew about it." And then Mr. Gray smiled; an unnerving thing it was, dry as dust, that smile of Mr. Gray's. "It is clear that Stalin planned also to have me killed," he said.

"And so you defected?"

"And so I defected," he said.


Mr. Gray was right; the plot to murder FDR was something we had known, but not faced. It was beyond us.

"But not beyond Stalin," Winters said, when I told him. "First Godinsky, and now Roosevelt?" He was holding a stolen cable in which Churchill acknowledged Roosevelt's promise to defend Polish independence.

Vladimir said, "Truman wouldn't dare use force so soon. He would need time to persuade the people, to get them behind him."

Winters was on the telephone. It was a rural line, with no direct dialing, and he had to wake the operator. When she finally came on the line, he gave her the number of the White House switchboard. The call had to be routed through Richmond and would take a few minutes.

Winters told her to hurry, that it was urgent, and hung up. He went into the kitchen, where our driver and one of the guards were having a late supper.

"We've got to get back to Washington at once," he said. "How fast can you make it? Your best time?"

"There's a shortcut," the guard said. "I'll write out directions."

The phone rang in the other room, and Winters ran for it. The White House switchboard was on the line. Winters knew that Roosevelt was in Warm Springs. But where was Max? Was he in Warm Springs? Was he near the President? Close enough to kill him?

"I see the name on the travel roster," the White House operator said. "Hinoy. Mauno Hinoy."

"Is he in Warm Springs now?"

"All I have is the travel roster," she said. "There's a booking for him, but I have no way of knowing if he's actually there."

"No phone number for him?"

"None listed."

Winters didn't hesitate. "I need to speak to the head of the Secret Service detachment," he said.

"In Warm Springs?"

"Yes. I want to know the condition of the President," Winters said calmly.

"There's no direct line," the operator said. "I'll have to go through the switchboard."

Winters held the receiver while the operator called Warm Springs. Time passed slowly, an excruciating few minutes, all of us in the room holding our breath. The driver called from the front door—the car was ready. "A gas station down the road stays open; we can fill up there," he said.

The Warm Springs operator came on the line. "The Secret Service duty officer says the President has retired for the night," she said. "He's asleep and can't be disturbed."

"Let me speak to the duty officer."

"He said you have to go through the main office in Atlanta."

"Then put me through."

"It's closed until nine tomorrow morning."

Winters kept his composure. He was considering a decision I knew was very hard for him. I watched him weigh the pros and cons. Finally, he said, "Can you put me through to Julia Winters?"

"I'm not familiar with the name, sir."

"She's a guest of the President."

"I'm looking for her name, sir. Julia Winters. It's not on the roster."

"The cottage across the road from the Little White House. She's staying there."

"Cottage A," the operator said. "It's listed as vacant."

"It's not vacant. Julia Winters is in it." Andrew took a deep breath. "I know she's in Cottage A," he said. "Please ring it."

"I have no phone listed for Cottage A, sir."

"But there's a phone there. I've seen it."

"It's unlisted."

"Ring it anyway."

"I need authorization."

"From whom?"

"The Secret Service office in Atlanta."

"They won't be open until tomorrow morning."

"I'm sorry, sir."

Andrew hung up. Over the years I've heard it said that in the next few hours he could have done more, acted more effectively. But could he? Was there any way the tragedy of the following day in Warm Springs could have been avoided? Vladimir and I were with him in that isolated farmhouse in the Virginia mountains, and neither of us ever doubted that Andrew did all he could. Yet hard as others were on Andrew, no one was harder than he was on himself. He blamed himself for Warm Springs, as he blamed himself for the murder of Godinsky. In both cases his efforts were frustrated by circumstances, by a fateful sequence of events, by simple bad luck.

The President was in bed and asleep, presumably safe, which gave us until morning. Andrew decided to leave immediately for Washington and hitch a ride on the courier plane that carried the President's mail from the White House to Warm Springs.

We left immediately, stopping only to wake the owner of the local gas station, who refused to fill our tank until our driver showed his government priority. If that hadn't worked, Andrew told me later that he was prepared to draw his pistol and take the gas at gunpoint.

But we got the gas, and while the tank was filling Andrew used the station telephone to call the airport in Washington to check on the departure time of the courier plane. It left at eight o'clock.

"We've got to make it."

"We will," the driver said.

But there were problems along the way. The mountain roads weren't clearly marked, and most of the trip was through open country, with few houses and no lights or anything to show us the way. All along we were plagued by bad luck—a blown tire, which had to be changed in the dark because the batteries of the flashlight in the glove box had been allowed to run down; a frayed fan belt, which snapped and caused the car to overheat. There was a spare, but changing it took time, and we stood helpless and impatient in a light rain by the side of the road while the driver repaired it.

Sometime near dawn we began to run perilously low on gas. Because of wartime rationing many stations had closed, and we had to hunt around to find an open one. By the time we did, and filled the tank, and had a look at the water and oil, it was morning, with forty miles yet to go.

On the main road to the airport, with time getting very short, we ran into a construction tie-up and a long detour. "One damn thing after another," Andrew said. "Damn rotten luck. Are the breaks all against us?"

"Against us or with Dolin?" Vladimir whispered to me in Russian. "Perhaps we're already too late."

"We're not too late." From the front seat, Andrew had heard and understood. "We're not too late," he said, "we can't be."

And as it turned out we weren't. We made it to the airport in time, but only by a couple of minutes, and only by racing through red lights and taking turns on two wheels. But there was more bad luck ahead, more frustrating delays. The courier plane was warmed up and ready to go, but the airport duty officer refused to let us board it. Andrew argued and pleaded but the young officer had his orders and there was no way to budge him. When Andrew showed him his White House pass, the young officer examined it and said, "That gets you into the White House, sir. But not on this plane."

Andrew argued and pleaded but there was no budging him. We watched the mail pouch being loaded on the plane, a stripped-down two-engine bomber, a B-25, the same model we had flown from Floyd Bennett. I watched the three-bladed propellers begin to turn, slowly at first and then building speed.

Over the roar of the engines, Andrew shouted: "Can you hold take-off long enough for me to make one call?"

"We're running late."

"One call."

The officer, Lieutenant Jamison—his name was printed on a tape sewn over his breast pocket—said there wasn't time for a phone call. One of the ground crew, crouched under the wing of the plane, took away the wooden landing blocks from behind the wheels, and the plane began to taxi slowly in the direction of the runway. I really thought it was over for us.

But not Andrew. Give him credit, he wouldn't give up. He grabbed Lieutenant Jamison and screamed at him to stop the plane. Lieutenant Jamison was startled and for a moment he didn't know how to react. Then he shoved Andrew away, and for a second or two I thought he was going to stop the plane. But Lieutenant Jamison reached for the pistol he wore in a holster on his belt.

Vladimir had been watching it all, and doing nothing. But when Lieutenant Jamison went for the pistol, Vladimir moved fast as a cobra. He grabbed hold of the lieutenant and pinned his arms to his sides. He was a strapping young man, but with Vladimir's arms wrapped around him he couldn't move a muscle.

Just then we got our piece of good luck. I looked up and saw that the pilot had feathered the plane's propellers. Something had gone wrong. As we watched, the B-25 turned off the runway and headed back toward the hangar.

Vladimir still had hold of Lieutenant Jamison. "Let Mr. Winters make his phone call, lieutenant. Give him a chance. Now there's nothing to lose."

Jamison nodded and Vladimir let him go. "The traffic officer at the White House is named Ferguson," Winters said. "Major Ferguson. Would you know his voice?"

"I've spoken to him a few times."

"I'm going to call him."

"If he gives the order," Jamison said, "it's okay with me."

Andrew was able to reach Ferguson, who cleared us with Jamison and gave the order. Jamison also called ahead to Fort Benning, and when we landed there, almost four hours later, a car was waiting to drive us to the presidential compound in Warm Springs.

At the gate, we were stopped by a Secret Service agent; behind him were two Georgia state troopers. I glanced at my watch: 1:45.

The Secret Service agent was agitated and perspiring heavily, although the day was cool. The troopers looked grim. As we drove through the gate, I heard the crackle of a radio transmitter and an excited voice calling a name I couldn't quite make out. Something was wrong. Vladimir and I both felt it, a sense of crisis; people were running or huddled together, their faces stricken and bewildered. In the car none of us spoke. We were afraid to, afraid to express what each of us feared.

The driver pulled up to the Little White House, where FDR lived and worked, and Winters jumped out of the car and ran for the front door. He never got there. Two brawny Secret Service men dashed out from behind the house and headed him off.

Vladimir and I also got out of the car, but stayed back, watching Andrew argue with the Secret Service men, trying to get past them into the Little White House. Vladimir started toward Andrew, with the idea of helping him, but I held him back. One of the Secret Service men had hold of Andrew and was shouting at him. Andrew was struggling, but the second Secret Service man said something, and Andrew abruptly stopped struggling and became limp, as if he were about to collapse. Something else was said, and Andrew nodded his head, and the Secret Service men let him go. Winters was pale and shaken, and Vladimir and I hurried toward him, but he suddenly turned and ran across the road to the guest house, Cottage A, where Julia Winters was supposed to be.

The door was wide open, and we followed Andrew inside, passing quickly through the empty sitting room to the bedroom. I had no idea what we would find. Surprisingly, the room was empty, the twin beds neatly made, bureaus recently dusted, wastebaskets and ashtrays emptied. Andrew pulled open drawers and closet doors, but he found nothing until he got to the bathroom.

"Here," he shouted. "It's Julia's." He was holding up a silver-backed hand mirror. "Do you see the initials? J.W. Julia's mirror. My mother gave it to her. Julia was here, there's no doubt of it."

"Where is she now?"

"They've made sure she's out of the way," Andrew said. "She's been hidden somewhere." He had begun to collect himself and to speak calmly, a flushed, artificial calmness. But his hand trembled, and in an instant that calmness could shatter like glass. "Now the lies are beginning," he said. "It begins with Julia and goes on from there. The lies, the covering up of the truth."

"What truth, Andrew?"

"What's happened?" Vladimir said. "Tell us what's happened."

"Julia wasn't here," he said. "There is no Julia, no conspiracy. But here's the proof she was here. And there was a conspiracy, we can prove that, too."

"Andrew, tell us, for God's sake."

"The President . . ."

"What?"

"They've done it," Andrew said. "Franklin's dead."

Two Secret Service men rushed in, a different pair from the two we had seen earlier. Andrew turned away from them and quickly put Julia's mirror in his pocket before the Secret Service men saw it.

The Secret Service men had come for Andrew, and when he went with them Vladimir and I were left on our own. We didn't know what was going on, or what we ought to do. I remember the phone rang—the unlisted phone in Julia's cottage—but when I picked it up the party on the other end hung up.

Outside the cottage, people were confused and disoriented, huddled together in little groups or wandering aimlessly from place to place. We tried to find out how the President had died, but either no one knew or no one would say.

Vladimir and I decided to leave Warm Springs, and managed to get a ride to Fort Benning and from there we hitched on a flight to New York.

By that time the story coming from Warm Springs was that Franklin Roosevelt had suffered a cerebral hemorrhage, gone into a coma, and died two hours later, never having regained consciousness. At the time he was alleged to have been with his cousins, sitting for his portrait while reading his mail in the Little White House.

That's all we read in the newspapers and heard on the radio and that's all Vladimir and I knew until about a week later, when we again met Andrew Winters in New York.

"What you've been told is the official truth," Andrew told us. "As to what really happened, that's being buried."

"And what did happen?" Vladimir said. "How did Roosevelt die?"

But Andrew wasn't yet ready to answer that question, at least not directly; I felt he wasn't quite sure of himself, and was trying to get the facts firmly in hand.

"The key to what happened is still Max," he said. "In the official version, there's no mention of him. He doesn't exist."

"But he worked at the White House," Vladimir said. "He was on the travel roster for Warm Springs."

"It can be shown that Hinoy was there in Warm Springs," Andrew said. "*His* name is on the Secret Service logs. He went off duty and checked out of the compound at two o'clock on the afternoon of April 10, and didn't check back in until just before midnight on the eleventh."

"According to Mr. Gray, Max was to meet Dolin on the morning of the eleventh," I said. "And on the eleventh, he was out of the compound."

"It fits," Vladimir said.

"Oh, it fits," Andrew said. "The only problem is that now there is no Max, no Hinoy. He's disappeared. No one knows where, and no one seems to care."

"Has he checked out of the compound?"

"Not since he checked in on the eleventh," Andrew said. "I went to his room, and it was empty; nothing of his remaining behind. But it doesn't matter—none of it matters because President Roosevelt died a natural death. His personal physician was there to sign the certificate of death. Cerebral hemorrhage. There was no autopsy, and there will be no investigation. The President died a natural death."

"What about Julia?" I said. "She was there. She stayed in the guest cottage."

"Did she?"

"You know she did. You found her hand mirror."

Vladimir said, "You've learned there's a plot to hide the truth, and you suspect that everyone is involved in it, and everyone is against you. But not us, Andrew. You're wrong to include Irina and me, or to suspect us."

But Andrew wasn't persuaded. He distrusted us; I saw the film of that distrust shift on the surface of his eyes. First Godinsky's death, then Roosevelt's, had changed him. Henceforth Andrew played a lone hand, told us only enough to keep our loyalty, and lived uneasily with his suspicions, his obsessions.

"By now I'm sure you've seen Julia," Vladimir said. "If only to express your sympathy."

"She was with him."

"When he died?"

"She was with Franklin," Andrew said. "There were no Roosevelt cousins. Claire Balaban was there, which is the only part of the official story that's true. The mail they say he was reading hadn't even arrived."

"Where's Balaban now?"

"With Julia, looking after her."

"What about Max? Did Julia see him?"

"He came in while she and Franklin were together. It was time for a treatment. Franklin was a paraplegic, in need of regular attention. Max wheeled him into the other room. It was getting on time for lunch and Franklin had asked Julia to stay and eat with him. They had been talking about the end of the war. Franklin had earlier talked about retiring before his term was up and building a house in Warm Springs and living there with Julia. But lately he'd changed his tune. He spoke of unfinished business—those were his exact words to Julia —'unfinished business.'"

"What was the unfinished business?"

"He never said."

"Had it to do with Poland?"

Andrew paused and then said, "Julia was told nothing."

"The President was taken into the other room by Max," Vladimir said. "What happened then?"

"Julia was left alone, and she waited for Franklin to return. They were going to have lunch," Andrew said. "Usually Max was with him only a few minutes, but Julia waited about half an hour, and finally became alarmed and called through the closed door. Franklin was very sensitive about his condition and she was reluctant to barge in. She called twice more before opening the door. When she did, she found Franklin slumped over in his chair, unconscious.

"And Max?"

"He was long gone," Andrew said. "Julia used the phone to call the Secret Service, and Franklin's doctor. She tried herself to revive him, but it was no use. Within a few minutes the place was full of people, and she was dragged out of the cottage, made to pack up and get out. She was driven to North Carolina and then put on a train to New York. The Secret Service stayed with her. She wasn't alone for a minute, and she was warned not to speak to the press or to tell anyone what happened. She was frightened, frightened even to tell me."

"Who told her not to say anything?"

"Hugh Leverett."

"He was ambassador to Moscow," Vladimir said. "Now he's head of Russian Branch."

"He went to see Julia," Andrew said. "She wanted me there, but Leverett insisted on talking to her alone. He knew all about her affair with Franklin, which had to be kept secret. The last thing she wanted was to have her love affair with Franklin dangled in front of the public. She had been humiliated enough and she wanted no more. Her private life was her own."

"Good for Julia," I said.

"Leverett is clever," Andrew said bitterly. "He knew Julia's attitude—in fact, he was counting on it. If her relationship with FDR was to be kept secret, then her presence in Warm Springs also had to be kept secret."

Vladimir said, "She was politely warned to keep her mouth shut."

"Did she agree?" I said.

"Oh, yes. Julia was officially nowhere near Warm Springs. She was in New York on the twelfth, in her apartment on Fifth Avenue. The doorman recalls getting her a taxi around noon. He remembers that she returned about two hours later. She had been shopping, there were a lot of packages. She was to have a dinner party that night. Leverett and his wife were coming, one or two other couples, all from the Russian Branch." Andrew tugged at his shirt collar, as if it were choking him. "It's a perfect story," he said. "A perfect tale."

"Has the family called her?" I said. "The President's sons—"

"No one has called," Andrew said.

I remembered that walk with Julia by the lake outside of Zurich when she first confided in me about her love affair; I remember Andrew waiting anxiously at the door of the cabin, and the photograph of Roosevelt that he'd hidden.

Andrew said, "Julia wanted to go to the funeral, but Leverett told her it was impossible."

There was more to Andrew's story, and much more to his relations with Hugh Leverett. Some Andrew told us, and some came later, after Julia died.

Andrew was with her the day of Franklin's funeral, and didn't leave her apartment until around midnight. The country was in mourning and Fifth Avenue was without traffic, dark and unnaturally still. Andrew spotted a Packard limousine across the avenue, and as he buttoned his topcoat, the headlights of the car came on and the motor was started. Two men were in the car—one was the driver, and the other, who opened the rear door and called out to Andrew, was Hugh Leverett.

"A few words, Andrew. May we have a few private words?"

"Come and walk with me. I'm going home."

"To Sutton Place?" Leverett said. "Do you keep up the big house?" They shook hands solemnly under a street lamp. "You could sell it for a packet."

"I'm sure I could."

"It's very clever to hold on until after the war. Prices will skyrocket, all that black money around."

"Have you been waiting long, Hugh?"

"Too long to pretend I'm here to blather about the price of real estate." Leverett was a head taller than Andrew Winters, a man of iron-gray hair and brushed mustache, of English wool and capeskin gloves. He was informed, clever, social, ambitious, and rich, although his wife was far, far richer.

"We need to talk frankly," he said. "We may not see eye to eye, Andrew, we seldom have. But now isn't a time for discord." The gloved hand grasped Andrew's elbow and drew him closer. "I've come to share certain secrets with you," he said. "These deal with matters of policy. When the war in Europe ends, Stalin has agreed to join us against Japan."

"And what do we give him in return?"

217

"We give him nothing. We only let him keep what he already has."

"Do you mean Poland and Eastern Europe?"

"We are still hopeful that those countries will be independent."

"Hopeful? Will we insist on it?"

"We have."

"Will we fight for it?"

"Absolutely not."

"Then we're whistling up a rain barrel," Andrew said. "Polish independence was dealt a blow when Godinsky was killed. But that tragedy at least opened Franklin's eyes to Stalin's real intentions. Stalin meant to dominate Eastern Europe and keep it as a buffer against the West. But he wasn't to be allowed to have it. Simple as that. Before he died, Franklin had made up his mind to draw the line."

"In Eastern Europe?"

"The Russians were to be made to live up to their agreements. They were to be made to pull their armies back."

"Made to pull their armies back?" Leverett raised his eyebrows and said, "Make them? Really, Andrew."

"There's proof of it—a cable from Churchill to Franklin acknowledging Franklin's decision to insist on an independent Poland. It is cautious, but explicit. Specifically, it does not rule out force."

"Against the Russians?"

"Against the Russians."

"No such cable exists."

"I've seen a photocopy of it."

"You've seen a forgery." Hugh Leverett's voice had risen; now he lowered it to a whisper, and the gloved hand tightened on Andrew's elbow. "All Soviet policy cables cross my desk. I read every one, and none can be sent unless I first initial it. I assure you that none was sent to Churchill or anyone else directly or indirectly threatening force. None. Never."

"Do you think it possible, Hugh," Andrew said evenly, "that Franklin sent that particular cable around you?"

"Around me and directly to the Prime Minister?"

"Yes."

"It's not possible."

"I know you had a man at Franklin's side," Andrew said. "And he read the cables *before* they were routed to you. But after Yalta, Franklin knew you were for placating Uncle Joe. When he stopped seeing eye to eye with you, it would be like him to go around you. So like Franklin to go around you."

"I don't suppose you'd let me see the cable copy."

"Not quite yet."

"Or tell me how you got it?"

"Not if you held my hand to an open fire."

"It doesn't matter," Hugh Leverett said. "Franklin's policy was to cooperate with Uncle Joe. The Soviets may be devils, but at the moment we need them more than we need Poland."

"There was a plot to kill Franklin," Andrew said. "A Moscow plot."

"Franklin died of natural causes," Hugh Leverett said. "He was worn out, his health failing. His blood pressure was dangerously high. The medical records are there. They are a fact, as the circumstances of his death are facts. He died suddenly, probably of a cerebral hemorrhage. He complained of a severe headache and collapsed while opening his mail."

"At what time?"

"Twelve-thirty."

' I was in the car that brought the mail from Fort Benning," Andrew said. "It didn't arrive until 1:45."

"When he died, three people were with him," Leverett went on steadily, implacably. Andrew saw a steamroller, leveling and flattening everything in its way. "His two cousins, one amusing and one literary, and a lady painting his portrait."

"Julia was with him."

Leverett said, "Julia was in New York."

"She was with Franklin."

"In Warm Springs? There's no record of it."

"She spoke to you," Andrew said. "She told you her story."

"Poor Julia. Poor, poor Julia. I don't want to be hard, Andrew, but between us she's had a long history of psychological difficulties. I doubt if she'd be considered a credible witness."

They had been walking south on Fifth Avenue and approached the fountain in front of the Plaza Hotel. Leverett said, "Is it true, the story of Scott and Zelda Fitzgerald?"

"What story?"

"Her getting drunk and jumping into the fountain."

"She sometimes got drunk enough to do it."

"Did you like them, Andrew?"

"He was all right," Andrew said. "She was a pain in the ass."

"But did she in fact jump into the Plaza fountain?"

"People say she did, so she did. Is that your point?"

"My point," Leverett said, "is that in history truth and belief are the same. One makes history by writing it. It's believed that poor Zelda jumped into the fountain and, on a far larger scale, that Franklin died of a cerebral hemorrhage."

"Put another way," Andrew said, "some stories are true and some are lies."

They walked around the fountain and farther along Fifth Avenue, and east on 54th Street. Andrew brought up Roosevelt's Finnish therapist and nurse, calling him by his real name—Hinoy—and asking where he was.

"Hinoy?" Leverett turned the name over in his mind. "The name means nothing to me."

Andrew ignored that. "By the time I got to his room, he'd cleared out," he said. "But he was there. He was in Warm Springs on April 12. His name is on the Secret Service logs."

"I don't think so," Leverett said. "No, Andrew. You'll find no Hinoy on the Secret Service logs."

They didn't speak for several blocks, but when they turned into Sutton Place, the Packard was there, Leverett's driver at the wheel, smoking a cigarette.

"We've been competitors quite a long time," Leverett said. "I think it may be the right time to put our outstanding differences behind us. I respect you, your dedication particularly. It doesn't matter that politically we rarely come down on the same side. I've been asked to create a permanent coordinating intelligence agency. I want you to join in and help me."

"And bring Living Memory with me?"

"Yes, of course."

"Put it under your control?"

"We'll go through it together. I'm sure it's in need of sorting out."

"I don't want to work for you."

"I'm asking you to work for your country."

"That's what I've been doing."

"What you've been doing is to impede national policy."

"*Your* national policy," Andrew said.

"It was Franklin's, too,"

"Not recently, not after Godinsky was murdered."

"Come off it, Andrew," Leverett said. "We need the Russians,

220

their cooperation. We can't go around accusing them of murdering our President."

"It's true."

"Damn truth."

"And Serge Dolin?" Andrew said. "What if he resurfaces? What if—"

"What if. What if. What if Dolin is only what he says he is, a journalist with connections to the French left?"

Leverett signaled his driver, who tossed away his cigarette and started the car. "Journalist or agent, if Dolin knows all you think he does, the Soviets will want to deal with him." Leverett stepped into the limousine and stretched out his long legs, arranging himself comfortably. The lamp in the roof of the limousine dramatically highlighted the planes and angles of his handsome face. All his self-possession had returned, and with it came an unmistakable smugness. "I'm reasonably certain the Soviets will want to deal with Serge Dolin in their own way." He closed the door and rolled down the window. "The bastard's life isn't worth a plug nickel," he called out. "Not a plug nickel."

# nineteen

☭ DOLIN HAD DRIVEN SOUTH TO NORTH CAROLINA, WHERE HE serviced the car, filled the gas tank, and counted his remaining ration stamps. There were fewer than he supposed, not nearly enough to reach Florida.

The car was registered to Barret Martin Fisher, and Dolin carried his driver's license; he was sure there was no police alert for the car, so that it could be safely sold. Gas had become a problem, and he was tired of driving. Cars in good condition were much in demand in the spring of 1945, and when he reached Charlotte, Dolin sold the Chevrolet to a dealer for $350.

He carried his bag to the station and doubled back on the first bus north to Winston-Salem. After waiting half an hour in the station there, he crossed the street to a diner, where he ordered scrambled eggs and drank three cups of coffee to stay awake. He noticed nothing out of the ordinary, saw no one who didn't fit in. But he made certain to stay alert, and to turn himself into a traveler who also fit in and wouldn't be noticed; he had become anonymous, not a drifter to catch the eye of a cop, but a working man, perhaps a bit seedy and down on his luck; a man careful to eat the last of his home-fried potatoes, the last crumb of his toast, but to leave an honorable dime tip under the saucer of his coffee cup.

He boarded an eastbound bus from Winston-Salem at five o'clock in the afternoon of April 11, and rode most of the night, with stops at Greensboro, Burlington, and Durham, arriving finally in Raleigh. It had been a cramped, lurching sort of ride, and he'd slept fitfully, with snatches of dreams from childhood and conversations in Russian. Several times he woke up alarmed, thinking that he had spoken aloud in Russian, and that he'd been heard by others in the bus, that he'd be noticed and remembered.

He had been too long without proper sleep, and that made him disoriented and unable to think clearly. In his lucid moments, he saw that he wasn't being followed, and doubted that anyone was looking for him. Fisher had left the States by way of Canada and used Serge's doctored passport to sail to England. If anyone was looking, that's what they'd find—Serge Dolin long gone to England.

But Max had still to act, and Serge was at times unnerved by the enormity and arrogance of the crime. He'd doze off, twisting and stretching in his cramped bus seat, neither asleep nor awake, but writhing in anxious gaps between the two. Fear came in short gasps, an abstract fear, an idea of fear, and all the more menacing because of that.

He changed buses in Raleigh, and went on to Charleston and Savannah, and along the coast to Florida on his way to Key West, the first stop on the escape route to Mexico.

It seemed an endless trip. Florida was damp and hot. In Jacksonville, midmorning of April 12, a man and woman got on the bus. There was something familiar about them, and something that troubled Dolin, but he couldn't place it.

The man wore a light-colored felt hat with sweat stains around the band. He carried a suitcase with a rope tied twice around it, and the sleeves of his shirt were rolled past the line where his suntan ended and the white skin of his brawny arm began. The woman had a bandanna tied around her head and carried a sleeping infant.

Before Dolin dropped off to sleep again, he saw his first palm tree through the window and felt a breeze, perhaps from the ocean. He slept for a couple of hours, opening his eyes when the bus stopped and passengers got off and came on, but closing them again and later awakening certain again that he had called out in Russian. Across the aisle, the baby had awakened and his mother, the woman with the bandanna, fed him and sang softly to him. Dolin closed his eyes; he went off to sleep and dreamed the song was in Russian.

The melody and the Russian words were part of Dolin's dream; the woman went on singing to her infant, an old song that he knew and that he had heard as a child and knew would end when he woke.

The bus had stopped, and the woman's husband had gone off to shop. He came back, looking grave, carrying a bag of oranges. He stood in the center of the aisle, the bag of oranges in his hand, tears forming in his eyes.

The President was dead. Dolin was awake now and heard the words clearly. The news swept through the bus. Roosevelt was dead. He had died that afternoon in Warm Springs.

The bus had started; when it stopped at the next town, Dolin got off long enough to buy the newspapers. These were early editions that

223

carried no details. He spent the night in Miami before going on to Key West and read the official story in the *Miami Herald:* Just before he was stricken, Roosevelt was opening his mail; he was sitting for his portrait; the artist was coloring his necktie, his Harvard tie. Such details made the scene more vivid, more credible, as in a literary work; so Dolin thought, and in this literary work the President complained of a headache, collapsed, went into a coma, and died without regaining consciousness.

There was no mention of Max, no autopsy, no hint of suspicion. The story was without loose ends and to Dolin again suggested a literary work whose author might be on to the untidy truth and might have seized Max, or even Fisher, before he left the country. And Mr. Gray, where had the old ghost gone? Dolin feared a gathering pursuit, felt its hot breath.

In Miami, he bought a chart of the waters between Key West and Cuba, and secondhand clothing—cotton shirts and pants, a pair of sneakers, and a canvas bag. He took what he needed from his suitcase—underwear and a shaving kit, pistol, cash, the Etienne Terrelle passport—and packed it all in the canvas bag. He tore the labels from his old clothes, repacked the suitcase, and filled it with rocks before tossing it from a deserted pier into Biscayne Bay.

Dolin had let his beard grow, but in 1945 beards still attracted attention, so he shaved it, leaving a mustache. He had his hair cropped and kept out of sight for a couple of days, before taking the bus that went along the causeway linking the Keys.

He needed to find a man named Berg, who was thought to be Belgian and had operated for a time in the Antilles, but now owned a charter boat out of Key West. Berg was a stop on the southern route used by Moscow to pass agents in and out of America. Fisher had gone to England, by way of Canada, in order to avoid Berg, whom he knew to be a cutthroat.

"If we are to be shot," Fisher had said, "if in Moscow the Little Father has ordered us to be shot, then Berg is the one to pull the trigger."

"Has he ordered us to be shot?"

"Perhaps, in order to wipe out the truth," Fisher said. "But what do you think, Sergei Dimitrovich?"

"I think I'd better watch my step," Dolin said.

"Stay clear of Berg."

Later, when they parted for the last time, Fisher said, "Tell me what it was like, the kiss?"

"Which kiss?"

"From the Little Father, our Stalin."

"It was damp," Serge said. "And on his breath there was a faint odor. Not strong, mind you, but still an odor."

"An odor of what? Of vodka?"

"Yes, of course. There was vodka on his breath. But something else. Herring. A smell of herring on Stalin's breath."

"That's natural," Fisher said.

"Exactly what I thought," Serge said. "Natural and reassuring. I was much relieved to smell it."

"It's a homey touch, all right," Fisher said. "But herring or not, I'd still stay clear of Berg."

In Miami Dolin hesitated, considering other routes. He could double back to Jacksonville, and from there take a bus to New Orleans and around the rim of the Gulf of Mexico to Brownsville, Texas, and then into Mexico. But that would take time, and to arrange the Mexican crossing would take more time. It was not without its risks. If he were to be betrayed, if the order had gone out to kill him, then the risks were everywhere. Better to face them now, with Berg, on a small boat in the Gulf.

Dolin took the bus to Key West and arrived there on the afternoon of April 17. Berg's boat was called the *Flamingo*; it was thirty-five feet long, with a diesel engine and extra fuel tanks. When Dolin arrived, it was on the water, and didn't return until late the following day.

Dolin and Berg met that night in a bar called Ruby's, where they were joined by a Cuban named Ambrosio, who worked on Berg's boat. They had drinks together and something to eat. Dolin was dressed in khaki pants and a loose sweater. He wore a black watch cap and hadn't shaved; there were streaks of white in his beard. He could have been taken for a South American, Italian, French, almost anything at all. Key West was full of people who had reason to come and go, people willing to pay dearly for private boats to run them to Cuba or across the channel to Yucatan.

To Ruby, the owner of the bar, Dolin seemed a man used to money, one who handled it carefully. He paid for the drinks and food, but ran his eye down the bill, quickly checking the addition in his head. Ruby noticed that he sat with his back to the wall, looking out at the restaurant, and that his eyes moved continually, and in them was a flat, cautious expression. Ruby saw the bulge of a pistol on Dolin's hip under his loose sweater. Berg was big, mean, and rough, and the

225

Cuban was known to use a knife; but Ruby, who was experienced in this sort of thing, suspected that Dolin was their match.

The three men left Ruby's place around nine o'clock and went on board the *Flamingo*. In a few minutes the Cuban untied the mooring lines and sprang back on deck, and the boat slipped into the channel. Dolin was in the wheelhouse. Ruby saw him beside Berg, his face lit by the greenish compass light as the *Flamingo* glided silently past the pier and into the deep channel, where darkness and fog closed around it.

They were seen the following morning off Cay Sal, a hundred miles to the southeast, where they put in for fuel, food, and fresh water. Berg owned an old tobacco warehouse there, and after taking on supplies, they sailed west, parallel to Cuba's coast. For a week nothing more was heard of the *Flamingo*, and it was not reported seen. If it came ashore anywhere on the Cuban north coast—and there were a dozen places where it could have—it was not discovered. In April of 1945, the Cuban navy patrolled the coast and demanded that every foreign boat register. But the Cuban naval logs contain no mention of the *Flamingo*. Nor is it known how many gallons of fuel were taken on at Cay Sal or whether, after the boat was finally found, tests were done to determine the size of its tanks or its range.

The next sighting of the *Flamingo* was recorded on April 28 by a Mexican coast guard cutter on patrol in the Yucatan channel. The *Flamingo* had gone aground in the reefs off Holbox Island, near Cabo Catoche, the easternmost point of the Yucatan peninsula. The bodies of two men, later identified as Berg and the Cuban, Ambrosio, were found on board. Both had been shot; both were armed with pistols, from which several shots had been fired. They had been dead at least two, possibly three, days.

The *Flamingo* had carried a rubber dinghy, which wasn't found on board, and it was assumed that the killer of Berg and Ambrosio had escaped in it. The Mexican coast guard searched for the dinghy along the beach for a couple of miles in both directions, but without any luck. The currents were strong and among the reefs were outcroppings of sharp rock, capable of tearing the dinghy to pieces. The Mexican coast guard concluded that the killer had drowned, and ended the search.

But later on, there was talk of a man, a stranger, speaking little Spanish, who had come ashore on the mainland, a few miles to the west, and wandered into an Indian village that appeared on none of the published maps but that was known locally as Chontalpa.

The stranger was said to be wounded in the leg, from a knife or a gun, and he was feverish, exhausted, and half starved. The villagers took him in and looked after him, and when he was stronger they led him to Rio Lagartas, where he stayed six weeks waiting for the coastal steamer.

To the Indians of Chontalpa he was only a white man, one of the few they'd ever seen, with his clothes torn, starving, wounded, and ill, and beyond that they provided no details. He was a white man whose ship had been wrecked, a white man saved from the sea—an Indian tale that could have happened last week or a hundred years before, or not happened at all. To the Indians it was all the same. A white man saved from the sea could have been real, or a dream or only a vision.

But in Rio Lagartas, where he waited for the coastal steamer, there was a market and a saloon run by a Chinese with rooms to let above it. Here people had learned to keep track of things and tell time, and here there are facts about the shipwrecked man. He was first thought to be a North American, but it turned out he was European, about forty years old, although his hair and beard were going gray. He spoke little Spanish but knew English and French. His right leg had been hurt and he walked with the aid of a stick. He had enough money to pay for his meals and a room above the bar. He had the local tailor make him a suit and two cotton shirts, and he bought a pair of sandals. He had his hair cut and his beard trimmed. He drank a lot in the saloon, but was never seen drunk.

He spent a lot of his time studying Spanish from a dictionary, and became a familiar sight with his walking stick, limping down by the dock, peering out into the Gulf for the coastal steamer. The children gave him the name Barbudo—bearded one; he was generous and friendly with the children, but stayed clear of the men who gathered to drink and play cards in the Chinese saloon.

In the market he bought a package of letter paper, a pen, and a bottle of ink, and wrote a lot of letters. He didn't hold them for the coastal steamer, but instead burned the letters in an empty Players cigarette tin, which he kept in his room and used as an ashtray.

This writing of letters and burning them was noticed by the Indian girl who cleaned his room. She thought it an odd thing, and wondered who the letters were written to. She guessed he had a wife or sweetheart, and was very curious about it, but too shy to ask him. Cleaning his room one day when he was out, she found one of the letters unfinished on his writing table, and tried to read it.

She had been taught to read Spanish in the missionary school in

Campeche, but this letter was written in a language she couldn't read. Just then, the door opened and he came in. She was frightened, but he wasn't angry.

"Can you read French?" he said.

"No."

"I didn't think so."

He was smiling and she remembers being fascinated by how white his teeth were against his dark beard. He asked her name and she told him the one given her in the missionary school—Feliciana. He said it was a pretty name and that it suited her, and he paid her other compliments, and in a short time she felt easy enough with him to ask about the letters.

"You write one every day," she said. "And at night you burn it in the tobacco tin."

"Yes."

"Instead of talking to someone, you write letters?"

She watched him working out the Spanish in his head. "Yes, I talk things over with someone," he said finally.

"Is it your wife?"

"No, not a wife."

"Then a sweetheart. Is she in Mexico City?"

"Farther away."

"Farther than Mexico City? That's unfortunate."

It will never be known if the Indian girl became his lover. Certainly she remembers him fondly. He gave her silver earrings, which he bought in the bazaar. She said he fixed the piano in the Chinese saloon and played old songs on it. He gave her money to visit her mother in Campeche. She regretted it when the steamer came finally, and he left on it. But to the end she claimed he wasn't her lover, only a friend.

Dolin boarded the steamer at Rio Lagartas and disembarked at Vera Cruz, and for nearly six weeks nothing at all was heard of him.

But it is known that he contacted the lawyer in Stockholm, the respectable and nonpolitical Jean-Marc Zauderer. On August 3, 1945, Zauderer received a thick letter from Dolin, postmarked Vera Cruz. In it was a second envelope, sealed, and a letter of explanation. The lawyer was to place the unopened envelope in the safe deposit box which Dolin had rented, and to which Zauderer had access. He would receive a letter from Dolin every three months, and as long as he did the envelope would remain sealed and locked in the box. Zauderer was instructed to open the letter and make its contents available to the world press only if there was no word from Dolin.

If Zauderer understood Dolin's instructions and agreed to do as he was asked, he was to place an advertisement in the *International Herald Tribune*, requesting a Spanish tutor for his children and using a box number of any three digits that totaled eleven.

After mailing the letter to Zauderer, Dolin made his way to Mexico City, where he stayed out of sight, contacting no one until the advertisement placed by Zauderer appeared on August 9. The following afternoon, Dolin went to a café on the Reforma, across from the offices of the Communist newspaper *El Machete*.

Just after five o'clock, Paul Cesar Duarte, the editor of *El Machete* and one of the founders of the Mexican Communist party, came out of his office and crossed the Reforma to the café, where he ordered his customary glass of red wine.

Dolin watched from behind a newspaper at a back table. When he was satisfied that Duarte was alone, he went to the bar and stood next to him, close enough to poke him in the ribs.

"Do you know what it is that I'm poking you with?" he said in Spanish.

"I think it's a pistol."

"It is," Dolin said. "And do you know who I am?"

There was a mirror across from the bar and Dolin stood so that Duarte was able to see his reflection.

"I've seen photographs of you," Duarte said. "The beard changes you somewhat, but of course we've been waiting for you, comrade Dolin. We've instructions to help you."

"To help me?"

"Yes."

"Orders from Moscow? Orders to help me?" Dolin said. "From the Little Father himself?"

Duarte said nothing, but looked straight ahead with his jaw set. Dolin jabbed him with the muzzle of the pistol, which must have hurt, but Duarte didn't flinch. He'd had pistols jabbed in his back before, this old revolutionary, and he'd been shot at as well, more than once. "I've been ordered to help you," he said, "and to show you every courtesy. You only have to tell me what you need. Money? Passport?"

"I'm to travel?" Dolin said. "To travel where?"

"Home, of course," Duarte said. "To the Soviet Union." The pressure of the pistol was steady in Duarte's back. He said, "May I turn around?"

"Slowly."

Duarte was a head taller than Serge, a heavy, unkempt man, with a mane of white hair and clumps of wiry white hair growing from his ears and nostrils; his eyes, when they fell on Serge, were the kind to give one a chill; the muscle of one lid drooped, and the whites were a muddy, yellowish color, the pupils nearly black, impenetrable, bottomless. "Go home, Sergei Dimitrovich. Go home to honors, to a promotion, to glory, all that."

The chilling eyes stayed on Dolin, bore down on him; Dolin jabbed again with the pistol and even drew the hammer of the pistol, and still Duarte didn't flinch and the eyes bore down.

"I was a delegate to the Eleventh Congress," Duarte said.

"I don't give a damn for the Eleventh Congress."

"I met your father there."

"Or him either," Dolin said. "I don't give a damn for him either."

Dolin's finger tightened on the trigger of the pistol. Duarte knew it, and stood without breathing; so a few seconds passed, and finally Dolin let up the hammer and loosened his finger on the trigger.

"I have a message that I want you to deliver to Stalin," Dolin said. "Tell him that I've written down the truth of Archangel, all the details, every scrap, and put it in a safe place. If I'm killed, it will be released to the press."

"And if Stalin doesn't believe it?" Duarte said. "If he thinks it's a bluff?"

"Bluff or not," Dolin said, "the secret protects me. Once it's told, I have no protection. Therefore, I want it to remain a secret. Have him work out the logic of that. Have him work out the logic." He backed away from Duarte, toward the door, the pistol bulging in the pocket of his jacket. "Have him work out the logic," Dolin said. "And tell him goodby, good-by to Stalin from Stenoviev's son."

Dolin went out of the saloon, turned, and vanished in the evening crowd along the Reforma. Duarte finished his glass of wine and immediately ordered another. Eventually, he paid for his drinks and returned to the office of *El Machete*. From there he composed a report on his meeting with Dolin, and that same night sent it on to Moscow.

The infamous Soviet defector known only as Prima Donna was still at his post in Moscow when Duarte's report was received, and he has described the panic of the intelligence officers who first read it. Prima Donna had shrewdly kept clear of all aspects of the Archangel affair, and there is considerable malice in his description of the reaction to the Duarte report; he talks of terrified senior officers running around and bumping into one another. Prima Donna had the talent of an actor, and his description was quite comic.

Stalin had ordered them to kill Dolin, and they had put Berg on to it. Berg had never failed. Set Berg to kill a man, and the man was killed. But not this time, not Serge Dolin. And not only was he alive, but he'd arranged things so that they dare not even try to kill him. In fact, they had to make sure that he stayed alive.

But how to tell Stalin? No one had the nerve.

Prima Donna claimed that he came up with the solution. "Stalin ordered us to kill Dolin in order to bury the truth of the Archangel conspiracy," he told his colleagues. "Alive he is able to reveal it, but dead he can't."

"Dead men tell no tales," it was said sagely.

"Except in the case of Dolin," Prima Donna said, "who has arranged things more to suit himself."

And so another conspiracy was constructed. "Dolin was again at the center of it," Prima Donna later said. "We conspired to keep him alive, so that his secret would be buried, at the same time telling Stalin that he was dead, so as to assure him that it was buried."

Prima Donna was pleased with himself. He personally went to Stalin and told him that his orders had been carried out. Godinsky was dead. Roosevelt was dead. Max, the Finnish nurse and masseur, had been intercepted by two agents of the Thirteenth Department, and was dead.

"And what about the other one?" Stalin said. "Stenoviev's kid."

Prima Donna didn't hesitate. "Dead and buried," he said.

"Everybody is dead," Stalin said. He sat contentedly in a deep chair, his feet in fur-lined slippers resting on an ottoman, a woolen shawl around his shoulders.

He soon drew Prima Donna closer, making room for him on the ottoman, benignly describing his plans for putting Poland and all of Eastern Europe under his protection. Later, they went in for dinner, and Stalin ate well, and that night he slept well believing all his enemies were dead.

# twenty

MAGDA HAD HEARD NOTHING FROM SERGE DOLIN. THE LET-
ters he'd written to her in Rio Largatas were never sent. She had no
idea where he was, or even if he was alive. Because she knew nothing
of Archangel, she didn't connect Roosevelt's death with Dolin's disap-
pearance. When the war ended in August, she had a moment of hope,
but no letter followed, no phone call.

When she parted from Serge in the bus station in Buffalo, she went
to stay with Christina Heller and her husband in a suburb of Toronto.
The Hellers had welcomed her and given her a spare room. She
opened an account in the local bank, depositing the thousand dollars
given her by Dolin. For five months she rode the bus into town every
morning and returned at night, working all day behind a counter in a
department store in Toronto. The people in the town and those she
worked with were told her husband was in the army overseas. At the
time I didn't know the story she had told Christina Heller, only that no
mention was ever made of Serge Dolin. I'm sure neither Christina nor
her husband heard his name.

From the first Magda had tried to resign herself to life without
Serge. She was a refugee and, like the rest of us, hardened to loss, to
packing up and moving on. But something told her that her life with
Serge wasn't over. "It's not the end for us," he'd said.

She hadn't quite believed him. But as the months passed and she
looked back on the time they'd spent together, she realized that Serge
had loved her. That was the secret she carried with her, and that love
was a fact, real as the baby growing inside her. She had loved Serge,
and he had loved her. Serge would get in touch with her and find a
way for her to join him.

But the months in Canada dragged by, and there were dark times
when she feared he was hurt, even dead, and her doubts would return.
She had a difficult pregnancy and was often sick. The only doctor in
the area was nearly seventy—the war had taken away the rest—and
according to Magda he reeked of whiskey and asked all sorts of un-
pleasant and insinuating questions: who her husband was, and where
he was, and if she had fled Europe because she was Jewish.

She knew I was living in Madame Berkowitz's house in Brooklyn, and a few times she telephoned, but always hung up without speaking. She also wrote to me, but like Serge Dolin in Rio Lagartas, she never sent the letters. I expect she wrote to him, and burned her letters, as he did his.

So I had no word from her all during the spring and summer and into the fall of 1945. Andrew Winters was spending his time trying to pick up Dolin's trail. He knew that Magda and Serge Dolin had left New York together, and he questioned me about places she might have gone. I knew she had spent time in Canada and there were people there about whom she was mysteriously silent. But I said nothing about that to Winters.

Winters was suspicious of me. "She must have mentioned friends somewhere," he said. "You must have heard a name."

"She didn't have friends. Not as far as I know."

"Are you sure?"

"I can't think of any."

"No names?" Winters said. "What about a place?"

"No, nothing."

Winters thought a moment and then said, "No friend but you? Such a pretty girl. How did you manage to meet her?"

"Through Willi Koder."

"What about him? Friends? Relatives? He introduced her to you, did he introduce her to somebody else as well?"

"Maybe he did."

"You don't know?"

"She never mentioned anyone."

But Winters' questions had reminded me of something. When I'd searched Willi's room after his murder, among the letters I found was one from Christina Heller. I thought the name familiar when I heard it later on from Magda, but at the time didn't make the connection. Now I did. I got out the letter and reread it. It was written in German and was full of news and questions about people Willi and Christina Heller had known. It was a letter between old friends—old friends or relatives.

I'd told Andrew part of the truth—Willi had never spoken of relatives, and after his death no inquiries had been made and no one had come forward to claim the body. Francis Keogh had wondered about that, but in the end we'd gone ahead and had the body cremated.

I decided to write to Christina Heller, on the chance that she had word of Magda. I wasn't prepared for what happened: Three days after

I mailed the letter, Madame Berkowitz appeared breathless at my bedroom door. I had a long distance call. It was Magda.

For a minute or two I couldn't believe it was she. There was a distracting static on the line, but it suddenly cleared, and I heard Magda's voice as if she were standing in the next room.

"I've been wanting to call you," she said. "But I went off so abruptly, and without even saying good-by. I thought maybe you were angry at me."

"You went off with Serge."

"Yes, we had a couple of days together in April."

"He's not with you now?"

"I haven't seen or heard from him since." And then she said, "Is it all right? I mean all right between us. Are we still friends? I hope we're still friends."

I heard the emotion in her voice, and I could barely speak or hold back the tears. I realized how worried about her I'd been and how much I wanted to see her.

"I have so much to tell you," she said. "I've told Christina about you, and Walter too. Walter is her husband. Can you come up? They want to meet you. Please, Irina. I must see you again. I know I demand things, like a spoiled kid. But it's true. Irina, my darling friend—I must see you."

"I'll have to get leave from the hospital."

"Can you? You must. There, I've done it again! Please, Irina. I'll never demand anything again." She laughed. "At least until the next time," she said.

Her defiance was gone, and in its place came a seductive and charming play upon my sympathy and love for her. It was probably contrived, and I should have been warned. But I believed her love was real—certainly the need to see me was—and I also needed to see her.

"I'll get leave this weekend," I said. "And wire you the flight number."

"When you come, bring your medical kit," she said. "I have a surprise for you."

"A surprise? Magda, what are you going to tell me?"

"That I'm pregnant. Damn pregnant."

I made Madame Berkowitz promise to say nothing about Magda's call. I had decided to keep it from Vladimir, and more significantly from Andrew Winters. The war was over and I was finished with the spy trade, with Living Memory—at least that's what I thought.

I went off duty from the hospital Friday night and took the morning flight to Toronto. Since her phone call, I'd thought of little but seeing Magda again. In the seven months since she'd disappeared I'd gone through moods of anger and jealousy. I resented her turning to me for help when she needed me, and putting me aside when she didn't. She could act selfishly, even ruthlessly. I sometimes felt exploited by her—exploited and then ignored. But I recognized that it was my fault as much as hers. I had recruited her for Andrew Winters and then asked her to spy on her lover. If she distrusted me, it was for good reason.

But there are friendships, as there are love affairs, that survive distrust and betrayal. That's how it was between Magda and me. When I arrived in Toronto, she was waiting in the airport, blooming next to the Hellers' old jalopy, Magda eight months pregnant, opening her arms and waddling toward me, and crying at the sight of me.

Later on she told me that I looked older, and that had shocked her, that I seemed grayer, thinner, and tired out, and she said it wrung her heart to realize that I was aging.

But all of that came later. At the airport we hugged each other and kissed, and she helped me put my bag in the car. She had learned to drive and was proud of that. She appeared rosy and more beautiful than ever, but as we drove I looked more closely, from a doctor's point of view, and noticed one or two things that worried me.

"How much weight have you gained?" I said.

"Tons. I eat like a horse."

I'd noticed that her ankles were swollen and I asked when that had started.

"A few months ago."

"What does your doctor say?"

"I don't have a doctor. With the war there's only one left around here, and I don't like him. He had me naked on his table, poking around inside, and asking if I were Jewish. He's just a damn old Nazi, if you ask me."

The Heller house was small and modest, but freshly painted and spotlessly clean. There was a flower garden in front—it was November and that far north all the leaves were long gone from the trees, and Walter Heller had lovingly wrapped his rose bushes in burlap against the Canadian winter. In back were a few acres of cleared and plowed land, a barn, and a kennel, where the Hellers kept a pair of German shepherds, who came out to sniff suspiciously at me, and wag their tails for Magda.

Christina Heller had lunch ready and had baked a cake, which filled the little house with the most marvelos aroma. Magda introduced us and we spoke for a moment in German—Christina Heller was Austrian; I recognized that, but not much else. My concern was for Magda's health, and I insisted she show me to her room so I could examine her. Before she undressed I had her give me a urine sample. I'd brought my lab equipment with me, and into a test tube I measured out 1 cc of urine and added two drops of Fehling's solution, which turned the urine blue. When I held it over a candle, within seconds the heat turned it yellow, indicating the presence of sugar. Using a second test tube, I used acetic acid to test for albumin. There were traces of that as well.

As I feared, Magda's blood pressure was higher than normal. I listened to her heart and that of the baby's and palpated her breasts and abdomen and was relieved to find nothing abnormal. She'd had a bit of vaginal bleeding early in the pregnancy, but none at all recently. Her pelvis was small, but not abnormally so.

"When did you last menstruate?" I said.

"The beginning of March."

"You probably conceived around the middle of the month." I calculated on a pocket calendar, adding 266 days from March 15. "You're due in a month, around December 6."

"Will it be a boy, do you think?"

"Is that what you want?"

"I don't care."

"Not at all?"

She only shrugged, and slowly began to dress. I said, "Does Serge know you're pregnant?"

"I told him."

"You said you hadn't heard from him."

"I haven't," she said quickly, and then added, "I told him when we were together last."

She was only half dressed, her hands in her lap, sitting heavily on the edge of the bed. "We had a couple of days together," she said. "I told him then."

I joined her on the bed and took her hand. She wore no marriage band, and I wondered if that had been noticed, and what people in the town thought. She guessed what I was thinking. "Christina gave me a band," she said.

"But you won't wear it?"

"Do you think I ought to? Is it proper?" It was said flirtatiously, with a hint of the old Magda, the Magda of Saturday nights in the Paris dance halls, the Magda whom everybody noticed and adored. "Would it make me more respectable?" she said.

"No question it would."

"Then I won't wear it," she said.

"Did you marry Serge?"

"There wasn't time. We looked around for a —what-do-you-call-it?"

"A justice of the peace."

"Serge wanted to marry, but I told him it was of no importance. Married or not married, it doesn't matter one bit. Not one bit. What matters is how we feel about each other, and there I'm secure. He loves me, and I love him—I love him totally, and I always will."

"In spite of what he is and what he's done?"

"I don't know about any of that," she said. "I don't think any of it is true, and if it were I still wouldn't care. He means everything to me. I only know that, and I only care about that."

I left her to finish dressing and went into the kitchen, where Christina Heller waited. "The baby's heart is strong and seems to be lying in the right position," I said. "But there are a few complications, things that might be a problem."

"With the delivery?"

"Possibly."

"Magda won't let the local doctor touch her."

"Have you any experience yourself, Mrs. Heller?"

"If you would call me Christina, please," she said. "I've had four pregnancies, but all miscarried. And now, I'm afraid it's too late."

She busied herself, pouring coffee, slicing cake, and serving it to me. She was a year or two past forty, a woman who must have been pretty, but had become worn and faded. Her blond hair was already streaked with gray, and she did it up in a bun, in a grandmotherly style. I noticed her hands, which were unusually white, surgically clean, the fingertips wrinkled as if they'd been soaked too long in water. She wore only a marriage band, a wide one with delicate carvings, which were also worn and gave off a dull glow. It was old, an heirloom, but a humble one.

"It's from my mother," she said. "There were two, and I gave one to Magda."

After she had put the coffee and cake in front of me she kept busy, rearranging the plates, brushing crumbs from the table, and never meeting my eyes. I felt Christina Heller's past, felt it hovering close by, impatient to be told; it was a past that involved Magda. I wanted to hear it, and Christina Heller wanted to tell it to me, but something kept her quiet while she went on avoiding my glance and brushing imaginary crumbs from the kitchen table.

Finally, I said, "Did you know Magda as a girl?"

"No."

"I thought you might have met, living in Vienna."

"I'm from Eisenartz. It's a small place. I heard of Magda's family, and also of Magda, but we met only here in Canada." I waited. Christina Heller wiped her spotless hands on her apron. "We were lucky to get away, my husband and I. So many didn't. And we are very grateful. To Magda also, we feel a debt to her." She became flustered, and her face colored, but the smile that covered her embarrassment transformed her and made her seem years younger. "I'm grateful to be able to help Magda now, and the baby, particularly the baby."

"Such delicious cake, Christina."

"Another piece?"

"Yes. Why not?"

"It's lucky you don't have to watch your figure," she said. "So slender, you could eat what you want. Like my husband, he eats and eats and never puts on a pound."

"Will I have a chance to meet Herr Heller?"

"Walter? Yes, at six-thirty, when he finishes work."

"On Saturday," I said. "A full day?"

"He's a hard worker."

"May I ask what sort of work?"

"He repairs farm machinery. He's taken an old barn and made it into a garage. Walter is very clever with machinery. In Europe he was an engineer."

I took another bite of the cake, which was indeed delicious. "Were you able to come to Canada directly from Austria?" I said.

"Oh, no. We were eighteen months in Lisbon, without a visa or money. A terrible time, too. But I don't complain; it was worse for others, much worse."

"How did you manage finally?"

"It was my brother."

"Your brother, Christina?"

"He got us the visa. My brother was a clever fellow."

"And also well connected?"

"Yes. And he gave us the money for the passage."

"Your brother isn't alive, is he Christina?" I'd noticed something familiar about Christina Heller, a resemblance, which I was now able to place. "Before you married," I said, "was your family name Koder?"

"Yes."

"Your brother then, was he Willi Koder?"

"You knew Willi?" she said, and would have told me more, would have told me the whole story, but the bedroom door opened and Magda came out, buttoning her blouse. A quick, warning glance passed from Magda to Christina, and for the time being I heard no more of the family story.

"What did you find when you examined me?" Magda said. "You looked so grave."

"I told you about the sugar and the albumin," I said. "Your pelvis is small, and you've put on a little too much weight."

"A big baby," Christina Heller said.

"Will I have a difficult time?"

"There's nothing abnormal."

"But it will be difficult?"

"It might."

"I want you here. Promise you'll be here."

"Of course"

It was late afternoon, and as soon as the sun went down it turned cold. We built a fire—there was a Franklin stove at one end of the kitchen—and Christina began to prepare dinner. I offered to help, and after much protest Christina let me peel potatoes and cut up beans. I liked Christina Heller's kitchen, which smelled so good and was orderly and clean. I thought I would like one of my own, and when later on Magda and I went for a walk, I thought about it again, owning a place with fruit trees and a vegetable garden.

We hadn't walked far when Magda complained of being tired and we rested on a fallen tree trunk at the edge of the woods to the north of the house.

I said, "They look alike, Christina and Willi."

"A bit."

"You should have told me he had a sister."

"He didn't want anyone to know. He was secretive. It was a way he had of protecting her. But he told me to go to her if I was in trouble."

"He must have trusted you, cared for you."

"Maybe. I don't know. He sometimes had an odd way of showing it."

"How does she think he died?"

239

"In Europe, on a mission at the end of the war. I made up a cock-and-bull story. She thinks he was a hero, a great man. It's for the best, no?"

"And the baby," I said. "Does she think it's his?"

Magda turned, her eyes fixed on mine. "Damn right. I told her Willi was the father."

When we returned to the house, dinner was ready and Walter Heller was there. He was between forty-five and fifty, with the kind of taut, muscular body and face that age slowly. When he chewed, the muscles and small bones moved visibly under the skin of his temples and jaws. He'd bathed, shaved, and put on a freshly laundered white shirt. His flat blond hair was neatly combed.

I noticed that he was self-conscious with his knife and fork, careful not to make a mistake, and didn't say a word through dinner, a shy man, touchingly so, used to working with his hands. I wondered what he thought of Magda and her unborn child, of Willi, and Magda's tale of his heroic death. I wondered if he believed her. Magda was animated at dinner and told funny stories about working at her job in the department store in town. I noticed that Walter Heller never looked at her. When she spoke, he stared at his plate. Was he aware of the intrigue around the kitchen table, and did he resent our intrusion into his home? There wasn't a word from him and nothing in his expression to indicate what he thought—not a clue. He studied each of us when he thought he wasn't being observed, and looked down at his plate when he thought he was.

The next afternoon—Sunday—Magda drove me to the airport. Nothing more was said of Willi, or of Serge Dolin either. We kept clear of both subjects. Magda had told me she'd heard nothing from Serge, and it's possible that at the time—November—she was telling the truth; besides, I really didn't want to hear any more about her feelings for Serge. I didn't want to upset her, or myself. I didn't want to fall out with her. I was worried about her, and I wanted her to take care of herself. I feared she was going to have a difficult time.

She pretended to be confident and in good spirits, and only after my flight was called, and I was about to leave her, did she admit how worried she was, and how frightened.

"You promised you'd be here to deliver the baby," she said.

"I'll arrange leave."

"You've got to be here in plenty of time."

"I will."

Back in New York I arranged with the hospital administrator for leave to begin on December 2. I kept in touch with Magda to be sure she was feeling well and looking after herself. Her letters were cheerful; and on the telephone she said she was looking forward to the birth of the baby and confident about the future. Things were going to work out. That's what she said, "Things are going to work out."

I suspected her lift in spirits had something to do with Serge Dolin. When I again asked if she'd heard from him, she denied it, at the same time making me promise not to tell anyone where she was. I thought that odd; no one had asked me about her, or about Dolin. It was as if neither one had ever existed. And of course no stories had surfaced about the way President Roosevelt had died—and no one seemed suspicious.

That is, until Andrew Winters reappeared. It was toward the end of November, just before Thanksgiving, another of those nasty, wet days that stand out so in my memory, when Andrew called and invited me to dinner.

We ate in a place on West 10th Street in Greenwich Village, where the owner, Albert, wore the rosette of the Légion d'honneur, greeted Andrew with a *mon cher ami*, and led us to our table, walking with a gallant but discreet limp.

"Albert," I said. "Is he a cell in Living Memory?"

"An old friend," said Andrew, with one of those smiles that told so much and told nothing at all.

Albert saw to it that we were served good food and wine and left alone to talk.

Andrew first asked after Vladimir. "You mean you haven't seem him?" I said.

"Not since August, at the party for VJ Day," he said.

"I haven't seen him either," I said. "He's the guest of the lady from Palm Beach. I think he's writing a book."

"About what?"

"I have no idea." That wasn't true. Vladimir had told me all about the book he was going to write, was writing; he had told me too much about it, and too often. But I didn't want to talk about Vladimir and the lady from Palm Beach. Instead, I asked Andrew about Julia.

"She's not well," he said. "Headaches, dizzy spells, even a loss of sensation in her right arm. None of the neurologists can find a thing wrong with her. Since Franklin's death, she's gone into a spin. The old business again."

"What will you do?"

"Take her to the clinic in Zurich. What else can I do?"

241

By the time the coffee arrived, we had brought each other up to date. Albert sent a bottle of cognac to the table, and Andrew got around, at last, to the reason he had asked me to dinner.

"Do you remember the club Willi took Serge Dolin to," he said, "the place Magda worked in?"

"The Danube."

"It's been sold," Andrew said. "The fellow who owned it bought a small hotel and restaurant in Deauville. Have you ever been there?"

"No."

"It reminds me of the Jersey shore," he said. "But the hotel isn't bad, and of course the food is pretty good. The point is the Danube fellow was able to tell me something about Willi Koder, your Willi the Mouse. It turns out he had a sister, who lives someplace in Canada. The Danube fellow said Willi was actually attached to her, and used to visit her, and sometimes he took Magda along with him." Andrew had been watching me closely. "What do you know of the sister?"

"Willi never mentioned a sister," I said. "When he died, none came forward."

"Was there a will?"

"A will? Willi hadn't two dimes."

"He might have had something squirreled away."

"Any of us might."

"Well, in fact he did have a sister," Andrew said. "The Danube fellow was right about that, and about Willi helping her. On June 3, 1940, he signed an affidavit in the American embassy in Lisbon sponsoring the immigration of his sister Christina and Walter Heller, her husband. He was told there'd be at least a year to eighteen months' wait for their U.S. visa. The second secretary, a man named Packard, remembers sending Willi around to the Canadians. He had a friend there who could open the door. Willi went, and Packard says the door was opened. The Hellers immigrated to Canada."

"Then she ought to be registered with their immigration," I said. "They'd have an address."

"The last address they had for her was in Quebec," he said, "but she moved from there after being naturalized. Immigration has lost track."

"It's Magda you want," I said. "Magda you're looking for."

"No." He shook his head. "I only want to find Dolin."

"But you think Magda knows where he is."

"If anyone does."

"If he's alive."

"Dolin's alive," Andrew said. "In Mexico City I heard he had a run-in with a comrade."

"What do you want him for?" I said. "See that justice is done, or find out the truth? You're not that concerned about either, are you, Andrew? It's that chasing Dolin is the only reason you've got to go on in life."

Andrew ignored what I said. I doubt if he even heard. He had become deaf as a monument, as stone, and I could have been the wind howling around him.

"Let Magda alone," I said.

"He hasn't really treated her well," Andrew said. "She must feel some resentment—some anger. Does she need anything, do you think?"

"Magda wouldn't tell you a thing."

"Friends in the Canadian postal service have put a trace on Christina Heller," Andrew said. "But I was hoping you'd help me save time."

"I don't know where Magda is," I said.

I'm sure Andrew didn't believe me. But he didn't blame me either—not for protecting a friend. Even though he had made finding Serge Dolin his life's work, he didn't demand that the rest of us join in. In fact, he chose to do it alone. He was born a spy, and as much a solitary as Serge Dolin. I used to think there was something missing, a vital human part absent from people like Andrew. But it wasn't so. It was only that he needed to follow a constant signal, a light of some kind. That was true of Andrew, and I thought it was also true of Serge. But it turned out to be different for Serge. He was the far more complicated man. Vladimir and I had, in our investigations of Serge, seen something of those complications, and were about to see more. Serge was about to astonish us.

I had made arrangements to leave for Canada the following week. But after dinner with Andrew, when I returned to Brooklyn, I found Madame Berkowitz waiting up with news that Walter Heller had telephoned; there was an emergency. Magda had gone into the first stages of labor, with pain in the lower back and contractions about half an hour apart. The water bag hadn't broken, nor had she expelled the mucus plug protecting the cervix.

"He called from the village," Madame Berkowitz said. "His wife is with Magda. She wants to know how long Magda has."

"It's impossible to tell from here."

243

"I've called the airport," Madame Berkowitz said. "There's a Detroit flight at seven that connects to Toronto."

I had made a list of everything that I'd need for the delivery and packed it all in a separate bag. I went over the list, doublechecking it against the bag, and then tried to get a couple of hours' sleep. It was impossible. After examining Magda, I feared there'd be complications, and dreaded to think what would happen if the delivery began before I got there.

"I ought to have stayed with Magda," I said to Madame Berkowitz.

"You calculated the dates," she said. "She wasn't supposed to deliver for another two weeks."

"There's no way to calculate exactly," I said. "I should have stayed in Canada."

"She'll be all right once you get there."

"And if I'm not in time?" I said. "What happens then?"

Madame Berkowitz made coffee and stayed up with me. She'd taught me to play gin rummy, and we played that, anything to distract ourselves. Because we couldn't get a cab, she drove me to La Guardia airport and saw me to the departure gate. Although she had met Magda only a couple of times, she knew how important she was to me.

"God bless you, both of you," she said, her eyes filling with tears. Madame Berkowitz was a loyal friend. What's the expression? The salt of the earth—that was Madame Berkowitz.

The plane took off a few minutes late, and didn't arrive in Detroit until ten. I telephoned Madame Berkowitz at her shop, but she'd heard nothing from Walter Heller. The Toronto flight was delayed by weather, and we didn't get in until just past noon. I was relieved to find Walter Heller waiting for me.

"Christina sent me and told me to wait," he said. "She was afraid you'd have trouble with a taxi going out so far."

"When did you leave the farm?"

"An hour or so ago. Magda was in labor." He had taken my bags, and we ran to the old car.

"Christina told me to tell you there has been a little bleeding."

"A little or a lot?"

"She said only a little."

We drove the rest of the way without speaking, Heller with the accelerator pressed to the floor, and the old car rattling and shaking as if it were going to fall to pieces.

It had been some years since I'd delivered a baby, but since I'd last seen Magda I'd reviewed the procedures and assisted at two births in the hospital. But those had been without complications, and the closer we came to the farm, the more nervous I grew. I kept telling myself that I must think of Magda's delivery only as a medical procedure— one that I was prepared for and competent to deal with—and put personal feelings aside.

At the farmhouse, Christina Heller was on the porch waiting for us. She had earlier struck me as a stoical woman able to cope, but now I saw at once that she was badly frightened.

"Thank God you're here," she said. "I was going to try to reach the doctor. She's having a lot of pain. Too much pain."

"Has the bag broken?"

"Two hours ago."

"And the contractions?"

"Every ten minutes."

I took instruments from my bag and told her to sterilize them in boiling water. "And bring clean sheets," I said, "pillowcases, and fresh newspapers."

I went straight into Magda's bedroom. Her face was white, and beads of sweat stood out on her forehead; her mouth was drawn tight, the lips bluish with pain. But as soon as she saw me, her eyes lit up, and she managed an exhausted smile.

I bent over the bed to kiss her, and held her face for several seconds. "First thing, I'm going to give you something for the pain," I said.

"Will it put me to sleep?"

"No."

"Only groggy?"

"Yes. Maybe a little."

"When you came in just now I thought we were in Paris, the time you found me in that terrible hotel. Do you remember the name?"

"I can't."

"The Morocco, on the Rue Hebrod," she said. "If you hadn't found me, I'd have died then."

"You're pretty tough," I said.

"Is it very bad?"

"I don't think so."

"I wanted to have the baby."

"You will."

I held up her head and gave her a 50 mg tablet of promazine, which she swallowed with a bit of water.

"Is that for the pain?"

"It'll help."

"Serge wanted the baby, too," she said. "We wanted something, something real. Do you understand? Something of us." She gasped and cried out in pain.

"Bear down," I said. "It won't last much longer."

"Do you understand about the baby?"

I was too busy to answer, too busy to be nervous or to think of anything but the job ahead. Christina Heller brought a basin of boiled water and I scrubbed my hands, and sent her off to sterilize sheets and clean newspapers by baking them in the oven. When she had gone, I shaved Magda's perineum and labia, parting the labia with my thumb and forefinger to bathe the area with warm water and soap. I administered an enema and saw to it that she emptied her bowels.

I listened to the baby's heartbeat and rhythm, and called out for Christina to bring the instruments I'd instructed her to sterilize. Magda began to moan and to writhe with pain. The second stage of labor had begun, and after a prolonged and agonized uterine contraction, the baby's head distended the perineum; I parted the labia, and there it was, pushing against the soft tissue, which refused to yield.

Christina brought the tray of sterilized instruments. Her face was as white as Magda's, and she was unsteady on her feet. "Pull yourself together."

"I will."

"I'm going to need you."

"I'll be all right."

I used the Tarnier's forceps, gently trying to widen the pelvic outlet. But the soft parts remained rigid and too narrow to allow the baby's head to pass through. Magda gasped, swallowing a scream of pain. The baby was in danger of suffocating. I tried again to widen the cervix, but the passage was too narrow. There was no time to waste. I prepared a syringe of xylocaine and turned Magda on her side, injecting her in the epidural space in the small of her back.

Again she gasped, and this time it seemed a whimper, and she said, "Will I die?"

Christina gently wiped her face with a damp towel. "You're in good hands, darling," she said in her soft German. "Irina is here, and so everything will be all right."

The room needed to be kept warm, but it seemed to have become stiflingly hot and airless. The odors of the human body, of blood and birth, were powerful. Christina used a second towel to wipe the sweat from my face, and to dry it.

Magda said, "I'm going under."

"Just relax."

"If I die, you must do something for me."

"You won't die."

"Will you promise? It's Serge . . ." The pupils of her eyes were contracted, and slowly dilated as the drug took effect. I watched them blur and go out of focus as she began to drift off. She came awake, with an effort of will, her eyes now full of panic, and again clutched my hand. "Serge is alive," she whispered. "I'm to meet him. He's arranged it." Her eyelids fluttered and the lids came down. But she still held tight to my hand, and again whispered, "I love him. Tell him I love him. Promise. If I die, tell him . . ."

When I was sure that the drug had taken effect, I opened Magda's abdomen and uterus and lifted out the baby. It was a boy, Magda's son. I quickly cleaned his nose and mouth of mucus, and inserted a drop of 1 percent aqueous silver nitrate in each of his eyes and washed them with sterile water. I laid him with his head lower than the placenta so that the blood from it could drain into his body. He sputtered and shook all over, and with a scream took his first breath. He was alive and, by the look of him, fit and robust.

I had felt Christina stirring at my side, and when I had opened Magda's uterus, I'd heard her gasp, a low sound from deep in her throat, as if the pain were hers. I feared she would faint; she wobbled, but held firm. I handed her the baby and she quickly bathed him and wrapped him in a clean blouse and a blanket. I turned back to Magda, removed the last of the placenta, and sewed her up.

While Christina looked after the baby, I sat beside Magda, monitoring her blood pressure and temperature. I had gone a night without sleep and, being emotionally spent, after a time I dropped off to sleep. When I awoke, Christina brought me a cup of tea.

"Is she all right?" she said.

"Yes, I think so. What about the baby?"

"He's fine," she said. "Come and have something to eat, and stretch out. I can have Walter bring in a cot."

I wasn't hungry but I was certainly tired enough to let Christina make up a bed for me. I slept a few hours, checked Magda, and went back to sleep. The next thing I knew it was morning, and Magda was awake. The xylocaine had worn off and she was in great pain, although she hadn't made a sound all the time I was asleep. I gave her something for the pain and she slept the rest of the day. I set up an IV, but by evening she had recovered sufficiently to take food. I brought the baby to her, and she nursed him for a couple of days, but without pleasure, I thought.

"He's a healthy specimen," I said. "Seven and a half pounds. We weighed him on Christina's kitchen scale."

"I don't have enough milk to feed him."

"Christina has some formula," I said. "And your milk may flow more in a day or so."

She shook her head. "Christina better get more of the formula."

"Have you decided on a name?"

"I haven't thought much about it."

"It's natural to feel depressed after giving birth."

"I feel fine," she said. "Some pain, but less than before. When I was drugged, did I talk a lot? What did I say?"

"You talked about Serge."

"What did I say?"

"That you'd heard from him."

"It's true, I have. He calculated the time the baby was due, and called in advance. Nothing has changed between us, you know. He told me that, and I told him—"

"I don't much care what you told him."

"I told him that nothing has changed for me either."

"There's the baby," I said. "That's a change, isn't it?"

She shook her head, turned her face away, and then said, "When I was delirious, did I tell you I was going to meet him?"

"You weren't delirious."

"That's right, I wasn't. I was only scared. The truth is, I am going to meet him."

"Good for you, Magda."

"And live with him."

"Live with him? Both of you on the run?" I said. "You're a damn fool."

"Don't judge him," she said. "You haven't the right. You don't know him."

Magda said it defiantly, with her eyes flashing, and I shouted back at her. "Nothing matters but your precious Serge. He's a ruthless, cold-blooded bastard, but nothing else matters."

"I told you—you don't know him."

"I know of at least two men he's killed."

"You know nothing. Not the truth, nothing."

"Tell me the truth, Magda," I shouted, forgetting Christina in the next room, forgetting the baby. "Tell me how kind he is, and how generous. Tell me how playful, how tender a lover. The bloody damn Chekist killer."

That got Magda's blood up, got her defending her beloved Serge Dolin. "I'll tell you nothing," she said, "because you understand nothing. You don't know how it is really to love. You never in your life felt it."

"Love? You invented it, eh? It came into the world with you?" I was furious, and shouting at the top of my voice. Magda knew how to get under my skin, no doubt of that. "Are you the first woman ever to be in love? The first woman ever to get herself good and screwed?"

"That's it," she shouted back. "That's exactly how it feels—as if I were the first woman in the world to get screwed. You pretend to love Vladimir, but you don't see him for months, and meanwhile he's off having a jolly good time in bed with the famous lady from Palm Beach. But so what, eh, Irina? What does it matter, as long as you've got your work? You don't love Vladimir, because you can't love any man—you never have, and that's because you're one of those with too much water in her milk. What do you say, Irina? Is it so?"

I said nothing. I had no answer. On her face was a triumphant little smile, and on mine—God knows what I looked like. She'd struck me a painful blow, more painful for being so near to the truth. No doubt I hated her at that moment; we hated each other.

The next day I removed her stitches, and went back to New York. I heard nothing from her for ten days, and then Christina telephoned. Magda had gone, leaving her with the baby.

"Gone? Gone where?"

"I don't know," she said. "Please, we must talk about things. There are complications."

"With the baby?"

"No, he's fine. A fine boy. I'm taking good care, and he's putting on weight. The complications are with Magda."

"I can fly up Saturday."

"Walter will meet you."

I was anxious to know what the complications were, and eager to see the baby. I filled my bag with diapers and bottles and rubber nipples, as well as stuffed toys and a mobile to hang across his crib, and took the first flight in the morning. The weather was fine for a change and the plane arrived on time. By noon I was admiring the nursery Christina had made for the baby; it was painted white, with yellow trim and blue cotton curtains. She'd bought a handmade crib, and the little lord was in it, blissfully asleep.

He woke shortly after I arrived, and I examined him; he was perfect, a strapping boy, with a lot of dark hair. "Did Magda decide on a name?" I said.

"I'm going to call him William, after my brother." And then she said, "Magda has gone for good."

William's diaper and shirt were changed and he was wrapped in a wool blanket. I fed him and held him against my breast, with his head resting on my shoulder. I gently and rhythmically patted his solid back. After he had fallen asleep, Christina took him and placed him in his crib. When she came back, we had tea and she gave me a letter addressed to me from Magda.

"Christina will give the baby a better home than I could," she wrote, "and be a better mother—a lot better, I think.

"I'm very sorry we quarreled before you left. Twice when I've needed you, you've come. Twice you saved my life. Forgive me, Irina, but I must go quickly before it becomes impossible to leave the baby. I beg you to forgive me, and try to understand."

I folded the letter and put it away. Christina said, "My husband has gone to Sherbrooke. It's a town a few hundred miles east, near Montreal, not far from the Vermont border. He's bought a garage there."

"And you're going to move there with the baby?"

"Yes."

There was no doubt or irresolution in Christina Heller—not on the matter of raising William as her son. She had held fast at his delivery, and she held fast now.

"You and Magda," I said. "Did you plan it all along?"

"From last spring," Christina said. "When she came and told us she was pregnant. We wanted a child, and she wanted hers to have a proper home."

"Was it Willi who brought Magda here first?" I said.

"Sure. She was his girlfriend, a pretty thing. But then it got to be more, although he always denied it, and claimed that she didn't mean that much to him. He even urged her to go out with other men, that's what she told me. Is it true, do you think?"

"I don't know."

"Willi had his ways, you know. But one thing, he adored Magda."

Just then she went to check the baby. She'd heard him cry in his sleep—I hadn't heard it but, of course, she was on guard, listening for it.

When she came back, she resumed talking about Magda. "Before she left, she told me that Willi wasn't the father. She wanted to be honest, and also she knew that I loved him as my own, and if Willi was his father or not didn't matter."

"Did she tell you who the father was?"

"She didn't have to." I watched Christina wet the tip of her finger and absently pick up crumbs of cake from her plate and eat them. I once had an aunt who did the same thing, but when I tried it, my mother had scolded me. "I know who the father is," she said.

"How do you know?"

"Because he came here," she said. "Magda left to meet him, and said she wouldn't be back. But then they both came back. The stuffed dog in the crib—his father brought him that."

"And you spoke to him?"

"He sat there, where you're sitting," Christina said. "And he drank two cups of tea with me. A handsome man, but with an injury to his leg. He walks with a stick, and always he's in pain."

It was quite a surprise; Serge had returned for Magda, and also to see his son. Just then I remembered old Yakov and his story of young Serge at the piano with his mother.

"What's the matter?" Christina said.

"It's a shock to me."

"That he came to see his son?"

"Yes."

"Well, why not?"

"Right. Why not?"

"He held the baby," Christina said. "And looked at him for a long time. I kept wondering what he was thinking." She slowly shook her head. "They both said they wouldn't be back, but I wonder."

# twenty-one

☭ MAGDA HAD BEEN RIGHT ABOUT MORE THAN ONE THING—I knew less about Serge Dolin than I thought, and I hadn't cared for Vladimir enough to rearrange my life for him. But was it true that I'd never loved him, never loved any man? I didn't like the sound of that. I thought back on the times I had been with Vladimir and it did seem that I had loved him with my whole heart. I wanted to love him like that again, passionately, recklessly, as Magda loved Serge.

"The first woman in the world to be screwed" is how she described herself. Who wouldn't envy her that? And so I astonished myself, even as Serge had astonished me, and telephoned Vladimir at the home of the lady from Palm Beach, using as my excuse the birth of William. Speaking in Russian, I began to tell him what had happened, but he cut me off.

"I'm very glad you called," he said. "I can't tell you how glad."

"Tell me anyway." I heard voices in the background, music, laughter, all from his end of the line. A maid had answered the phone, and I visualized a party, one of those society bashes I'd read about; the lady from Palm Beach was famous for her parties. "I want you to tell me how glad you are I called," I said.

"Later," he said. "*Lybimaya*, I can't talk now. Everywhere are spies listening."

Later that night, he called back, reversing the charges. "I'm in a phone booth," he said. "And without enough coins."

"Who are the spies listening in?"

"Gregg, my hostess. She picks up the extension and listens in out of jealousy."

"Is she jealous of me?"

"Jealous? To make her furious, I have only to mention your name."

"How marvelous."

"I want to come up to New York for Christmas," Vladimir said.

"What's stopping you?"

"I'm broke," he said. "I didn't even have the coins for the telephone."

I sent Vladimir an air ticket, and met him at the airport. I'd bought a car—the first I'd ever owned—and we drove to Sherbrooke in Canada for the christening of William. I had helped register his birth as William Heller, son of Christina and Walter Heller, and Vladimir and I served as godparents.

On the drive back, I confided in Vladimir, telling him all that Christina had told me about Magda and Serge.

"Will you tell Andrew?"

"Not a word."

"He's been to Vienna is what I hear," Vladimir said. "Looking around for family traces left behind by Willi and Christina. From Vienna he went to Palestine, and to South America. He's hoping Magda's been in touch with somebody."

"She rarely talked about her own family," I said.

"They're all dead, mostly in the camps."

I remembered Magda telling me how she loved only Serge—no one else. "Will she regret what she's done, do you think?"

"Going off with Serge?"

"On the run all the time. It's not much of a life."

"It depends what happens between them," Vladimir said. "How that works out."

"Andrew won't let them alone," I said. "What if he finds them, what will he do?"

"He'll kill Serge," Vladimir said, without hesitation. He was looking absently out the car window, his wide-brimmed hat low over his eyes and his long legs drawn up. "In Palm Beach there's no way to tell it's almost Christmas," he said. "Why not stop and buy a tree—a Christmas tree?"

"At the next town."

"Next Christmas, I'll buy you a beautiful present," he said. "I finished writing my book, and I'm going to make a lot of money. It's the story of my life and adventures, and some of it may even be true, but only the incredible parts."

"Is the Princess Natasha in it?" I said. "Was there in fact a Princess Natasha, or have you only stolen her from Tolstoy?"

"Of course there was a Princess Natasha," he said. "Although I also made a little bit up."

He was about to tell me more—it was the right moment for him to tell me about his Natasha, about all the loves of his life; both of us were ready to let down our hair, to reveal our secrets once and for all, and even settle things about our future.

253

But just then we came to a roadside stand selling Christmas trees. Vladimir called out, and we stopped, bought a little tree, some wreaths and pinecones, a bushel of apples, and a gallon of fresh cider.

By the time we got back into the car, the mood had changed, and he didn't tell me about his Princess Natasha, and over Christmas when I tried to get him to talk about her, he wouldn't, but made jokes and evaded the subject.

He had kept his apartment on Third Avenue, although he was a couple of months behind on his rent. I loaned him the money to pay it, and we spent the holiday there. Our favorite bakery was gone—in its place was a bank—but certain things were the same. If I were secretly lonely and unhappy, and if I lacked confidence in myself as a woman, and if I were foolishly shy—well, as in the old days, with Vladimir all that was forgotten. We had been separated long enough so that novelty played its part, and we could return with passion to making love and, after passion, with comfort and the fondness of old friends.

We might have stayed together, even married. We talked about it—not seriously, or rather so seriously that we had to pretend it was a joke. Madame Berkowitz was to be matron of honor and hostess at a party afterward. The ceremony was to be in a Russian church, conducted by a priest with ties to Living Memory. But the more we joked, the more serious it got. Vladimir wanted to marry me, and I got cold feet. I was used to my life, comfortable with it, and now and then fleetingly satisfied with it.

I had been made chief resident in pediatrics at St. Monica's Hospital, opened a clinic in a brownstone not far from Prospect Park, and moved to an apartment of my own, although Madame Berkowitz and I still saw a lot of each other. My new place was very like the one I'd had in Zurich, and later on in Paris. I'm best off in compact rooms that let the sun in and are on the top floor near the roof.

After Christmas with Vladimir, I went back to Brooklyn; there was a flu epidemic that winter, and when Vladimir called I was too busy to see him. I was too busy all that winter, and Vladimir eventually stopped calling.

His book was bought by a publisher, and when it was brought out later that year, it became an instant success. The most glowing reviews and long interviews with Vladimir began appearing in the newspapers. He was good copy, and the radio talk shows picked him up. He was suave and witty, and his accent charmed everyone. With television, he became even more in demand. Madame Berkowitz bought one of the first sets. I remember sitting with her and peering at the tiny screen, watching Vladimir and listening to him go on about his adventures in the White Guards and the gallant, but doomed attempt to rescue the Princess Natasha from the Bolsheviks.

Vladimir became a darling of international society, attending the most glamorous parties; there would be his picture in the paper with Princess So-and-So and Countess Such-and-Such, with opera singers and well-heeled widows. He'd grown a distinguished little beard and had taken to wearing the Cross of the Order of St. Catherine, although where he got that I don't know.

He bought a home in Florida and traveled all over the world, sending me postcards from the most exotic places, and occasionally he'd telephone, and when he came through New York, we'd have dinner.

I marked the years by those dinners, by the lines in Vladimir's face and the gray hairs in his beard, and by my visits to my godson, Billy Heller, as I watched him grow. It seemed to me the years were passing quickly. Madame Berkowitz and I spent more time together—two aging women. We bought a house and some land in New Hampshire, and spent our holidays there, close to the Hellers.

If I sometimes missed Vladimir and regretted not marrying him, at least my work in the hospital and the clinic made me feel useful, and sometimes I was able to eat my dinner and go off to sleep feeling I had done something worthwhile that day.

But there were more days on which I saw things in a harsher light, with a sudden and penetrating understanding, and I suspected my own motives and scoffed at the noble sacrifices I made for the poor who needed me. I remembered that there were other doctors, and that more and more the city and state hospitals were taking over. I stayed in Brooklyn and worked long hours and sacrificed myself, out of choice, not because I was needed, but because I needed to feel worthwhile.

I was tired of the dreary and increasingly dangerous streets of Brooklyn, but I dared not leave them. I dreamed of the warm sun, not of the cold and rain of those early days in Zurich and Paris. I dreamed of a flower garden, and even a swimming pool of my own, a heated one, with tropical flowers planted all around. I wanted to live in that paradise with Vladimir. I saw myself working in the garden, digging and planting while he wrote in a room nearby, and with all my heart I wanted that. But I stayed in Brooklyn. I don't know why.

I did manage to spend part of every summer in New Hampshire, and as he got older Billy Heller would stay with me, working in the fields and with the animals, which we kept on the place and boarded on another farm in winter.

He was a clever, happy child, a pleasure to be around. He looked a lot like Magda, although his hair and eyes were darker—an energetic, sturdy little boy, as Serge Dolin must have been.

He was like Dolin in other ways. He loved music, and I can still see him on the couch with Misha, our cat, asleep in the bend of his arm, while Billy listened dreamily to my records on the phonograph.

I thought often of Magda, and wanted to get in touch with her, but didn't know how. And if I could reach her, was it the right thing to do? The Hellers were good parents who loved Billy. Eventually, he would have to be told the truth, but that was a few years off. My thoughts, though, were of Magda, and what I imagined was the restless, troubled nature of her life. There must have been times she regretted what she had done, and flayed herself for abandoning her son. But she had done it out of love for Serge Dolin. When I compared my life with hers, my life of routine and hard work, I found that I still envied her Serge and that single, irresistible passion.

During the first years after she left, I expected to hear from her. But as Billy grew older, as we grew older, I began to think that she had put all of us out of her mind. I wonder now if I was resigned to never seeing her again. I can't believe that. I knew that she was alive—I don't know how I knew, but I knew; and watching Billy grow, and seeing how he resembled her and even took on some of her manner-isms—there was no way to explain it, but the older Billy got, the more he reminded me of Magda, and the more I wanted to see her again.

Then one morning there it was, a letter from her, postmarked Dublin. It came in a plain envelope, prestamped, the kind sold in any post office in Britain.

She wrote in German, I don't know why—her English was quite as good. It was a short letter, without preamble or explanation, as if we had been in contact all along. There was no word of where she had been living, and no mention of Serge Dolin. Not a word of him. She only included a name and address in Dublin where I could write her. I knew it was a drop, like the one I'd run in Zurich. She wanted to know about the *boy*. She didn't know his name, and she didn't say "my son." She wanted the *boy's* photograph.

"If you would be so kind," she wrote in her best German, "please try to send all snapshots taken over the years, so I can see how he has grown."

I was angered by the letter, exasperated by the coolness of it, by

Magda's self-centered indifference to anyone but herself. Then I thought how many times she must have started the letter and torn it up and started again. How difficult it must have been to have waited so long and finally written to me about Billy. And in the end she must simply have said, "The hell with it," and treated it as if it were a business matter, an inquiry to an estate agent or lawyer in Vienna.

When I thought of the letter that way, it was funny, and I wished I had a phone number so as to call Magda and share the joke with her. I wanted to put my arms around her and assure her that she was forgiven, and more than forgiven, she was admired; cheeky and self-centered, she was a damn heroine.

But I put none of that in my return letter. I knew to go slowly with Magda, to let her think the moves were hers, and so I wrote a short, cordial, but formal note and sent a batch of photographs.

I didn't hear from her for nearly six months, and when I did the letter was postmarked Lisbon. Its tone was far friendlier and more relaxed. She thanked me for the photographs and asked about Billy—she liked the name because it was so American. She wanted to know about his school and what his interests were. She had, of course, shown the pictures to "someone," and he had thought the boy was very handsome and looked healthy and happy, and he wanted also to thank me.

That was her only reference to Serge Dolin, that "someone" who wanted to thank me. There was no hint of what their life together was like, and nothing beyond the postmarks on the envelopes to indicate where they lived or where they'd been. I read the letter over several times, looking for a clue. I don't know why, but I concluded that their life was hard.

At the end of the letter, she'd written, "I'd like very much to see Billy, but I don't know if I ever will. We still have to be careful." And then she added cryptically, "There is such a lot to worry about."

I answered her the same day. My letter was full of news of Billy, with more snapshots, and I wrote about myself and the difficulties that I had begun to have living and practicing in Brooklyn.

Soon, Magda and I were writing to each other regularly; I wrote long, chatty letters, the kind I knew she wanted to read. I was consciously drawing Magda back into my life.

It was successful. Her letters became less reserved and cautious. I picked up details of her life with Serge. They had been in South America and Mexico, and for a time in the islands off Italy, where they bought a house but had to sell it and move quickly. She didn't say why. They had been in London, where Serge had gone for medical treatment. Magda was tired of moving from place to place. "After all these years," she wrote, "I still have an electric ring on the bureau. I'm still a refugee."

She never discussed Serge, rarely mentioned him at all. Did she love him still? Did she regret going off with him? On all of that she was silent. She wrote only of wanting to see Billy.

In the fall of 1958, just before Billy's thirteenth birthday, Magda wrote suggesting that she and I meet in Paris. "It's been such a long time," she wrote. "I thought you might like to see Europe again, particularly Paris. We had some good times there."

I thought it was a marvelous idea and wrote her that I would take leave from the hospital starting the last week in November. A few days later there was a call from Air France in New York. An open ticket had been bought in my name, and a room reserved for me at the Hotel California on the Rue de Berri.

Madame Berkowitz, who was always after me to dress up, insisted I buy new clothes and presented me with a set of matched luggage. I even went to her hairdresser, the first I'd been to since I was a child in St. Petersburg. I liked it so much I decided I would go again, perhaps in Paris, just to have my hair washed and set.

The flight across the Atlantic was thrilling. I was eager to visit the old places in Paris, but most of all I was excited about seeing Magda again. I was disappointed that she wasn't at Orly to meet me. Neither was she at the Hotel California. A room had been reserved for me, paid up a week in advance, and in it were fresh flowers and a bowl of fruit. But no sign of Magda.

I unpacked, bathed, and changed into a new tweed suit. We had flown overnight, and now the sun was out. It was warm for November; no rain and cold this morning. I had coffee and a croissant and walked along the Champs Elysées, crossed the Seine, and wandered through the Old Quarter. Hardly anything had changed. I even recognized some of the faces in the street. A tailor had taken the storefront where the clinic had been; I saw him in the window at work on his sewing machine, a youngish man with russet hair and a full beard, wearing a yarmulke. The Jews had come back to the Old Quarter. I sat on the terrace of a familiar café on the Rue St. Dénis; the red wine and sandwiches tasted the same, although the prices were higher. I had a second glass of wine.

An American had told me a story. Before the war he had lived in Paris and stayed on until just before the Nazis came in. He enlisted in the American army, and because he spoke French and knew France, he wound up in intelligence—and was with the first Allied troops into Paris.

He rode across the Seine on the hood of a jeep, leading a caravan through his old neighborhood. The streets were jammed with people who had come out to greet the Americans. Everywhere he looked were young girls to kiss and men offering bottles of wine. In the middle of it all, he spied his old landlady, and when she saw him riding on his jeep, she nudged her husband and said, "*Alors, Marçel, voilà le petit Juif qui habitait le troisième étage.*"

I had a third glass of wine, feeling quite gay and glad I had come. When I returned to the Hotel California the concierge told me I had a visitor in the writing room just off the lobby. I rushed in, and there was Magda. My instinct was to throw my arms around here—I loved her, and started for her, but stopped when I saw her hold back, out of either that self-protective shyness of hers or something deeper, a feeling of unworthiness. We faced each other for a second or two, more than that, a breathless eternity it seemed, and then I could stand it no longer and ran toward her with my arms out, and we hugged each other, kissed each other, and cried and laughed in each other's arms.

We stayed talking in the writing room for hours, until it was dark and we were hungry. I don't remember what we talked about—Billy, I suppose. I'd brought more snapshots, and later we walked up the street and had dinner in a restaurant on the Champs Elysées.

She had looked through the photos once, and in the restaurant went back to them, and took one aside. "This one of him . . ." I saw her struggle to hold herself together, to control the surge of feelings that had risen up in her unexpectedly. "In this one there is such a resemblance," she said.

In the photo Billy was standing in an orchard in New Hampshire in front of a wooden fence, his arms folded, trying to look serious and grown-up. "He does resemble you," I said.

"No, not me—that doesn't matter. He's like my brother, very much like my brother."

"I didn't know you had a brother," I said. "You never mentioned him."

"Two years younger than I," she said. "I was sent to school in France. He was still at home when the Nazis came in." She studied the photo under the light from the table lamp. Magda was one who shields grief as if it were a flame that could not be allowed to go out. She had a brother, whom the Nazis had murdered; his loss was hers, never to be shared.

"I have not even a photo of my brother, or one of my parents either," she said. "But you once told me it's the same with you."

"I have no photographs, but I remember my mother and father," I said. "Sometimes, their faces are vivid, as if I could reach out and touch them."

"What's awful is when you can't remember what they looked like," Magda said. "It puts me in a panic. I wake up in the middle of the night, and there are no more faces, no past. I can't bear that. And it's the same with Serge. The same emptiness, the same panic."

"With Serge, it must be his mother he thinks of."

She stared at me. "Could you have known her?"

"No. But I met a man who knew her—the janitor in their house in Moscow. He told me about Serge's mother, and once described seeing them playing the piano together."

"Yes, it's true." She was smiling then, although her eyes were filled with tears. "Serge has told me the same story. And the janitor, was his name Yakov?"

"That's him."

"An old soldier with a wooden leg," she said. "And he lived finally in Pennsylvania. Is he alive? Yakov with the wooden leg, is he alive?"

"No, he died."

"Serge liked him, you know. He was very fond of his Yakov. He even visited him."

"I'd heard that, but I didn't know if it was true."

"Certainly it's true. Serge will be unhappy about old Yakov."

"Is it still the same between you and Serge?" I said.

She only nodded. She wasn't ready to talk of her life with Serge. "Tell me, is Billy good in school? Does he study?"

"Yes. He's a serious boy," I said. "He's clever, and picks things up quickly. He's best at mathematics and languages. He's got good French from school, and German at home. Lately, I've been teaching him Russian."

"Has he been told about me?"

"No."

"Does he know Christina isn't his mother?"

"He's not been told," I said. "I'm sure he suspects it, but isn't quite ready to face it."

"Then he must be curious. He must want to meet his real parents."

The waiter brought menus, and while she was deciding what to eat, I had a chance to study her. She was older, thirty-eight by then,

260

but I really think she had never been as beautiful. Her hair was darker, her figure a little more full, and her features softer, her eyes particularly, the light in them more gentle and reflective. She had been uninterested in clothes and I remembered an intentional drabness; she had wanted not to be noticed. Now she dressed stylishly and it was impossible not to notice her. Wherever she went, there followed behind a sexual stirring. When we had entered the restaurant, I saw it in the reaction of the proprietor, in the waiter who served us, the men at other tables, even the women.

Beside her, one became invisible. In one way that suited me. I liked standing aside in order to observe the effect she had on others. She was indifferent to that effect, not quite aloof, but independent of admiration—as I knew her to be contemptuous of those men and women who depended upon it; at times I thought she was tired of being beautiful, and always concerned that it not be used to distract from more serious matters.

I wondered at the changes she saw in me. Even in my new clothes, beside her I felt dowdy. I had thought of myself as taller than Magda, but now I saw that we were the same height. She was saddened by the lines and fatigue in my face; when I talked, she'd look at me with eyes full of unhappiness.

After dinner we strolled a bit on the Champs Elysées and returned early to our hotel. We were both tired and slept well, meeting the next morning for breakfast. I told Magda about going to the Old Quarter on the other side of the Seine.

"Do you remember the clinic?" I said.

"Your clinic on the Rue de Babylone?"

"We lived on the Rue de Babylone."

"The clinic was there, too."

"It's nearly twenty years ago."

After a moment, she said, "You're right, it wasn't Babylone. The clinic was on Rue Alphonse. When I'm wrong, you never tell me. Why is that?"

"You're wrong, Magda," I said. "The clinic was on Boulevard St. Marcel."

We had a good laugh; until then there had been some stiffness between us, and we had been occupied by observing each other. With that laugh, the stiffness fell away, and it was like old times.

"I liked that clinic of yours," she said, "and helping out there. I never told you this, but at the time I thought of going to medical school. I was young enough, and I wanted to be like you."

261

"Like me?"

"Sure, why not?" she said. "I had a fantasy of the two of us in practice together. I admired you so much, a woman on her own, starting out with nothing, doing work that was worthwhile, and being independent, not needing any man."

"Not needing any man?" I said. "Or simply lacking the passion to sacrifice for one? What was it you said? I had too much water in my milk?"

"I was talking through my hat."

"Were you? You gave up everything to go off with Serge. I wouldn't have the courage to do that."

"One changes." She shrugged. "You could be describing a stranger," she said.

After breakfast, we decided on a long walk, a look in the shops, and a bit of sightseeing. We started out for the Champs Elysées, and turned in the direction of the Place de la Concorde. As we walked, arm in arm, she began to describe her life with Serge.

"He's nearly always in pain," she said. "And lately it's been getting worse. He was shot in Mexico, shot or stabbed; he won't talk about it. That part of his life is put away—yet it torments him. The pain is there, and the torment also."

She talked about the rootlessness of their lives, how they moved regularly from place to place, and how she had no home, but always lived in hotels. She had no friends. Serge had money hidden, but for a long time it was too risky to go near. "Serge said it had to be allowed to cool," she said, "and in the meantime we had to lie low, and take any kind of job. I didn't mind, I was used to it, yet for Serge it was humiliating. He waited tables, played piano in a dive. He was a travel guide and washed dishes and worked as a busboy one time when I was sick and we were up against it. He took abuse from men whom he could have swatted like a fly. He swallowed his pride; he was able to do that—he had that sort of guts too."

Magda had kept everything bottled up, and when she finally began to speak, it came out in a rush. "And all along somebody was after us. We were hunted." She shook her head. "At first I didn't believe Serge. I thought he was imagining it, that it was a ghost he'd raised out of his own guilt. But then I saw him for myself."

"Who did you see?"

"The American. Your old friend."

"Andrew Winters."

"Two years ago in Vienna," she said. "After Stalin died, and

Khrushchev denounced him, Serge decided to take a chance and dig out our money. I wanted to go back to Vienna to see if anyone had survived, and what was known of my family. I went alone."

"And Winters?"

"He had been over the same ground," Magda said. "He was looking for a way to find me, and through me to locate Serge. Along the way, he talked to a lot of people. He knew one day I'd be back. Most of us go back in order to see with our own eyes what we remember, and to learn whatever we can of the end of those we loved." She took a deep breath, a sigh, full of pain and resignation to pain. "Andrew Winters left behind a lot of shillings, dropped into the right palms," she said. "If I came around, he was to be contacted. It worked. The day I was to leave, he appeared at my hotel."

"You saw him?"

"We had a long talk," Magda said. "I told him I was leaving for Israel. I'd located a cousin, who'd survived and was living there. It was true, I was going to see her, and to find out what she knew of my family. He said it was no affair of his, and that I was free to go where I wanted. His only interest was in meeting Serge."

"What did you tell him?"

"That Serge was dead, that he killed himself." She shook her head, and said, "It's what I fear, you know. That one day he will kill himself."

"Did Andrew believe it?"

"I don't know," she said. "I think maybe he wanted to believe it. He wanted Serge to be dead, and himself rid of the obsessive need to find him."

It was getting cold, and a few drops of rain began to fall. I said, "Andrew won't rest until he finds out what happened."

"What do you mean?"

"He needs to know the truth about FDR's death."

"He asked me a lot of questions," Magda said. "Had I ever heard the name Godinsky? Did I ever meet somebody called Max? All sorts of questions, and names, lots of names."

"What did you tell Andrew?"

"That I could tell him nothing. I knew nothing."

Was it true? I searched her face for some clue, but there was none. Had Serge confided in her—during the thirteen years of their life together, had he managed to hold it all back? Or had she lied to Andrew, and was she lying to me now? I said, "When you told Andrew you knew nothing, did he accept that?"

"He drove me to the airport when I flew to Tel Aviv," she said. "He even gave me the names of some people there—people who might have information."

"And what did you find out?"

She shrugged. It was a gesture of hers that hadn't changed. "A dead end," she said. "I spoke to the people Winters had mentioned, but they had no file on my family. My cousin remembered only that my father and mother, my brother too, were taken away. After that she didn't know what happened to them."

We spent that day and the next in Paris, visiting places we had known and enjoying ourselves in the restaurants and shops. We planned to travel to Zurich, but the morning we were to leave, Magda knocked on my door.

"I've had a call from Lisbon," she said. "Serge isn't well. He's had an accident." I had ordered a pot of early morning tea, and offered Magda a cup. When she took it, I noticed that her hand shook.

"The call was from the woman who owns the pensione," she said. "Serge was having a bath and fell asleep, flooding the damn place." She took a deep swallow of the tea, drew a deep breath, and sat with her head back and her eyes raised to the ceiling. "The landlady isn't a bad sort. She knows I'll make good on the damage. She said it could have been worse. Serge could have drowned."

"Did he faint?"

"He passed out. He was drunk."

"Where is he now?"

"God knows where. Probably gone someplace for more to drink. He won't talk to me. He's ashamed." She slowly lowered her eyes from the ceiling and shook her head. "He does awful things to himself and others. He goes to the worst dives and gets into brawls, and sometimes he gets beaten up. It's as if he's punishing himself. I'm afraid one day he'll be killed. Do you see how it is? I can't leave him."

"What will you do now?"

"Take the first plane to Lisbon."

"Let me go with you."

"No. If he sees you, it'll only be worse," she said. "He went to the Americans, you know."

"I didn't know."

"American intelligence. Serge knew a man in Madrid, and went to talk to him, to tell him all he knew. He did it for my sake, so we could go back to America and see you and Billy. But the Americans weren't interested. They didn't want to hear what Serge had to tell. They treated him as if he were a crackpot. They wouldn't listen to his story."

We arranged our flights—hers to Lisbon and mine to Zurich—so that we could share a cab to the airport. I'd have to wait a few hours, but it didn't matter. I feared only that she would retreat again into her troubled life with Serge and I'd never see her again.

"If I can arrange it," I said, "would you like to meet Billy?"

"Can it be done?"

"He's mature for his age," I said. "It's time he found out about you, and got to know you."

She had brought a photograph of her and Serge. Serge had changed so much I wouldn't have recognized him. His hair had gone nearly white, and he seemed so much smaller, barely taller than Magda. He looked distressed, and uncomfortable, as if he had been obliged to dress up for the photograph; his collar looked too stiff, and I noticed a handkerchief folded neatly in the breast pocket of his jacket.

Magda said, "Will you show our picture to Billy?"

"Of course."

"We still can't travel to America."

"I'll try to arrange for him to have a holiday in Europe."

"All I want is to meet him," she said. "To get to know him. And Serge too. It's all he wants."

We said our good-bys in the airport lounge, before we got to passport control. Magda didn't want me to see the travel papers she used. That was a reminder to me of the kind of fugitive life she had been living with Serge. Yet she was anxious about Serge and eager to be on her way to Lisbon, to return to him. He was still the center of her life. I resented that, and was disappointed that our holiday had been interrupted.

On the plane to Zurich I took out the photograph Magda had given me of her and Serge. I remembered whom they reminded me of: Nadine Berne and the murdered Pole, Godinsky. What was it that had caused me to connect the two photographs? They were people a world apart. Yet something in the photograph, some psychological clue, had jogged my memory and caused me to think of the other pair, both long dead.

The air hostess brought me a drink and I sipped it, leaning back with my eyes closed. In the photograph of Nadine and Godinsky she had worn flat heels so as not to appear taller than her husband. I took another swallow of my drink, and realized what had linked the two photographs: It was the wifely handkerchief folded so lovingly in the breast pocket of both men.

# twenty-two

I HAD LOOKED FORWARD TO ZURICH, TO SEEING OLD friends and the places I remembered so well. But those of my friends who were still alive had gone elsewhere. And visiting the cafés and standing in front of the house with the attic room where I'd lived only made me miss Vladimir and wish he were with me. I went by Lowenstein's jewelry shop, where I had gone to sell my father's fake diamond, and in the way of such things, the weather was again raining and cold. Lowenstein's shop was unchanged, and inside was a man who startled me, he looked so much like Lowenstein; I went in and impulsively bought a gold watch for Vladimir, and found out that the man who sold it to me was Lowenstein's son.

The same day, out of loneliness, I telephoned Vladimir in Florida; but he wasn't there. His housekeeper told me he was traveling. She expected him back in a few days. I wrote him a letter—"a love letter from one old fool to another" is what I called it. It was a difficult letter to write, and I must have started it and thrown it away a dozen times. I wanted to tell him how much I loved him, how he was an inseparable part of my life, and to at last confess I needed him. As I say, a difficult letter to write. I had to tell him I feared growing old with nobody to care for, and nobody to care for me—and perhaps most important of all, nobody to chew over old times with, no "first witness," which was one of Vladimir's names for me. I was his first witness, and he was mine. Without a first witness to testify to the past, it might not have happened.

What a chilling thought that was: All that we loved, all that made us happy and broke our hearts—none of it real, all of it so much smoke. I tried to get all that in my letter, and then to wind up proposing marriage. I actually wrote it—a marriage proposal. But then I got cold feet, and didn't mail it.

I folded the letter away and kept it with me on the flight back to New York. I argued with myself all across the Atlantic. It came down to being reluctant to give up my work at the hospital and the clinic, to retire and live comfortably with Vladimir in Florida.

Yet I can't say I liked my life in Brooklyn, which was becoming more harsh each day. After Paris, and particularly Switzerland, where things seem never to change, the burned-out houses, the litter in the streets, and the drug addicts in the hallways of Brooklyn were a shock.

Madame Berkowitz told me while I was away she had been held up, robbed, and beaten.

"I know the one who did it," she said. "I've seen him before, the big one they call Zombie."

"He's been around the clinic, looking for drugs," I said, "and threatening to smash the place if I don't give them to him."

"The police were helpful, but I was afraid to identify him," she said. "I'm going to close the shop, pack up, and get out. Enough is enough. I've got a little money saved. I thought I'd go to one of those spas out west and spend a little time with my sister in Beverly Hills. We've been talking about a Pacific cruise, stops in Hawaii, Hong Kong, Bangkok." Later on, she said, "I don't want to go back to Europe, too many lousy memories."

"I'm going to miss you."

"Then why not come along?" she said. "The place in New Hampshire is worth a pretty penny. If you want to sell, it's okay with me."

"And sail away to the South Seas?"

"What's bad?"

"The land in New Hampshire keeps going up every year," I said. "One day we'll be rich."

"One day we'll be old hags," Madame Berkowitz said. "Irina, for once give yourself a break."

I listened and said I would, but for the time being I did nothing about leaving, and the letter to Vladimir stayed in my desk drawer. Madame Berkowitz packed up and left for California, but I stubbornly hung on. The city cut the staff of the hospital and refused money for new equipment, which we desperately needed. When I complained to the director, I was told the administration was considering closing the hospital.

One night on my way home from the clinic, I saw a man shot to death on the street. He was young, seventeen or eighteen, and he'd tried to hold up a liquor store; shots were fired, and he staggered out of the store, the owner chasing him with a pistol. He turned back for a moment, and the owner stopped and pointed the pistol at him—I was only a few feet away, unable to move, powerless as in a dream, looking on as the store owner shot him in the chest.

Once it was over, I tried to help. The robber was crumpled up on the sidewalk, blood pumping from a hole in his chest. I tried to plug the hole, to slow down the bleeding, but there was little I could do. People stood looking down at the dying man indifferently. By the time the police arrived, he was dead.

That same night I mailed my letter to Vladimir, and the next morning I told the director I'd be leaving the hospital at the end of the month. I called Billy and arranged to drive up and visit him that weekend at school.

I had planned to drive to New Hampshire late Friday afternoon, sleep at the house, and go on to Billy's school the next morning. Before leaving, I went to the clinic and was doing some work on my insurance forms when I heard someone at the door. I had locked it from the inside as I always did when I was alone. But as I watched, the knob turned and the door opened. It was Zombie; he'd picked the lock.

"You see how easy it is," he said. "Any time I want, I could do the same over at your apartment." He knew my address, the apartment number. "And the locks on the door—one's a Segal, the other a Medeco, no problem."

"What do you want?"

"Drugs," he said. "You got no money."

He paced back and forth as he spoke, circling me, as if he were about to pounce, watching me out of the corners of his eyes. He was of medium color, with a droopy mustache and a tuft of hair between his lower lip and chin. His cheekbones were high and his eyes narrow, a point of cold light in each pupil.

"You don't use drugs," I said.

"I sell them."

"I don't have any here," I said.

He stopped circling me and stood without moving. I could feel the tension quivering in him. He slapped me, his hand lashing out so quickly I didn't see it. "Talk nice," he said. "Tell the truth."

My cheek was numb where he'd hit me, but in only a few seconds it began to burn. "Let me put some ice on my face," I said.

"You're a tough old lady," he said. "You don't scare."

"I'm scared enough to tell you the truth," I said. "All I keep here is aspirin."

"I know that," he said. "I'm talking about the hospital. They keep the drugs in the safe, right?"

"I'm not given the combination."

"You're a doctor."

"The way it works is, we write a requisition for every drug and give it to the security office to fill."

This time I saw the blow coming and managed to get my hand up, which only infuriated him. He punched me in the ribs and kicked me, at the same time shoving me against the wall. He began to smash things, deliberately, maliciously picking things he judged to be most precious—my diplomas from the wall, my instruments—and never taking his eyes from me, those narrow eyes with their cold light.

He hit me a few more times and did other things to humiliate me, but I shut my eyes to them then, and refuse to recall them now. They are not to be recalled. They are part of the evil that is in the world, as he is part of the evil. Finally, he went away, threatening to return, and I got slowly to my feet, bruised but with no bones broken. I washed myself and treated the bruises, swept up the mess he'd made, and walked the few blocks to my apartment. From there I telephoned Vladimir in Florida, but there was no answer. I quickly packed a bag, carried it around the corner to the garage where I kept my car, and drove that night to the house in New Hampshire.

I slept a few hours, and the following morning drove on to Billy's school, St. Stevens outside of Middlebury, Vermont. I had a fair-sized bruise under my eye and bought a pair of dark glasses to cover it; the promise of seeing Billy cheered me up. He was in his freshman year, and though his first months had been difficult, he was settling in well. St. Stevens was not only academically demanding; it also had an exacting code of dress and conduct. Most of the boys came from wealthy or well-to-do families and were more sophisticated than Billy. But he caught on quickly. He wasn't one to curl up or quit, or hide in a corner; a good athlete, as well as a good student, he was the kind of boy others are naturally drawn to.

He'd grown since the last time I'd seen him, and it seemed he looked more like Magda than ever. He'd spoken German since childhood and studied French in school. I'd always spoken Russian with him, and now he'd begun to study it seriously. St. Stevens had a Russian instructor, and he'd encouraged Billy.

"He says I have a good accent," Billy said. "And he wanted to know if my parents were Russian."

"Did he?"

"I told him my grandmother was Russian," Billy said. "And then I told him all about you, the story of the diamond sewn into your coat and how your parents sent you off to have a new life. I told him how you met Uncle Vladimir, and lived in Switzerland, Paris, and Cuba, and finally came here."

"You told him I was your grandmother?"

269

"Yes. And he's dying to meet you. When I told him you were coming this weekend, he invited us to tea."

"Tell me his name again."

"Mr. Davilov. Yuri Davilov."

"How old is he?"

"Not so old. He's strong, like Uncle Vladimir—well, maybe not *that* strong."

We went to tea with Yuri Davilov. His house was just off the campus, on the main road to town. He spoke American English and Russian like a Muscovite, an urbane man, I thought, at work on a new translation of Turgenev and an anthology of Soviet writing after 1946. He talked easily about his work and was never pompous or self-conscious. He was obviously a good teacher, and I understood why Billy liked him.

"I knew a Davilov," I said. "He was an officer with the Whites."

"My uncle was in the army, and later was wounded at Kazin with the Whites."

"What was his full name?"

"Igor Andreivich."

"I knew him in Paris."

"A small world," Davilov said.

Davilov's wife was American, from Columbus, Ohio, an attractive blond woman several years younger than he. She was a painter, and several of her canvasses were on the walls. They were sophisticated paintings, very skillful. She also baked good brown bread and put up her own jam. We had a nice tea, a nice afternoon. Billy adored Davilov, and I saw no reason to be suspicious of Davilov's motives, or of the way in which he encouraged Billy. I thought it natural. I was sure it was innocent.

Later on, when we were alone, Billy said, "I want to know about my real mother and father." I had told him about meeting with Magda in Paris, and gave him the photograph of her and Serge. At first Billy only glanced at the picture and hastily put it away. There was something furtive in his gesture, and I was sure he wanted to be alone when he looked his parents over carefully. But a little later on he surprised me by taking out the photo and studying it; I watched his face for a clue of what he was thinking. I was struck by how he had grown up and again by how he resembled Magda.

"Are you sure that's my father?" he said, at last.

"Yes."

"He doesn't look the way I thought."

"He hasn't been well," I said. "He's changed a lot."

"Did you know him well?"

"Not as well as I knew you're mother."

"He was a soldier in the Russian army, wasn't he?" Billy said. "But you said my mother met him in America. If he was in the Russian army, what was he doing in America?"

"It was during the war," I said. "Your father had gone to work for their foreign service."

"Did you like him?"

"I didn't know him all that well."

"But you love my mother?"

"Yes."

"Is she as beautiful as the picture?"

"More beautiful."

"Do I look like her?"

"Quite a bit."

"But I don't look like him," Billy said.

"I told you, he looked very different when young."

"I don't look a thing like him," Billy said.

"Would you like to meet them?" I said.

I had expected him to be eager for it, to jump at the chance to see them at last. But Billy again surprised me. "Do you mean she'd come here?" he said.

"I was thinking you'd go to Europe next summer."

"By myself, do you mean?"

"If you want."

"I don't know." He put the photograph in his pocket. "Can I think about it?"

"You'd like her."

"What about him?"

"You can meet her alone," I said. "If you want to meet your father later on, that'd be up to you."

"Did she say she wanted to meet me?"

"Of course," I said. "She's eager to meet you. Very eager."

"You mean she's invited me to meet her in Europe?"

"In Paris."

"All right," Billy said formally. "If you give me her address, I'll write to her and accept her invitation."

Because I was not a spy, because I had long ago stopped being a spy, I incautiously wrote out Magda's address and gave it to Billy.

271

# twenty-three

ON THE LONG DRIVE TO NEW YORK, I THOUGHT ABOUT THE letter I had finally mailed to Vladimir, and wondered what he would think when he got it. Was he involved with another woman, another like the lady from Palm Beach? I began to regret sending the letter. I felt like a fool.

Worse than a fool, I felt old and unloved. Billy was growing up, Madame Berkowitz had gone off on her South Seas adventure, and the hospital was about to close, leaving me out of a job. No gratitude in the world and no place for an old lady to lay her head, and no companion on a long solitary drive like self-pity.

By the time I got to New York I had made up my mind to pack up and move on. I decided to return to Paris or even Zurich. But just the thought of Zurich brought tears to my eyes; I was again in that attic room with Vladimir and the romance of my life was beginning. How I loved him—and why had I been so foolish as to lose him?

But of course I hadn't lost him. How could I lose Vladimir, who would never let me down?

He had received my letter, my marriage proposal, and was overjoyed, and had tried to reach me at the hospital, the clinic, at home. When he couldn't get hold of me, he'd sent a telegram, which was waiting for me under my door.

"*Lybimaya*," he wrote, "pack up. "Your life is about to begin."

I spent the rest of the night filling cartons and suitcases. Vladimir had instructed me to pack up, and so I packed up. I didn't know where we were going and it didn't matter, for I was certain it would be an adventure. Driving home, before I received his wire, I had felt that all good times were past, that all I loved was lost, and that I was an old woman with nothing left but to lay down her head.

And now it was all changed. My life wasn't over; it was beginning. I scribbled a note to Vladimir, stuck it in the door, and, happy as a bride, went off to the clinic to collect a few of my instruments.

But I had forgotten something. I had forgotten that when you're feeling gayest and most confident of the future, that's the time to watch your step. I hadn't noticed that the weather was nasty, cold, and raining. I hadn't noticed the scratch marks on the outside door lock of the clinic. I hadn't noticed the muddy footprints or the litter in the hall, and so when I opened the inner door, I was shocked to see that the clinic had been broken into, and everything smashed to bits, and the walls covered with spray paint, and even the furniture broken and torn, the stuffing of couches and chairs ripped out. The fury of it, the rage, left me dazed.

I had forgotten Zombie, and the beating he'd given me, and the humiliation I'd endured. It suddenly came back. I screamed with fear, and stood trembling in the middle of the wreckage he'd made.

Then I heard something—the chilling sound of broken glass ground under a heavy foot. It was Zombie.

He shouted and shook his fist and threatened me, as he had before, but now he was furious, and I looked around for something to defend myself with, but there was nothing. He lunged at me, and I jumped away. He had come to kill me, and truly I thought my end had come.

Just then I heard another heavy step on shattered glass. Zombie heard it too, crouching and starting, and with a mad look in his eye. Before I could see who it was, I knew it must be Vladimir, and I knew that once again he'd come to save my skin, and come just in the nick of time.

Vladimir faced Zombie, an old man now, but half a head taller than Zombie, just as broad, and far more resolute. Zombie didn't know what to make of him. He stopped his shouting and his endless circling, and crouched with his fists clenched at his sides, panting with his mouth partially open.

"Come, *Lybimaya*," Vladimir said, holding out his hand to me. "Come, my dearest."

I took his hand, and stepped lightly over the smashed furniture and broken glass, and we started for the door. Zombie revived, and snarled something at Vladimir, who ignored him. To be ignored infuriated Zombie most of all. He cursed Vladimir and called him every vile name, and still Vladimir ignored him. Zombie decided that Vladimir was afraid. This hoodlum thought that my Vladimir, the hero who had fought Lenin's thugs and Stalin's thugs and survived both their prisons—this hoodlum thought my Vladimir was afraid. And so the fool went too far. In front of Vladimir, he dared to lay his hand on me.

At that Vladimir gave a great roar—I tell you it was a roar that made the walls shake—and his huge fist shot out and hit Zombie in the middle of the face, and he staggered back, his nose spurting blood. Vladimir was after him and grabbed him with one hand, drew back his

fist, and again struck him, and once more, before hurling the hoodlum across the room, where he curled up in a corner, bleeding and
moaning, and that was the end of him.

But the fight had taken something out of Vladimir. Across from the
clinic was a broad avenue with benches the length of it—Eastern Parkway, it was called—and I had to put my arm around Vladimir and
help him to a bench.

"What is it?"

"A pain in my chest," he said.

He smiled weakly, helplessly, and the stricken look in his eyes sent
a chill through me. All the color was gone from his face and he had
begun to sweat; the pain in his chest spread through to his back and the
length of his arm. His breathing was labored, his pulse rapid and
irregular.

"Ahh, *Lybimaya*," he said in Russian. "I'm no spring chicken."

I loosened his collar and wiped his face. A light rain fell.

"Stay close to me," he said.

"Is there much pain?"

"Ahh, stay with me."

"I'm going for help. Hold tight, I'll be back in a second."

I ran into the middle of Eastern Parkway, and waved at passing
cars, trying to get one to stop. But none did. Just then, a stroke of
luck—I saw a police car at the end of the street. I ran toward it, shouting and waving. They caught sight of me, and made a sharp U-turn
and pulled up.

"I'm a doctor," I said. "My husband is having a heart attack."

There were two policemen, and both were out of the car and running along the street toward Vladimir, who had slumped over on a
bench.

"St. John's is closest," I said.

His color was worse, and he was only semiconscious. The policemen took hold of Vladimir and carried him to the car. I got in next
to him, tore open his shirt, and with the siren screaming, massaged his
chest, and talked to him in Russian, pleading with him to breathe, to
live. But I could feel the fibrillations of his heart under my hand, its
pathetic fluttering.

Within minutes we were at the emergency entrance of St. John's.
The police had called ahead, and an emergency team was waiting for
us. Vladimir was carried from the police car and placed on a stretcher,
a portable oxygen unit wheeled beside him. I knew the doctor on duty,
an Indian, a good doctor, and he went right to work on Vladimir, even

as they carried him into intensive care. I ran along beside him, clutching his hand. The oxygen had brought him around a bit; he was conscious, aware of everything and in great pain; his eyes, those eyes that I had known forever, they never left mine.

For the next week I slept at the hospital and stayed near him, so that when he was awake he could see me. The doctors thought a main artery was involved and it was very grave. He ran a high fever, and there was no way to know if he would live or die.

The cardiologist said the first week was crucial, and that his chances improved every day after that. Toward the end of that first week, I dozed off in the chair next to his bed, and either heard or dreamed something that made me think Vladimir had died. If it was a dream, it was nothing I could remember, only a shade that passed through me and left me shivering and frightened.

I said out loud, "No, he's not dead." Then I whispered, "He can't be dead."

It was my old feeling that there was more to our lives, that more was to come, and now added to that was the faith that what was still to come would turn out to be the best time of all.

He recovered slowly, then more quickly. Soon he was sitting up in bed for short periods, and at the end of the second week was moved from intensive care. The color gradually returned to his face, but he had lost weight, and I was struck by how thin his arms seemed in the loose short-sleeved hospital dressing gown, and how the cords in his neck stood out. In his eyes I saw something I had not seen before. He was afraid, dependent, even helpless; all of that was in his eyes. When I was in the room they never left me, and if I got up and moved around they followed me, and if I left they pleaded with me to stay.

When he thought I wasn't around, his eyes took on a contemplative, distant look. I would wonder at what scene of his life he was remembering, and if I were part of it. I sensed that at those moments, when his thoughts took him far away, he was without terror or pain.

When he was well enough to leave the hospital, he had his lawyer rent a suite in the Gramercy Park Hotel, on 21st Street in Manhattan.

I was given a room of my own and for a time looked after him. He held court for people I didn't know—his lawyer, his accountant, his literary agent and publisher, all those who collect around a rich and famous author. The actor who had played him in the movie made from his book came, and got so drunk he had to be put to bed. The actress who played his Princess Natasha sat on the edge of his bed, held his hand, and gazed deep into his eyes, crossing her beautiful legs. A man arrived who was writing an opera from Vladimir's book. Every day there came a stream of people—writers, violinists, and head-waiters, as well as Russians of every description, all hovering around Vladimir and fawning on him as if he were Czar.

They had to be fed, and with the food came wine and vodka, and always the bill went to Vladimir. I tried to put a stop to it, but if I chased that bunch out the front door, they came in the back. Some even asked Vladimir for money, and if I wasn't around, he gave it to them.

He was unable to say no. "Anyway not to a Russian," he said.

"You gave fifty dollars to the little fat one with bread crumbs in his beard," I said, "and he was a Pole."

"A Pole down on his luck."

"And the Frenchman?"

"A worthwhile man," Vladimir said. "He plays the fiddle and sings like an angel."

Now I sat on the edge of the bed, and held his hand, like the actress who played his Princess Natasha. "But you don't gaze deep into my eyes," he said. "And you don't cross your beautiful legs."

"They're no longer beautiful," I said, "if they ever were. In any case, your heart couldn't stand the excitement."

"Then we need to go where my heart can mend," he said. "Just the two of us."

It was exactly what I wanted to hear, so I packed up, shook off the parasites and chiselers, and went with Vladimir to Florida, to live in his beautiful house in Palm Beach. Every day I swam in the pool and worked in the garden, while he read and sunned himself. As he re-covered, we went for long walks along the beach, and shopped together in the markets for our dinner. People took us for an old married couple.

Vladimir liked to play the part, and claimed that it had become necessary for us to be married. "My tax lawyer says so," he said. "It'll save us a lot of money."

"I thought you had a lot of money."

"I do."

"Then what do you want to have more for?"

"You're being deliberately unreasonable," he said. "And playing hard to get."

"I'm content the way things are."

"So am I," he said. "But I want you to be my wife."

"How long is it we know each other?" I said. "Thirty-five years?"

"Thirty-seven."

"All right," I said. "Let's get it over with."

We were married without fanfare, in the office of a local judge, with his wife and clerk as the only witnesses. Afterward, Vladimir and I went home, opened a bottle of wine, and ate dinner—fresh pompano broiled on the barbecue on the patio next to the pool. After dinner we played checkers, read a while, and stretched out side by side in the same big bed. A television set was at the foot of the bed, and near at hand was a bowl of oranges and bananas, and in the morning, by the mere press of a button, the curtains opened on our own swimming pool. Life couldn't have been more different from the way it had been with us in Zurich and Paris, and even in New York. But much of what we said to each other was the same; we still spoke in Russian, and what we felt for each other was the same. So if there was a swimming pool, and bowls of fresh fruit, and a curtain that could be opened by the press of a button, it was lovely, but really it mattered very little because nothing vital had changed.

I had been corresponding with Magda and talking to Billy on the long distance phone, and it was arranged for him to go to France to meet his mother. When his school year ended the following June, I went up to New York and put him on the plane for Paris.

Before he went, Billy told me he hadn't talked about Magda with any of his friends. I judged he was already one who kept things to himself, and believed that only the Hellers knew where he was going that summer, and who he was going to meet. Yet I hadn't cautioned him to be quiet about it. I thought there was no reason. Andrew Winters, and his obsessions, was a long way from my thoughts; I had lost track of him, and didn't know how he spent his time. That part of my life, and Vladimir's as well, was a long time past. I didn't think of Living Memory. I didn't think of Billy's Russian tutor, Davilov.

I spent a day and a half with Billy in New York. He seemed to take meeting Magda in stride, and was more excited about traveling alone to Europe and was pleased with himself at being so grown-up. That's how it seemed until the last minute, just at the boarding gate, when he said, "Will she be there to meet me?"

"Of course."

"How will it be do you think? Shall I speak to her in English?"

"Sure."

"What if we don't like each other?"

"Oh, you'll like her."

"What about her? Will she like me?"

"Oh, my darling Billy." I took his face in my hands; it was such a great moment in his life, and he looked so serious, so worried. "Oh, my darling," I said again, and kissed him, and waited with him until his flight was called, and watched him walk through the landing gate. From a distance, he turned and waved, looking quite grown-up.

Magda was at the airport in Paris to meet her son. She said she'd never looked forward to anything as much, or been so nervous. She knew him at once, although her first sight of him coming through customs was a shock.

"If I'd never seen a photograph, I would still have known him," she told me later. "But I hadn't expected him to be so big. I kept thinking of him as a little boy, although I knew he was fourteen. He was taller than I, probably as tall as Serge. And with a deep voice and hair on his upper lip. I couldn't get over that."

Billy behaved very formally toward her, shaking hands at first, and then awkwardly offering his cheek to be kissed. What a strange, remarkable moment it must have been for both of them. She spoke to him in French, and he answered in English. She switched to English, and he responded in French. It was comic. Both saw the joke at the same time. The tension relaxed.

Magda had booked two rooms in a small hotel on the Left Bank, off the Rue Dauphin, not far from where she and I had lived before the war. She took his arm in the Tuileries and listened gravely as he told her about his school and his friends. She walked him around to our old haunts, pointed out the house where she had lived, and even the notorious Hotel Morocco, and the cafés where we went to dance and have a little fun. She was at her most delightful, and he was enchanted, listening breathlessly to the story of his mother's life before he was born. Her adventures were to him like fairy tales, real and not real, adventures in a world that existed before he did.

He soon fell in love with her. She was his mother, and at the same time a beautiful and exotic woman, or so it seemed to him. And what about Magda? What were her feelings? She held tight to his arm—he had a powerful arm like his father, although he most resembled her. She looked too young to be his mother. People thought they were brother and sister, and I think they pretended they were.

It was several days before he asked about Serge. He needed to screw up his courage, to feel more secure with her.

"What is it you want to know about him?" she said.

"Where did you meet? Was it here, in Paris?"

"In New York," she said. She was conscious of moving cautiously, of putting one foot down at a time, as if she were at a party where the dance floor had just been waxed, made slick as glass. "I was introduced to your father in New York," she said.

"Who introduced you?"

"Do you call Irina grandmother?"

"Yes."

"She introduced us."

"Then he was a friend of hers?"

"Hasn't she told you about him?"

"Not much. She prefers to talk about you."

Magda told Billy that she had first seen his father at a party in New York. "A very glamorous party. The woman who gave it was a well-known entertainer named Mitzi Roth."

"I never heard of her."

"It was a long time ago."

"What did you think of him?"

"Of your father? He was handsome and had very good manners. There was a big fuss made over him by lots of pretty women in fancy dresses. I didn't have any money, any job, and my dress was an old rag."

"Grandmother Irina said you were the most beautiful woman there."

"Did she?"

"And that he ignored the other women, and took you home from the party."

"I thought she didn't talk about him."

"She told me that much."

Magda began to talk to Billy more easily about his father. She kept as close to the truth as she dared, and spoke honestly of her feelings for Serge. She tried to get that part exactly right, so that Billy would know just what she had felt. Because he trusted her, she was responsible for every word and every word weighed heavily on her. What he heard now, at the age of fourteen, would become the truth about his mother and father, and would stay with him all his life.

"He was a soldier, wasn't he?" Billy said. "Grandmother Irina told me that also. He was a Russian soldier. But why did he leave the Russian service?"

"He lost faith in it," she said. "But he wasn't a traitor, so he didn't defect. He just disappeared."

"And you followed him? You left me and followed him?"

"Yes." She nodded, but said nothing to defend what she had done. It was the moment she had dreaded, and the moment she was relieved to have done with. "I left you and followed him." She had lowered her eyes and when she raised them it was to look directly at Billy, and to deny nothing. "I followed him," she repeated.

"You must have loved him."

"I still do."

Billy said, "Does he want to meet me?"

"Very much."

"Where is he now?"

"We've been living on an island off Spain."

"What's it called?"

"Ibiza."

"Are they still looking for him?"

"Probably."

Billy had a troubled look, but it was gone in a moment.

Magda said, "Have you told anyone about meeting me?"

"No. I don't think so."

She suspected he had told someone, but she didn't know him well enough to be sure. All the time they'd been together, she'd been looking around corners. Her life with Serge had made caution second nature. And she had seen someone, felt something. Then there was the troubled look on Billy's face: Had he told someone?

She had seen the same familiar face in different places; an ordinary-looking man of about sixty, possibly older—she wasn't a good judge of age. He wore a soft brown hat and belted raincoat. She never managed to get a good look at him. The first time she saw him was on the Champs Elysées, when she had a feeling of being watched and turned around suddenly. The following day, seated in a café across from their hotel, was the same man drinking lemonade. It could have meant nothing, a simple coincidence; but instinct made her suspicious, instinct and fourteen years with Serge Dolin.

She waited a couple of days and kept an eye out for Brown Hat. That's what she called him to herself—Brown Hat. But there was no further sign of him. She decided she had been unduly suspicious. She had only imagined he was following her. It wasn't the first time she had imagined being followed. Serge was the same. He saw them too, the men in brown hats. He had made her pack up in the middle of the night, and move from one hotel to another, from one city to another. Serge owned a pistol and slept with it under his pillow.

Billy returned to the subject of his father. They had been on a day trip to Versailles, and at dinner that night, Magda said, "Would you like to go to Ibiza?"

"To meet him?"

"Your father, yes."

"All right."

Air France flew to Madrid, where they connected with an Iberia flight to Barcelona, and from there flew by small plane to Ibiza. She and Serge owned a small hotel in the interior of the island, in a village called Santa Eulalia. In a few years the island, and the village along with it, would become popular with tourists—the weather was good in summer, and there was excellent swimming off the rocks, where on a clear day one could make out the coast of Africa. Eventually the place became a haven for the international bohemian set, and notorious as a bazaar for cheap drugs from North Africa.

But when Billy first went there with Magda, it was still largely undiscovered, cheap and fairly primitive. The only transport between the town of Ibiza, where their plane landed, and Santa Eulalia was a bus that the Russians had given to the loyalists during the Spanish Civil War. It broke down more often than not, so Magda hired the one taxi on the island, an ancient but splendid Hispano-Suiza driven by a former Luftwaffe officer who had settled in Ibiza after the war. Lots of Germans had come in 1945.

Magda's faint Austrian accent was largely ignored on the island, and Serge persuaded everyone he was German by refusing to speak anything but Spanish. Their hotel was just across from the village square, and Serge was on the porch when Magda and Billy were driven up in the back seat of the open Hispano.

Billy watched Magda wave and smile in the direction of the man on the porch, who leaned on his cane and waved back. But Billy didn't believe that the bent, white-haired man squinting into the sun was his father. His first thought was that he was an employee of the hotel, possibly a porter.

If he were a porter, he seemed too frail to manage their bags. Even after Magda introduced them, Billy was unconvinced. He had imagined his father differently, and was disappointed, and in some way embarrassed. He shook hands with Serge, not meeting his gaze. They spoke in English, polite questions and answers about the difficulty of the trip from Paris. By way of greeting, Magda kissed Serge and squeezed his hand, and the boy turned away.

He had picked up only bits and pieces about his father, but he had thought a lot about him—thought a lot, wondered a lot, but said little. The reality was a shock.

According to Magda, his father had been a soldier. "Is that how you were hurt?" Billy said that night at dinner. "Were you wounded?"

"No. It was an accident."

"Your father doesn't like to talk much about the war." Magda had stepped in quickly, too quickly, Billy thought; being around Serge made her jumpy. "I was thinking we might go swimming off the rocks tomorrow," she said.

"What sort of accident?" Billy said.

"A boat accident."

"In Russia?"

"No, not in Russia."

"Where, then?"

"In a boat," Serge snapped. "A boat accident takes place in a boat."

Billy looked as if he'd been slapped. He seemed more like a young child then, and Magda wanted to reach out for him. The silence around the table was heavy. Serge looked down at his plate, and when he finally looked up, there was an expression of such remorse in his eyes that all Magda's sympathy shifted to him.

"I'm sorry, Billy. Forgive me," he said. "It's hard for me to talk about my life. I'm certainly not used to discussing it. But I've been looking forward to meeting you, and now I'm spoiling it."

It was too much for Billy, who didn't know what to say, and looked for help to Magda. She sat between them, and reached out for both, taking hold of both at the same time, as if to complete a circuit and make the current of her love pass through both of them. Again, she fell back on the amusements of the island, particularly the swimming.

Serge was good in the water, for there his leg didn't bother him. He and Billy spent the morning snorkling, and then he took Billy out in the sailboat, while Magda, who didn't care much for sailing, sat on the rocks, shaded from the sun by a broad straw hat, reading and looking at them far out in Serge's boat, its sail a perfect white triangle against the light blue sky and darker sea.

She had brought a picnic basket, and when she saw them heading in, she prepared the lunch. There was cold chicken, cheese, bread, and wine in a cooler. Billy joined in a glass of wine—Serge poured it out for him; after lunch when the wind came up, they built a lean-to and had a nap.

For the next few days, at meals or on walks along the cliffs or to the village and through the little park across from the Café Flora, Serge spoke Russian to Billy, and even taught him songs and poems from Pushkin. It was years since Magda had seen Serge laugh and enjoy himself as he did with Billy.

Serge also acted differently alone with Magda. He began to talk about himself, and to tell her things that over the years he had kept from her. He had cut himself off from his past, claiming that Serge Dolin had died in Mexico City and been reborn with her, that he owed his life to her; and when he was morbid, drunk, and self-pitying, he said that because he owed his life to her, he owed his misery as well. It was then he would lash out at her, and sometimes even hit her, and then crawl back remorsefully, begging her to forgive him.

But with Billy's arrival, he began to talk again about his past, stories of his childhood, part memory, part fantasy, and all of it in Russian, which she could barely follow and doubted that Billy understood any better. But it didn't matter. He listened enthralled to his father, his eyes shining.

"He'll remember me, won't he?" Serge said to Magda. "If this is the only time we meet, he'll still remember me."

"It's not the only time you'll meet."

"But if it is, he'll remember," Serge said. "It's important to him."

"And to you," Magda said. "It's important to you, too."

"Yes, very important."

One night, as they were preparing for bed, Serge said, "I told him about my father, and he'd heard of him. He's studying modern Russian history, and he knew who he was. He had heard of Stenoviev. Can you imagine? He was proud, and thrilled. He asked me why with such a famous father, I changed my name."

"What did you tell him?"

"That I wanted to live quietly, without politics." Serge said, "but he's clever, and has guessed that I'm covering up. I don't blame him for wanting to find out the truth from me. First the truth about one's father, and then hopefully the truth about oneself."

All through it, Magda was shaking her head. "I don't like the truth you're talking about," she said. "I don't want him involved. It's all buried in the past. Let Billy alone. I don't want him involved."

"He wants to know what I was. Don't you see how it is between us, between a father and son?"

"Take him sailing," Magda said. "Help him with his Russian. That's also between a father and son. I don't want him involved. I won't let you do it, Serge."

"What if we have no choice?" Serge said. "What if we have no choice at all?"

"You want him to know who you were," she said. "You want him to know what you once were."

"Tell me, do you ever think about Vienna? You grew up there, do you ever think of going back?"

"I don't know what you're getting at," she said. "And why do you say we have no choice?" She shook him. "What's happened, Serge?"

"Would you go back to Vienna?"

"I told you, there's no one there. It's a dead place, at least for me."

"Israel, then. You can claim citizenship—"

"What's happened?"

"America," Serge said. "You'd be able to travel to America, see your old friends, visit Billy whenever you like."

"It's the man in the Café Flora," she said. "When I saw him in Paris, I didn't recognize him. I should have, but he's changed so."

"You met him before?"

"In Vienna."

"It's Winters, isn't it?" Serge said. "Andrew Winters."

The next morning Winters was again in the Café Flora. He'd changed his brown hat for a straw one, and bought espadrilles, cotton trousers, and a colored shirt. He had done himself up like a tourist, sipping coffee and reading the English papers.

But tourists were still rare in Santa Eulalia, and those who came were noticed. Serge had friends in the village, patrons of the Café Flora, who brought him gossip and kept their eyes open for him, and he set one to keep an eye on Andrew Winters.

"He's sickly," Serge said to Magda. "He looks even worse than I do. No wonder you didn't recognize him."

"Why is he showing himself in the café?"

"He expects me to join him for lunch." Serge even laughed. "He thinks it's time I threw it in. He's got an instinct, old Andrew Winters."

"We can pack up and get out," she said. "I can give Billy a story."

They were near the head of the jetty leading to the rocks, which made a sheltered cove around the tiny beach at the back of the hotel. Billy had taken his mask and fins and was snorkling against the rocks.

"He's a strong swimmer," Serge said.

"What does Winters want?"

"I don't know exactly," Serge said. "Once he was after blood. But no more."

"You don't know," she said. "He swore to kill you."

"Years ago."

"You don't know what he'll do." Serge used his hand to shield his eyes from the sun and peered out at Billy swimming near the rocks. "I like him, you know." When he turned to Magda, he was smiling. "He's a good kid," he said in English.

"How did Winters find us?"

Serge shrugged; it no longer made the slightest difference. He said, "I'm going to the Flora for lunch."

She tried to stop him, to talk him out of it. She pleaded with him. "It's for me, isn't it?" she said. "You're doing it so I can be with Billy. If Winters has you, he won't want me. It's to release me."

But he only smiled and kissed her. She followed him through the hotel, and onto the porch, to the steps leading to the road to town. With his bad leg, steps were difficult, and halfway down he stopped and turned back to her, squinting into the sun and shading his eyes.

"You've forgotten your sunglasses," she said.

"I'll come back for them later."

From the bottom of the steps he smiled and waved, and just then, in the midday sun, in spite of his white hair and cane, he looked much as he had years before, when he was so handsome and she had fallen in love with him.

"I love you, Serge," she said. "I always have. Every minute."

But he made light of it, and waved, and called out to her not to worry, and told her he'd be back, and told her that Winters was an old man, and he was an old man, and assured her there was nothing left to fear.

She let him go. She thought: In spite of all he's done, there's good in him. "Please," she whispered, so that only she could hear, "please judge him for the good in him."

Leaning on his cane, he walked slowly along the hundred yards of road and across the square to the Café Flora, and went straight up to Winters' table. They spoke. Winters didn't stand up, didn't offer to shake hands, and didn't seem surprised. It was true Winters had an instinct; it was true he knew when a man was ready to throw it in.

Serge pulled up a chair and sat down. He ordered a drink. Around them were empty tables, and Serge saw no other strangers in the square. The Hispano-Suiza was parked in the shade under a clump of trees at the north end of the square.

Magda had gone back into the hotel, through the lobby to the back porch. Billy was walking toward her along the jetty, a towel over his shoulders, the mask and fins dangling from his hand.

"Can we have lunch?" he said. "I'm starving."

She went into the kitchen with Billy, where the cook was busy with the guests' lunch. She fixed something for Billy, and while he was eating, Magda walked to the village, to the Flora.

Winters' table was empty. She looked up and down the square; there was no sign of him or Serge. The shutters of all the houses were closed against the afternoon sun. Nothing stirred in the café except the waiter snapping at crumbs on the table with the corner of his towel. She looked to the east, the direction of the road that ran along the beach out of town. The white road was empty. She shielded her eyes from the glare on the surface of the sea. There was a sudden turn in the road as it came out from behind the cliffs, and there she saw the Hispano, raising a column of dust on the dry road. Serge had gone with Winters.

# twenty-four

SERGE WAS GONE. FOR FOUR DAYS SHE HEARD NOTHING. SHE told Billy that he had gone to Majorca on business. A German was interested in buying the hotel—there was some truth to that—and Serge had gone to talk it over with him.

But Magda was unable to conceal her anxiety from Billy, who soon realized that something was wrong. "Is he sick?" Billy said. "Something like that?"

"No. He's gone on business."

"I guess it's a secret," Billy said. "Something between the two of you. And I'm not supposed to know."

"Billy, a man has shown up. A man your father used to know—I can't tell you the whole story."

"You don't have to tell me anything."

"Billy, try to understand that it's difficult to—"

"It's none of my business, right?"

"Take it easy. Try to be patient."

"I'm going swimming," he said.

That same day Magda telephoned me in Florida, told me what had happened. "I want to go after them," she said. "I know the driver of the taxi they went off in. But Serge wouldn't want me to look for him. And Billy's upset, and doesn't know what's going on. I don't know what to do."

"Don't do anything right away," I said.

"Something awful has happened," she said. "I'm sure of it."

"You'd better stay put," I said. "Serge might want to get in touch with you."

"I need a great favor," she said. "Can you come over?"

I glanced at Vladimir, listening on the extension. He nodded. Since his heart attack I was reluctant to leave him. But with his hand covering the receiver, he urged me to go.

"Where's Billy now?" I said to Magda.

"He's gone swimming."

"Stay put," I said. "I'll make flight arrangements, and call you back."

I was able to book an Avianca flight from Miami to Madrid, and to connect with Barcelona, where I telephoned Magda. She still had no word of Serge. I slept in Barcelona, and in the morning flew to Ibiza, where Magda and Billy met me.

"I'm afraid the taxi is occupied," she said. "We'll have to take the old bus."

"It's a Russian bus," Billy said.

"I spoke to the taxi driver about Winters and Serge," Magda said. "But he's not much help. He took them to the airport, and after that he knows nothing."

"He didn't see what plane they took?"

"He claims he didn't stay around."

"What about luggage?"

"Winters had a bag."

"And Serge?"

"He carried nothing."

We rode the Russian bus to Santa Eulalia. It was crammed with local people, their parcels and livestock, and rattled and shook over the unpaved road, threatening to fall to pieces.

Billy teased me about the Russian bus. I realized he had been told part of the story, and during the long flight over I had made up my mind to tell him more—all of it if need be.

But when I started to describe his father's work during the war, Billy shook his head and turned away. He had changed his mind, and wanted to hear no more. He'd had a good time with his father, and in those few days had come to like him, and perhaps to admire him, and he refused to listen to anything that threatened to change that.

The bus let us off in the village square, and we had to walk the hundred yards or so to the hotel. As we came closer we noticed a small green-and-white car parked at an angle to the entrance. It was a police car. Magda was the first to realize it, and ran for the hotel, Billy and me following with my bags.

"Have they come about him?" Billy said. "Is it bad news?"

Two policemen were at the front desk talking to a waiter Billy called Paco. A man in a wicker chair, his back to them, read a French newspaper and looked out at the rocks, the jetty, and the tiny bit of beach.

The police were from Santa Eulalia and Magda knew them. One was old, the other young, and she could tell from the face of the older one that the news was bad.

He spoke in Spanish, and I could only get the drift of what he said.

There had been a call from Barcelona. The police in Barcelona. News of Serge.

"What news?" Magda said. "What's happened to him?"

It was bad, he told her. *"Malo, muy malo."* Just then he remembered that his cap was on his head, so he took it off and gestured for the other cop, the younger one, to take his off.

It was all happening in an ordinary way. The man in the wicker chair went on reading his French newspaper. It was on to lunchtime and from the kitchen came the smells of food cooking. The younger cop was bored and let his eyes wander around the lobby before settling them on Magda.

The news was that Serge had checked into a hotel in Barcelona and stayed four days. On the morning of the fifth day, when the maid came in to clean the room, she found him on the floor of the bathroom.

Magda looked at the older cop, and from him to Billy. She said, "What had happened to him?"

"He was dead, *señora*," the cop said.

We had to wait for the morning flight to Barcelona. I stayed up with Magda, but we talked very little, and when we did it was only of practical matters. She and Serge had been thinking of selling the hotel, and she would go ahead with that; and she thought she would move to Paris and live there.

"Why not come to the States?" I said. "You can visit Billy at school, and spend time with Vladimir and me in Florida."

"My passport is a problem," she said. "Serge was trying to work it out."

She wouldn't talk about herself and Serge, and what she felt she kept to herself. His death had sealed her off. For so many years they had lived as two fugitives, confiding in nobody, with no life apart from each other, depending on each other and trusting only each other. Without him she felt disoriented, bewildered.

That night in the hotel, and the next morning on the Barcelona plane, her face was taut, white, and remote, the perfect features immobile as a carving.

"There was good in him, you know," she said. "The last time I saw him, I thought about the good in him."

I said nothing to that. Perhaps I should have reassured Magda and agreed that there was indeed some good in the man she had loved. True or not, it would have been kind and generous, and I had learned to care less for the truth and setting the record straight than for the comfort of those I loved; but my thoughts just then were on other deaths—"works of art," in the language of the assassins. There had been "some good" in Willi Koder, too; and Nadine Berne had also lovingly folded a handkerchief in the breast pocket of her husband, the murdered Pole, Godinsky.

In Barcelona, the police were courteous and helpful. They explained that Serge had checked into a hotel called the Astoria. He had been alone, although he dined in the hotel with another man, and the same man visited him once or twice in his room.

"What was the name of this man?"

"It's not known."

"Has any attempt been made to find him?"

The policeman shook his head. "It's of no concern," he said, "as your husband died naturally, of heart failure."

"Did he go anywhere in Barcelona? Did he visit anyone else?"

"It is of no concern." The policeman liked the phrase. "It's of no concern."

I waited until Magda was out of the room, led off to collect Serge's personal property. I said to the policeman, "Was there an autopsy?"

"No. It's not required in such cases."

"What sort of case is that?"

He was young, spoke excellent French, and wore a tiny gold cross in the lapel of his suit. For a policeman, he had a comforting rather than a knowing smile, and his perfect teeth were white as breakfast china.

"While it's true that no autopsy was done," he said, "the body was examined by a police surgeon. There were no wounds, no bruises or contusions, and the external evidence was consistent with heart failure." His lovely smile dimmed, flickered briefly, then shone again, comforting as ever. "And the room in which he died was locked from the inside," he said.

"How did the maid get in?"

"By means of a passkey." He carried cigarettes in a silver case; there was a matching lighter, and the business of offering a cigarette, tapping the end of one on the back of his hand, and striking the lighter—all of it was learned from old-fashioned Latin movies, preposterous in the smelly offices of the Barcelona police.

"Are you a relative of the deceased?" he said. "Or of Madame—" He made a point of glancing at Serge's Canadian passport, open on his desk. "Or a relative of Madame Terrelle?"

"She's an old friend."

"Are you also Canadian?"

"I'm an American citizen."

"Do you know the nature of Monsieur Terrelle's business?"

"He owned a hotel."

"Yes, a hotel. He owned a hotel." I wondered what he knew or suspected, and what he had been ordered to ignore, this Spanish cop with his fluent French, his swell manners, and a gold cross in his lapel. "Monsieur Terrelle's passport and personal possessions will all be returned to Madame," he said.

As far as the Barcelona police were concerned, there was no more to it. Serge had died of a heart attack in a hotel room locked from the inside. He had dined with a man whom nobody remembered. He'd had no other visitors and never left the hotel. What had he done, alone in that room, for three days? It was of no concern—it was all of no concern.

Certainly someone had influenced this smiling Spanish cop, but if it was Winters, American intelligence, or the Soviets, I never knew. Perhaps it was, finally, of no concern. Serge was dead, and the police released his body to Magda; and though burial for foreigners is usually difficult, they helped us arrange for him to be buried in the English cemetery in Barcelona.

Only we three—Magda, Billy, and I—followed the coffin and joined the minister for the brief service beside the grave. Be sure that it rained, that a cold wind blew, and that the rain poured out of a black sky the day we buried Serge.

Afterward, we went to a restaurant for a glass of something to warm us. Billy was on his best behavior, seated stiffly at the table with his fingers laced, as if in church, and it seemed to me he hadn't spoken a word since we arrived in Barcelona. I don't know what Serge's death meant to him. He'd hardly known him. But he liked being allowed to drink a glass of sherry. After the rain at the cemetery, we all welcomed it, and the bowls of vegetable soup that followed. We were hungry enough for omelettes and platters of fried potatoes.

All through the meal there was no talk of Serge, no talk of why we were in Barcelona. The death belonged to Magda. But grief hadn't taken her over. She had prepared herself for Serge's death.

"It could have come at any time," she said. "We both knew it."

Later that day, after we returned to the hotel and Billy went out for a walk, Magda and I were alone, and I got her to talk about her life with Serge.

She admitted that her passion for him had cooled over the years, that she saw all his weaknesses, and that gradually she took over, earn-ing the money and keeping both of them going. As Serge faded, her love became protective and self-sacrificing. Eventually, self-sacrifice and denial were all that remained of that love.

"It got so we were hardly talking, and for a long time there'd been no sex. Sex seemed to go out of Serge's life," she said.

"But not you," I said. "Sex didn't go out of your life."

"I certainly missed it, and thought about it," she said. "Other men. There were some I was attracted to, one or two I could even have loved. But I never encouraged them, I never even let on. And when they were clever enough to guess how I felt about them, I discouraged them."

"But why?" I said. "Why discourage them?"

"I had given up Billy for Serge," she said. "I couldn't give up Serge, too. If I did, it would all have been for nothing.

I said, "What about a life of your own?"

"You mean without Serge?" Her smile was patronizing. "Should I have left him because I'd stopped admiring him? Once in Lima, Serge was carried home drunk. He'd picked a fight and gotten beaten up. He was a mess. I had to bathe him and patch up his bruises, and put him to bed. I held him until he went off to sleep. I don't remember that I got any pleasure out of his dependence. Maybe I did. Maybe lying next to him I got some pleasure out of it."

I began to think I had left Vladimir alone too long. When I telephoned him, he sounded cheerful and assured me he was well. I told him about Serge, and he pressed me for details, but took care on the overseas phone to improvise a code made of private allusions and ellipses.

"Something like the old days in Zurich." I heard his familiar laugh over the long distance wire. "You did tell me it was summer there."

"Summer?" I was being dense. Summer, as in summer, spring, et cetera? Summer equaled winter—Andrew Winters. "Summer was here," I said. "Come and gone."

"There was talk he'd returned to the States," Vladimir said. "He's supposed to have migrated down here, the west coast around Sarasota." There was a crackle of overseas static, and Vladimir gleefully said, "He winters down here, don't you know."

I had booked Billy and me on the New York flight the next day, but before we left, Magda took me aside to show me what she had discovered among the things Serge had with him when he died.

It was all in a cardboard carton given her by the Barcelona police.

Aside from the usual things—a spare shirt, underwear, socks, a paperback book, and a toilet kit, all of it bought in Barcelona.

Serge's wallet had been given to her separately, and when she went through it, she found a few hundred pesetas and an international driver's license. It had been issued less than a month before, although she didn't remember Serge mentioning anything about it. "He didn't like to drive," she said. "I was the one who did it."

She carefully slid the license out of its plastic holder. There were actually two licenses, the top new and the bottom old, the two sides carefully glued together. Magda got a razor blade and separated them. She told me Serge had taught her the trick of making glue out of soap and talcum powder. With the edges glued, the center of the two halves made a pocket, and in the pocket was a sales slip from an electronics shop in Barcelona. It was for a tape recorder and four cassettes of tape.

But no recorder appeared on the inventory of Serge's possessions; no recorder and no tape had been found.

"Is it with the police?" I said. "Or with Andrew Winters?"

"I don't know."

"Four cassettes of tape," I said. "Serge was alone in the room for three days—time enough to record all he knew."

"I don't care," she said. "I don't give a damn for those tapes, or for what Serge knew." She held the receipt in her hand, staring down at it, and then crumpled it up and threw it into the wastebasket. "I don't care how he died, or why he died. He's dead, and only that matters. When he was alive, I loved him, and now I'll never see him again . . ."

She would not hear another word about the tapes, or what had happened to them. The next day at the airport, her thoughts were on Billy, on having to part from him. When she kissed him good-by, she clung to him, but for only an instant, and fought back the tears, and even managed to smile. Then it was my turn to say good-by to her, but I could not hold back my tears.

"When is your flight to Ibiza?" Billy said.

"In a couple of hours," she said. "Don't worry about me. I'll be busy there, arranging to sell the hotel."

"Can you come to America?" Billy said.

"I'm going to try."

"I'll do all I can to help," I said.

"In the meantime I'll get a place in Paris," she said. "With an extra bedroom. Even an attic room, with a skylight." She managed to laugh to show us that she was okay.

On the flight back to America, I thought about the problem of Magda's visa to the States, and decided to contact a lawyer I knew in Miami whom I trusted and who specialized in immigration cases. With Serge dead, I expected that whatever difficulties there were could be worked out, particularly by the clever lawyer from Miami.

I was more anxious about Vladimir, and regretted having left him alone so long. Since his heart attack, he'd begun to weaken; on the long distance phone, I'd heard a new quaver in his voice. Vladimir would be eighty in a couple of months. I drank a martini, and thought of Magda, who would never see Serge again. With the second martini, I closed my eyes and saw myself in the last act of my life; I was without Vladimir, whom I would never see again.

Self-pity rose with the alcohol in my bloodstream. I needed dinner to set it right. The stewardess brought it around, and Billy and I had a good talk with our meal. I gave him my dessert, and resolved to shake off my dark mood. Vladimir was alive, and I vowed to take good care of him—"to prop up his old bones," as he himself would say, and to make sure he lived quite a long time.

In New York, I said good-by to Billy and put him on the plane for Montreal, where the Hellers would meet him, and I flew to Palm Beach.

Vladimir was all right, at work on the second volume of his memoirs, and soon we settled into our usual routine. I kept busy around the house, swimming twice a day, gardening, reading, and always keeping an ear cocked for the clacking of Vladimir's typewriter through the open window of his study.

Unfortunately, the lawyer in Miami was unable to get a visa for Magda. She'd been out of the country and had not renewed her green card, which had expired. Applications for a new one and a visa had both been turned down. No reason given.

Magda wrote from Paris that the problem of a valid passport was becoming urgent. Serge had gotten her Argentinian documents, but these would expire in only a few months. Without him, she didn't know how to get new ones. She could travel to Vienna and try to establish her original Austrian citizenship. But that would involve a thorough investigation, which she feared.

"I don't know who was looking for Serge," she wrote. "Which side? Both sides? I realize there was a lot he never told me. Perhaps there are secrets in every marriage, but I kept nothing from him and I wish he had told me more of the truth about himself." It was the closest I'd ever heard her come to criticizing him. "I tried to put Barcelona out of my mind," she went on, "but it's not possible. I don't want to think about how he died, and yet I want to know. Was he killed, do you think? If he made tapes before he died, what was on them? And who has them? I keep looking over my shoulder for those men in brown hats."

There was more to the letter; she'd heard from Billy—he was a clever boy, he wrote good French. He was busy and happy at school.

But at the end she returned to the tapes, and what had happened to Serge. The meaning of the letter was clear: She was alone in Paris and frightened; around every corner was a man in a brown hat.

I didn't want to leave Vladimir again for another trip to Europe, but I had to help Magda.

"I think we ought to get in touch with Andrew Winters," Vladimir said.

"Can you reach him?"

"If I dip my beak into Living Memory," Vladimir said.

In a couple of days Vladimir had an address for Winters on Longboat Key in Sarasota. I wrote and asked if we could drive over and talk to him. He didn't answer immediately, but when he did it was to say he was ill, but would write again and arrange something as soon as he was better.

In November I still hadn't heard from Winters, and was thinking of writing again, when Billy telephoned. There was to be a Thanksgiving party at his school—relatives were invited, the Hellers were coming, and Billy wanted me and Vladimir to join them.

"Do you remembr Mr. Davilov?" Billy said.

"Your Russian tutor?"

"He specifically asked me to invite you."

Vladimir wasn't up to the trip, but wanted to know more about this Davilov. "There was a Davilov in Paris," I said. "Do you remember?"

"The waiter at the Odeon."

"He wasn't a waiter."

"He wore a waiter's coat and a black tie."

"If he heard you call him a waiter, he'd be mortified," I said. "My Davilov was a *maître de salon*."

"And he was your Davilov?"

"The poor fellow," I said. "For a franc or two he was anyone's Davilov. But once he was an officer with the Whites."

"An officer with the Whites." I could see Vladimir turning that over and rummaging through his immense memory, as if it were a card file. "There was a Davilov on the mathematics faculty at the

University of Moscow. But that was in my time. How old is Billy's Davilov?"

"About forty."

"Young enough to be his grandson," Vladimir said. "And Living Memory knows nothing of him. He stays clear of émigré society, yet he knew Billy's history—even the connection to Stenoviev."

"He also managed to learn about Billy's trip to meet Magda."

"And perhaps passed the word to Andrew," Vladimir said.

By Thanksgiving, Vermont was already covered in snow, and more fell the day I arrived. I had flown up, arriving after the Hellers, who had driven down earlier and were at the airport with Billy to meet me. Walter Heller had prospered in the years since the war; he drove a Buick and had even managed to put on a few pounds. He was still a man to rely on, laconic and trustworthy. As for Christina, the years had also been good to her. I noticed that she now wore a touch of makeup, and had even done something to her hair. She was immensely proud of Billy. He was at that age when boys seem to grow overnight. Yet there was nothing awkward about him, and he had developed naturally into a poised man. He still resembled Magda— perhaps a little less so as he matured, but he kept her fineness of features—and had a surprising lot of the mannerisms of Walter Heller. I realized it only when I saw them together. He was physically strong in the same unobtrusive way Heller was, and competent, the way Heller was, and scrupulous, again like Heller. During the weekend, I saw that Heller was aware of how Billy had grown like him, and greatly pleased by it. It pleased me, too; it was just.

There was a round of parties, but on Thanksgiving day the Hellers, Billy, and I were invited to dinner by Davilov and his wife. Davilov kept horses in a large barn in back of his house, and one of the mares had foaled. When we walked through the snow to have a look, Davilov took me aside.

He told me that he had been in touch with Andrew Winters—it was said boldly, without any explanation, as if there were nothing in it underhanded.

"We write to each other regularly," he said. "And I spoke to him yesterday on the telephone."

"Then it was you who told Winters about Billy's trip?"

"It was me."

"And made friends with the boy in order to spy on him?"

"No, it wasn't like that."

"It would seem as if it were like that," I said. "Exactly like that, Mr. Davilov."

"Billy is my friend," he said. "I feel toward him as I would toward a nephew, even a son. He's a gifted boy, and he told me about you, and his interest in Russian things. He came to me to study."

Through the open door, I could see the others—Walter and Christina Heller, Billy and Mrs. Davilov—standing in a semicircle in front of the mare's stall. Fresh snow fell heavily, large flakes turning slowly in the moonlight, settling silently on the branches of trees and on the ground.

Billy turned and called out, "Come and see, Grandma."

"Who are you?" I said to Davilov.

"I teach Russian," he said. "I translate the classics. And that's all I am."

"What do you want?"

"I have a message for you from Andrew. He's very sick. The doctors say he's dying. He wants you to come. He's says it's of the greatest importance."

"It's none of my business."

"But it is." Davilov had hold of my arm. "Please, listen to me. He trusts you—the Russian Woman. It's for Billy's good, and for the mother—Magda Renner, wasn't that the name she used?"

"It's her name, Mr. Davilov."

Billy had come out of the barn and started through the snow toward us. Davilov let go of my arm. "It's for her that you have to see Winters," he whispered. "For Magda Renner."

From the airport the next morning I called Vladimir, and told him that I had decided to go to Sarasota and see Andrew Winters. Vladimir suggested I fly home, and that he and I drive to Sarasota.

I liked the idea, and caught the first plane to New York, and from there flew to Palm Beach. After a good night's sleep, we started out first thing in the morning. Vladimir liked to have breakfast on the road. He owned a collection of maps and touring books with the names of out-of-the-way hotels and places to eat, the smaller and more modest the better. He liked to talk to people along the way—America was still an adventure to him—and to eat food that was cooked in a kitchen, not prepared in a factory. And, of course, Vladimir's car was a special car, a 1952 Bentley, which he had bought from an old friend, a tenor with the Los Angeles Opera. Although Vladimir no longer drove, he still tinkered with the engine, and bragged about it all the time. "Listen to it," he said. "That engine sings better than the tenor."

"Is that why he sold it?"

We drove around Lake Okeechobee and drank fresh orange juice from stands along the road. Later, we ate breakfast in a tiny place off the main road—country-cured ham, cornbread, and fresh eggs. The woman who served us was a great grouch, but Vladimir charmed her and told her jokes, and soon had her bringing us little treats from the kitchen.

Our trip had started off well, both of us in good spirits, but as we got closer to Sarasota the mood in the car changed. Vladimir was silent for a long while, and finally said, "Andrew is eager to see us, particularly you."

"When did you talk to him?"

"After you called from Vermont. He said to hurry. He had no time to spare."

"Davilov said he was dying."

Vladimir nodded. "He's got cancer. Last year he had an operation, and then chemotherapy. Then that tutor Davilov came to him with the details of Billy's trip to meet Magda. We were right about Davilov."

"And Andrew got up from his bed and went after Serge?" I said. "But why after all these years? Was it to learn the truth? To kill Serge?"

"I don't know," Vladimir said. "If Serge made tapes, I don't know what's on them. If Andrew knows, perhaps he'll tell us."

"Is that why he sent for us?"

"We'll have to wait and see."

"Aren't you curious?"

"Yes, very. But also apprehensive," Vladimir said. "Some things are best left alone."

We were driving through marshland and swamps to the north of Okeechobee, and just then, rising from the tall grass on Vladimir's side of the road, came a pair of large blue-white birds, wading birds with astonishing long legs; they had been feeding in the shallows, and suddenly took flight, their legs folded straight back and their huge wings beating the humid air that hung heavily over the swamps.

Vladimir had rolled down his window and watched until they were out of sight. "How beautiful," he said. "What are they called, those birds?"

"Herons."

"Do we have them in Russia?"

"We have cranes."

"Yes, cranes. It was cranes I was thinking of."

We arrived in Sarasota just after noon, and crossed a bridge above a small harbor filled with pleasure boats. We were on Longboat Key, where Winters lived in a tall, modern building in an apartment with a terrace overlooking the Gulf of Mexico. The day was clear, and there was a view for miles along the beach as far as the horizon, although the stench of dead fish hung heavily in the air.

Winters received us on the terrace, where he lay in a steamer chair, wrapped in a blanket, although the sun was hot and there was hardly any breeze. From the first glimpse of him, from the haunted look in his eyes and the cold touch of his hand, it was obvious that he was dying.

And the first words were the accusation of a dying man, one unreconciled to his fate and convinced that it was unjust. "You're older than I am," he said to Vladimir, and looked around for others to bear witness. "He's older and stands there, look at him, a picture of health."

"I have my aches and pains," Vladimir said, and calmly pulled up a chair next to Andrew.

There were lots of people in the apartment, enough for a party or a wake, many of whom I recognized, faces that had wandered in and out of our past, survivors of Living Memory. There were some who were younger, and who resembled people I had known, relatives of Living Memory, a second generation hovering near Andrew Winters, hoping for one last favor, a crumb from his table, a final word in the right place.

Julia was there. I hadn't seen her in years and was shocked by the change in her. It wasn't only that she was older—we were all older—but that something essential and vital had gone out of her. She moved around the apartment straightening things, and taking away empty glasses. I heard her humming to herself. I knew that Balaban had died, and that Julia had moved close to Andrew. I tried to talk to her, but it was no use; she had retreated within herself, and barely remembered me at all.

Andrew motioned Vladimir and me closer. "How old are you, anyway?" he said to Vladimir.

"Eighty."

"Eighty. Imagine. And look how healthy he is."

"Touch wood," I said.

"It's because of her," Andrew said, pointing to me. "She takes such good care of him, that's why he's so healthy."

"What did you want to see us about?" I said.

Andrew waved the others away and they filed off the terrace, disappointed at not being able to hear what was said. They were spies of one kind or another, parasites and gossips who swam around like a school of ravenous fish, on the lookout for any bit of information, eager to tear frantically at any rotten little rumor.

When the last of them had left the terrace, I closed the heavy glass door so that we were alone with Andrew.

"You have a lovely view," Vladimir said. "But why does it stink so?" He took a deep breath. "A stench of dead fish, my dear old friend."

"It's something in the water," Winters said. "It colors it red, do you see? So it's called the red tide, and it kills fish."

"Is it a joke?"

"I sometimes think so," Andrew said.

"Why have you asked us here?" I said again.

"To help Dolin's wife, your friend Magda Renner." He had to stop and catch his breath. "They took out one lung, but the damn thing has spread to the other."

Gently, Vladimir said, "What about Magda?"

"It was because of her that Dolin agreed to go with me to Barcelona," Andrew said. "He recorded his confession there, in the hotel room in which he died. He put the whole story on tape, including the part about Max. He was to give me the tapes, and I was to arrange travel documents for the wife."

"For Magda."

"Yes, the Renner woman." Andrew caught his breath again, and rested, looking out at the horizon. "It does stink here," he said.

A maid came out on the terrace, carrying a tray with a pitcher of ice water and three glasses. Andrew waited until she had gone before he said, "Dolin loved her, you know. The Renner woman. He did love her."

"The bargain he made with you," I said, "Magda's travel papers. Were you able to arrange it?"

"Yes. But Dolin didn't trust me," Andrew said. "He made four tapes, and gave me only two. The other two are with a lawyer named Zauderer in Stockholm. Very respected, quite old now, Zauderer. Do you know him?"

"No."

"Well, maybe not." Andrew wanted a drink of water. He didn't ask for it, he only pointed, rather rudely; but I gave it to him, and after he drank it, he said, "What is it you call those old-timers, all my hangers-on?"

"Ghosts," Vladimir said.

"I have something they want," Andrew said. "Money, a favor of some kind. That's why they stick around, and wait on me."

"Will you help Magda?" I said.

"When Dolin gave Zauderer two of the tapes," he said, "his instructions were to send them to you. And when Renner has her papers, you're to send them to me."

"I don't want the tapes," I said. "You can have them."

"They won't do me any good," Andrew said. "This time Dolin has outsmarted himself." He began to laugh, then cough, and his eyes watered from the red tide. He dabbed at them with a tissue, and went on laughing. "Dolin outsmarted himself. I won't bargain for the two tapes because I won't be alive to hear them." He shook when he laughed, and the tears from the red tide rolled down his cheeks. "Dolin outsmarted himself," he said.

"Let me help you." I wet a tissue, patted his eyes, and wrote a prescription and asked one of the Ghosts to carry it to the druggist.

"You take good care of Vladimir, don't you?" I had pulled my chair closer, and he took hold of my hand, and kept it in both of his. "Mr. Gray is alive," he said.

"Do you hear from him?"

"Once in a while."

"And Max?"

"He survived." I dabbed again at his eyes. "Gray survived Stalin; Max survived, too. Moscow faked his death, so that we would stop looking for him. American intelligence went along with it because they wanted the matter dropped. Franklin Roosevelt died naturally, and that was to be the end of it."

"How did you learn Max was alive?"

"From Serge. He had deposited Max's money in a Zurich bank, in an account known only to him and Max. But when Serge tried to withdraw the money, he was told that the account was empty. Max had withdrawn it."

When the medication arrived, I put three drops in each of Andrew's eyes, and afterward fixed a cold compress; he was more comfortable and he liked being looked after.

"In Barcelona, Dolin and I had a long talk. He wanted to get things off his chest. He even laid off the booze. I got to like him. I wanted to kill him, but I got to like him. There was no remorse in him. He

301

wasn't blind to what he had done, but he took the responsibility. And he loved her. He loved Renner." He closed his eyes; I noticed how thin the blue lids were, how they fluttered, and the delicate tracery of veins. "Can she make it to Lisbon?" he said.

"Yes."

"Tell her to go to the embassy there, and speak to a man named Ranger, Mitchell Ranger. He'll arrange papers for her."

"What can be done for you?" I said.

"Nothing." He was very tired, but still a smile crossed his lips, a yellow smile that was death itself. He motioned me closer. I leaned over him, fearing him; I forgot I was a doctor and became a superstitious Russian woman, frightened of the death close by.

"I didn't kill him," he said.

"How did he die?"

"He was a murder artist," Andrew said. "A murder artist."

When we left Andrew Winters and the Ghosts, the survivors of Living Memory, we decided to take a little time and not go directly home. We drove south along the Gulf coast, which neither of us had seen before, and decided to stop where we pleased. We needed to shake off the ghastly memory of Winters, and to forget the Ghosts.

I telephoned Magda in Paris, giving her the name of the officer to contact at the American embassy in Lisbon; and we continued south to Fort Meyers and drove across a long causeway to Sanibel Island, where we stayed the night.

In the morning we swam in the Gulf, Vladimir gleefully pointing out that the noxious red tide had receded. After a couple of days of idling on the beach, reading, and gathering shells, we drove across the peninsula and returned to the house in Palm Beach.

With the accumulated mail was a notice from the post office that an insured parcel had arrived for me from Sweden and was being held at the customs window. Vladimir was eager to get back to work on the next volume of his memoirs, and when I left the house in the morning to go downtown to shop and pick up the mail, he was already at his typewriter. The sound of him pecking away reassured me that all was well with him.

The package was about the size of a small cigar box. It had been mailed from Stockholm, but the only return address was a postal box in that city—there was no name, and none on the insurance form or the attached customs slip. Thirty-two cents in extra postage was due.

It was an intriguing package, reminding me of those I had received when I worked for Winters in Zurich. I didn't open it, not in the post

302

office or in the car, but decided to wait until I was home with Vladimir.

I spent an hour or so shopping at the supermarket and stopped to get a cold drink and to buy Vladimir his newspapers before heading home. I never let the package out of my sight.

Vladimir was waiting at the door. From his face, I could see that something had happened. The news was solemn, but not unexpected: Andrew Winters was dead.

Davilov had called not long after I left. "He wants to come and see us," Vladimir said.

"Does he?"

"He has something urgent to discuss with you."

I had put the parcel on top of the bag of groceries, and now showed it to Vladimir, who got his paper knife and opened it. Inside was a sealed manila envelope, and a letter from the lawyer Jean-Marc Zauderer.

"The enclosed parcel was sent to me by Serge Dolin," he wrote. "I have represented him in matters of an extremely delicate and confidential nature over a period of many years. When I informed Monsieur Dolin of my intention to retire from active practice, he instructed me to send the enclosed parcel to you. Its contents are to be regarded as your property; your rights to it are absolute and you may do with it as you wish."

After Vladimir and I had both read the letter, I said, "It's not quite as Andrew thought."

"Not quite."

"What does it mean?"

"It means you're stuck with the tapes."

The manila envelope was sealed with transparent tape, across which Serge had written his name. Vladimir cut the tape, and removed two audio cassettes bound by a rubber band.

"I can get the player," Vladimir said, "if you want to hear them now."

"Not now."

"They're yours. You can destroy them and be done with it."

"Why has Serge given me the responsibility?" I said. "I don't want it. Damn the tapes. The responsibility isn't mine."

"Serge trusted you."

"And I trust you," I said. "Help me decide what to do."

"Put them away."

"And then?"

"One day we'll listen to them."

Vladimir had a safe in his study and he locked the tapes away. Then he told me there was more news, good news for a change: A telegram from Magda had arrived. She was in Lisbon, had been to the American embassy, and was having her papers processed. She expected to be in America by Christmas.

That night I called Billy, and although he had promised to spend Christmas with the Hellers in Canada, he said he would come down between Christmas and New Year's.

It seemed that everything had worked out well—Magda was coming to America, and we would all begin the new year together. But I was still troubled by the tapes and what to do with them. I was worried that someone else knew of them, wanted them, and would inquire after them.

And shortly someone did inquire—the tutor, Davilov.

He telephoned and asked if I would see him—"on a matter of the greatest importance," as he said, in his old-fashioned and formal Russian. It had occurred to me before that he'd not learned Russian as a child around the dinner table, but had been taught it later on.

He arrived after dinner, and I politely offered him coffee and slices of cake. He wasn't a friend, this Davilov, but neither was he an enemy. An adversary, I thought, and a man I would never trust.

"I've been in touch with Serge Dolin's lawyer," he said, "Monsieur Zauderer. According to him the two missing tapes are with you."

"Yes."

"What's on them?"

Vladimir had greeted Davilov and then excused himself to work in his study. Through the open door I could see the light over his desk and hear the clacking of his typewriter—the sound that so comforted me and assured me that all was well.

"The tapes," Davilov said again. "What's on the two tapes?"

"I don't know. I've not listened to them."

"Not listened to them?"

"I'm not sure I want to be involved."

"Not sure." He repeated everything I said, and stared at me with his eyes wide.

"Is anything wrong, Mr. Davilov?"

"No—except. You've not listened to the tapes. But you have them?"

"I said I did."

"And not destroyed them?"

"What do you want?"

"Max is alive."

"I've heard some such story."

"It's true." Davilov's face was white, and his hand shook so that his coffee cup rattled. "Dolin met Max again only a few months before he died. He knew the name Max was using and how to reach him. It's on the tapes, all of it is on the tapes. Don't you see? We can get hold of Max and prove that Roosevelt was murdered."

While he spoke, I watched the teacup rattling in the saucer in his trembling hand. Now I reached over and took it from him. It was an antique Russian cup, one of an irreplaceable set, a wedding present from Vladimir, and my only concern was that Davilov not drop it.

"We must find out the truth," he said.

I put the cup safely on a table. But now I was uneasy about something else, and it took me a few seconds to realize what it was. Vladimir had stopped typing and the lamp over his desk had gone out. I excused myself and went into the study, but Vladimir wasn't there.

He was in our bedroom, stretched out on the bed.

"I'm all right, *Lybimaya*," he said. "Just a bit tired."

"I'll send Davilov away."

"Finish with him first."

I found Davilov wandering around our living room, pretending to look at the titles of the books on the shelves.

"Andrew left a lot of money," he said. "But he had no heirs, so he's created a foundation to perpetuate Living Memory. There's a large endowment and I'm to administer it."

"And you want the tapes for the foundation?"

"It's the proper place for them," he said. "And once and for all we can solve the mystery of Roosevelt's death."

My thoughts were on Vladimir in the next room. It had been an exhausting day, but Davilov continued to talk about the tapes, and the great secret in them, and the great mystery they solved.

I was very tired, too tired to talk any longer, and asked Davilov to excuse me. We were adversaries, but whatever was to come later, we were still polite to each other. He apologized for keeping me up, and I apologized for being so tired and politely took him to the door.

As we said goodnight, he unexpectedly took hold of me and kissed me on both cheeks. I stepped back, my cheeks burning.

"You never answered my question," I said, "my question when we first met."

"What question?"

305

"Which side do you work for, Mr. Davilov?"

I locked the door behind him and prepared for bed. I turned off the lights in the bedroom and lay down beside Vladimir, who was asleep. I listened to his breathing, and put my ear against his chest to monitor the steady beating of his heart.

I took his warm hand in mine. For so many years, I had loved him and now wondered how much longer I would be permitted to love him, and when one of us died how our love would survive. I thought it would survive, that it must.

When I closed my eyes, I saw Davilov's trembling hand, and heard him going on about the secret of the tapes, and of the great mystery they would finally solve. But lying beside Vladimir, that mystery was distant and unimportant. Another mystery possessed me. Would Vladimir and I be together forever? As a young woman, I was unable to believe in *something*; now it was impossible to believe in *nothing*. Yet I didn't know. I wasn't sure. It was a mystery after all.

But was I afraid? No, not afraid. I put my head against Vladimir's shoulder, held tight to his hand, and was reassured; the mystery was solved, for it was as if we had stepped together into the darkness.